GLYN HUGHES

Glyn Hughes has lived in Yorkshire for many years and has enjoyed a distinguished literary career. He has written an autobiographical work on Yorkshire, MILLSTONE GRIT. His first novel, WHERE I USED TO PLAY ON THE GREEN, won him the *Guardian* Prize for Fiction and the David Higham Prize for Fiction in 1982, and was followed by THE HAWTHORN GODDESS and THE RAPE OF THE ROSE. THE ANTIQUE COLLECTOR was shortlisted for the Whitbread Novel of the Year Award, the Portico Prize and the James Tait Black Memorial Prize.

Glyn Hughes

THE ANTIQUE COLLECTOR

For Jane

·1·

L ET me be sorry for myself, just a little, just at the start.
Please. Even though I know self-pity doesn't pay; it gets
you chased off-stage. Let me shed a tear like a – lady. I don't
think my worst enemies would say I indulge too often, but I'm
in mourning for you, dash it, Mr Dodds; the first and best of
my 'antiques', as someone once most unkindly called my line
of elderly gentlemen. Though there were only two of them;
yourself and then Mr Palmer.

It's not Palmer whom I miss, no sir, no! Only you, Garrick
Dodds, who joined your mother in the burial ground of St
Jude's where we used to attend Sunday service together.
You were buried in an atmosphere of hush and black
crêpe where they whispered, 'passed on', 'at rest', 'at peace',
'gone before', and only I, though I have spent a lifetime on
unrealities, said, *dead*.

There's a funny thought. But we'll come to the funny
thoughts later.

*

In May 1915, a hopeful month of the year though not
perhaps of this one, I pen these lines in a gypsy vardo;
a solid, safe, wooden caravan decorated with arabesques
of gold like a music-hall stage. I picked it up cheap from
gypsies camped on Mr Palmer's estate. In this humble vehicle,
a change after Mr P.'s Rolls-Royce motor car I can tell you,
I am wandering yet again, yet again. How many times in
boyhood and in . . . later . . . have I travelled these ways by
one means or another?

It is night, when anyone, especially an ageing drag-artist,
feels vulnerable in a caravan. The door is locked against
what I fear. Pursuit. The candles flicker in what were your
mother's candlesticks. My open notebook is soaking up the
light. Shadows elsewhere. A few moths have strayed in.

1

Yesterday, Tuesday 18 May, I left Halifax and travelled the Calder Valley. The moorlands above are as bare and unpopulated as the moon, but cutting through them is this crammed, industrial scar. Road, canal and railway are twisted into one thread, spun through the jumble of textile-workers' terraces, mills and some fine houses of tradesmen and factory-owners. All working places, caked in soot. Familiar districts; I have spent my life in these parts. What a place it is for an entertainer, for they need one here!

At the moment, the main entertainment is the War.

You know what it's like all over England these days, but as it's sure to be forgotten, I'll set it down. Every village, Pye Nest, Friendly, Luddenden, Mytholm, is excited with the fever to recruit, as day by day over there in Flanders the blood drains away. These crowded valleys are a rich source of cannon-fodder. The more the black-bordered telegrams pour into the villages, the more eager they become to sacrifice their young. The grief is hidden, a subject for shame, but sacrifice is a public and joyful entertainment. I even came across a tram requisitioned as a recruitment office. Decked with flags and bunting as if for a fair, a wakes or a circus, it trundled down the valley between cheering crowds. Every church hall is advertising a dance or a sale of work, 'to aid the war effort'. The recruits gather at the photographers' studios, afraid to go away without leaving a reminder with their wives. They have their wives and sweethearts taken, too; some of them, I know, in ways they wouldn't want their daughters to see. Lewd photos are carried against the breast to turn away bullets. (I have heard of prayerbooks stopping bullets, but never a wallet of naughty pics.) 'We'll be back by Christmas!' – chanted like a music-hall chorus, while the churches send them forth with brass bands and death-worshipping hymns. I'm glad to be a woman, as it were. Or, as a man, one just too old for this madness.

After Todmorden, I reached the head of the Cliviger Valley, Burnley waiting on the other side. I am now in a bleak but, hopefully, peaceful place. No recruiting sergeants here, to inspect a thirty-nine-year-old drag-queen. No ladies energetic nowadays, as they never were on ballroom floors, with the pleasure of driving young men to the trenches. No one at all. In this district, out of dense habitations one climbs into regions that are like the world before creation, barren, stony, covered with a hair of coarse, sooted grasses; for the chimney smoke still pours all over the hilltops. Places where life does not yet seem to have happened. If you call war, 'life'.

My destination: in my transportable dressing-room, with my mementos, I, like many in my profession, trust that I'll find a better season on the Lancashire coast, in Blackpool for the summer. Turn into a pierrette on the sands. Find some colleagues with whom to get together a revue. When there is no one else to perform for, I'll entertain children, or fishermen at the end of the pier. If you can distract them from staring at the sea, you know you're damned good, for there's nothing more difficult than gaining the attention of a fisherman; which is interesting, when you think there can't be a more uncomfortable, boring business than fishing. But they're stubborn about it. I know them, because Mr Palmer was fond of fishing – the flies and trout sort.

> . . . *Oh, I do like to be beside the seaside,*
> *I do like to be beside the sea,*
> *Oh I do like to stroll upon the Prom, Prom, Prom*
> *Where the brass bands play, tid-de-ly om pom pom . . .*

That was written about Blackpool, you know. There I hope to revive my finances, after a year of hopping about the North like a blessed flea on the back of a snapping dog, pursued by –

I'll come to that later.

Most important of all: with the sea air and by eating the fresh vegetables that they grow in west Lancashire (Blackpool tomatoes and celery are famous), perhaps I will renew my health, find the peace and strength to finish my *writing . . . writing . . . writing*. There being two sides to everything, I must, from my side of it, *explain*.

Get it down, before it is too late.

For I've a feeling that in one way or another the net's tightening. 'Armageddon hangs above us all,' as a Salvation Army man at the Pye Nest crossroads declared.

My façade is crumbling under the weight of creams, powders, rouges and raids upon superfluous hair. Don't they play havoc with a gal, these fellars! My dressing up has replaced *everything*. Touching ... love ... everything ... But at least I have my *writing*. Dare I say: I am writing for both of us, Mr Dodds. I'll try to be fair.

*

Tonight I had my dream again. This is one I've had of my origins, oh, many times, though less often as the years have gone by. In fact nothing is known about them except that I was found by a railway track, but I think there might be a lot of hidden truth in these dreams that fade.

I see a woman in a first-class carriage, as such were in 1875, forty years ago. She is a poor woman with problems, so I don't understand why she is in such a place. Can only surmise. She is alone except for her baby cocooned in a shawl on her arm. Her little baby boy: that's me, I was a boy, then. I imagine that, in classic fashion, some well-off chap has set her up and then deserted her, or rather sent her and her, that is, their, infant packing. With a first-class rail ticket, to make himself feel generous. I've met so many of these cads, I know the type well. With difficulty against the tilt of the rocking train, immediately before it enters the Standedge Tunnel through the Yorkshire moors between Saddleworth and Huddersfield, she opens the window and thrusts out the baby which unrolls from its garment and drops like lead. She performs her act hurriedly, seemingly on impulse but of course it must have been premeditated, the culmination of a huge and insoluble grief. Perhaps the train does not stop at Diggle, the little station at the tunnel mouth. She slams the window shut before reaching that black hole in the earth.

The smoke and soot is passing by the window on the other side of the carriage, down to which the floor slopes. She has chosen a moment when they are travelling round a bend, thrusting forth the baby on the outer side of the curve. Presumably because that is how she can ensure that no one, peering through another window, is likely to be able to see her: not without leaning a long way out and maybe not even then.

But, dash it, this is only likely, it is not infallible. She is not an experienced criminal and also she is too distraught to plan her act well. The curve that the train is following means that the child will roll down the embankment. There is no certainty of death that way. Presumably she intends to destroy her offspring, otherwise she might have left him on a doorstep. Therefore she would have done better to have thrown him out when the curve was in the other direction, to fall on to the other track and probably be killed, without a trace of the deed, by a train coming the other way. Also, scattered along the side of the track are factories and farms from which what happened might have been observed. She could have waited until they entered the tunnel and thrown it out with no one to see her.

At the last moment, was the thought of splattered blood and tissue torn from her own heart too much for her? Or did she both wish to kill it and want it to live, like some ancient Greek mother leaving a babe on the bare mountainside, giving the gods a chance to decide?

That thought is a door into my mother's soul.

And it comforts me that, from the beginning and before I was taken into account, there were already two sides to everything in my life.

*

As always, I awoke in the middle of the night, sweating and also shivering. My fingers are so soft and wrinkled, it is as if I had taken a hot bath. It is not sickness, real sickness, so much as – oh, I miss you, dash it! I miss you! I am trapped in my grief, listening for sounds because of my dread of pursuit and detection by your sister, Liza Buckton.

No matter what you left me, dear Garrick Dodds, in truth I lost everything, that is, everything that mattered, when you died. At any rate, I lost far more than did that envious Liza who while you were alive hardly came near, because of your 'carryings on' as she called them, and now she claims that *she's* been cheated! So now I have to run. *Her dratted lawyers!*

Sometimes, when I wake so abruptly, I imagine I hear the voice and the familiar footsteps of you who were so kind, so kind. I hear it most clearly. I *have* loved . . . well, you at least; but I've done none of the unnatural things Liza Buckton is trying to stick on me, I swear! For you were as pure as the driven snow. In honour of your mother. 'Mere' dressing up has been the sum of my thrills. The fear was so great. But even to have associated together can get you penal servitude, so they tell me. We ourselves hardly discussed it, for, despite the Oscar Wilde case, you poo-poo-ed my fears.

I woke thus an hour ago and only after a moment did I realise where I was. Outside, there was only the looming moor, those rocks and cliffs. I was beating the covers in panic and despair. At such times – they have occurred before – I am a beetle on its back, a fly in a web. I cannot breathe. I cannot breathe and I panic. There is heartburn. I am alone.

Health is a mysterious essence. It depends upon happiness. It does not flourish in loneliness. It is like soul, in that you cannot say where or precisely what it is but you certainly know when it has fled. The vacuum! You never think about your health until one day you find it gone. You realise then that something has left your body, that a spirit has flown, or seeped into the ground to await your corpse. From then on, your heartburn and breathlessness are no longer temporary troubles to be noosed in a joke. They are the leering faces of that ghost in your body: mortality. I am not George Formby, laughing at his consumption. I saw him only a short time ago. 'I'm coughing better tonight!' he joked as he spat blood in front of the curtain. 'It's not the cough that carries you off. It's the coffin that they carry you off in!'

But I – I am frightened. With what time is left, I have to write it all down: the truth.

But just look at me.

In the mirror: move the lamp and see. Gypsies' caravans are full of mirrors, fitted not for vanity, nor as instruments for examining yourself so as to settle matters of doubt, but in order to give the illusion of space. For one reason or another, mirrors have turned out to be the settings of my fate. They're always present. Mr Palmer's mansion had drawing-room walls, dining-room walls, bathrooms and dressing-rooms made of them to reflect the goings-on. Once it was my delight to be always peering in them. When I first went into the old Folly Theatre in Peter Street, Manchester, and found it full of mirrors, doubling everything that happened, I thought that they made it the most magical place I'd been to in my life and it was a great disappointment I never got round to treading the boards there before it was all done up afresh and re-named The Tivoli in – 1897, I think it was. Mirrors have filled theatre dressing-rooms, they have been the essentials in my bedrooms, *and* I have faced the camera's lens, which is nought but a moving mirror. In public salons, it is impossible for me to be secure and comfortable without checking my appearance from time to time. Yes, the Fates attendant at my birth brought me mirrors whether I've wanted them or not. Now I try to avoid them, but I can't. Glasses. In this tiny, only-nest that I have, I cannot avoid reflections of myself and my tatty drag-act except by burying my head in a pillow.

Which I do when I am not bent over these pages, for reflections show horror incarnate. They truly do. Oh, my looks are fled! After having dressed up (merely for my own pleasure) in the caravan last night, now I see my grotesque make-up, still cruelly smeared over my – I need a shave. Without my wig, I see the thin, flattened, natural hair receding. My teeth going. The ridiculous, frilled night-gown, purchased in my palmy days from Leak and Thorpe of York, hiding softly hairy thighs. The chest, when truth is out, without breasts; I don't bother to shave nor wax-treat my chest anymore. Nobody's going to see me so close.

Oh, my dear one, what a mess! It's the way of life that we lived that's made me ill, I know it; and, if truth was out, it was what killed you so suddenly, stopping your heart. Living in a fantasy is so nervy, so exhausting. You have been hugging yourselves in the egg of an artificial world, but you never know when your partner, or you yourself, is going to come to his senses. A fantasy is much kinder, and becomes more real-seeming than the real world, because you have made it yourself, but its thin shell is easily broken. You never know when your dear friend is going to abandon the treaty that makes the madness work. '*Get out of those ridic-u-lous clothes!*' Where are you then, may I ask?

Of course, you never said it – not that one. But I always feared it; that or some other expostulation. Imagine the scope there is for cruelty. You might find yourself saying something. You bring tears to Mr Dodds' eyes. You wish you hadn't done it. You didn't mean it. You did. Which one of you did; which self? You never know where you are. Nor what you are. Your deepest desire comes to be for – security.

To know who you are.

Something like that eats at you and the illness grows inside.

Just look at me! *Look at me!* Is this tattered rag doll that same youth, who, if a strange path had not unrolled before him, might have grown into a decent man with a wife and family? With my temperament, with the example of my beginnings (or rather, lack of them), could I ever have been a good father? Whatever else I see, those questions, those ones, are always there, looking for me. Hunting me.

Which one is me; who am I? Frustrated male, husband and father; or merely a derelict drag-queen? If I try to hide, I cannot escape it for long before the question pounces on me. Is *that* me! Is that me, dash it, or isn't it? It can't be. It must be. That grotesque! Jack Shuttleworth, alias Camellia Snow . . . that wriggling, desperate creature, squirming in the night like a worm in the soil, that *thing*, with its mask that is taken by the world as being *me!*

I don't want to end up repulsive.

But perhaps that's how we all end up.

*

The nights are not warm, yet. I shove some scrap wood and coal, scavenged from behind the mine in Halifax, if you care to know, into the little stove.

There were these two brothers, see. Archibald had a terrible st. . . st. . . st. . . utter and Cyril had a limp, because one leg was shorter than the other. They were walking along the road when Archibald said, 'I kn . . . kn . . . ow how to c. . .c. . .ure your l. . .limp. You should w. . .walk with one. . .ne. . .ne leg on the f. . .footpath and the other in the r. . .r. . .oad.' Cyril tried it and was run over by a cab. When Archibald visited him in hospital, Cyril told him, 'And I know how to cure your stutter! You should keep your flippin' mouth shut!'

I rehearse it on the moorland night. Get the intonations right. The pauses. The emphases. The things that make the difference between a well-told joke and a boring one. Do a sentence again. *They were walking along the road when . . .*

Nobody laughs. The stalls are empty. The moorland is nearly silent. But does that mean *safe*? Lawyers inform constables, who send spies. Lawyers send their own spies; Liza Buckton has enough money to pay for them. Palmer supports her. Any stranger looking at me twice could be tracking my whereabouts or looking for evidence, couldn't he? *I* should be hunting *her* for my rights. Instead . . . I know what the case is that they're getting together, because a friend of mine who works in Palmer's lawyer's office told me, when he came into The Mitre public house.

'Attempting to defraud Mr Dodds and influencing his Will when he was senile.'

You were *never* senile!

'Stealing from The Hollies.'

That's because I took away *our* things . . . the gramophone, tea-service, album of snaps, plus my dresses and a suitcase of memories, which Liza would have thrown on the tip.

Finally, 'False appearances.'

False appearances! It was your idea!

'Let me tell you, as your friend,' said this acquaintance of mine. '*You* know, *I* know, that none of it's true, but she won't stop short of accusing you of unnatural practices nonetheless, even though it means casting aspersions upon her own brother. I don't care what your sort gets up to, but take this from me, as your friend – be careful. Greedy, she is.'

You know what they do to people like me, once we're accused? We *'perverts'!* It doesn't have to be proved. Imagine what the tommies would do to me if I was stupid enough to be swept into – all that lot.

Oh, forget it for a moment, forget it! It is a lovely, starry night. My horse, Taffy, a Welsh cob, is quiet, tethered on the road verge outside, giving out the quiet and companionable pulses of his breathing. What spiffing weather we're enjoying, aren't we? It makes the tragedy of the War more poignant, over there where apparently it's so muddy. There is a thin, new moon, unusually clear for this misty part of the world. It is steely-white and as sharp as the clipping of a fingernail, glowing through my little golden curtains. On the hillsides, if

I peep, are moonlit splashes of hawthorn flowers. I enjoyed looking at them as I travelled yesterday. Some of the bushes were incandescent with blossom, like a theatre's gas lamps when their mantles first glow. Mr Oscar Wilde said that 'nature is middle-class', but we used to love it, taking drives in the motor car, sitting in the gardens of tea-rooms in Harrogate or in Ilkley, by the River Wharfe, or strolling; hands openly touching, at times. We did touch one another in public, you know, taking a risk, fingertips to fingertips, sometimes.

In the sunset yesterday I heard the first curlew of the summer. It is still crying and besides that plaintive bird, disturbed by the moon in its new, summer home, only I am restless. I *wish* I could sleep, but for years I have got into the habit of being alive mostly at night and in the twilight, or among the vague and tricky effects produced by paraffin flares and candles, or in the dim electric lamps of theatres when I cannot be inspected too closely.

I dip into my pages. Even when I bury my face away from mirrors, I, that *I* whom I do not possess, is reflected in my own imagination, to haunt me.

I miss you, Garrick. After you died, Mr Palmer asked me how I felt. I could not tell him; could not utter a word. But after some time, I found myself able to speak lightheartedly (which was, after all, how Palmer always wanted me to speak) about what was still breaking my heart, and the way I put it was to say that those years were now as distant as if they'd been lived by someone else.

But all my life, I said, looking back on it, fell into periods that I had lived as quite different people. I wondered, then, as I wonder now, which one of me would be living the next stage.

The choices are still before me, at least to think about; for one does have to go on living, doesn't one? Jack Shuttleworth, Camellia Snow, Rose Gay, Lily Dreams, Iris Vane. . . . What a lot of names I've had, and Blackpool awaits them; my last fling?

I always choose flowers. All of them pretty names for one who does not even own his . . . her . . . own body; which has been given twenty-four hours a day to be the slave of whatever invention pleases others!

To please some old man!

Some antique!

But here is my real secret (perhaps you've guessed): the truth is that often, even now, on seeing some pretty girl in the street, I could throw off my glad-rags, abandon the treaty, thinking, *what have I missed, what have I missed?*

*

A fallen woman with a girl child can find a husband more easily than she can if she has a boy. If I had been a girl, maybe my mother would not have needed to cast me aside. But, if I had been a real female, I should not have known you.

Before you condemn my mother's abandoning me, please bear it in mind that her own child does not hold it against her. By Jove, I've seen too many dastardly acts to condemn human weakness!

I was found in a bush at the back of a factory in Diggle, by the railway line. My natural mother has never been traced. I used to daydream that in some theatre or public house a smiling, tear-smeared woman, still pretty, fair-haired like myself, of slender build like me, would step forth and 'Mother!' I'd exclaim, 'Mother!', as I instantly recognised her. I'm sure she goes to the theatre or the music hall, for most people do. Do you think she might have seen me perform? But that perhaps, after all, she crept away?

Do you think she might have seen me projected by a bioscope? My performance as a nervous tart in Mr Bamforth of Holmfirth's *Kisses in the Train*, perhaps, which they often show during music-hall intervals?

I'm sure I'd recognise her, yet the truth is that nothing is known about my mother except what I can tell from the not insignificant (*not insignificant*: I like that form of expression, it was one of your favourites) track she has left across my mind; and I honestly don't know if this is another of my fantasies, or truth; an image of her laid down before my memory began. At any rate, she glows like a comet in my reveries, in my recurrent dreams, and you used to talk this way about your mother, too; I am not alone.

As time has gone by, my picture of her, my idea of her world, of the way she moves and speaks, of what she loves and what she fears, has filled itself out and I'm sure it's not merely whimsical. Pictures of her have sprung into my mind, unexpected, unasked for, and have stayed there. Perhaps it is *actually* she who visits me in dreams, giving glimpses of herself; I have known madder ideas than this peddled by showmen and many have been proved true. Shall I paint her picture for you? Her swan's neck, her fair ringlets, her laughing eyes? Better not; I would get carried away and it would take up too much time. But I tell you this: I have a clearer idea of her, whom I never actually knew, than many have of the mothers who they live with.

With whom they live, as you told me I should say.

I suppose that, as according to Dr Malthus the poor are multiplying so superfluously (another idea that you taught me), whoever it was who found me might have left me to die, which would have needed only an hour or so of neglect. But at the back of a spinning mill it was more than likely a woman who lighted upon me. I've always been able to rely on genuine women, you see; only I've met so few.

She would have handed me over to someone with more authority, but perhaps whoever he was would bear it in mind that there was this female witness in the background. A motherly woman with a tender heart, perhaps.

At any rate I was taken up the hill and handed over to a lovely, fat wet-nurse, whose huge body I could sink into; name of Mary Shuttleworth, in the women's dormitory of the Saddleworth workhouse in Diggle.

It was she who stuck the name *Jacky* on to me at a rough christening, together with her own surname. As it could be short for a woman's name, *Jacqueline*, it was also the first one that I used for my impersonations.

What was she like? As I read of the ideal wet-nurse in *The Mother's Medical Adviser*, one of the volumes on women's ways I was exhorted to read when first entering your – service: *Her breath should be sweet, and perspiration free from smell; her gums firm and of good colour; teeth fine, white and perfect. Her milk should be white, inodorous, inclining to a sweet taste neither watery nor thick, of moderate consistency, separating into curd over a slow fire.*

Did Mary Shuttleworth offer all these things?

I believe I remember that she did; if only 'remembering' as Moses, or whoever it was first wrote about it, remembered Eden: in dreams.

I must have felt at the time like a grub curled up in a juicy apple.

Beginning of my conscious life.

Mary Shuttleworth had been admitted to give birth to an illegitimate baby of her own; and this goes to show that I had been let into a kindly spot for not every workhouse in the country opened its doors to such women. They usually took the moral tone and let them suffer their disgrace among their neighbours. Mary's natural-born infant had died and I was there to sup the milk. I have not always been unlucky, you see; and thereby I was given two mothers, the first of the soul and the second of the flesh.

*

How I talked to you about the workhouse, Mr Dodds! For as we could not go out on so very many evenings, considering the difficulties of the way I was dressed, like Scheherazade I had to entertain you with stories for my bread.

What else could we do? We played draughts, chess, snakes and ladders or cribbage; we enjoyed living in the artificial world of games, as anyone can imagine. You sometimes used to play piano arrangements by Parry, Stanford and Coleridge Taylor. Despite your sharp, educated wit, for which I so loved you, underneath you were full of soft-centred melancholy and I thought it was overblown, soggy stuff. Sometimes we sang together, or to each other. I rendered the turns that I knew: *And her beauty was sold for an old man's gold,/She's a bird in a gilded cage*, which was a hit, if I recall correctly, of 1899; or *The Future Mrs 'Awkins: At first she said she wouldn't,/Then she said she couldn't,/Then she whispered, 'Well, I'll see . . .'.*

Most of all, it moved me to sing *Little Yellow Bird*. You, in your beautiful tenor voice, did *Come into the Garden, Maude*.

But someone whose mind has explored the twilight of sexual doubts and uncertainties finds it difficult to get sustenance from sentimental songs and I preferred true stories.

13

I kept it up for hours in the evenings, in your parlour lit by too few lamps for us to read by, or later by those terrible electric lamps which used to catch fire – do you remember how we used to throw cushions at the ceiling? You wanted to fashion an atmosphere for your creation; I was dressed in black silk or crêpe perhaps, and certainly so after Queen Victoria died.

You could have made me into anything you wanted . . . yes, you could have turned me into anything. I was always game to be led. It was what I needed. My only fear was that you would become bored with me. Like Scheherazade, I feared that if I ceased to entertain you, you would boot me out. It took me until your death to realise that you were in truth faithful: oh, isn't that always the way?

You were so ignorant of my early world and so shocked. Your type could never understand Mary Shuttleworth who laughed at everything.

She laughed because whatever it was that she remembered, what she thought was, 'It could have been worse'. When she told me how she had been dragged by the edge of her caught skirt into a spinning machine, a common occurrence, thus losing a finger which was why she was never dexterous enough to work in a mill again, and she a girl of only fifteen, she laughed and laughed because 'It could have been worse for me, couldn't it?'

She was mother to us all, adults and children alike, until she died when I was nine. Kept on at the workhouse to cook, to clean and stitch, to iron and mend, Mary used to entertain children and strangers as she sucked and blew at her clay pipe by the kitchen fire, telling stories, just as I recounted them later on the music-hall stage and as I told them to you; or as she sipped the ale that she was permitted to drink at all hours. You would find her at it for breakfast; oh, couldn't she put it away! She was granted the privilege not merely because she cooked, but also because of the size of her body and of her personality. She was a big woman in every way. And intimidating.

Some used to play the fiddle in the kitchen; others used to clog-dance; Mary, like the statue of a goddess, used to sit in her throne by the fire until the hour came when she

14

was moved to tell us stories. From her smoking, her strong voice was an impressive octave below the usual for a female. If anyone interrupted her, "Old your noise until you know summat!' she'd declare, silencing them with her low, modest but authoritative tone as she pointed the stem of her pipe. 'How old was she?' I hear you ask. At the time of which I write, she must have been turned thirty.

She had got herself into trouble through stitching a sampler, depicting Christ and the Lamb. Her mother showed it to everyone who came to the door, especially to a mill-engineer named Joe Gaukroger.

"'I like it enough but I make nowt o' the sheep," Joe said. "She ought to 'ave done a dog. I'm right fond of a dog." When Joe had gone, Mother said, "Thee go and stitch a dog. Thou never knows." She meant that at twenty-five I was growing into an old maid. "The size you are, there's not many men around who could suit thee. If you don't catch someone now, it'll be time for you to get into a bonnet and take to religion instead.'"

By this stage of her tale, Mary would have to relight her pipe, pour some fresh ale and wipe away a tear with a corner of her apron. I learned the dramatic pause and most of the rest of the art of story-telling from her.

Mary continued. "'But . . . ." I interrupted. "No *buts!*" Mother shouted. "Get out thee silks and start on a dog and 'old thee noise 'till thou knows summat!" So I started on a dog. First time that I saw Joe after, I said, "I've done its 'ead, you'd best come round and see." So Joe come round and set his feet under the table. I made 'im some tea, with a bit o' cake. My mother asked 'im what sort o' trade mill-engineering was at the moment and 'e answered, "Very fine." So the next week, I says to Joe, "I've done the dog's feet, now. Thou mun come and see." And so on, until, though as is the way wi' big chaps 'e was a bit backward at coming forward wi' speaking, 'e promised me all sorts. "I seem to be getting into the way o' coming and folk are getting into the way o' nodding and whispering," 'e says wi' a smile on 'is face. "I'd 'appen better do summat about it." And 'e did, too. At the back of our 'ay barn. It were the annual Wakes' 'oliday. Folk stopped work and got drunk, at 'ome if they didn't go to Blackpool. 'E was drunk. So was I. Then 'e disappeared over the 'ill to another job, as mill-engineers do . . .

'Thou doesn't know what I'm talking about, does tha?' she added for my benefit, I suppose because I was staring at her so intently.

'No, Mary.'

'Thou knows what a Wakes Week is, though, doesn't tha?'

Yes, I did. Was I five years of age when these memories began? For Mary told her stories year after year, polishing them as time went by. The Wakes Week holiday reached even into the workhouse. It was a different week in each town, according to the saint's day of the parish church. It was called a 'wake' because you could stay awake all night if you wished to on a holiday, so Mary teased me; and I believe it was true. The mills shut off their furnaces and by the end of the week the sky nearly cleared of smoke and soot; get a fine week, the sun breaking through, and it showed up the muck gathered on everything.

'Thou knows what a Wakes is 'cos it means sugar sticks and being taken to t'fairground and comic bands when chaps black their faces and wear silly 'ats wi' flowers on and tell silly stories,' she teased me, and then she turned back to the others.

'Eh, well, never mind,' she said, stroking my head. 'If I've not a chap and a family, I've got this one, who will do for both a boy and a girl.'

The workhouse is still standing today. It is a collection of stone buildings on an acre site, alone and visible for miles across the moorlands on a hillock named Running Hill. With irony, Mr Dodds. For there was no chance of running anywhere. Every outside window was barred and the gate kept locked. The name was a temptation to defiance, a daily reminder that there must be places and things to run to, if only someone could show me.

There were about a hundred of us in there, many not permanently, and in fact the Board of Guardians spent most of its money on relieving trouble outside its walls. People were always coming to its gate. You were very conspicuous when you went up that bare hill, so no one would search it out who

16

wasn't truly in distress. Do you think that was why it was built in such a spot: to put misery centre-stage?

But also, tramps who had crossed the Pennines from Huddersfield would have their spirits raised on seeing the workhouse and its chimney mounted like a castle on the hillock, for they could stay there overnight, maybe a little longer if they were willing to work. We had vegetable gardens, an orchard, plus one or two small fields growing oats for porridge and bread. We also grazed four or five milk-cows and a few sheep. We kept poultry and work-horses, besides having our own bakery, dairy and laundry. Some of the other hill-dwellers said that we lived in a palace. They envied us our cows, our big cast-iron bread-ovens, and our walled garden which meant that we could grow vegetables and greens despite the wind. Everyone else lived mostly on a monotonous diet of oats and even people's skins had the texture of porridge.

Oh, how you tutted over my distant hardships, Mr Dodds, you who were brought up on roast beef! You cried as over, say, *Little Yellow Bird*. Though to me it had not seemed like hardship, with such as Mary Shuttleworth singing around the place, so proud.

It was after all a proud system that allowed us to sustain ourselves and not be too great a strain on the Guardians' resources; leaving the bowl spilling over for others. There I was taught at the beginning of my life to exist through self-sufficiency and not dependency, I'm glad to say. If I'd been in a more common type of workhouse perhaps I would have turned out institutionalised and always happy to have found a prison for myself. 'What's most striking is how often you have gone scuttling for shelter!' I hear you say. Both are true, probably, but the point is that, as you see, I've always broken away in the end.

It was, in fact, only its prison-like character which I resented; and did I resent it! We could have withstood a siege and the place was built as if we expected one. I don't know whether we were being punished, or being trained to be as inward-looking as monks so as to discover the secrets of our 'sorry state', but there was no way that even an adult could look out without standing on something and straining. The

17

design of the windows proclaimed that they would choose to do anything rather than let in light or air, so just be grateful for what little was offered! They were as narrow and as deep as possible, which made you feel that you were at the end of a tunnel or at the bottom of a well rather than looking from a building and were made not with small bricks or stones but with huge slabs that wouldn't let you forget weight, size and superhuman oppression. A great many bars, of course, strong enough to resist a horse but close enough together to confine a rabbit, let alone a child.

Dear Mr Dodds; you could not imagine it and Saddleworth Workhouse might have been as far away as Africa from your home in Savile Park, Halifax. Even its smell was unimaginable to you, its human smell of sweat and dirt; you who lived in The Hollies in your own peculiar aroma of eau-de-Cologne mingled with fat and suet produced by Mona, the cook!

But we agreed in our opinions of men even though, unlike me, you yourself had a father – whom you hated. Similar men did briefly descend into my life with rules and punishments. In years I hardly saw a male except as a patriarch for me to suspect and fear. When you described your father, I knew exactly what you were talking about. What are called 'manly' features – being always aggressive, alert for a fight – naturally disgusted and frightened me.

Of course, I dreamed also of an ideal father; that word drummed into us through the phrase 'God the Father', conjuring up strength and security. These qualities have been searched out by me more desperately than by those who take their families for granted. That was why I went to such lengths to please you. Surely only a person desperate for security would have done the things I did. That is what I was *really* looking for, in Mr Palmer and in you; a model man, a model protector. Someone to show me the way.

As you had been, I too was compensated by being over-mothered. Not only by Mary, who alone could swallow the whole world, but by many women. For I was held in the women's dormitory, where frustrated motherly instincts were poured upon me. In contrast to my ignorance of men, I knew all about women through growing up in the company of so many of them. From the start I felt, saw, smelled and heard them in all their varieties. There were no 'female mysteries' for me. Women kept no secrets from a child they assumed could not be interested in them, yet on the contrary I was taking in the keenest observations of my life.

I was absorbing, in the fashion of a daughter, a woman's ways.

Yes, it started as early as that. How to walk, how to sit, how to be mendacious. How to pull my face, to get my own way. How to put on a look of vulnerability so as to draw sympathy and avert a blow.

How stupid men are, who seem never to understand that there is a guerrilla war being conducted inside their camp! It is women's only way. They think of men as an army of occupation. Men lay down the rules and do as they wish with women who have no recourse to law over most of what is done to them. I can hardly have been more than four or five when I started to overhear details of random, drunken beatings.

'Perhaps I 'ave no' missed so much,' Mary used to say. 'If I've been short of a man wanting to set 'is feet under my table, yet I know that I can agree best wi' myself! That way, there's no one to 'arm me. Even if I'd been favoured wi' a good 'usband, we might still 'ave both ended up 'ere, after a lifetime of being together now kept apart as punishment for the crime of poverty.'

Like all the women, I had an endless desire to cheat one man in particular: the workhouse master, that patriarch with sweat and hair all over his face.

For instance: for some reason, we were forbidden to look out. Therefore my rebellion took the form of climbing up out of the circus of sweaty petticoats and aprons in order to peer through the window. Down the green slopes to the valley where Delph was; across a mile or so to Saddleworth Church; and a few miles away, above the hidden town of Uppermill, the higher hills toothed with boulders called, as I knew long before I was able to visit them, Pots and Pans. I would see larks spring out of the fields and hang, quivering black stars, on the blue. The curlews would sweep and cry, over such distances!

19

So easy! Oh, if only I had *someone* to take me, to lead me through it all; the magic and mystery of the world.

But a strap would land on my backside and with a grazed shin, or a crack on the back of my head where I had caught the lintel of the window, I would yelp and fall back into the pit, hearing the sneer of the master.

'He's a lovely voice!' some of the crueller women joked at my cry. They were not *all* softness and kindness!

This was because I used to sing around the place, and it was noticed.

'Let him be, he's nobbut a girl, isn't Jacky Shuttleworth!' other women said and laughed.

Even though the master knew perfectly well what sex I was, yet the mere suggestion that I was a girl made him hold his hand. What a defence it was! The instinct to protect rather than punish a female is so strong, is it any wonder that I began to make use of it?

*

'Saddleworth', twenty miles over the other side of the Pennines from Halifax, is the general name for the villages along the valley of the River Thame. *Dob Cross, Denshaw, Diggle and Delph.* They are hard, stony, smoky places but their names running together make a sweet, metrical sound that I was taught to say over and over; mysterious villages which I had not yet visited, but when Mary Shuttleworth lilted them, they formed the first line of song or poetry that I knew.

Saddleworth was typical of the valleys burrowing into the Pennines, ending at a hamlet of textile mills and a sooted wall of starved moorland: the places where all my life I have rooted for a living. I could have been a starved thorn myself.

'Nobody blows into the Thame Valley without they've a reason, trading i' wool, building a mill or summat,' Mary used to philosophise. 'Even more so wi' the coming of the railway, they generally pass straight through. The Tunnel blacks out all memory of Saddleworth. We seem a lawless set, especially those still living by 'andloom weaving on the 'ills, as we've been doing for centuries, keeping our distance from both strangers and neighbours.'

Yet I knew that, as in all other valleys, this would be broken by the men getting drunk for days on end, during a Wakes Week or a rush-bearing; most usually when they had sold a woven piece and were supposedly returning home. Few could resist celebrating at an inn for days.

Mary tapped out her pipes on the back of the stove, where she often broke them. There collected a white, limey heap of her old, bitten stems and bowls, until they were eventually thrown out with the ashes.

'And no stranger gets th'ang of our names,' she continued, for the entertainment of some poor strangers who were tramping across the country from Liverpool to Hull. 'Walk into a tap-room, ask for "James Bradley" and they'll pretend not to know who the d——l you are talking about. Everyone's called by their Christian name, but as there's only an 'andful of 'em we've to link 'em to a father, grandfather, great-grandfather or a farm or cottage. "Does tha mean James o' Jack's o' Bill's o't' Gate, by any chance? Or ar't' looking for James o' Bill's o' John's o' Sarah? Or 'appen it's James o'Bills o't'Moorside thou's wanting?" They know well enough who simple James Bradley is, for 'e's 'is name written over 'is shop, but they like to tease. I was always known as "Mary o't'Gate".' She laughed. 'And sometimes I think I've left the gate too wide open!'

Thus she explained to me the history and character of the world that I had entered. She it was who began my education.

There was a gruff kindliness, a strong-speaking attitude in Saddleworth that has taught me to be uncomfortable with dissemblers and hypocrites. Also, the dwellers of what I proudly think of as my 'native valley' weren't as lawless as at first they appeared. Differing from their plain-dwelling neighbours in Lancashire and separated from Yorkshire folk like themselves by the wall of moorland, they held to laws of their own. This was based on a common decency that in many instances was a good deal kinder than the Acts passed by the London Parliament.

About women, for instance. Although a man could neglect his family through drinking in the alehouse, on the other hand if he overstepped the mark his own drinking mates wouldn't be slow to hand out justice.

'There was a man we carried tied on a ladder through a jeering crowd for a mile from 'ome to 'is favourite pub and back again,' said Mary. 'There 'e was dumped on the doorstep for 'is wife to let 'im in or not, as she wished. This was because 'e'd knocked 'er about and cursed 'er loud enough for the neighbours t'ear. I doubt if 'e did it again.

'Then there was the effigies of a man and 'is wife who were burned in front of their own 'ouse because they'd so badly treated a six-year-old girl that they'd broken 'er legs.

'And there was something more,' she said. 'Once . . .' What she was about to say made even her nervous to speak of it. She tapped out her pipe too fiercely and broke the stem. Her hand was shaking. 'They killed a man. One of two who were living together, as . . . well, we were suspicious, and it came to a head when they took a young boy in one evening. *Nobody* can abide that sort of thing. One of the men – if you can call him such – was found chopped in bits on the moors. The other one fled. The community closed its doors and nobody ever found out who did it.'

She spat in contempt, while something –a prescience, I suppose – gripped me with fear. No, I could never do that!

Mary o't'Gate had been bred in one of the handloom weavers' cottages which are scattered over the hillsides to monopolise a watercourse and to surround themselves with a bit of a field for drying cloth in and grazing a pony. The sprinkling of small, unembroidered huts (you could not claim that their cottages were anything more), made of dark stone, is characteristic of this Pennine region. Some cottages, but not Mary's, had a special loom shop built either as a third storey or as an extension. 'But we used to weave in our bedrooms. After a Wakes Week when a wool merchant called round to see the pieces 'e'd to step around us asleep in our beds.'

The men did the weaving. The women and children went down to the spinning mills in the valley. At that time, there were very few factories engaged in weaving and employing men. If they were not spinning cotton or wool, the factories were making shawls and flannel to sell in Lancashire, or perhaps carding wool for firms in Rochdale.

Morning and evening, I'd see through my cell window the women and girls threading their way down the hillsides, among fields white with cloth stretched to dry on tenter frames. Mary could look out without too much straining on her toes. Sometimes she lifted me up and held me, her cheek against mine. Tough as a carter though she was, she'd see the girls picking their way down the hillsides and would grow sad. 'Can you see me doing that?' she'd say. 'Can you see me when I lived that life? Ah, I was young then! You should've seen me.'

Gathering lower down, they formed single lines following the footpaths between the walls. In their white aprons and shawls against the dark landscape, I fancied the sight was very like that of threads of cotton spreading from a spinning machine.

'We mixed with a different sort when we got down in the valley. Wi' folk who lived in terraced 'ouses near to the mills and who didn't keep looms in their bedrooms. It was the men from these places who worked in the factories, weaving by steam-power. They lived among machines and sometimes seemed closer to machines than they were to people. They were very strange to us, who were still on th'illsides. Up there, we still kept to different ideas. Old-fashioned, you might say. Two breeds of people were forming.'

But it struck me that, one way or another, their whole lives were about work; and what work was I, Jacky Shuttleworth, to do to get out of the – yes – *work*house?

*

What were the choices, dash it? Near by, there were four coal pits. I couldn't think of a fate worse than to be sent to toil and worm in dark underground tunnels. I have enough trouble with living in a caravan! Claustrophobia: isn't that what they call it?

I can still see you shudder at the idea of me in the coal mines. 'And you so delicate,' you say. 'Such a golden child, you must have been, for such a destiny! Your lovely hair . . .' Instead of ringing for Mona or Sarah, which would interrupt our mood, you lean forward and poke the fire yourself, to shake off these unpleasant thoughts.

Reservoirs were being dug on the moor tops. In 1883, when I was eight and the need to be employed was first on my mind, they started on that reservoir at Greenfield for the Ashton-under-Lyne and Oldham Corporations and a year later, when what was termed my 'years of dalliance' were over, they were talking about signing on 'hands' – including boys' hands – for the reservoir excavations at Castleshaw. The fresh air on the moorlands would have suited me, except that nobody could ever have imagined me growing up to be a navvy.

There was the Dob Cross Loom Works, which was growing bigger all the time because of James Hollingworth's patents. By now, they've made twenty-five thousand looms, to be found in all sorts of places abroad, Indian villages, Africa. But to swing a hammer in a foundry required strength, too.

All through my life there has been an immense amount of making and building taking place in Yorkshire and Lancashire; railway viaducts, cotton and woollen mills, factories of all kinds, mansions for the manufacturers and terraces for the workers. If I went anywhere else, I don't think I'd get over it being so quiet and still! In my time, the world around me has been quite remade – an astonishing change – and parts of it still seem to be nothing but mud, scaffolding, building sites, camps and drinking places for the navvies.

But such work is only for the strong. There was nothing else for me except to be apprenticed as a factory weaver, learning to weave by steam. Which was frightening enough. A few years before I was born a mill chimney up Friezland way collapsed, killing all eleven members of one family. They were aged from eight months to forty-five years and they have a plaque with mourning angels in the church, modelled upon something Italian, although others say that it's Turkish.

But I couldn't stay always a coward avoiding manly ways of earning a living, could I? Or so I was told.

When I was nine, Mary Shuttleworth was taken with a tumour. Her death was big, and quiet, and impressive, like her life. No moaning, though she quickly became only skin and bone. As she sat by the fire, she had a way of clasping her hands over the growth in her stomach and of turning her mouth away. Soon, she could not leave her bed. She still struggled to amuse us; until thoughts of Gaukroger strayed across her mind, whereupon Mary's expression was transformed by that experience which I heard people call 'love'.

So that was love! I could never forget it — the look on her face. She spoke so softly, so tenderly, yet her moments of recollection were quite frightening to me, because of the way in which the pain of love changed her.

Then those last little comets of thought, coming out of nowhere and vanishing quickly into the same darkness, also ceased. When I saw her for the last time, in the hospital, she looked straight through me for a long time, before she gave me a smile and lifted her hand the inch she was able to lift it, so that I could hold it.

She delivered her last advice. 'My boy-girl, I was very fond o' thee! Take care. Take care. But you canna get by in life through always trying to please other folk and getting to depend on them. Try to please yourself, in your own eyes, not other folk, in theirs. Being so timid'll be your downfall, mark my words.'

I think that is what she said, for it was difficult to make her out. At any rate, I understood what she was telling me, though I find that I haven't learned the lesson. More than once, on looking back, I wish that I had remembered, for I have altered and adapted myself to please you, to please Palmer, so as to be warm, to be safe; have tried to please audiences when I might have done better by behaving like Marie Lloyd, flaunting my boldest self.

Mary died in a space of weeks. Top and bottom of it is, I've spent my life in a sort of panic ever since, wondering where to regain her protection and her love, trying to buy it by pleasing people. Pleasing men, since no women came my way.

In some moods, yes, I believe that is what all my entertaining has amounted to: buying love.

*

Shortly after my Mary died, I was sent half time to Holingdrake's New Delight spinning and weaving mills. Can you see me, with my blond looks, my pinched and dreamy face, my big moist eyes, my delicate build, bereft of a mother for the second time and not even sure whether I was a boy or a girl, making my way with the other workers up the mile-long cobbled track to the factory and its group of dependent buildings — houses, chapel and mansion?

They were huddled remote from habitation, far from

humanity, high up towards the head of a poisoned stream. Why were they built in such an isolated place?

My apprenticeship in that hell of machines was supposed not to end until I was twenty-one, which was so distant it might as well have been a life sentence. A hollow eternity in which all I imagined being able to think of was Mary Shuttleworth; Mary o't'Gate, that had been left too wide open.

I was shown my indentures because I had to sign them, being among the not so very many there who could actually write his name. At that time I could read less than half of the paper, yet I found it impressive. I had never seen so many colours brought together on one sheet, for neither the workhouse nor the Methodist chapel was remarkable for its art. Such lurid colours, too. Reds, blues, crimsons and golds. The same as my caravan – I wonder if, without realising, the memory was the reason why I was so happy to have it painted in those colours? With its arms and other drawings, my indentures looked to me like a royal proclamation. It made me feel very important, but all it was doing was turning me into another kind of prisoner.

The other half of my days was supposed to be spent in getting a bit of schooling and all that's worth is just a word in passing. Schooling it may have been, but it wasn't education! Except that I learned from Miss Shingles the term, 'years of dalliance', and a few other words and phrases that advanced me in society later. The Reverend Johnson, and Miss Shingles in a silk cloak that had a quite devastating effect upon me, took it in turns to come up Running Hill. We depended upon the weather for them to turn up, as it was a bleak climb; or, in Miss Shingles' case, upon her 'indispositions', to which she was regularly prone. If they did face us on our two rows of hard pine-benches in the dining-room, they were supposed to teach us to read at least our prayer books. I learned practically nothing and how I acquired what in the end turned out to be an education belongs to a later part of my story. Even if one or the other of them came to save us from an afternoon of weeding in the gardens, the children who were over ten years of age were mostly so tired from their morning at factory or farm that they fell asleep and our teachers, either from kindness or from the desire for a peaceful life, wouldn't wake us.

I found out much later that in 1876 a law had been passed that children under ten should not be sent to work and that between the ages of ten and fourteen they should be provided with a certificate of their educational standards before being employed. This explains why, especially when the mills were in full production, if I was kept on to labour in the afternoons and a factory inspector or someone from the Saddleworth School Board called, I was hidden and nearly suffocated in a basket of shoddy.

But at least I was still among women. For although you would never guess so from seeing the clerks in the offices, once you got inside it was clear that all the spinning was done by what is called 'the fair sex'. Though few who have ever worked in a mill would call them that. Pale they certainly were, but fair in any other sense they were not! So striking were they in all sorts of ways and so unforgettable that my main problem in later life hasn't been the ability to behave like a woman; it has been not to shock drawing-rooms and café tea-rooms by behaving like one of *them*.

Also they taught me not to be glib about the female character. If many of the ladies I have met since could have dropped what they think of as being feminine and had learnt from what I saw, they wouldn't have half the problems which they think are inevitable for members of their sex; though their new behaviour might upset all the establishments for gentlemen, such as the London clubs.

The spinners were the true heirs and sisters of Mary o't'Gate. They had qualities which those gentlemen and ladies who contribute pained articles to *Tit Bits* consider evidence of the immoral influence upon women of working in manufactories: I could see them only as strengths and virtues. They could fight and drink like navvies, repair machinery as well as any male mechanic and also thread cotton with a delicacy beyond almost all men; spend their money like drunken sailors, and then weep like . . . women. And mother me into the bargain. And go home and look after families. Those especially broad hips that women have so as to cradle and care for us even before we are born – they seem to have need of bigger hips all through life, sheltering men who never cease to behave like nursery-room babies. I mean: look at this War!

I even felt that women's opinions, like their cradling hips, were broader than men's. For example: when I first dared to express my picture of my origins, it was Mary Shuttleworth who had told me that only a man would throw his babe from a train or dash out its brains. What had I been imagining? she asked. I dreamed it all, I told her, but I was sure that it was true. Well, she said, she had once heard of a mother who murdered her baby the moment it was born, before she had taken a look at it or given it its first suckle. After this point, no woman had ever existed who would not try, however hopelessly, to secure a future for a child she was forced to abandon. Mary suggested that my natural mother had perhaps taken the opportunity of the train travelling at walking pace because of a signal, and had laid me carefully into the bush at the side of the track in a place where one of the women from the mill was bound to find me. But why should my having been found on a railway embankment have anything at all to do with a train? Why couldn't my mother have worked at the factory?

A woman can make a chap feel a frightful fool.

The female sex seemed capable of everything, every range of mood and behaviour, those of 'men' and those of 'women' too. They kept most of it secret, except from the eyes of watchful children like myself, and put on a different act as soon as there was a man in the room.

Women were employed because, supposedly, they were more biddable and could be paid less than men. How little the men understood! For, just as in the workhouse, these females were waging a secret war against the males; against mankind with its steam trains and ships, its guns and bridges. They were trying to hold intact something, some way of knowledge or of life, some ancient way, perhaps, that men knew nothing about. Is it any wonder that I wanted to be one of them, a member of their secret society?

Was my sex automatic — or did I have a choice of two ways in which to go?

Though for a long time I didn't even dare think of such a strange thing.

The girls used to sing in the factory. Because of the noise of the looms and the spinning frames, you couldn't hear a word of the songs. In any case, every child working there grew up a little deaf. But all of them learned to lip read. In Lancashire and Yorkshire mill-towns, everywhere you see half-deafened women communicating across crowded market squares or streets of traffic, pulling their mouths into exaggerated expressions like tragic actors and gesticulating to make their meanings clear. 'Mee-maw-ing,' they call it; try saying that, and you'll understand why. I, too, was eventually able to lip read. It is an art that has saved my bacon more than once; but I'll be coming to that.

I learned many of the songs of the day, as well as folk tunes. The spinners, and the men, too, the engineers and weavers, talked about the music halls, especially Liston's in Manchester and the Peoples' Music Hall in Oldham.

And I remember the day I learned some verses that, though they are as simple as nursery rhymes, chilled my blood:

> *The spinning frames a spinning*
> *The bobbins never still*
> *And a thousand threads are carried*
> *In the clatter of the mill.*
>
> *No loose tongues, girls,*
> *No loose ends*
> *Or the teller to the cellar*
> *The loose girl sends.*

The New Delight was mostly engaged in spinning, but Holingdrake's had recently opened a weaving shed to manufacture shawls out of shoddy and cotton. I didn't get far towards weaving a single shawl. I never got beyond being a 'piecer', for three years dashing among the looms and spinning-frames doing errands and dirty work for others. I couldn't stand the noise, or the fluff in the air which made me cough, or the hard work. I can hardly say it too often: all I had ever wanted was *out, out*; anything to feel free to move where I willed or felt inwardly driven to go.

I soon learned what Mary had meant when she told me, 'Folk are relating better to machines than to people; times are changing and a machine madness is upon us.' In the first day there I began to understand what factory life was and it maddened me that so many of these supposedly experienced and wise adults couldn't see the future lying before them. You would think that anything but a donkey could see it. Like donkeys, in the midst of times which in this district had never been so prosperous, they were simply being used up on their labour. They talked so much about their coming weddings or holidays, you'd never guess these events were months away and of such brief duration. How fond they were of saying, philosophically, 'You only live once', whenever they wanted an excuse for someone's drunken or mad behaviour and yet how carelessly they used up twelve hours of every precious day unpleasantly toiling for the benefit of others, gaining for themselves merely the sustenance to spend another day at it!

Meanwhile, they were acquiring all those ailments that, soon and irreversibly, made them unfit not only for work but for life itself. Arthritis, worn-out lungs from breathing dust and fluff, and poisoned blood from the chemicals. They used to walk home covered in white fluff. It smothered their hair, their shawls and their dresses as if it had been snowing. Imagine how much of it they were taking into their lungs. There was also a disease of the mouth contracted by many women. It was caused by spending a working life kissing the lead-tipped end of the shuttle in order to facilitate threading. They literally died of kissing the shuttle that enslaved them.

Did I say, they did it carelessly? No, I should not have said that. It is unfair, for what else could they do, poor things? And that was why they performed uncomplainingly, suffering for the sake of no more than a daily carrot, watching the full profits of their work go into building ugly churches and mansions, into polluting the river and blackening the hills. Yorkshire valleys are full of contentious people, it's 'built in with the bricks' as they say, and there were regular mutterings from trade unionists. In 1890 there was a strike at Rasping Mill; and there were others. Nevertheless, 'Revolution' held forth a weak and palsied hand hardly worth the bother of grasping, in my opinion.

I felt that the women, by themselves, were a good deal more determined and tough, even though they were secretive about it. In 1905 a mill-worker from Saddleworth, Annie Kenney, made a stir by joining forces with Christabel Pankhurst and starting the Suffragettes. Reading in the newspapers since about the Suffragettes frightening folk all over the country, I realise that women have more power because their organisation isn't restricted to the working class. But I wasn't yet a woman so I couldn't join their cause.

I knew it would kill me sooner than it killed most if I stayed in that mill.

*

As with so many factories in West Yorkshire, just outside its walls was a chapel, erected by the Holingdrake family. This stood in a treeless, grassless yard that was crammed with blackened stones. The graveyard, with the Holingdrakes' monumental tomb at the head of the slope, the workers' graves ranked below it, 'in death as in life', was so full that hardly a blade of grass could have fought for a place, had anyone allowed it to try. I passed it every day before I was swallowed into the mill gateway; this, too, seeming like the opening of a tomb into the hillside. From an upper storey, if I wiped away the grey dust that was thick upon the windows, I saw the rows upon rows of headstones.

The mechanics and spinners sent me out every day to fetch meat-and-potato pies, or dishes of hot peas, from a cottage which they called a 'pay oyle' (that is, a 'pea hole') where, as so often in the shadow of a mill, there was a widow making a living from her baking. Upon these errands, I more than once stole into the grounds of Holingdrake's mansion to stare into his fish pond; or I went into the graveyard, noting the ages of those who were buried there and how youth had been so markedly struck down. I discovered that the ability to read can be quite a pain and a burden. A greasy mutton pie gagging my mouth, a can of steaming peas in my hand, I was awestruck by those graves. A single stone might hold a whole list of young wives, a man sometimes having three, four, even five of them, dying from childbirth or consumption. There

31

were boys and girls there, many younger, others hardly older than myself. Their gasps of pain bled in sentimental verses upon the gravestones. Various white, stone angels were, I fancied, the winged spirits of some of those children.

And one grave, especially, I stared at, the memory of which horrifies me still. In lettering as brusquely eschewing ornament as a government mandate, upon a single headstone were listed the names of boys and girls still in their early teens who had been brought from Liverpool as orphans to labour in the factory and who had died during a typhoid epidemic in their dormitory.

I sometimes heard the harmonium being played and a choir practising. From the workhouse we were led to a chapel every Sunday and by listening to hymns I had already formed the belief that religion consisted of pretending, while you were alive, that you were already dead.

Among all my fantasies, I never indulged *that* one!

The factory that killed, the graveyard that buried, and the chapel, from which I heard them singing praises to death as a better place than life, were all that existed at the end of the long track through the soot-blackened moorland.

I realised that, even if I survived for longer than I imagined, all I could hope for in the end was what a Self Help Society could offer me on the lip of the grave, provided I had kept up my lifetime payments of twopence a week.

Instead, I ran.

*

I ran away on the evening of Queen Victoria's Jubilee in June 1887, when I was twelve.

By midday we children were free of our morning in the mill. At the workhouse, instead of school we spent the afternoon cleaning the place, while the women cooked and the men decorated the dining-room with bunting. We polished our clogs. We scrubbed ourselves thoroughly at the pump – thank God it was summer! A gentleman who had prospered from investing in the railway had left a sum of money, I believe it was five pounds per annum, to equip us with 'Sunday clothes', and we changed into these. The girls had smocks with aprons.

We boys were given medium quality worsted suits, breeks buttoning on to stockings above the calves, soft caps, heavily blackened clogs and distinctive, broad, white collars that had some lace decoration though nothing too fussy; outfits which clearly indentified us as being from the workhouse. At five o'clock the children with the women, and the men in their ward, too, were given a special feast. I don't know what the men's was but from my experience of their likes and dislikes I hope they were provided with a generous supply of tobacco. We were filled up with the wholesome produce of our own garden and farm, potatoes, cheese, vegetables, milk, plus meat (shambles meat, admittedly) and also there were salted herrings. And cakes.

What a time we had! Miss Shingles was more of an old sport than you might imagine. For instance, it was she who during Wakes Week led us in crocodile fashion to throw wooden balls at coconuts in the fun fair, and now she did something amazing. She abandoned her Band of Hope meetings and made some jellies. I know how long she spent in preparing them, or rather in supervising her cook and maid, because she delivered a speech at table making sure that we knew.

I can see the shapes of those jellies to this day. As she informed us, she borrowed the moulds from the kitchen of one of the finest houses in the district, from Mallalieu's, members of the Jubilee Committee itself, and we were very impressed. Everything from rabbits to castles, ships to steam trains, quivered before us, raspberry pink, lemon yellow and lime green.

It was my good fortune that from the beginning I never was in circumstances in which I depended upon others for my entertainment. The women all taught me songs and verses. Mary had used to put on quite a performance, mimicking the workhouse master behind his back. On this day, after we had consumed our jellies, men, women and children were brought together for the 'music hall'.

My first music hall! Masters and inmates did their turns on the platform in the dining-room. Miss Shingles hung her cloak up in the back-room and played two hymns on the harmonium. Then, putting on her other, far from solemn expression, she told a couple of those anecdotes that she was fond of drilling into us during classtime. They were mostly about, of all things, 'the servant problem' and, I realise now, she had read them up in *Tit Bits* or *Punch*. They were my first examples of a genre I was to find typical of theatre-plays and of all middle-class amusement. Working people were caricatured for being ignorant and were even expected to laugh at their own ignorance, in the company of those who kept them so. Just as we were, in the workhouse on this day.

'Bridie,' inquired her mistress, 'How long are you going to take, filling the pepper pot?' 'Sure, I don't know meself, ma'am, how long it'll be afore I've got it through all those little holes at the top'.

Believe it or not, a few of us laughed, so Miss Shingles broke into another one. I will abbreviate. *Mistress: 'Do you know, Bridie, that you have broken more china this month than the amount of your wages? What are we to do about it?' Bridie: 'I don't know, ma'am – unless you were to raise my wages.'*

After Miss Shingles, the workhouse master himself did a few conjuring tricks and sleights of hand, obviously to demonstrate to us how quick-witted he was; how he saw everything that was going on and could stay several moves in front of everybody else. He was a solidly built, but nervously twitching man, wild-eyed, savage-tempered, forever tugging at his profuse hair and whiskers.

He was followed by Ammon Wrigley, a local bard who recited verses that he had written in the dialect. He knew his work by heart and could perform, I should think, hours upon hours of it. Didn't he seem well satisfied with them! But he was a bright, humorous character and I liked him.

Then I took my turn. Fourth on the bill, which was no bad start in life. Yes, I now sang my first song in public. It was one of the many folk melodies that the women had taught me, very often illicitly at night, but until this moment I had only sung, recited and done comic or sentimental turns more or less spontaneously and secretly for them.

Singing and performing were from the start associated with rebellion and with what was illegal. The Reverend

34

Johnson and also our Methodist preacher in flamboyant terms associated entertainment with Godlessness. Now, for some reason, it had been plucked out of darkness and set up centre stage. I had even been rehearsed, during the previous afternoons after the school hour was over, and I was *publicly introduced*. 'Ladies and gentlemen, we now have Master Jacky Shuttleworth who has been prevailed upon to recite and sing one of his favourite pieces.'

Our Methodist preacher, if he could have been 'prevailed upon' to do such a thing as introduce a turn, even for the Jubilee of the greatest Queen in the world, or King for that matter, might have done it with some grandeur; for he had great style, rolling about the pulpit and banging his fist like a gavel. Miss Shingles would probably have done the job quite saucily. But the Reverend Johnson was no music-hall artist. He announced me in such a solemn voice that I might have been about to be publicly flogged. The result was, everybody looked deucedly serious, even bored, before I began.

Also, the tune I had chosen to sing was a tricky one. All my maternal ladies had advised me against it. On looking back, trying to understand why I picked something so difficult, I realise that it was because, already, I was ambitious.

There was another interesting thing, too, that I discovered as soon as I launched into my piece. While I was as nervous as was to be expected and every part of the preparations was designed to make me even more so, once I had got over the first couple of bars something happened that I did not anticipate. I lost all my fear. I was a fledgeling bird flung over the edge of a nest and expecting to sink like a stone, but finding itself flying, elated. I sang the better because I was excited by the presence of an audience, their expressions changing from charitable indifference to interest, pleasure and even excitement. I had a sensation that a loom had never given me: that of discovering what I was born for. I thought of more than simply getting to the end, which is the mistake made by untalented beginners. Though I had chosen a difficult piece, an easy tune might have floored me by giving me nothing to think about except my own nervousness.

They say my love has listed and wears a white cockade,
He is a handsome young man besides a roving blade,
He is a handsome young man, and he's gone to serve the King,
Oh my very, Oh my very, Oh my very heart lies
breaking all for love of him.

The way the ordinary public-house singer tackles such a moving song is with a great deal of sentimental emphasis, yet paradoxically he is embarrassed by the emotions and probably he even nervously laughs his way through. Thereby the poetry is evaded; and when the audience joins in the chorus, they turn the most tender lyric into a mechanical hunting song. There is a wonderful variation of metre in the last line which the bad singers fight and try to flatten out, but when I was repeating *Oh my very, Oh my very, Oh my very heart lies breaking . . .* I did not gloss over the words in embarrassment. I dwelled on them, remembering what Mary Shuttleworth had told me about Joe Gaukroger, and of her life. People think that a child of twelve has no experience of love, which is nonsense.

I don't say my rendition was all that wonderful nor that it contained this understanding at the time. I do say that it was better than they normally heard in the workhouse and that, judging from the reception I was given, I must have shown at least some seeds of a future.

Oh, may he never prosper, and may he never thrive,
With anything he takes in hand as long as he's alive,
May the very ground he treads upon, the grass refuse to grow,
Since he's been, since he's been, since he's been the
cause of my sorrow, grief and woe.

And then, by Jove, they started to clap. Imagine the effect of that on a lad who'd never been praised for anything in his life!

Instead of being emotional, running away and crying, I launched into another piece without even being asked. The Reverend stood back amazed. No one had ever dared upstage him in history.

It is of a farmer's daughter so beautiful I'm told
Her parents died and left her five hundred pounds in gold,

36

She lived with her rich uncle, the cause of all her woe,
But you shall hear this maiden fair did prove his overthrow. . . .

My head was stuffed with such sentimental songs about the ladies. I must have heard many kinds of verses but these had stuck. I never have had any appetite for ballads about Lord Nelson and the Battle of the Nile.

When I stepped down, the women were all smiles, saying to each other for no reason that I could understand, 'Hasn't he grown?' while the men were remarking, 'Who's this, then, we've got among us?'

Fame. I could not bear to sink tomorrow into being Jack Shuttleworth, the piecer.

I asked the Reverend Johnson, 'Please, sir, may I get a drink of water?' and being in a good mood he nodded amiably.

I was excited and felt braver than I'd ever been in my life. The nearest jug and ewer was in the cloakroom where Miss Shingles hung her cloak. I calmed myself with a quick swig of water, and moistened my mouth that was as dry as the desert sands.

Many people keep secrets and if they were all brought into the open perhaps I myself would not seem so very strange. I lifted the cloak from the peg. The combination of fear and silk gave me a tingling in my groin that I had not experienced before. Something was happening that was totally absorbing. I pulled the cloak across my shoulders and fumbled for the arm-slits. The huge cloak trailed over the ground. I crept about the room, not because it was a place from which I could be overheard, but because what I was doing felt holy. Did I look like the 'real' Miss Shingles? Did I feel like her – the usually pious, sometimes jaunty, fox-faced Miss Shingles, but shining in silk? It was a devotion. Also I was captivated by the noise of the material and wanted to listen to it.

I was looking for a mirror in which to see myself. Before I found one, someone else was there. Yes, Miss Shingles!

The earth was not kind enough to swallow me up.

*

I guessed that the gates of the workhouse would not be locked, because several important people had to make their way out.

The gatehouse keeper was enjoying the free ale in Oldham and no one suspected that anyone would choose this great holiday to run away. I knew also that I would not be picked out among the celebrating crowds.

I did not report to Miss Shingles and the workhouse master 'later'. I ran. I was determined to reach something that I had only been tantalised with but had never seen: the music hall.

I had been accused of hunting for the schoolteacher's purse, which filled me with a prickling sense of injustice. Dressing up as a woman was too great a disgrace for such an accusation even to be uttered; it therefore left me wondering whether Miss Shingles had or had not realised what in fact I had been doing. People knew my character even if they did not speak about it. The uncertainty of it all made me feel hot and then cold.

Not wanting to get lost on the moors with darkness falling, I made my way down to the valley bottom, along the river and the railway line through Dob Cross to Delph. Instinct, as always, took me not to lonely places but to where people were enjoying themselves.

Bonfires were being lit upon the hills and although they were for Queen Victoria's Golden Jubilee, they made me feel that I was escaping through Hell, as I had seen it depicted in a lithograph in a Bible. Fireworks spurted and lit up the clouds.

I raced as if the constables were already on my heels, though I knew this was unlikely for at least a few hours and maybe they would not check the inmates at all on such a special night. I ran while looking over my shoulder so that I got a crick in my neck. I paused to pick up sounds of pursuit and heard them, of course, as you always do if you grow afraid of the dark, then I raced on with heart pounding like a steam-engine. Wooden clogs with iron tips are not the easiest footwear for running in. I believed that I would be running for ever, for I could not imagine a place of rest; yet running, running, running was preferable to being imprisoned.

When I had crossed the river at Dob Cross and saw Knott Hill looming like a great tombstone, with its bonfire atop, be d——d if I didn't hear a cannon. I thought they were hunting me with it! I had hardly ever been out of the workhouse and I was as innocent as a cage-bird or a tame rabbit let out into the wild. I was without resources except the one that had emboldened me, that is, performing and singing. I was ready for any trap, ones I knew nothing about and others that I imagined. But nothing would make me turn back except force.

When I reached Delph, there wasn't a single constable looking for an 'unnatural' boy who had dressed in a woman's cloak. I was easily identifiable in my workhouse clothes, and was surely the more suspect because I wore a 'Sunday outfit' that was splashed with mud. I had tried to rip off the tell-tale collar, but had merely torn it, which made me feel more conspicuous. But one comfort was obvious even to a frightened, over-imaginative innocent: nobody was interested in me. Unlike on a normal weekday, there were no idlers short of amusement, no ladies and shopkeepers whispering and talking about the passers-by. Even if the crowds had noticed me, they were too drunk to care. In places devoted to amusement, I was safe.

I was told later that six thousand people had gathered in the centre of the village, mostly around the foot of Knott Hill Lane where they were watching the fireworks. In front of the Swan Inn was a greased pole with a leg of mutton on top. The Mechanics Institute clock told me that it was ten in the evening and so far no one had reached the mutton, nor were they likely to, because the young men were becoming increasingly drunk as the evening wore on and they attacked the greased pole so recklessly that they tired before they got half way up. They were not interested in me.

Because I looked so tired and thirsty, an old fellow sitting against the pub wall offered me a sip of his beer. I emptied half his tankard and when I lifted my eyes from its lip I saw that he was staring at me. Naturally I believed that he had guessed what I had done. His eyes travelled up and down my workhouse clothes, but he did not speak. That was even more intimidating than being questioned. Then he said, with a smile, 'Thou'll be all reet, lad, in th'end. Dunna worry. Never mind.'

But I did not understand him. They talk like that in Yorkshire – mysteriously. You're supposed to know what they mean before they say it and what they're putting to you is a password or code to test whether you're one of them or not. (It's the way that working people have been treated that makes us clannish, in self-defence.) I would not trust him and I ran into the crowds.

The public-house keepers were rolling barrels of ale into the street. They were handing out free beer. It was going to grow into a yet more wild and drunken night in Delph. Not for me, though. I'd had scare enough and I was already tiddly from the old man's half-tankard. You know how a tipple goes straight to my head; you know it from our quarrels. I wasn't hungry, because of the workhouse feast, but I was tired.

It was quite dark by then and very late, at least by my standards; in the workhouse we were in bed by nine o'clock, even in summer. I made for the nearest hill, thinking that on a hilltop would be the safest place to fall asleep. Not able to run anymore, I climbed for about three miles, passing through a hamlet which I did not explore. The road flattened out through bare country. It passed between the rocky sides of a gloomy cutting. It was a clear night and one could see for miles. The hills bulged in the moonlight like the backs of the grey carp turning in Mr Holingdrake's fish pond. A small amount of fast, light traffic carrying gay passengers sped by; I was obviously on a main road. Beyond the cutting, the road sank steadily down again, towards towns full of lights. I felt safe, for I had crossed the hills.

Isolated on the far side of the cutting, above the drop, was a public house named The Fleece. There was not much sign of life and I assumed that most people had gone into town for the celebrations. It had unlit outbuildings in which I guessed I had a chance of being safe. I was tired enough to take a chance on almost anything.

I poked around the empty yard until I detected a smell of warm hay. I followed my nose, shut myself in and fell asleep, without even remembering having done so, on a horse's fodder.

Anybody who looks at a map will see that I had merely travelled in a circle. I was on the top of Standedge and I had only to retrace my steps to the other side of the cutting to be able in the daylight to see the workhouse and Diggle Mill.

·2·

I WAS wakened by a shaft of sunlight from a suddenly opened door. Screwing up my eyes, I took in the wavering impression of something like a post against the light. A tall, thin man. I'll tell you how I think of him, on looking back: he was loose, light and floating, like a strand of sooty wool caught on a fence. He was like that famous will-o'-the-wisp, the Brocken, which in a certain light is seen upon the moortops and which I believe is merely one's own shadow, thrown by the sun at one's back upon a wall of mist in front.

'Poor b——r,' the Brocken said, slowly and with emotion.

What else could he have seen, but a lean moorland rat? I expect he took it all in at a glance.

The first thing I did was to run. Try to get past him, through the door. There I found the substance in his skinny arms. Without trouble and laughing, he caught me. He played me out, letting me struggle for a few minutes until I was tired, then he set me down. He stood back from me, his arms spread, his bony fists clenched on the jamb.

Apparently he could read my mind.

'I'll not send you back,' he promised, 'wherever it is you're from.'

From the way he said it, I thought he knew where I was from or had guessed it. Perhaps my clothes were identifiable even all these 'miles' from Diggle.

'So come into th'ouse for a half a mo'. Come on. And tell me what you've done. Or not, just as you wish. Oh, deary me, it – nobody knows, do they?'

With his last sentence, I didn't know what he was talking about. He was obviously referring to some preoccupation of his own; but it was his having a problem that gave him sympathy with mine. I felt that I could trust him. I recognised a kind person, even though a man.

Anyway, I couldn't refuse. He took me by the shoulder

and firmly but not cruelly led me through the yard. Daylight showed me what moonlight had suggested: that I was in a grim, high spot, fifteen hundred feet as a matter of fact, on the top of the Pennines. Not a tree nor bush was in sight, except one tattered thorn bush by a stream full of brown and foaming water pelting through rushes, which were also more brown than green, and square miles of rushes all around. There was a dismal reservoir on the far side of the road. I knew that it was early because of the angle of the sun but even at this time, the road was busy with all sorts of traffic, from slow, heavy carts to fast traps. Half a mile away across the bogs I could see the vents of a railway or canal tunnel.

Into the public house. I remember rubbing my nose on my sleeve, which is what we common children did when we were nervous. Over the door, on a board that listed the lodging, stabling, billiards, music, ales and porter that the pub provided, I read this gentleman's name, presumably, as the licensee. John Haigh. Indeed it turned out to be he. Though needless to say, no one called him that. He was known as John o'Jack's o't'Fleece.

As I was shot into the dark passageway, I took it in that the pub was moderately clean. Being with women had trained me to have a keen eye for the domestic offices, such as males and especially young boys do not usually possess. I observed that, although over the flagstones in the hallway lay bits of straw brought in on the boots of carters and work people, the flagstones were scrubbed underneath. Some busy woman, or someone strict with the maids. Through the door of the empty tap-room at the back of the building came a smell of beer and tobacco. From another, larger and better appointed room at the front came a smell of stale food.

'Tha should open the windows in there,' I said, solemnly. 'Let the air in to clean th'place.'

I spoke in the dialect, in those days. And I shouted boldly, giving full weight to consonants and vowels as one did in the factories and on the moorlands, even though it offended refined taste.

Mr Haigh let go of me and started laughing. I was in a temper because he had not taken me seriously; then I began to smile, too. I didn't know how I'd caused it, for I was only commenting in my usual way, but I was pleased to have made him laugh. I had already realised that there was something sad about him. You can tell that sort of thing, almost from a smell. The whole pub had a dolorous air. That must have come from someone: that is, from the owners, and children have instincts about such things. In the shells of their rooms in the mornings, after the customers have left, all public houses are dejected, but in The Fleece it was more than that. Sadness came from the smell and cut of John o' Jack's clothes and from the sunken look of his face when he failed to find something to laugh at or engage it. He turned out to be the kind of man who is always struggling to find something to laugh about, something to keep up his spirits, but too often not succeeding. As he gently pushed me along, he was determinedly chuckling and repeating what I had said. 'Let the air in to clean the place! Deary me! Thou'd 'appen turn out a better pot-house maid than Ethel Ferret, t'hear thee talk. Tha prattles like an 'ousewife! Oppen winder, let the air in to clean the place, deary me!'

I was propelled into the scullery, still rubbing at my sleeve with my snotty nose. It was a damp place, given over to all the things that one does with swillings of water: washing crockery and clothes, mixing basins of food for the hens, storing wet mops and buckets. Even the surface of the deal table was wet. The only thing which was, perhaps, dry was an unmade day-bed, still not folded back into the wall.

At a stone sink by the window, a pump at the side of it, the occupier of this bed, I assumed – a thin girl, not much older than me and also about five feet tall – was wiping the insides of some large earthenware jars. She looked up and her face held an expression that later you taught me to call 'wistful'. This could not have been the first time that I had come across such a look, for surely many a girl and woman in the workhouse had her pensive moments, but as I had never noticed it before, this perception must have been a landmark in my puberty.

She looked away quickly. I was left with only her clothes to examine. She was wearing a clumsily made dress of off-white calico reaching nearly to her ankles, over it an apron of the same material. A bonnet of that same putty-coloured calico hid every strand of her hair so that I did not know whether she was fair or dark. Humiliating clothes. Her dress without adornment or variation of the same cheap material, as well as the resigned way she returned to her work, made her look as though she, too, had come from an institution. A place where they had taught her to hide everything in uniform, humble clothes, ashamed.

Her pinched, yellow features showed that she had been brought up on the plainest food and not very much of it, either. But then, the moorland cottages can be as grim and imprisoning as any institution. She shot a glance back to see if I was still watching her and I was. She looked away again, frightened. I, in my shameless lad's way, kept on staring. At the time I could not reconcile the picture of this drudge with the idea I was forming of Mr Haigh's kindness. I discovered later that Ethel Ferret's appearance had more to do with her nature than the way she had been treated; not that she'd ever been treated easy.

'This is Ethel Ferret,' Mr Haigh announced. 'Ethel, say "Hullo" to . . .'

I couldn't be cheated and I didn't tell him my name.

Another brief glance from Ethel. We could play this game for ever. This time there was a smile on her lips and in her eyes which was unexpected from the first impression. A secret brightness and a welcome were peeping out, not at all suitable to the role she appeared to be playing.

Once more, she returned to her part, calmly and steadily wiping the jars.

Mr Haigh waved his arm. ' 'Ow long would it tak' you to scrub this floor?' he asked me, jokingly. 'It tak's Ethel abart a fortnight and t'place is still a mucky oyle when she's finished. How long would t'job tak' you, d'yar think?'

'Do it in a morning,' I boasted, believing his joke about Ethel. Then, wanting to defend her, '*I* don't think it's a mucky hole,' I added, speaking posh, like Miss Shingles.

I had been taught that you had to speak posh to get a job, and it was beginning to dawn on me that there was a chance of employment here. Possibly I'd find variety in the work and wander the moors in my spare time. Mr Haigh and I might well get on swimmingly. So might Ethel and I.

'A morning, eh?' Mr Haigh found this *very* funny. 'Not this morning, you wouldn't. You're tired. You don't need to fear that I'm going to drag you back to Running Hill.'

I jumped.

'Nor am I going to make a prisoner of you. If you don't believe me, then run and see what 'appens. Before you've gone a couple of miles you'll go down wi' tiredness and fright and you'll be picked up by someone not 'alf as good to you. Either that or you'll die of starvation. Why don't you sit and talk to Ethel for ten minutes? 'Elp 'er, if you like. I'll give you a permanent position if you want one. If you don't, you can run. Otherwise there'll be a breakfast waiting for you in 'alf an 'our in the kitchen. Ethel'll show you.'

He left down a different passageway and I heard him shout, 'Maggie, we've got a runaway!'

'Is it a boy or a girl?' his wife answered. Hers was a hard voice, like stones rubbing together; not loose and willowy, which was her husband's tone, matching his physique. I could not see the woman, but a strongly different personality pervaded what was, very nearly, fun in the scullery.

'I wish I knew,' Mr Haigh continued to joke. 'It'd depend on 'ow you dressed 'im. On balance, I'd say it was a lad. But 'e can speak lardy-da when 'e 'as to.'

That made Ethel smile to herself.

I sat timidly on the edge of a damp rocking chair, afraid of disturbing her concentration. As with a wild bird, a rash movement might make her fly away.

Delicately, Ethel put down one of her jars and started to work the pump. Everything in the room, perhaps in the whole public house, radiated from the pump. The little heaps of clothes and linen waiting to be washed were strung out in lines from it. Likewise, the crockery placed upon the floor. Humble Ethel officiated at the fountain of the house. She seemed to feel that she ought to be as quiet as possible. The pump handle squeaked and that was the only noise until the water ran. She took another, more searching look at me. She turned away to put another jar under the spout. Staring at the water, she told me, 'It's not too bad here. John o'Jack's alreet.'

I gathered that was her way of making me welcome and of advising me to accept. I knew that we had clicked.

From the direction taken by Mr Haigh and which evidently was towards the kitchen there came a smell of bacon frying. *Bacon!* I don't think there's anything more seductive and appetising than the smell of frying bacon on a morning when you're hungry.

'I'd like to stay,' I said.

'Mr Haigh knows everybody. He'll be able to fix it with the workhouse governors. What do they call you?'

'Jacky Shuttleworth.'

*

As it was the most God-forsaken spot that you could dream of for a public house, you may be wondering how The Fleece came to be there at all. It was certainly not one of your village alehouses with regular customers who had lived in the district for generations, knowing everybody and censoring everything with their gossip. There was not even a hamlet near by, only bleak cottages scattered over miles of moorland. Yet it turned out to be a remarkably busy place. It had a unique mixture of travelling clients. On the one hand, it catered for a rough element, dating back to the navvies who seventeen years previously had built the second railway tunnel from Diggle to Huddersfield, who had lived in the rain-and-wind-bitten shacks of a shanty town and who were now building reservoirs. Even if working five miles away, still they trekked to The Fleece to dry their clothes, to sing, to play fiddles or melodions. They held union meetings in the tap-room and they fought about matters that they treated more seriously, such as women, around the latrine in the back yard.

Meanwhile, the front of the pub catered for a genteel clientele. We were on a trade route through the Pennines. It had been a stage-coach route before the coming of the railway, but was still much used, the strangers cheering what would otherwise have been a gloomy hole. Some were family parties: fathers, mothers, children, grannies, hangers-on and nursemaids who stuffed themselves with stodgy meals in the privacy of the cubicles. Others were carters or commercial-type travellers. Many passers-by were, I am sure, using false names.

I had thought I was the only one in the world who was on the run but when I'd been a pot-house boy for a few months I learned that it doesn't take much to get people to take to the roads. If you've worked at feeding them, bedding them down, cleaning their boots and pots, you hear all sorts of excuses for being peripatetic. I found that people will leave their families for weeks on end to sell almost anything, just to excuse getting away. Engineers in the last gasps of hopeful poverty, going from Huddersfield to Manchester or vice versa, arrived on the backs of worn-out nags with their panniers full of still unpatented spindles. In The Fleece, they would give all their useless secrets away in one forgetful night; being the only sober one among them, because I had been filling their tankards and emptying their pockets, I was the only one to remember anything in the morning. Grocers, tailors and ironmongers, who had become Methodists or Baptists so as to get out of their shops, turned into itinerant preachers and enjoyed having their say, even if only to a few broken-down beggars in the rain, and appeared at our door to sip nothing stronger than what they termed 'honest water' – a quotation from Shakespeare himself, but few of them knew this; nor did I in those days. The self-righteous travelled in the causes of Temperance or alternatively of medicinal wines; in the causes of the end of the world and the coming of the New Jerusalem. The less imaginative would wander to gather the wool that sheep left on walls and fences, to bundle rushes into a sack, or to collect lichens for dyes and would beg to sleep, as I had done, in the outhouse. The swarming poor of the North are always having to devise some means to keep body and soul together.

*

Mr Haigh was a decent old stick. For hours on end sipping at his slowly sinking tankard of ale, he chatted with his customers about nothing and about everything; about the Queen's wars and with equal concern about a lamb that had got its head stuck in a fence. John o' Jack's never knew whether it was eleven in the morning or four in the afternoon. You had to tell him whether it was Monday or Friday and whatever it was, he would be surprised. He didn't know whether his work was earning him a halfpence or five shillings.

Mrs Haigh nagged him about it. She herself was interested in one type of customer. Carters.

Some of our trade was with the carters who took wool over the Pennines in carts that swayed like Spanish galleons, with teams of decorated horses to hold them on the steep hills; such exotic vehicles have disappeared now. The drivers held high opinions of themselves and showed off most when Maggie Haigh was near.

This lady, severe and unhappy one minute, as flighty and silly as a girl the next, had a magical effect upon navvies and carters. She found their travels, their tales of stupendous drinking bouts and of fights on the road or in the bogs, a romantic aphrodisiac. It was in comparison, I suppose, with her tame and Fleece-haunting husband, who could have no fresh, interesting news to exchange from the locals. What did *they* know of Manchester or Leeds; those fabulous cities that were like Venice and Florence? And looked like them, too, I discovered when I went to take a peep at their banks and textile-exchanges, built beside the River Irwell like palaces on the Arno.

Mrs Haigh was one who felt that having a good time meant following her roving eye. She imagined something brighter and gayer existing over the horizon. Who could blame her, when confined in such a dreary place? I was of the same temperament myself; although I never shared my dreams with Mrs Haigh, but experienced personally only her severer side.

The landlady was sweet on one carter especially whom Ethel and I, and most of the inn's patrons, knew only as Jim. Customers laughed about the affair, even to John o'Jack's mild face, and although Mr Haigh did not seem to understand what was going on, I am sure that he did. Eventually I was to meet some striking examples of those who pretend not to see what is before their eyes, for the sake of some other benefit that is a mystery to the rest of us. I think it was from loneliness that Mr Haigh was so kind to me and to Ethel. He spent his whole life looking for a friend.

For such a whore, Mrs Haigh most of the time kept herself surprisingly quiet, plain and severe, dressing to make herself look even duller, in greys, blacks and whites. There was one exception to this; one weakness that magnificently expressed the other side of her nature.

Hats. If I had a fondness for silk, Maggie Haigh made a fetish of her headgear. She presented a divided appearance. Her main, sober dress represented what she thought about her home, but the hats with which she crowned herself embodied the glamour of the imagined existence beyond The Fleece to which some stranger might lead, as I am sure she hoped. Perhaps she had dwelled too much on the phrase used to express a lady's capturing of a suitor: 'I threw my cap at him.'

John Haigh was devastated by her yearnings. Unreal yearnings do cause devastation all around; you and I, above all, should know that! Yet he used to encourage her extravagances. I don't know why he was afraid of displeasing her, for she wouldn't have been half so bad without his encouragement. 'There's nowt so queer as folk,' as they say. As a result, it was amazing what a variety of hats she possessed; astounding that she could keep them on the top of her head in that windy, rainy place; but most surprising of all was the quantity and variety of her talk about them. It was one subject that could unbutton her tight lips.

'I'd wear my blue un with the osprey that cost me seven shillings if it wasn't leet to rain, and if it wasn't for having to sit in the homnibus tram. It tickles folk and they get upset. It makes them so nowty,' she rattled on in her sharp voice, being pretentious. She pronounced each *h* as if it was as heavy as a bag of potatoes.

At one o'clock on a workaday morning, after the last customer had left, we were sitting by the tap-room fire. You would think then that there had never existed a word of dissent between the master and mistress. John o't' Fleece was smoking his pipe. Ethel and I, having cleaned up, were sitting with them as if we were their own children.

People who have families take them for granted; but I knew that this was one of the charmed moments of my life. Every minute is still vivid to me.

'I reckon it looks stylish wi' the feathers, Maggie!' John o't' Fleece egged her on.

He was a regular sport, the way he encouraged her.

'Not everybody minds it i'the tram,' he said. 'Isaac Turner's lass won 'erself a chap from 'aving some feathers in 'er 'at that tickled 'is ear 'oyle. She were sat by 'im and every time she turned 'er 'ead 'e said politely, "I beg your pardon, Miss!"'

John Haigh, a proper comedian when he got going, imitated Isaac Turner's voice.

'She turned 'er 'ead again t'ear 'im and then 'e got the feathers in 'is eye or 'is mouth, until at t'finish 'e lost 'is temper wi'er. "Nay dammit, Miss!" 'e exploded at last; and so 'e 'ad to walk along wi'er apologising all the way to 'er 'ome, they both laughing their socks off and they've been laughing ever since and 'ave three children by now. Or is it four? I canna remember.'

Ethel and I were laughing, too. I was so pleased to see it that, if she stopped, I poked her in the ribs and, sure enough, she would start giggling again.

However, neither Mr Haigh nor I could make the mistress laugh. We had to admit that we had failed there.

'Well, I still think my blue with the osprey feather is getting such an old thing now. I've had it since last season and don't know whether to have it turned up at the front and down at the back, or up at the back and down at the front, or make something of it with an amber brooch or something. Mrs Womersley said a hat suited me best when it covered my face up. 'Covered my mouth,' was what she hactually said but I think she were being cheeky. My green's like that and I can get it on grand and firm, too. I could walk to Huddersfield in a hurricane and it'd never budge. You know how I like to feel that my hat's *on*, don't you, John Haigh? *John Haigh, you're not listening to me!*'

'I were, though!' He jolted awake out of his chair. 'T'every word yo' said to me. You were on abart your 'at.'

'Well, I wish you wouldn't speak so common when you address me.'

Despite her isolated home, Maggie Haigh's flirtatious silliness or mysterious severity, depending in what frame of mind, or rather, under which hat you encountered her, won her fame as an intriguing, incalculable *femme fatale* far beyond The Fleece and the nearby farms. She was known right down to Meltham and Huddersfield; and, on the other side of the Pennines, through Saddleworth and into Oldham, why, even in Manchester, where so far only her dreams and her reputation had reached.

People found pleasure in imagining more about her than she offered, and her incalculable-ness encouraged speculation. Even sermons were delivered including her. These, said the men laughing in the tap-room, were to entice women into the chapels. They wanted to hear the details. You need a scarlet woman or two in order to keep chapels full.

The pub was also the object of the women's tongue-and-head-wagging in cottages and farms. The gossips wondered how Maggie Haigh could 'get away with it, and her so plain'. 'It just goes to show,' they said. I heard that phrase often when I was sent across the marshes on an errand for milk or meat. It struck me, most memorably, that 'it' went to show nothing.

Maggie Haigh behaved as if she had no idea what people said or thought about her, yet she knew how to advertise even though she hardly ever left her station on those moors which so intensified her dreams. Of course she was perfectly aware of what was said. That was why she stayed put, knowing that mystery encouraged gossip. Except for her occasional trips to the posh emporia of Huddersfield, she relied upon Ethel, or me, or her husband, or the passing carters to bring her goods and shopping. She hardly ever served in the bar, but stayed hidden in the kitchen until the hour when she made a dramatic appearance in her neat nun's dress, crowned with some crazy hat.

'Mutton dressed as lamb,' Mrs Womersley remarked, standing over me in her kitchen. Hers was the nearest farm, half a mile away across the rushes and pools of black, stagnant water. There Mrs Womersley, like many local women, kept her husband from even thinking of daring to go out for a drink in The Fleece. She was Temperance with a vengeance, she was, and Right was on her side; she let you make no mistake about that.

'I'd say a prayer for 'er in chapel but I don't think it'd be much use. You know who I'm talking about, don't you?'

'Yes,' I admitted, guiltily. She glared at me as if Mrs Haigh was my responsibility.

'It's that beesom over yonder I'm talking about,' she emphasised to make sure I wasn't making a mistake. 'I've tried praying afore, but all I've got for my pains is to wear my knees out. There's many a one 'ave wore out their knees praying for folk when they would 'ave done better for themselves scrubbing their own yards. Though there's none o' that sort over *there*. 'Ave you seen 'er with a new 'at lately?'

I didn't want to be disloyal and I didn't answer.

'What's up wi' you? Cat got your tongue? She brought one back from 'Uddersfield last market day, didn't she? *Didn't she*, young man? She bought it at Kay and Monnington's. *Didn't she?*'

She prodded me and I nodded back.

'Yes, indeed! There's nothing else would get her out except to buy a new 'at,' Mrs Womersley said. 'And only Kay and Monnington's would sell something grand enough for 'er. She reckoned she couldn't afford to go 'alf wi' me for my dog licence, but she can pay for a new 'at. It's no trouble for 'er to go in for a new 'at, oh, deary me, no.'

Because the Womersleys' dog barked whenever anyone came across the moors, she thought that Mrs Haigh should contribute to the licence.

'Any news?' Mrs Haigh grimly asked me, when I got back from my errand. So I had to tell her. Watch her go up in the air. That was fun.

'You can just go tell her, Jack Shuttleworth, that if she wants me to pay half for her dog just because it hasn't gumption not to bark at everything whether it's coming to her doorpost or mine, in that case she can pay half towards my new hat, as I give her the pleasure of looking at it! The beesom! So *common!*'

It remained a mystery, Mrs Haigh's power over men, for which women hated her. I studied it. I was already wondering, fascinated – could I, too, possess that female essence; her mixture of extravagance, daring, but also of unpredictable silence, mystery and restraint that brought the travelling-men around her as bees come to a rooted flower?

The public house was always busy because of her. If it had been left to John o't'Fleece, the business would have collapsed and I'm sure she made certain that her husband did not forget this.

But I was telling you about Jim the carter; and if Scheherazade doesn't get on with her flipping story I guess she might find herself tied up in a sack at the bottom of the canal.

Such is the oddity of life, Mr Dodds, that Mrs Haigh managed to hold Jim the carter's heart, the hearts of several other travellers and also the devotion of her husband who was so atrociously spurned.

Ethel, who was bedded down in the damp scullery, and I, who slept in a box-bed which was like lying in a little coffin, my nose only a couple of feet beneath the leaking, draughty slates, could hear what went on, if wind and rain did not compete too loudly with it. After the evening noise had died down, when humans and animals were bedded, when the elements muttered and whined around the building, you knew that you were imprisoned in an isolated and eerie world, up there on Standedge. There we listened to the carter with Mrs Haigh giggling through the night and Mr Haigh prowling, restless and futile.

Matching these sounds of restlessness, misery and mockery, with Mr Haigh's wrecked appearance during the morning, I again became aghast and awestruck by this unholy fury which adults called 'love' – just as I had felt on being witness to Mary's feeling in the workhouse. Myself, I had never yet felt these emotions. I was baffled by them. But were they, then, to be my fate? I loved women. But *love*, what I had seen of it, terrified me. It was like an incurable disease.

While John Haigh, who never did much work (it was his wife who was the worker) seemed exhausted and drained, the carter fed off his rival's despair and became proportionately extravagant with gaiety and bullying talk. Neither party would give an explanation. After his tormented nights, John o'Jack's looked tired and sheepish, merely throwing out the phrase which he often used to fill a vacuum, 'Nobody knows, do they?' For some reason, his phrase chilled me to the bone.

Eventually, I discovered the cause of this strange relationship; drained dependency on the one hand and strutting power on the other. I found out about it because of my factory-worker's ability to lip read; and it was not the last time in my life that this gift was to help me explain the otherwise inexplicable. Mr Haigh was being blackmailed by the carter for the robbery of a mill's wage office, a stupid and, I believe, isolated crime that he had committed some years before. I could pick up only the crudest details of the conversation between the two men at the far side of the room, but it was enough.

Mrs Haigh obtained from the carter rolls of that putty-coloured institution material that I had found Ethel wearing and which he was delivering from a factory near Manchester, his masters having business with orphanages, workhouses and servants' outfitters in Leeds and York. Mrs Haigh could find no use for it other than for dish-clouts and to dress us in it. My 'best' workhouse suit proved hard-wearing enough for me to grow out of it before it became threadbare, after which I wore breeches and shirts made of the carter's itchy stuff, full of knots and slubs, thick and difficult to sew, as Ethel was the first to tell me; for she was the one who sewed it, until she taught me how to make my own shirts.

In our similar dress, only I had my hair free so that you could see my curls and I wore breeches instead of a gown, you could hardly tell which was which. Which one was maid and which was boy. If you'd made a guess for the girl, perhaps you would have chosen me, instead of Ethel.

*

As I was soon to realise, especially from the attitudes of some of the less respectable travellers. Let us call them that and finish with it, for I hate looking back and seeing where my innocence might have led me, spoiling me for you, my dear. The ones wanting something unusual in a place where no one knew them; who were interested in a bit of adventure in a private place among the bogs, often staying for a night or two longer if they saw any chance of finding it.

A new phenomenon entered my life; one which stayed with me until I was in my early twenties, by which time I had learned to understand it. Men stared at me. They haunted me with stares. Palmer did it. You did it, before you spoke to me. Once or twice they dropped improper suggestions until I blushed. You know the kind of thing I mean. Ethel and

I, discovering that we could be mistaken for one another, sometimes tempted providence by exchanging clothes, as children will when they discover a way of teasing adults. As twins do. Oh, I can hardly bear to think about what might have happened; for I was always too eager to please people, as Mary had told me. But I remembered too well that icy moment when Mary talked about the fellow who was chopped to bits and buried in a peat-hole, with no one to bring him justice. I was saved because at the last minute I was also 'quick with my lip', as they say. I could never go that far, I told myself. But the more dangerous and horrifying the fate, the more it can hypnotise. Oh, you know how I was drawn . . . and we could have done more, if you hadn't been so . . . *Victorian!*

Was it to tempt some of these oddities that Mr Haigh had offered me a job with such alacrity, do you think? Could it be that his first thought was to keep himself in his wife's good books by promoting a bit of business for the pub; then he grew to like me and perhaps changed his mind?

That would be something to spice up another of the stories with which I filled our thousand and one nights, wouldn't it? Bung-ho! Oh, it makes me blush to think of it! Yes, I think I must have been a bait laid by the Haighs. A victim, unbeknown to me at the time.

Actually, now that I know more about such types, it is the weird customers themselves for whom I feel sorry. Even more, for their dependents. The foul ways that some men flow into, helplessly flushed down the sewers of a satisfaction that they cannot keep themselves from! I have seen all of that. The sacrifices that such make of those who love and depend upon them. Wives and families are sacrificed to satisfy some indulgence for the man – it was always men – alone!

And it always ended with *their* being alone, too. There should have been a lesson for us in that, my dear Dodds, but I did not weave the moral into my stories soon enough.

Though nothing so very bad happened to me, as it turned out. I was lucky. Yet this strange phenomenon had much to do with why I have always fallen into something whenever the occasion has clicked; this seems to have been what had happened for me to slip into a home at The Fleece, for instance. This facility may be my good fortune, or has it turned out to be a web of misfortunes that entraps me?

It was all because of my looks – not because I was handsome but because I was what they called 'pretty'. By instinct and not conscious of what I was doing, I was helping myself along this path by imitating Mrs Haigh, just as I had followed the women in the workhouse and the mill.

As I was given little opportunity to mix with other growing lads, I thought that the way I instinctively behaved and the fashion in which I was treated at The Fleece was usual for boys. Tickled under the chin as often as I was slapped on the back. Gently stroked, more often than jokingly thumped. Laughed at, sneered at, contemptuously hailed as 'slavey' or 'skivvy' and without a thought sent off to do a maid's work as often as a lad's. A great joke made of their not knowing, or pretending not to know, whether they were addressing Ethel or me.

Mrs Haigh herself joined in this kind of fun; though in the end her cruel streak has turned out to my advantage, for if she was in a good mood she would get me to do quite personal services for her, in public and in private. Here, again, my upbringing with females stood me in good stead and I was acquiring more knowledge that would be useful to me later. Through Mrs Haigh I began my education in the subjects of hats, hair brushes and toilet soap; in the ironing of finer clothes, lace and so forth.

I faced up to it: I was a male with a female trapped inside me. It caused me pain, but thrilled me with its mystery. All boys dwell on the changes taking place in their bodies, but my broodings were for something more than normal, I realised. The guests at The Fleece teased me about my moods and my strangeness, until I either blushed like a girl, or at other times I would be quick with my fists and display a temper. A proper mix-up, as people sometimes said. Travellers of a better class called me 'an enigma'.

I did not mind the fun I caused; I already liked people to laugh at me. It was that other kind of interest. I learned to recognise a particular type. I could see them coming. 'Half a mo',' I'd tell myself. 'There's trouble here!' These types were both generous and overbearing. They tried simultaneously to impress and degrade me. It was most distinctive. Also, although they could vary from the manly to the effeminate themselves, they were noticeably exaggerated in whatever they were. Sometimes they fondled me and even put me on their knees. I felt very much a girl then. Sometimes they slapped me. This often occurred when they found me in their rooms. At other times they were cruel with their tongues. One actually suggested that I become his 'slave'; that was the very word he used and he offered to take me away with him.

The master and mistress were almost as bad and encouraged this behaviour. It went on until at last I stood up to Mrs Haigh over one suggestion made to me, though I shall not name it and, yes, with a tear at the corner of my eye, I insisted, '*I'm not doing it, Mrs Haigh, I'm not! I'm not! I'm not!*'

With hindsight, that moment when I dug in my heels was probably the beginning of the end for me at The Fleece.

But mostly I put up with it because I was free, too, in a way I'd learned to appreciate in the workhouse and the woollen mill. At any moment I could walk over the hills to another stony little hamlet and find a job in a public house. Only someone brought up in a prison could understand how important such a freedom could be.

Second, whatever else my patrons or persecutors were, they were rarely boorish and with their little acts they were not monotonously brutal, whereas boorishness and unwavering brutality had been precisely the characteristics of all the male overseers and officers whom I had met before.

In my heart I was still hoping for a father.

Meeting such a man as Mr Haigh, despite his sadness, had made me believe it was possible that, somewhere, one existed.

*

Although Mr Haigh had told me that he had squared things with the Guardians of the Poor, it did not take me long to see that Diggle was only a mile or two away on the other side of Standedge. I was constantly afraid of some hand reaching over the hill to grab me. Those smoking vents on the moor were those for the Standedge Tunnel, at the mouth of which I had begun my life.

Yet it would have taken a very positive alarm indeed to wrench me away. Did it strike you that Mrs Haigh in her nun's dress and her preposterous hat sounded like a music-hall turn? You were right. She loved it all. Stranded among the water-filled holes of the moor, the only way she could make her dreams of Manchester come true was to turn that large front room where travellers dined into a hall for singing and entertainment, a couple of nights a week at the weekend.

This was also more than enough to keep me at The Fleece for three years.

The ailments of the factory, the worn-out lungs, the blood poisoned with chemicals, the graveyard with its memorial pomp waiting outside the mill gates and the chapel there, too, its hymns shot through with praise of death as the very purpose of life, had sickened and horrified me. If you get into the frame of mind of those multitudes of death-worshippers, as one so easily may, death-worship can seem the true expression of these trench-like, tomb-like valleys. Did I have to reconcile myself to such a thing? *No*, said the music hall. *No! No! No!* All that dark earth-boundness was but a springboard for this other vitality; the entertainment in which I wanted to make my career.

Also, the fiddle-playing in the public houses, the jokes, the monologues that I too learned to deliver, gained their sword-like power to cut the heart because they were antidotes, they sprang out of what otherwise haunted the valleys. They opposed the downward pull towards death.

The word got around when a well-known singer, musician, comedian or conjuror was expected to be passing by The Fleece and such news would crowd the place out on *any* night of the week. For its more usual entertainments, the pub depended upon locals or regular travellers who would sing, tell jokes or do tricks, for drinks and a few pence or maybe simply to impress Mrs Haigh and the customers.

Unlike at theatre plays, if people didn't like what they heard, they didn't listen and an entertainer had to thrust himself forward to grasp their attention. It's ironic that the amateur who performs in the local pub cannot afford a flop, whereas your professional, though booed off stage, can heave a resolute sigh and pass on to another town. Your local must provide the same standard in order to stay in business. All of them derivative acts, of course. But The Fleece on its trans-Pennine route was well placed both to have a regular offering upon which people could rely and yet also the pub did not grow stale, being continually revived with a flow of new travellers, as both performers and audience.

This was a milieu in which, although I say it myself, my talents shone when I dared let it be known that I was willing to have a go on stage. As it happened, entertainment at The Fleece boomed at the time I fell upon it. Jim the carter helped by boasting about his experiences of the London music halls. Winking and leering over his hints of what went on there, he used what he knew to cement his bond with Mrs Haigh, to inspire her yearnings and to shut out John o'Jack's who was ignorant of these things. The carter also dazzled Maggie Haigh and the drinkers who gathered around him with tales about the halls and theatres in Leeds, Bradford and other towns. He entranced me, too. I was bewitched and could never hear enough. The girls at the mill had enticed me with snippets of information, but he was the first to be fulsome about the music hall. It is a pity I associate my first knowledge of the great performers with him, as I did not like the man, but it was from his lips that I first heard the names of Jenny Hill, 'the vital spark', of Vesta Tilley, Vesta Victoria, Kate Carney, Katie Lawrence, Bessie Bellwood, Dan Leno, Gus Elen, Eugene Stratton, Florrie Forde, and Marie Lloyd – all my stars.

Mrs Haigh, soaking all this up, longing to bring a 'real' music hall to The Fleece, got excited over her schemes with the carter. She could not go as far as erecting gilded pillars and an auditorium in the style of a Moorish temple. She did put in mahogany tables with wrought iron legs. She purchased some very artistic oil lamps, too, with dolphins fashioned out of brass, and she complained loudly that the public gas supply did not reach Standedge to light us up with something even finer.

As decent women would not go near The Fleece and as it was filled with spendthrift men who were far from their homes, tinker-women, gypsies and prostitutes filled the vacuum. To control them and to put on an appearance of respectability, Mrs Haigh devised regulations. She would not allow 'ladies' to enter her pub in bare feet; this kept out the rush-gatherers, tinkers and all other poor types who combed the moors. If she felt that the place was getting close to its quota of loose women, she would have Ethel, myself or someone else posted at the door to say that the house was full.

Her final trick for turning The Fleece into a 'Tivoli', a 'Hen and Chickens' or a 'Liston's': she learned from the carter to issue 'refreshment tickets'. Originally at The Fleece you either ate a large meal at specified times in one of the cubicles, or you stayed at the bar and drank ale or porter. When the room was used as a music hall, Mrs Haigh abolished the large meals, but to get around the licensing regulations governing entertainment she made everyone pay twopence for a token refreshment, a piece of pie or a slab of bread and cheese.

Six months after I arrived, it was my good fortune that a mere singing room, such as any pub might have, was turned into a regular music hall, dubbed 'the sod's opera' in the farms and villages. When the place was barricaded within snow or ice, sometimes the entertainment continued for days.

*

Take a further look at the list of artists above, a list that fell so easily from the tip of my pen dipped into an inkwell rocking gently as I stir my caravan with my movements on a moorland night: almost all are female. In The Fleece we depended mostly on male comedians, singers, accordionists, fiddlers and clog dancers, but many of the most famous names nationally are female. You once told me, Garrick, that music hall has that characteristic of Ancient Greek drama: its *great* figures are women. A stage that was dominated by Medea, Clytemnestra, Antigone, Helen and Cassandra, next to whom all the male characters, Agamemnon and that lot, seem weak despite their bluster, is today matched by a theatre led by the likes of Marie Lloyd, Florrie Forde and Vesta Tilley.

The music hall tips upside down our society in which women are supposed to be meek and mild, while men are powerful. In the music hall, men are weak, but women become larger than life. Which was my view of my experiences, exactly; so what else should I want to be on the stage, but a woman?

There is the true dream-home of the oppressed women whom I felt for in the workhouse and in the mill. In the music hall, women can do the unthinkable. They roll about drunk, show their thighs and knickers, openly make jokes at the expense of Father, the Boss and the Vicar, even poke fun at sex. Men's part is to be stooges for the women's attack. The men on stage are anything but powerful bankers and builders, soldiers and engineers. They are set up to be laughed at as drunken, immoral, weak, hen-pecked or in debt. George Robey plays a clergyman with a drinker's red nose. Deflating snobberies and hypocrisies on behalf of women: that's meat and drink to the music hall.

*

At the age of thirteen I discovered the existence of men becoming women on stage: of the drag-act. It was after a stroke of great good fortune had blown my way. Dan Leno, of all people, with a trunk full of props for a whole gallery of male and female impersonations, stayed overnight at The Fleece on his way from Manchester to Huddersfield. I'll never forget my debt to that genius; oh, if only I now had the chance to tell him so! A tiny man, five feet three inches. But he was the biggest creator of laughter on the stage that we've ever had, I'm sure of it. I recognised the authority of his dedication to his art as soon as I met him and it was this that excited me more than anything.

I had never before met anyone with a *vocation*. I had not even known that such a thing existed. Yet here it was – a calm, absorbed professionalism, showing itself even in the way he could turn aside the unctuous bullying of the carter, who wished to take him over for the evening.

Yet, just as with Mr Haigh, I could smell his melancholic nature, too, as soon as he came in. That cadaverous face, cheeky and alert it seemed at first glance, then you noticed that it was haunted. When I heard in 1904 that the poor chap had died of insanity at the age of forty-four, I was not surprised. It was said that he was broken-hearted because his little group of music halls had been swamped by the big syndicates. But it was really because he had tired of fighting his black angels, his ghosts. In the 1880s, I had yet to learn that comics die mad, die sick, or kill themselves and that they become comedians in order to drive off their intuitions of a melancholy future.

Now I understand better why Dan, who could be billed in New York as 'the funniest man on earth', was miserable with a failed ambition to play Hamlet.

The carter took on the role of Chairman for the evening, as he usually did. He wore a top hat, sported a cane and a cravat, used a tradesman's rolled-leather hammer as a gavel and while the great man was out of the room he informed us of his repertoire: the fireman, the railway guard, the huntsman, the recruiting sergeant, the Beefeater, Charles I, Nelson and Abdulah the sheikh.

Dan didn't do any of these turns. He had also won a competition to become 'the greatest clog dancer in the world', an art that didn't go down well in London, so in general he had dropped it from his act. What better place than a Pennine alehouse for him to dance in once again? I might have been back at one of those happier hours in the workhouse kitchen, as he pranced in iron-tipped shoes on the stone floor of the tap-room.

Following this, he disappeared for five minutes while we refilled our tankards. After he had changed into some token female clothes, he announced himself as a 'drag-act' and it was the first time that I heard the term.

He had us in fits with his 'Mrs Kelly' impersonation. Dan wore a crumpled plaid dress with short, puffed sleeves displaying his thin but sinewy arms. He had a pinny fastened on his breast and a most peculiar wig that had two ridiculous twists of hair sticking out like horns at the side. He folded his arms, clamped his jaws to make a disapproving pout, looked very severe and then, like a slattern gossiping on a kitchen step, he poured out a jumble of comic nonsense.

Except that it wasn't really nonsense. It was a wry view of the world, knowing the pits of despondency that lay on either hand of his razor-edge of cheerfulness, but never tumbling. A tightrope act, such as Dan himself walked through life.

He possessed huge, arched eyebrows, so that he always looked surprised. That poor, downtrodden 'woman', 'Mrs Kelly', was a female Don Quixote, taking on a huge world that baffled but would never defeat her.

*

I can see it now; my life was illuminated as if with a flood of electric lighting. All you had to do, in order to get away with dressing up as a woman in sight of everyone, was to tell funny stories on stage! And there you were! Bob's your uncle! I grasped that I would not even need to look convincingly female, to have the pleasure of feeling like one. Comedy made it acceptable to be in drag. Surely I could do that? As well as Miss Shingles' anecdotes, I knew lots of low-life tales, having overheard them from the woman's side in workhouse, mill and pub.

I worked hard to absorb Dan's tricks, watching every detail, memorising them; I studied his mannerisms as if I'd never watched a woman before. I had only my familiar pot-house costume which hardly needed altering to make me female, and so my first drag-act was born effortlessly. I only needed to swop Ethel's gown for my breeches, tie my hair up under one of her bonnets and put on a squeaky voice. I first went on during the following week, straight from carrying around pots of ale, to sing from my repertoire of sentimental ballads and to mix them with Miss Shingles' jokes about servants. It was as a slavey laughing at myself; not, mark you, from my, but from their point of view – the problems that employers have with slaveys.

I learned from Dan's 'Mrs Kelly' that not only dare I dress publicly in drag. By creating a character I could go far beyond sentimental ballads, or Miss Shingles-type, prissy anecdotes. I could go on as a working woman, breaking up her yarns with sentimental songs; announcing myself not as Jack but as 'Jacky' Shuttleworth. Everyone in The Fleece having seen Dan Leno made me, too, acceptable as a performing-girl. Though I despaired at not having access to props, having to make do with Ethel's and my own poor clothes was a blessing, making my act economical. This had the effect of giving my words and actions room to breathe.

If 'Mrs Kelly' hung over my act, yet also my performances developed their own, Yorkshire material, mentioning people and places known to the audience. I gained most of all from the fact that, unlike Dan, I had a girlish appearance and my voice had not yet broken.

It also entertained people that I was so young. There were lots of other homeless thirteen- and fourteen-year-olds hopping about the towns and villages doing juggling, sleight-of-hand and mimicry (more often than singing), in order to hold body and soul together. You'd come across these scamps everywhere, doing their turns on the steps of pubs or down back-alleys where if you didn't pay them they would rob you. But few of them had their hearts in the entertainment business. They had merely discovered a trick by which to get by and might as well have been out-and-out thieves. Though I say it myself, what gripped my audiences was what one gentleman described as 'my nascent professionalism which is quite astonishing'. Yes. They stared boggle-eyed at my smooth, small, unlined and inexperienced young face (I weep for it now) doing an imitation of a middle-aged, experience-soured woman.

But, though I had discovered the basis of a workable act, at heart I was not the servant type. I was pursuing the wrong line and in the end that was what turned out to be most funny about it.

I realised what a comical model I had in the pretentious Mrs Haigh, trying to better herself through wearing hats. I retrieved some of her cast-off headpieces from where she had thrown them on to the midden of chicken manure at the side of the house. As my performance developed through the winter months, I added more elements of the absurd, and began to tower out of my oatmeal-coloured calico. The more humble my anecdotes, the more I strutted like the Princess of Wales.

The 'Princess of Wales' telling yarns like a village gossip, and the audience gasping because she was in fact a fourteen-year-old boy!

It was already quite bizarre.

For perfection, all that I needed was a proper lady's wardrobe, and some first-hand experience of a lady's life.

·3·

I WAKE up in the dawn and my first thought is gratitude: I have slept. I could not have told you for how long, without consulting your fob-watch hanging from a hook above my bed. It was as good a sleep as that. The stickiness, the shivers, the wrinkled skin of the steam-bath, yes; but *sleep*! Four hours, four complete hours. That is about as much as I expect, nowadays. Yet again, I have got past it: the awful chasm that opens, always, in the middle of the night when I awake abruptly, brilliantly awake, as my heart for a second stops and then, to make up for the stopping, beats furiously, in those seconds when I realise what hunts me, what loneliness, and with the terrible disappointment of again not having made it to the morning. Am suspended in this blackness. *Nobody knows, do they?*

Stop it, Camellia! Take a grip on yourself, gal! Stop feeling sorry for yourself, dash it! You'll end up dying all alone, of self-pity.

That is when I write myself up. Or tell myself jokes, in a fury of trying to forget – reality.

I simply do not wish to stir. But the only thing to do is to get up quickly. Everyone who has been in grief knows it. It used to be a delight to linger in bed. Lie there now and you'll die, Jacky Shuttleworth.

Camellia Snow.

Rose Gay.

Iris Vane.

I climb out of my drawer-bed, slide the drawer into its place above the cupboard and pull back the window's inner curtain. One gold giving way to another: that of sunlight coming through the lace screen. Oh, the dawn, the dawn, so beautiful! The sunlight plays upon the India rug on the floor, for all the world like a fountain of water.

A Halifax lady's husband was dying, so she got the ham

sandwiches ready.

As he lay in bed, she asked him tenderly, 'Now is there anything tha fancies, love, before tha pops thee clogs?'

'Aye,' he answered, 'I'd just love one o' them 'am sandwiches.'

'Nay, my love, thou cannot have them. Them's for t'funeral!'

I try this one out while I warm coffee on the stove; warm myself, too, clutching my night-dress around me. I take a spoonful of Phosferine for my health. I see from *The Times* that they even recommend it for steadying the nerves in Flanders.

Nay, my love, thou cannot have them! Them's for t'funeral . . .

I try the turn again, with different emphases and a little faster. I pace out the rhythm, using my finger as a baton. Go back a sentence.

Now is there anything tha fancies, love, before tha pops thee clogs?

That absurd sentence must be uttered with unctuous sentiment and sweetness.

Now is there anything . . .

It's make-up time.

Dressing-rooms are usually foul, from too many people using them. They are half boudoir and half public urinal; messes of spilled powder, scattered eyebrow-pencils, screwed-up handkerchiefs stained with make-up smears or tears; littered with tarnished mirrors and wobbly stools. I'm glad to be out of all that, actually. (No, I'm not!) But I decided from the beginning that my caravan, though it *is* my travelling dressing-room, was going to be different. You have to be tidy in a caravan. And the consolation is: it is all of it entirely, entirely mine! For once, for the first time, my own home!

Boil water for a shave, meanwhile pack things away ready for setting off. My notebook, my bottle of ink. My copies of *Era*, the stage magazine. Your mother's needlework basket; another present from you. How precious things become in a caravan! The final essence of my life jogs with me along the road. Such loved things, now. It took me some patience to learn to pack my mementos carefully each time I move on: a gypsy's art. Here are some of your books. Manuals on being a lady. On etiquette. Here are picture-postcards of me in drag, professionally taken, signed 'Sincerely, Camellia Snow' and now pinned above my bed.

The water's boiled upon the spirit stove. Pour it into my little ceramic ewer, decorated with blue flowers. I'm so glad I'm fair and have no problem with a shadow. For the same reason, my eyebrows don't let me down, neither. Though I have some lovely creams, because I've been lucky; I've had the opportunities to find out.

It's a funny thing, but males have more profuse sweat-glands than females; I don't know why that is. You can betray yourself, make a wobble in your act with a stink of sweat, or the secretion of some other gland that it is not possible to uproot. And over-all washes are a problem for me, these days. Expect me to go to the public baths, do you?

I dip my face in a bowl of warm water and shave. I don't go the whole hog anymore and I'm glad I've now given up shaving my chest; a shaved chest gets very prickly in warm weather. Lord! Not long ago my maid, Sarah, was adding Rimmel's May-Dew to my bath! Merely bathing used to take all of a blessed hour. After caressing my cheeks with glycerine cream, I would apply Blanc Marimon, a stage-whitener but, dash it, I needed it, and next, Hebe Bloom Rouge. That was after spending all afternoon removing hair with wax-treatment and picking out my eyebrows with Rimmel's pencils. Rimmel's stuff is the best, you know.

Still talking to myself. Talking to you, that is. Can't stop. You've no idea, have you, because you died, what it's like to be talking to someone all the time, in your head? I catch myself at it and realise I've been doing it all morning or all afternoon, until I tell myself, God, you must stop it, give yourself a blinking rest!

Before I do, listen to this one: this is a true story, but you have to know that locally 'War' is pronounced 'Woor'. Taffy, listen to this one.

There was once a bachelor decided at last, at the age of fifty, to leave his mother, see. He bought a terraced house in Wakefield Road and called it 'War House'. A chap asked him why he'd called it by that name and he answered, 'When

I told my mother I was moving home, she said, "Well, I 'ope you're not going to turn it into one of them whore-houses!"'

What shall I wear? I can't be too extravagant these days because I have to go out and tackle up Taffy. Stumbling about on the grass after a horse, life's not easy for a girl on her own. No good my dressing like Scheherazade, a slave bangle on my ankle, anymore. Can't carry it off. I just about keep myself up to scratch by taking doses of Phosferine and Wincarnis.

> If those lips could only speak,
> If those eyes could only see,
> If those beautiful golden tresses
> Were there in reality . . .

Away we go. Sit on the shafts, release the brake. *Click, click* to Taffy who bends her shoulders to our future and with a smell of crushed grass we lumber on to the stony highway, *rattle rattle* down off the moor.

Soon, the road verges are dancing with mayflowers. Through a spring dawn, I go through Holme Chapel and Towneley, before I drop into the cotton-town of Burnley. My entry into Lancashire is through a passage of the real countryside of farms, fields and woods. What the *toffs* call 'countryside'. You could catch trout here. Shoot pheasants. Tear foxes apart. Slaughter partridges.

Taffy is enjoying life, too. On the gentler, downhill slopes, she manages quite a brisk trot. She shakes the white blaze on her forehead at a horse in a nearby field, who, following an impulsive affection, runs, neighing, the length of the hedge after Taffy. Love at first sight. A music-hall theme.

I, also, feel something. Oh, it would be good to be alive in the spring of this year of Our Lord 1915, if only one were young! If only I were young!

Suddenly, the sun has risen through pools of mist; scattered wombs, warm and still, in which everything sweats with growth. Those cottagers I watch coming out of their houses: if they would lift their heads from their dull concentrations (which they do not do), they would observe, in a mere hour between their entering the cows' shed and coming out again, the woods change. Beauty can be so great, it seems to be without substance. An inner glow has become so powerful that it has consumed the substance on which it feeds.

Since leaving Halifax, I have travelled twenty miles. How long will it take me to reach Blackpool? A little over a week?

I am following the route through Burnley, Accrington, Blackburn and Preston, though I can't think why. If I'd gone through Rochdale and Manchester, I could have seen the most interesting acts that are on in Lancashire theatres at the moment, so *Era* tells me. Jack Pleasants at the Manchester Empire, Mrs Langtry and Company at the New Palace.

So why am I following this desert road?

I know why.

This was the way I used to go by railway to Blackpool with you, my dear Dodds.

*

Down in Burnley, the chimneys of the cotton mills are already smoking heavily, stoking up again at the end of the night shift. The firebeaters must get a head of steam on time for the women coming to work in the morning. There is so much soot filtering through the air that dropping into the valley is like putting your head into a chimney. No sun here, only a grimy screen with a pale disc hung faintly behind it. 'The beds never grow cold,' they say of these towns, for one half of every family is now about to tumble into the beds being deserted by those about to report. The town is busy, with men returning from night duty and women, dressed in shawls and clogs, going in for the day. Well, I doubt if any of *these* are Liza Buckton's agents. Little groups are coming along, with a huge noise of clog-irons on the cobbles. While I feel that I bring with me a memory of life as it was out of town, golden, majestic, flower-filled. That, also, makes me an oddity. It is a secret I might have shared only with you. You would understand what I am saying.

I pull up Taffy so as to pop into a shop to buy a copy of *The Times*. I have regained my nerve now. The beauty of that fringe of countryside between town and barren moorland has given me courage.

Some young soldiers are gathered in the square; recruits to the Duke of Lancaster's Light Infantry, seemingly without a care in the world and lounging with nothing to occupy them at the moment. A woman, better still a chap in drag, stepping out of a gypsy's caravan would be a gift, wouldn't it?

Mr Dodds, this is what you're longing to know, even though you're up there playing your harp: what am I wearing? Am I in this year's fashion of sloppy clothes, especially in the silks, taffetas and cottons? Or, so as to be my age, do I go in for 'matron's wear', say a walking-outfit of navy cloth and braid under a dark, silk-lined coat? I can see the gleam in your eye. But I keep you waiting.

Sorry to disappoint you, old chap, but I'm in none of these things. Without even a wig, I slip from my caravan wearing a pair of your own old tweed trousers, a red silk shirt which I'm afraid I can't resist as I am, after all, a 'gypsy'; with a red silk scarf round my neck. Maybe there is, yes, just a trace of make-up left from doing myself up last night.

I step across the sunlit cobbles to the shop.

You used to say, 'What the British are best at is *Being Closed*, at saying *No,* at *Not Having Any*, at *We've No Call For It.* These are their best acts,' you said. Oh, Mr Dodds, I can hear your dear voice now! Your dear voice! These things used to drive you mad, because you'd been in Paris and Vienna. But, surprise, surprise; the shop is open, for its trade in selling tea, pies and breakfasts to the mill-workers. It has a stock of yesterday's newspapers. In the shop, a real *We Don't Have Any* type, you would think, a real chump, in fact sells me a *Times* but he hardly looks up. It's too early in the morning for him to expect anything interesting.

When I come out, the soldiers and the mill-workers don't turn a blinking hair and I set off down the road, heading towards Padiham, but first of all looking for somewhere to park and to graze Taffy while I pop round to the Palace to see if I can find work for myself.

I read *The Times* on my lap over Taffy's bobbing rump. On the two hundred and ninetieth day of the War, Lord Kitchener calls for more blood to be poured into the trenches. That's not the way he puts it, of course, but I know what's going on and none of that junk about the 'bloodthirsty Hun' impresses me! There's a letter in Kitchener's handwriting. '*I have said that I would let the country know when more men*

70

were wanted for the War. The time has come and I now call for 300,000 recruits.'

There follow the new conditions for enlistment. They would even take me, now. The age limit is raised to forty, the minimum height reduced to five foot two (*Forty! Five foot two!*), and they'll have you with a narrower chest. My chest, thank goodness, is *very* narrow, but I'm five foot six and I'd scrape in easily. If I was foolish enough to try.

But, every day, elderly bigwigs write letters to *The Times* calling for conscription.

At the foot of the page, in Gothic letters redolent of civilisation and tradition, I read:

God Save The King

Elsewhere, the paper's a more cheerful read. '*Perhaps the most wonderful thing in the War to us women,*' reports the fashion page, '*is our realisation of the indestructible power of life. In spite of everything, we go on with our everyday lives and the importance of ordering dinner is only slightly lessened. We even find, as the spring develops, we are going to take an interest in clothes.*'

Mr Dodds, how you would have drooled over the illustrations on the fashion page, thinking of me! A tea frock and a tea gown, both long and loose, for £2 18s 6d and £3 18s 6d, respectively, from Debenham and Freebody. Marshall and Snelgrove's Grecian night-gown in crêpe de Chine, worn with a négligé cap. Afternoon coat in black silk poplin from Harrods: £5 19s 6d.

Burberry advertise 'summer wear for Flanders'. They show officers shining in the rain of the trenches like medieval knights in armour.

There has been a gas attack at Ypres.

*

Ethel repaired Mrs Haigh's cast-off hats for me; I have one of them to this day. In her wet scullery, Ethel spent her little spare time in stitching by the fireside. It was possibly because she was so nimble at repairing hats that the Haighs employed her. It was lovely to watch her fingers working. They were

71

what wings are to a bird. They fluttered and floated. They lifted her, through her concentration, above her earthly self.

'What are you thinking?' she asked, when she caught me staring.

'I like watching you.'

She smiled. I believed that I was getting her to smile more and more as time went by.

'What are you watching? I'm not doing nothing. I'm only laiking.'

'Laiking' means *playing*, Mr Dodds. (As you never understood the dialect!) If you were not improving the world materially, you were 'laiking' which was synonymous with doing nothing.

'I'm not watching anything. But it's nice. Mary Shuttleworth used to sit by the fire like you, telling stories.'

'You told me she was a big woman. Not like me. And I've no stories to tell.'

But she was pleased. She knew what I meant, no matter what she said.

I got Ethel to add turkey feathers that I picked up in the Womersleys' yard, bunches of rowan berries and dried heather, which turned the old headgear into fantastic stage props. Marie Lloyd would have gone mad for them.

Wearing these creations atop working clothes borrowed from Ethel, I stood on stage pretending to be not one but two women, enjoying a right good gossip. I had seen a comedian do something similar on Friday nights at The Fleece. By changing hats and ruffling his clothes he pretended to be two men, a dude and a tramp. Similarly, I only had to turn my head in different directions and to change my hats, to be first of all Mrs Sykes, next her friend, Mrs Bolton. The pair settled permanently into my repertoire. Mrs Bolton had a whinging, squeaky voice and was the stooge to Mrs Sykes who boomed and was overbearing. Mrs Sykes' hat was the more extravagant. Mrs Bolton's was, in time, reduced to a little felt skull-cap with a single, long, drooping feather.

I did everything straight-faced and understated. In some stories, I was a bride deserted on her wedding night, or an old woman lying about having lost sixpence when they came round with the church collection plate. Sometimes I told the story of Joe Gaukroger and Mary's dog. I also developed a routine in which the two women discussed purchasing a gas oven and Mrs Bolton wanted to find out how much Mrs Sykes had paid. I was building up a repertoire of turns that with variations would take me, in time, through strings of halls in the north. I could make a cat laugh. I could bring a tear to a glass eye.

Not everybody listened; not always. There was generally a noisy crowd at the back, drinking and talking under clouds of smoke. If they took notice of me it was only to make fun in the way I didn't want it. I was learning that I couldn't please everyone, but to have the nerve not to bother about them until I had an answer ready that would turn the tables. What mattered was to hold the attention of the front rows.

I discovered also that the more dry and melancholic I was, the more they found me funny and entertaining. Sometimes, when I delivered anecdotes about the workhouse, I was falling apart with sadness, inside. Especially in telling Mary's story.

Here were another two people inside me, you might say; one happy, one sad; one of them skating upon the character underneath.

*

A gentleman started to make a habit of coming to see and listen to me. He sat at a few tables' distance and he came alone. He stared so that the first time I spotted him, all that I was aware of was his burning eyes which were dark and large underneath neatly trimmed eyebrows. He had smooth-shaven cheeks and neatly trimmed hair, black tinged with grey, combed in a dashing fashion. It was some time before I saw him stand and discovered that he was tall, with an elegantly slight stoop.

He stared in such an intent fashion that I had to think about him, and I believed he was the kind of man with breeding whom I would have chosen as a father – strong in the world and therefore, I assumed in those early days, strong in himself.

When he had to make his way out to the white-washed wall in the back yard by the midden, the insensate crowd made way

73

for him in awe and he did not need to say a word. Looking down upon them, he behaved as if they didn't exist. Only I, so you might believe, existed. In this public house which was so conspicuously not his element, he never moved far before he was haunting me again with his stares.

He never smiled at my act. My demotic humour could not move him. He was equally unstirred by the sentimental songs with which I finished my turns; the popular women's numbers with which I could charm sentimental hearts, before my voice broke. Why, I wondered, was he drawn to the music hall, to the public laughter and the filthy conviviality; to the place where the rawest experiences of the sweaty proletariat are banded about? Why had he come to stare at me?

In between my appearances on stage, Ethel and I were serving drinks or food and mopping tables. The visitor sipped small glasses of sherry, which we had on tap because of our trade with genteel customers, and he never touched the slice of pie that he'd paid for; not many were like that in Saddleworth.

I could examine him more closely, then. He possessed one of those skins that are preserved with frequent washings, using fine soaps and eau-de-Cologne. In The Fleece, he really was a fish out of water. He and his valet had obviously spent hours upon his appearance. He never spoke to me, but if I came close, for once he looked away. I never dared to initiate a conversation; he froze me. He was preoccupied with looking down to flick the ash from his black cigarettes clear of his suit and to keep his knees out of the way of having beer spilled on them.

Some of the other customers were able to tell me that his name was Palmer. It is amazing what a sense of being pre-armed that gave me. When I was performing, our eye-lines would become entangled. Before many weeks had passed, the temptation to exchange glances had become like an itch that we both had to scratch. I did not find anything sinister about him. His restraint added to his air of breeding. I was hoping that he might turn out to be a scout for the Leeds or Bradford music halls; perhaps even for Mr Tom Barrasford or Mr Oswald Stoll, whose names I had heard dropped weightily from the carter's lips.

Watching each week for the arrival of Mr Palmer, who might open so many doors, you can imagine what agonies I went through. You know what I'm like when something might be coming my way! I could not sleep on Thursday nights, though we still had not spoken to each other beyond the most meagre politenesses. Our greatest intimacy was that I had served him sherry, when I who was so confident on stage was tongue-tied with fear at having to speak to him directly.

I set Ethel on to find out more. She had seemed so subdued, but had turned out to be a chatter-box when she got going and all her silence, her keeping her head down, was mostly the camouflage of, underneath, a determined young woman. But she could not find out very much, either, and she was as tongue-tied as I when it came to conversing with such a gentleman. All she discovered was that he owned 'estates' on the other side of the hill.

It was ridiculous of me to put such faith in so very little, but I had a hunch that something was in the wind. I needed it, for things were worsening at The Fleece and I had to grasp at straws. Mrs Haigh told me I was getting too big for my boots, that there was something very peculiar about me, I was the sort something should be done about, I ought to have a hoperation, it was time I was on my way, et cetera, et cetera. More and more she was finding fault and confining me to the kitchen. Jim the carter had started to kick me around. He was doing it more and more, with a lot of cruel teasing – you can imagine.

Also, he tried to upstage me. Before he collapsed into his drink and began to snivel about the death of his wife, also from drink three years previously, the elephant used to do a few turns himself. He tried to be a swell, to swagger with a cane and sing George Leybourne's song, *Champagne Charlie*. I'm convinced that he actually thought of himself as a Leybourne or the Great Vance, a '*lion comique*' as that type of entertainer was called; a rake, a spendthrift man-about-town, loved for his generosity. A dude.

I belonged to the other music-hall tradition: that of self-mockery, taking on the mantles of working women challenging a world bent on reducing them but not succeeding in doing so. The carter and I could never have hit it off

75

together. And his act! He weighed seventeen stones, most of it beer fat, and wouldn't in a month of Sundays develop the finicky lightness of touch necessary for *Champagne Charlie*. Neither could he disguise his Yorkshire accent. He would bounce on stage with his overbearing grin, and try to sing a typical '*lion comique*' song,

> *Whoever drinks at my expense*
> *I treat 'em all the same,*
> *From dukes and lords to cabmen down,*
> *I make 'em drink champagne . . .*

His thumbs stuck proudly in his lapels or into his waistcoat, he did not realise what people were thinking about him when they laughed, even though they started putting on their coats. Not until half had left the building did he understand. Naturally, he took his failure out on me afterwards. The jealous cad, oh, he was green with it, started to knock me about something awful.

A Friday came when Mr Palmer did not turn up. Yes, I cried myself to sleep.

But he was either teasing me, or some genuine delay had occurred. For he appeared on the following day, Saturday, at a quiet time. It was in the early afternoon when the diners were dozing off their lunch, while our usual clientele of deadheads were too drunk to notice anything. A pub at that hour is like the end of the world, especially on Standedge. I had not known how Mr Palmer travelled but looking through the window I saw him driving himself in a light, polished, very fast pony and trap, setting Mrs Haigh's hens squawking, the horses racketing in the stable and the dust rising.

I slipped out to offer my services.

'You're the actor, I'll be d——d if you're not the actor!' Mr Palmer most surprisingly blurted out, as if he hadn't been staring me blind for weeks.

Hens and ducks wandered around, a sow rooted in the midden and two laughing chaps watered the gatepost. But me -- what I could smell was the tide turning; you know how it is, in Blackpool, and how you feel. Mr Palmer stood there so dapper. He looked me briefly in the eye and then flicked his glance over my head. He played with his gloves

76

and the buttons of his smart coat. I did not at that moment sense anything fatherly about him, but rather someone like a workhouse-keeper or a vicar. Only he swore. I do not think that a gentleman should swear.

'As a matter of fact, it's you I've come to see,' he continued. 'You're jolly good, aren't you? Oh, yes, you are. Tophole.'

'Thank you, sir.'

'I've been watching you, you know. You're d——d good. *Now . . .* ' he said emphatically, in order to announce serious intentions, 'over at The Lumb we're getting up a play and there's a part in it for you if you want it. What do you think of that? It's not a terribly grand part, but an important one, don't you know! In fact, fulcrum of the plot, rather.'

I was able to look up boldly into his face. He had come with a definite purpose, and I had grasped that *he* wanted something from *me*.

And I was fixed on the idea that once I got out of The Fleece a great career lay before me in the theatre. I had seen Dan Leno do it. If that sparky, melancholic, but otherwise ordinary-seeming little man could do it, why shouldn't I? In the way of romantic boyhood, I happily lacked the doubts about my genius that haunt me now. Here is my chance, I told myself.

I was lost in what I have learned since is the way of a born fantasist; I had no grasp of the difference between what I imagined and what in reality I could expect, so my imagination ran away with me.

*

A restless artist, who was getting around by doing inn signs to pay his way, stayed once at The Fleece and painted my portrait in oils to hang outside a public house called The Golden Child for which he had a commission. He used sound, tongued-and-grooved, pitch-pine boards, decent paint and several coats of good varnish which the landlord has fortunately renewed every summer since. I passed it the other day and was stabbed with memories. From the years of hanging out in all weathers the sign is cracked and flaked, but still swinging, and I now perceive what it was that the artist, as well as Mr Palmer and others, saw in me. As we always say of the things of our youth, I wish I had understood this at the time, for I could have made better use of it.

The painter has portrayed a mysterious boy-girl; you'd have a job to tell which one I am. He has caught me in that ambiguous stage through which, as a matter of fact, most boys pass and which for me occurred between when I arrived at The Fleece and the time that I left, when my voice had broken. At that stage it is, you might say, a matter of who it is that grasps the helm. Which inner person – or which outer one.

I can see the female, inner me, so clearly in that portrait. He's painted me looking so beautifully maiden-like, I might have spent my whole life sighing in a garden-arbour. Thin chin; girl-like long neck with sloping shoulders. The artist has emphasised my gold tresses which were freshly washed for the pose, as they generally were for weekends at The Fleece, and which I had parted down the centre of my crown. He has given me lovely dabs of rosy cheeks, which he has exaggerated. How could anyone immured in a workhouse, a mill, and dwelling upon a soggy, northern moor, look like that? But I excuse his poetic licence and as a matter of fact my roses, even at my present age, are still just visible, as I could show you any day; though they've turned a bit brown with time, as rose petals do. But it's the eyes that have lasted best. They are those of a musing and perhaps love-lorn virgin, you might say. Very Swinburne, I might tell you. But a lot of purposefulness also – as you often get in the expression of someone who has some peculiar way of his own to go in life.

How you used to like to motor to The Golden Child, Mr Dodds, to take not alcohol but tea on a table by the stream at the far end of the garden, from which point you could keep your eye on the sign and sigh, 'Ah, if only I had met you then!'

*

Mr Palmer offered me a winter at The Lumb, otherwise called Lumb House. Of course I wondered what would happen in the spring, but I could see little choice for me but to move on *somewhere* from The Fleece.

Ethel and I parted after taking a walk towards Castleshaw, as we had often done in our spare time, when Ethel would pluck posies of wild flowers for all the world as if she was a well brought-up young lady, while I practised my songs. Often she was as lively as a sparrow. She had been brought up, not in an institution as I had first thought, but at a poor moorland farm, and she was in her element on the hills.

Don't think that I wasn't, somewhere inside myself, fond of girls in a boyish way, too. Even though it wasn't very powerful, not compared with some — well, I'd have to say with most — yet I used to see daughters of families breaking their journeys to dine at the pub and I had my feelings. I could get quite sloppy. You know that Ethel was nothing much to look at, except that she was a bit of a charmer around the eyes when she lifted her head and didn't take fright, yet I had grown to be very sweet on her.

It was spiffing autumn weather. That misted sunlight you get in the Pennines. You couldn't tell whether those were ranges of hills in the distance, or whether it was veil after veil of soft, dove-grey curtains.

We walked slowly along the rim of the valley, where below us they were digging a reservoir. It was as if these very footsteps were tearing us apart.

'Why don't you leave with me?' I suggested.

I longed for her to come with me. It was all that I needed to complete my happiness.

She waited several minutes before she shook her head slowly and mumbled her negative reply. It wasn't like making a decision. It was more like being resigned to knowing what she was not capable of doing. Ethel, as I think we both realised without saying so, simply had no future. Some people don't, you know.

'Mr Palmer would find you some work at The Lumb,' I persisted.

She did not answer.

'They've started on another tunnel under Standedge,' I continued. 'There'll be hoards of navvies drinking in The Fleece. How safe do you think you're going to be with that crew?'

'They're out-of-work slate quarry workers from Wales. Religious. All they're interested in is finding a chapel where they can sing.'

'Until a wilder lot follows on their heels. When the mist comes down it's like a prison up here. And when it snows. The frost . . . '

The wind would skim the surface off the reservoir and blow it over the side of the building where it encased the pub in a wrapping of ice.

'I know you can put up with boredom better than I can, but . . . '

I brought up everything I could think of to persuade her. But she was too timid. Nothing would make her take the risk of leaving. She clung like a limpet in a rock crevice, awaiting the breakers.

She knew all this herself. With gestures and nuzzlings, she stopped me from saying anymore. She wanted to spoon. I tried to respond. It was all right when she fluttered lightly over my lips; but next she pressed herself upon me, most brusquely. If I had felt anything before – I think I had felt something – I was repelled now. I tried to hide my expression, but what I wanted was to wipe my mouth.

'Why don't you want to kiss me?' she pleaded.

Should I tell her the truth, or make something up? I decided to tell the truth.

'I like you very much,' I said. 'But the reason I can't kiss is that I'm sure that you're just like my mother was.'

'But you never knew her!'

'I know exactly what she was like. She was an actress.'

'How do you know that?'

'I . . . know. Maybe you don't believe me, but I dream about her.'

'I believe you.'

'So I can't spoon. It would be like doing it with my own mother.'

Under the great moorland sky there was a quiet breeze brushing the heather and thyme, and the occasional clank of spades from the navvies below. I was miserable because I was sure that she couldn't understand, or wouldn't believe me. I looked at a clump of flowering heather as if it was the last one I would see in my life and the most important ever, so I must burn it into my memory. I can still see it today. Ethel looked at it, too. But we did not speak about it, as we had been used to talk excitedly about the things we saw and experienced together. This struck me as being particularly sad. Now we were lonely in each other's company, as we had never been before; looking at the same things and feeling the same about them, yet saying nothing.

I'd never before seen Ethel cry. If you thought about it you'd probably say that she was the sort to bottle it up, but probably you wouldn't think of it, for she was the inconspicuous type about whom it doesn't occur to you to consider whether they even have any emotions. Yet her cheeks were wet and her eyes were bulging.

'You're the only friend I've ever had,' Ethel said. 'You're the only friend. The only one . . . '

'We can see each other.'

'No,' she said, firm again quite suddenly.

'Why ever not?'

'It won't 'appen. I don't know why.'

I tried to spoon again. I put my arm around her. She was the first girl I had ever touched in that way, and I found it easier when it was I who made the approach. I loved the feel of her delicate shoulders and the smell of her washed hair in the sun when I brought my lips close. Again she turned her lips towards mine. This time when I kissed her, she smelled and tasted of whinberries, because she had been plucking at the little, low bushes as we walked along.

I *did* think it was beautiful, you know; I did.

I took away my lips, and then my arms. Ethel sighed. I realised that I had stopped too soon. But it was too late for me to say that I wished I had hung on.

'You'll go on the stage,' she said. 'You like performing, most of all. Don't you? You've a gift. You like that much more than you like girls, don't you? You prefer all those disgusting things that go on in the concert room.'

'Disgusting?'

I'd had some tricky moments, I'd seen some interesting things, but I'd never thought of them as disgusting.

'That's what Mrs Womersley says,' Ethel said. 'I think she's right.'

I was amazed at Ethel agreeing with Mrs Womersley.

'Well, I hope you become famous and I can come to see

you in the music hall that you keep talking about, after you've forgotten all about me,' she continued. 'You won't even know who I am. You won't even be able to remember my name.'

'Of course I'll remember you.'

I caught her biting her lip.

'No, you won't. You won't even be able to remember my funny name.'

'I expect that by then *you'll* have forgotten *me*. You'll be married and have a dozen children.'

'Whose?' she said, and then she shrieked like a mouse in a trap, '*Whose?*'

I had never before known her be emphatic and it startled me. When at last she faced me, I saw that she had blood on her lip from biting it. She looked desperate and helpless.

We walked back to The Fleece, mostly without speaking. It was hopeless. I can remember every step of the way. Everything. The sparrow that flew across our path – everything.

I held her hand. It was a light hold, but for the last fifty yards she gripped me tightly. Through her fingers I felt her fear. Presumably of her future.

She turned her face to me, even though there were tears in her eyes.

'Promise me that you won't make fun of me in the music hall,' she said.

'Of course not! Why should I ever do that?'

'You do now.'

'I do?'

'Yes.'

I suddenly realised that, because I wore her clothes, she thought I was making fun of her. She had kept her pain at it to herself, all this time.

'It's only because I wear your clothes!'

'You copy my voice, sometimes. You tell them things that I've said.'

I do imitate voices and accents without knowing it. Can't help it. I remembered that I had picked up phrases and jokes from her.

'I didn't mean to.'

'*Please* promise me that you won't do it. I can't bear to think

82

of you laughing at me when I'm not there.'

She was holding back from reaching the door, until I promised.

'I promise.'

She let go of my hand and ran ahead of me, disappearing. I can feel the grip of Ethel's fingers upon my flesh to this day.

But how on earth do I get my material, except from listening and watching people?

*

I learned my basic acts at The Fleece, but I took away very few material belongings. The main possessions I cared about were my props. Mr Haigh gave me a big canvas seaman's bag to put them in. He also gave me one of his coats for my journey and Ethel cut it down to size. When I said good-bye to Mr Haigh, he hugged me. He said nothing that was of any significance. Only kindly platitudes fell from his lips and I replied in a similar way, but I knew the depth of his feeling. I stared back at him for some time without speaking, because I, too, could not find the words. His look is before me now, and today I know what it was telling me. It was of the disarray of his being, day after day, under the pangs of jealousy and unrequited love.

And I do not know what has happened to him since. The last time I passed by The Fleece, a few years ago, the whole place had been gutted by a fire. I wondered who or what had caused it and whether anyone had died. I went to the Womersleys' farm, but strangers were there who for some reason would not speak to me. Nobody could or would tell me what had happened to Ethel.

My bag over my shoulder, bulky but not heavy, I struck across the moors. I had to ask my way many times and Heaven knows for how many miles I stumbled around until I found myself in the Palmers' valley. I kept forgetting the instructions I had been given. I was preoccupied with fears for my future and with my doubts about Mr Palmer, who was almost of a different species to the humans I had known, so that I thought we probably never would be able to understand one another. I was thinking about Ethel. In fact, I was still talking to her, in my head, all the way and it took me many weeks before I stopped doing this.

Yorkshire is divided into its valleys as securely as if they are neighbouring countries, their ways of life different to one another. Even before I reached Lumb House, the Palmers' mansion, I had realised that it was they who ran everything to be seen between the two moorlands walling in either side, and the grouse moor out of which the stream rose at the head. I saw that I was on an estate which only he could have owned. My God, what a difference there was to Saddleworth, or indeed to any other of the spoiled valleys where the rivers slide black, oily, and odorous as sewers! Along the river were the usual soot-blackened worsted mills, but, curiously, no mess upon the greenery, other than that it was sooted, and you can't help that in the North. Nowhere was untidy. In regimented rows or avenues, trees had been planted by a previous generation of Palmers, their upkeep continued through Sampson Palmer's time. There were artificial vistas – in accordance with the rules of an Italian pattern book, I learned later. The place is, still, a peaceful country seat. The inns are embalmed in quiet. None of your singing rooms there. No brawling weavers and navvies. The tradespeople have nothing to quarrel about, because butcher and saddler, innkeeper and blacksmith, hold their premises and trade by aristocratic grace and favour. They wait for what the Palmers have decided, as Irish farmers wait to see what rain falls upon them from Heaven. You can sit peacefully in a corner of a hostelry and smoke a pipe, talk about guns or dogs, or tut over the doings of the Prince of Wales. The mills themselves look like country mansions surrounded by lawns and parkland. There are even deer grazing under the long sausages of smoke and within earshot of the thunder of looms. Everywhere, notices threaten trespassers and poachers with 'the full rigour of the law'.

This, I found, was what Mr Palmer called 'keeping the countryside pure'. Uncontaminated by the scramblings of his own workfolk that meant, when translated out of Palmer language. Anyone found supporting a trade union or speaking well of Mr Bernard Shaw would immediately lose his position, or would discover that his tenancy was not to be renewed next quarter-day. Anyone not supporting the Anglican church that had been built by the Palmers and who was found creeping off to a Nonconformist chapel would have a hard time of it. The creed of Anglicanism was as firm as an extra park wall for keeping out the rabble of West Yorkshire.

Setting themselves apart in The Lumb, surrounded by lawns and trees, their three worsted mills discreetly embedded in woodlands along the river bank, socially the Palmers existed midway between those factory owners who stayed where they were born, among the grime, and at the other extreme those who carted off their wealth to pretend to be country squires in the hunting counties of Leicestershire or Norfolk. Though the Palmers set themselves up as landowners, they, in the fashion in which they understood it, lived among and were neighbourly with their own industrial proletariat. The Palmers think of themselves as frightfully good patrons of all that they survey from the commanding, polished windows of Lumb House and are not aware of anything wrong. While glad to boot out those whose truculence brings misery upon themselves (as the Palmers see it), yet when any case of undeserved misery is humbly brought before their attention they rush to salve it with charity. It makes them popular with their own vicar and his bishop. They have soups delivered. The ladies send around blankets and flannel, the kind designated as being suitable for 'charitable purposes' by Leak and Thorpe of York, the fashionable department store.

You could envy that peaceful way of life and agree with the Palmers in holding it up as a model for society, did you not, like me, come to know it from the underside; know what butcher, saddler and even more those who toil in the worsted mills think but dare not say in the hearing of anyone with influence.

Though the men take off their hats and the women curtsey to the mill-owners on their way to church, in fact they're an emasculated, secretly grieving, frightened, muttering bunch.

*

I was to get to know Lumb House and the Palmers well, especially years later when time made me, against all the odds and quite unimaginably, its mistress, after a fashion. If I was to sum up the place I would say that, like its master, Sampson Palmer, it was all deception; a false front and nothing underneath.

A black gothic pile, matching the church that they had built, it was a lie from the time it was thought up on an architect's desk. It was what the novels which you taught me to peruse called 'a forbidding edifice', Mr Dodds.

I approached across a terraced park, all the lawns shaved, with rare trees dotted upon them. The soot-blackened building had two grotesque towers at either end and, congregated between, more spires and turrets than I could be bothered to count. There was a huge conservatory clotted with palm trees and cacti, various other glasshouses, and several walled gardens. There was a grotto made of bits of the replaced medieval church.

I cockily went to the front entrance, which itself had a porch the size of a mansion to protect the carriages. Gargoyles peeping at me. From there, I was led by a maid, who was full of suspicion.

Talk about having your breath taken; I felt that I had never seen mirrors before in my life. Vista after vista of ingenious deception unfolded. You could hardly tell which was real and which was a reflection; which was a real bowl of fruit or dead stag and which a painted one. A hall the width of a carriage drive reached to the far end of the building. Or I thought that it did; I learned later that the second half was merely a mirror image of the first. It was lined with mahogany and mirrors and had several huge fireplaces along its length.

I was led in to meet a few of the Palmer clan, who were gathered in the greatest feature of the house: a suite of four interconnected reception-rooms on the right-hand side of the long passage. These were divided by mirrored doors that slid into the walls. When the doors were open, the vista was spectacular. The huge chandeliers, eight of them, made a forest of crystal. There were massive drapes, portraits, busts and vases placed around. Though I was finally to spend quite some time there, I was always spotting something that I felt sure hadn't been in the room before, only to find that it had been standing, untouched, for years. As well as the sliding panels there were false doors painted upon the plaster and the illusion made you gasp; a style of art that I was told was called *trompe l'oeil*. *Trompe l'oeil* (I could never say those words correctly) pictures, too. Powder blue skies, golden clouds, and 'the muses' floated over the ceiling, while lower down, yards upon yards of silks and embroidery were painted. It was like a market with fruit, wine, fish and meat. That was where the muses went to do their shopping, I suppose. Whole dead stags appeared to flop with their butchered heads hanging over the edges of tables. And in an immense frieze were dozens of stuffed heads of bison, tigers, rhinoceroses and lions. It took five maids a whole day upon ladders to dust them; they did it every week, and there was one who couldn't stand heights and used to get dizzy. The suggestion was that Mr Palmer had shot them, but he hadn't. (Not the maids – the animals.) I don't know why one family should want all this stuff, especially in West Yorkshire, for most of it had come out of India, China or Africa and had no usefulness or meaning whatsoever, here.

Several equally useless members of the Palmer family were scattered around, like strangers in a railway station, having in common only that they were waiting for the same train. You could say, the train was Death; even though some of them were young. They were not assembled to meet *me*, of course. Half their lives were spent stuck in this room. One was embroidering, one was reading, another was sipping brandy, I think. They seemed as lost and disconnected as I was.

What a family I had stumbled into. Most of them don't concern my story so I won't take up time with them. In any case, the fringes of the tribe were constantly changing. Governesses and poor aunts came and went, only half-noticed, like mice that steal into a house during the winter. I believe that a stranger, given the correct dress, manner and sufficient cheek, could have walked in, found a corner, a bed, and not been noticed. The house was a zoo of maiden aunts, widows, marriageable and unmarriageable daughters (the major distinction between them), old soldiers and retired officials of the East India Company who had fossilised out in Poona and were as stiff and yellow as old bone. The important ones were Sampson Palmer's unmarried nieces, Beatrice who was known as 'Booboo' because she was a 'mistake' and Diana known as 'Didi' so as to chime with 'Booboo'. Then there was Mr Palmer's sister, called 'Nana' though she was not much older than himself, and Uncle Clarence, 'who got chased out of India'.

All this I only found out much later. The maid abandoned me at the door and I slipped into the room for one yard only, afraid to go farther lest the polished parquet floor turned into a lake that would swallow me up. I was wearing clogs and they made a terrible row. Nobody introduced me. For a long time, nobody inquired who I was. One female eventually slid forward noiselessly, like a wind-blown leaf. Her extended arm and hand were as limp as a trail of honeysuckle over a hedge, as she said, 'You must be Sampson's protégé. I'm Didi.'

Until then I had been too shy to look at any faces. Still I could not look at her, so high born, so close, but I did now glance beyond. From a great distance they were all staring at me and it was like being on stage, which helped to put me at ease. Didi led me across and at last introduced me to Clarence, Nana, Booboo and others.

Booboo was snivelling into a handkerchief. I don't know what it was about and nobody took any notice, which I learned was sensible of them for she cried over nothing and was always doing it. Sampson Palmer, his long legs wrapped around him, sat like a king among his relatives. He wasn't staring at me anymore – not hauntingly. He was merely looking. His attitude had already changed, I sensed, although I had yet to experience it. I was a possession, now; something which he had purchased for a specific use; something which, therefore, he no longer *desired*. No longer was I a tantalising mystery, possibly unattainable.

*

And so I settled in. Although this was a mill-owner's family, the one thing you didn't find anyone talking about was the production of woollen goods. They were infatuated with the theatre and especially so was Mr Sampson Palmer, who had been enamoured since his boyhood at Winchester College followed by his Cambridge days when he had been a star of what I'm told they call *The Footlights Review*, with his picture in the papers. Yet the first recorded Palmer was, of all things, a handloom weaver who in the seventeenth century got a few pounds together so that he could invest in warps and he let his impoverished neighbours have them on credit, so as to be in a position to buy woven pieces back from them at his own price. If they wanted warps, they didn't have any choice. He kept the local weavers poor and therefore dependent but he made a fortune himself, investing, so I believe, in slaves and sugar. With the profits he established a family tradition of a different kind. Once Lumb House had been built, filled and surrounded with every luxury and ornament imaginable, the Palmers started to send their sons to be hacked to death in Africa, India or South America. And some call *me* perverse!

Sampson Palmer, too, had 'lived'. In fact, it was on his conscience. It was whispered that his first wife, Pamela, had died of grief and strain because of his excesses.

Upon meeting his second wife, Cynthia, you would expect her to go the same grief-stricken way; if not because of him, then through her own character. This second Mrs Palmer was brooding and strange, with hardly a twinkle. Yet I liked her from the very moment I saw her, sitting next to but clearly not *with* her husband. I felt that there was something underneath which could have been sparked into life. She was clearly frustrated and restless, otherwise she would not have got into the habit of snapping at servants whenever she came across them. Sampson Palmer must have known what she was before he married her and I decided eventually that he had made his choice in order to make himself unhappy; to give his conscience something to work upon because he had treated the first wife so badly. She was a test for him to prove that he could be a good husband.

And didn't she challenge him! She tormented the whole family with what they called 'powtry', swallowing the 'o' and pronouncing the remainder with great weight as if only they had a right to the lofty word. After the theatre, the second obsession of that family was Cynthia's 'powtry'. It turned into an obsession because she was no good at it and could not publish the stuff, except by paying for it herself. She blamed her failure on her husband and 'the rest of the Ps' as she called them. She loved to creep off into a private silence and write verses about roses, knights and so forth. She also delivered yards of what I call 'mortuary verse'. She gave me one of her pamphlets:

> *One last, long look ere the grave seals up*
> *Our dead till the Judgement Day.*
> *The earthly garb of the soul we loved*
> *Will soon be with the clay.*

That's one example. And:

> *O speak a kind word to the lost one*
> *With heart overburdened with care.*
> *To the one who has fallen a victim*
> *And is ready to sink in despair.*

Every member of the family was a dilettante in one form or another and she was a dilettante of death; for I could see no reason for her to be dwelling on it, in her comfortable life.

She was the only one there not devoted to amateur theatricals – with a proud emphasis on 'amateur'. The Palmers, one remove from trade themselves, separated from it only by the buffer of their mill managers, pretend to despise all forms of selling, and especially trading in art. It's only your real traditional aristocracy, Lord Rosebery and so forth, that hobnobs with actresses, usually posh ones, Maxine Elliott and the like. The female members, especially, of our local mill-owning families shudder at the thought of professional actresses and would rather be struck dead than be discovered in a room with one; or so they say. The men speak the same way, though I believe them even less than I do their ladies.

The family was scattered over the valley in half a dozen smaller houses besides the huge, central one and most of them had theatres built in their upper floors or out of their attics, where they 'got up' their plays. To fill a Sunday afternoon in the season, which was mostly Christmas or Whitsuntide, Mr Palmer and whoever else had gathered would construct a plot. A wink at the church porch when the world before one seems fresh, bright and beautiful again because the sermon's over for another week, and the men were on their way to 'getting up', after being invited home to lunch. It was always the men who made the play, but the ladies were obliged with charming parts to perform. By the time they had got round to constructing a plot, the Palmer gentlemen were in a bibulous state, quite carried away with play-crafting, forgetting all practicalities and as a result sparing neither expense nor, even more likely, their serfs' time in the construction of scenery and in the provision of props. Estate carpenters and village tradesmen who wanted to suck up to the Big Family wasted weeks upon these absurd productions.

If the Palmers ever suffered fits of modesty about their talents, as dilettantes are apt to do, they justified their theatricals as part of their other avocation, charity. 'Bit of a flop, what? It's all in a good cause, though. We're not professional, thank goodness!' All their productions were benefits. 'What are we going to get up for the Primrose League this year, old chap? Why don't you come over, quite informally, get free of those deuced petticoats for an hour and we'll discuss it?' It kept them out of the way of being involved in the Sunday afternoon Bible classes that the ladies ran to stop the wilder valley-children robbing their orchards or nutting in their woods. The chaps had an excuse to shut themselves away in the study, which opened into the billiard room; to drink port and to smoke Havana cigars.

The Absent-Minded Dowager, that d——d silly 'comedy', composed or perhaps cribbed from some London success by Mr Palmer, for which I had been sucked out of the squalor and Friday-night brilliance of The Fleece, is best described by quoting its eventual, grovelling 'review' in the local paper. 'The plot is based upon a series of misunderstandings. These, however, all come right in the end, having proved the moral, that when matrimonial affairs go awry, sometimes it's the fault of the ladies and sometimes that of the gentlemen. Suffice it to say, that when all is done, they live happily ever after.'

I expect you've guessed what sort of part Mr Palmer had singled me out for. Right first time, Mr Dodds. His 'plot' made use of a gardener's son whom some young blades disguise as a 'fresh young maiden' to deceive one of their fellows, the heir to an estate. Their high jinks go astray when the 'misguided gallant' falls in love with the imposter. I was picked for a role of mistaken sexual identity. I was selected, not merely because I could act it convincingly, but also because I could be relied upon to sing a ditty to break the monotony of a plot that everyone could see through from the beginning.

I was also being cast to play a member of the lower orders making a fool of himself through trying to better himself. My acts at The Fleece had involved laughing at skivvies and ordinary women, but I was not doing it to amuse members of what some of my later, rebellious acquaintances in public houses termed 'the oppressing classes'. If I'd understood beforehand that it would be assumed that I was poor and hungry enough to insult my own kind, I would never have left Ethel Ferret and our berth among the heather and cotton grass above the Standedge Tunnel, I tell you that for nothing.

The other roles were designed flatteringly to employ every member of the family. All except myself were cast to display either their beauty or their wit. The main interest of the author of *The Absent-Minded Dowager* was not dramatic content, but costume and fine words. Fine words rolled about Lumb House like brandy in a glass being carefully rocked to warm forth its aromas. This kind of language, then unintelligible to me, smothered the play like thick treacle.

All except in my own part. I found it a lonely and embarrassing business to be the only one cast as ignorant and plebeian. I thought I was going to be happy, have the chance of a lifetime, but I was miserable. Outside the play I was hardly spoken to except condescendingly, which soon bored both them and me, so they left me alone when they could. Hardly noticed me. Until the first performance I never had a chance to understand the whole of the drama, because as soon as my bit was finished at rehearsals I was sent down to the kitchen for my reward, a piece of cake or whatever else I could scrounge from the servants.

I'd had no experience of the staff of a mansion, who are so different to working people in a factory. Innocently, I approached them as I would have gone to the women in workhouse or pub: with my arms open and expecting to tumble into their opened arms.

The first time I broke into their private world was when they were assembled for dinner in the servants' hall. A silence fell around the table. All through the meal, not a soul would speak to me with any ease. Yet this was where I was supposed to eat every day. They were also frigid with one another, because of my presence, I'm sure.

I found that they actually *did* see me as one of their own sort who was making a fool of himself and they took an even more frosty view of it than did their betters. It was at this point I learned that servants are more hierarchical than their masters. The butler and the housekeeper required maids to wait upon them, and everyone was harsher than their masters would be to those who were lower in the pecking order, expecting even more servility from them. You should have seen how the second housemaid treated the third housemaid, for instance.

I was lonely with my betters, I was lonely with my equals, but there was one person with whom I became as intimate as two people can be.

That was with 'Sylvia' – the name of my part in the play.

Within a week or two of being born, she was for me not merely a figure of Mr Palmer's feeble imagination. I inhabited her so fully that she *became me*. I had no sensation of acting and from time to time, in order to please myself, I turned into her off-stage, whenever I dared let her out. She was so powerful that it was difficult to keep her in and only Jack's fear succeeded in doing so. She was a person whom Jack could observe, or reflect upon after she had passed through his body, as being more total than himself. She was a friend who never accused him, who could never desert him. She was as secure and pacifying, in her own way, as Mary Shuttleworth had been. Whenever I was afraid or worried, whenever I could not sleep, I turned to her to divert my mind. I thought of her and through my fantasy I could rest.

The other appeal of Sylvia was that, being born so completely, yet without a past, she was without the guilt that haunted Jack. Quite without wear and tear.

Sylvia was vulnerable, submissive, delicate in her movements and eager to please. As well as these, what might be called negative, characteristics, she was more receptive and sensitive than Jack, especially to other people's feelings.

As is the way with submissive types, she could be more firmly and completely herself than Jack could be himself. It is amazing how submissive people get their own way. As a result, it could seem that Jack was a figure of Sylvia's imagination and not the other way round.

And perhaps he was. Perhaps he was. Nobody knows, do they?

At any rate, a stupendous change had taken place for me. I had emerged as two people, two sexes and two names, inside one body. From now on, in every single moment of my life I was going to be asking myself who I was, or what I was; and sometimes making a mistake, through approaching Jack's tasks in Sylvia's frame of mind, thus to be confused with a dilemma.

*

Sampson and Cynthia Palmer had rows about me from the moment I arrived. I heard them, from behind closed doors, a long way down the corridors. Often, one or both was clearly drunk. I once heard the noise of glass being thrown, I think against the wall, I think by Mrs Palmer. When she got out of her silent moods, had a drink, could she blow! Didn't I learn some things! 'Sampson, you b———d! Why can't you take an interest in a *real* woman? No wonder we have no children! You're not even *unnatural*! You're not even a Sodomite! You're just a *mite*, Sampson! You're *empty*! Pulling this waif off the streets and making him a princess, all you want is an ornament, another stuffed head on the wall. To buy him. You can't *buy* a relationship! What are you going to do with him when he needs something? Are you going to dump your toy?'

She fought her husband by adopting me herself.

In the whole household, she was the only one with whom it could be said that I held a conversation. This strange lady, her hair and other features as dark as her soul, hated theatricals. But she treated me as an equal and I was the only one at whom she smiled.

I spent afternoons with her, when she worked at improving my reading. Being enthusiastic, I made great steps forward, so that after a month I could digest a newspaper. She improved my vocabulary. She talked to me about, of all things, Socialism, which I gathered was a mixture of vegetarianism, trade unions, going for hikes, bicycling, red ties and Rational Dress. I'm afraid that I was and, despite Cynthia Palmer, I remain an enthusiast for the S-bend in fashion, so it's a matter of regret in my life that corsets and Socialism are such

94

unhappy bedfellows. But there you are — it doesn't do for us all to be the same!

We would shut ourselves away in what the family, with shudders, called her 'den'. Perhaps we would stroll through the Gothic tracery of the grotto, or lounge in wicker chairs among the palms, cacti, orange and lemon trees of the conservatory where the servants, who were happier seeing me there than in the kitchen, brought us tea and biscuits, just for the pulling of a bell-rope. How well-trained they were, you think: don't believe it! I knew what they were really like; they knew that I knew, but, like well-drilled troops, they didn't blink an eyelid. To the devil with them, I thought. It was beginning to dawn on me that, if my eccentricities made me unacceptable to my own class, then I'd rather be on this upper-class side, thank you very much. I could develop quite a taste for it.

Meanwhile, Mrs Palmer introduced me to the great questions of the universe. Where do we come from? Where are we going? What is infinity? Is there a God?

I had to confess that I did not know. It turned out that neither did she. I don't much mind not knowing these things, but Cynthia Palmer was lost without the answers.

Cynthia Palmer also led me to the problem of deciding who or what was the 'greatest' example of this, that or the other, in music, art and literature. I loved it that she tinkled on the piano for my benefit and a great door opened for me, but be damned if she didn't slam it shut again by making me worry about whether Mozart was 'greater' than Beethoven. Over engravings, I had to decide whether Raphael was greater than Michelangelo. When reading her poetry — her poetry, mind — it had to be questioned whether Dante was greater than Shakespeare. I felt a stone of worry laid over my heart.

Though Cynthia Palmer lived in a fantasy world, just as I did, I never managed to penetrate hers. She was interested in the occult and the mystical as, I have found, such people often are. It is because the occult offers a form of knowledge, underwritten by tradition, in which nothing that's said can be either proved or disproved and it will 'verify' anything you wish to believe in.

There were moments when I was not sure whether it was Jack or Sylvia who was speaking. I would be sitting there as

Jack, when Mrs Palmer said something that appealed to Sylvia and I would be most confused.

There were times when, after a rehearsal, I deliberately visited Mrs Palmer still dressed in my 'Sylvia' clothes, letting it be assumed that I was too lazy to change.

There was nothing ambiguous about Sylvia's attire. I was quite a doll, after Booboo had taken me 'treasure hunting' through the attics, pulling out frills and flounces belonging, probably, to the eighteenth century; petticoats and hairpieces. I had an excuse to wear as much silk as I liked. Dressing me up to look like a fairy on a Christmas tree made Booboo dab at her eyes with joy. 'Don't be silly, Booboo,' Didi commanded, tartly. Didi was the one with fibre. With that toughness underlying surface sweetness, she could have been a schoolteacher had she been compelled to earn a living. But both of them, with years of their lives become static in this asylum from normal problems and experiences, behaved like children still. 'Oh, I think there's room for a little feeling, a little sentiment in life, Didi.' '*Nonsense!*' retorted Didi, and Booboo burst into tears.

Cynthia Palmer was so self-absorbed that she hardly took any notice of how I was turned out. 'Oh, you've been playing!' she commented, abstractedly. It was unclear whether she saw that I had been performing in theatricals, or was haunted by some memory of herself as a girl, going out to play.

Whenever verses looked like being the order of the evening, I would definitely turn up in Sylvia clothes. In fact, when overwhelmed by a need to be Sylvia, I would ask Mrs Palmer in advance if she would read to me that evening. She never refused. Thus I led her into indulging a fantasy with me. I became most intrigued by corrupting the guileless Cynthia. We would chatter away and quite forget that I wasn't a girl.

With little planning, I had stumbled upon a way of life in which Jack Shuttleworth could float around a grand house dressed as a young lady, in all the finery that thrilled him, and nobody questioned it! Mr Palmer enjoyed it, too. My being a girl, even without the excuse of theatricals, was more than he had hoped for and he complimented me. There were even some delicious moments in which, when I was sitting with Mrs Palmer, a new maid mistook me for a lady, addressing me as

'Miss' without a shade of suspicion. It was never long before the other servants disenchanted her, but I was delighted to discover the possibility of convincing someone of my chosen identity. Oh, it was fun.

On the other hand, it was Jack who could be decisive and when it seemed that Cynthia Palmer was getting too miserable for her own good, it was he who would shoulder the responsibility of pulling her out of it with a funny story.

There was this woman in Saddleworth, see, whose husband died young, and she was very lonely, I began.

'How sad,' she said, seriously. 'Tell me about it.'

Cynthia Palmer had no idea of how to even *listen* to a joke. But she did like melancholy stories.

'She went to this doctor and said, "Doctor, Doctor, my poorly husband's died young and I get lonely." "Thou needs a pet, then," says the quack. So t'woman goes to the pet shop. "Thou mun buy a little dog," says the pet shop fellar.'

'That was a very good idea. I had a little dog, once.'

'"No, I don't want a dog. I'd 'ave to take it for walks," says the woman. "Then thou should get a kitten!" "I don't want a kitten. It'll grow up to be a tom cat and be out all night and leave me."'

'How true!' Cynthia commented.

'"In that case, thou should buy a parrot and it'll talk to thee. That'll be thirty shillings . . ."'

'Goodness gracious! That's expensive!' Cynthia interrupted.

'. . . She pays over her thirty shillings. "Thou'll need a cage to put it in," says the shopkeeper. '"Ow much'll that be, then?" "That'll be another pound."'

'That's far too much!' Cynthia said.

'The woman take's the parrot 'ome, see, but after a week she brings it back. "Parrot's said nowt yet," she tells the shopkeeper. "Thou'll 'ave to buy it a ladder or summat to climb up and down on, then it'll talk," he says. "And 'ow much'll that cost me?" "Ten shillings." She pays out her ten shillings. Parrot goes up and down the ladder but still never says nowt. She goes back to th'shop again. "Parrot still says nothing," she complains. "Then thou mun buy it a mirror to look at itself at t'top o't ladder." So she buys a mirror . . .'

'Deary me, how will this end?'

Cynthia, taking me seriously, was growing very anxious and I was getting exasperated. It would never have turned out like this in The Fleece.

'*So next she buys a mirror. Puts it at the top o' the ladder. Parrot climbs up, one, two, three, four, five, six, seven and looks at itself. "Flippin' eck!" parrot says and drops down dead. So she goes back to the pet shop. "Parrot's dropped down dead," she tells him. "Well," he says, "Thou should 'ave bought it some bird seed!"*'

'What a sad story. Is it true?'

'No, I don't suppose it's true.'

'Why do you tell it, then?'

Cynthia Palmer couldn't get the hang of a joke if it jumped out and bit her. Some people are like that.

But she enjoyed my stories, nonetheless, in her own way. At any rate, she listened. And whatever I told her, she took it as the gospel truth.

I could no more understand her poetry than she could grasp my jokes. But as I was grateful for her attention, I made the effort to be polite. I could always hope that she would unexpectedly break off into another train of thought.

One day, for instance, she paused in mid-line and, as a glaze fell over her eyes, she said, 'Do you know why those Palmer women wear lace collars up to their ears? Why it's the fashion?'

'No,' I admitted.

She turned her face to the wall as if she had penetrated a ghost.

'It's because of Princess Alexandra.'

She made a motion with her finger across her neck. 'She set the fashion when she had to wear something to hide it after she tried to cut her own throat. Because of Prince Edward's doings. But she made such a mess of it. I could not imagine a lady killing herself in such a way – spoiling her features.'

A full five minutes later, she added:

'Sampson's first wife killed herself, you know.'

And then, with tears in her eyes, Cynthia Palmer plunged back into her verses. I felt I could ask her no questions, for she had withdrawn into a world which no one else could enter. Whenever her speech stopped suddenly, like that, it was because her soul had flown back into her inner world, like a bat into its tower. Her dark master of fantasy and grief had called; the occult, the mystical, was the only source of messages from there.

*

When I was off-stage another role, one of continuous gratitude, was expected from me. I was nothing more than a temporary amusement for Lumb House. Just as such people are with pet dogs, nobody cared about what I was to do with myself when Sampson Palmer had ceased to be intrigued by my turning into a girl or when Booboo and Didi had finished their hours of petting; what sufferings I had to put up with when banished to join the servants; even, where I was to sleep after each long day was over. The housekeeper had found me what I'm sure she believed to be a most humble attic room, but unlike my place in The Fleece this was under-drawn and held a fireplace. The fact that it seemed luxurious to one used to sleeping in a workhouse dormitory or beneath the open slates was no thanks to any of the Palmers.

It was the performances themselves that were the biggest embarrassment. There were three pre-Christmas showings of *The Absent-Minded Dowager*. The first, at Lumb House itself, was by invitation to a hundred of the 'better' families in the district. Leaving carriages and coachmen shivering outside, the toffs entered dressed up for the occasion and settled precariously, like over-feathered birds, upon gilded, stiff-back chairs. On the cushions, they found programmes displaying half a dozen typefaces, the Gothic in preponderance. Instead of slamming down pots of ale, spilling puddles over the floor, belching and spreading their chests, picking their noses, roaring, swearing, rattling money and ordering drinks during the performance, be d——d if I wasn't faced with the amazing spectacle of an audience quiet even before the show began! Nothing but whispering, coughing half-audibly behind dainty fists, and shuffling programmes came from them.

You never quite knew what my nervousness was like, did you, Mr Dodds? As I'd never been in or seen a play before, I knew little of what to expect, but my reflections upon the experience were, if *that's* your play-performing, then you can keep it so far as I'm concerned. I can't see why people go all the way down to London for something so dull and I'd cry my eyes out with boredom if I was stuck with watching it.

One thing I did learn, though; there's nothing like a bad play for highlighting human nature – in the audience. The first night they were indulgent, because the play was for charity. That was a killer: charity again, which I had loathed in the workhouse, murdered any life there might be on stage before it had a chance to give a wriggle. Though they were so quiet, it wasn't because they were enjoying the play; or, if they were, they were making a virtue out of necessity. Before me, clear as a picture, were displayed the two types of human kind. Those who expected to suffer the worst were dozing with eyes tightly closed, longing for it to be over. Those intending to wring fun out of everything were tittering over what was not meant to be funny, or were giving the kind of 'encouragement' that is meant to unnerve one. 'Jolly good, Booboo!' – after Booboo had tripped up in her old-fashioned dowager's clothes. 'I say, Charles, isn't spooning on stage a bit over the top?'

For the second performance, the Palmers had props and scenery carted to the dining-hall of one of their mills. This was better for me, though it wasn't for the audience. The workers knew right enough what they would have to put up with. The weavers and spinners, who had never travelled beyond their valley, were annually brow-beaten by stage-characters with whom only the Palmers were acquainted: the heiresses and poor cousins, masters of foxhounds and clergymen, dowager countesses and lords, housekeepers and 'companions', who were the stock of their plays. Even the supporting roles of servants, always either comic or faithful, were played by people who wouldn't know how to peel a potato. But instead of starting a revolution, nobody dared even yawn.

The performances held under the Christmas decorations in the mill were a very different affair to our appearance at Lumb House. Although the mill-workers had been described to me (*me!*) a hundred times during rehearsals as 'a rough bunch, yet with no harm in them, actually', it was my fellow actors who were nervous of their captive audience; while the mill-workers were afraid of losing their positions if they stayed away. You could have cut the atmosphere with a knife, as they say; although there was nothing to be afraid of. They had been conditioned for a hundred years to attend boring chapels and churches. Lurking malcontents, trade unionists, Suffragettes and the like had been put in a softer frame of mind with a ham tea, just in case. Life was not so prosperous for workers in Palmer Land that free food wouldn't soften the most bloodthirsty spirits.

This audience, too, sat through the show either stolidly or looking for fun, depending on their temperaments. Very few found my portrayal of a poor lad tumbling over himself in his efforts to pull himself up by his boot-laces either affecting or funny. The whole play was dead; stillborn. A few of the girls and women sniffed, for doffers and spinners can have sentimental hearts. The others either despised the character I portrayed for his pansy affectations, or they just couldn't be persuaded that it was funny to try to better yourself and fail.

I learned a lesson from this; didn't I just. That night I lay restless in bed calling as bitterly as Voltaire for a revolution. Until a plan formed itself. Cynthia Palmer had introduced me to Socialism and I decided to strike a blow.

The third night's performance, held in the same dining-hall, was for tenants, farmers and tradesmen of the estate and villages who were expected to pay into the Palmers' charity box, fourpence for a front seat and twopence to sit at the back. For them I decided, without rehearsal or preparation, to play my part quite differently. I played it, not as the Palmers saw it, but as I did. I showed them that it was a tragedy to make a fool of this poor gardener's lad.

It's amazing what different meanings you can give to words when you try. I brought the house down. I had three curtain calls when they were shouting and whistling just for me.

Nobody at Lumb House knew how to address me that night. Not many spoke to me at all. I was supposed to sit in a corner feeling ashamed, but I fought off the pressure to be guilty.

Instead of staying for the last-night celebrations, I slunk away. I had learned enough about the working classes not to expect the servants of a country house to thank me for striking a blow for their freedom, so I didn't go to the kitchens. I spent the evening talking to Cynthia Palmer in her 'den'. She had spurned all the productions – being 'selfish', they said. She had some bottles of wine brought, then some gin and together we got drunk. We talked very intimately and, much to my regret, almost all of it I have forgotten.

When the show was written up in the newspaper, my performance was demolished in a contemptuous sentence. 'It is a pity that Jack Shuttleworth, having the good fortune to play his first role as the gardener's boy upon whom Mr Palmer's plot revolves, chose to insult his patron and to exceed the bounds of good taste.'

Except perhaps for chastising the audience from time to time for not being sufficiently appreciative, the newspaper, being owned by Mr Palmer, normally praised *everything*. Such phrases as 'the comedietta was capitally presented in every department', 'Mr Palmer is possessed of an easy but incisive style of elocution and rendered his part most effectively', were used throughout the same column that gave only me the raspberry. Otherwise, the sweating journalist, who could so easily lose his job, paid a compliment of the same brief length to every member of the cast, lest someone be offended. They had to be kept brief because anything longer than one sentence is liable to hint at either favouritism or criticism, after the piece has been mulled over for days by the unmarried daughters and unemployed aunts up at Lumb House. When he ran short of compliments, the frightened author filled his long and lonely column with a list of the names of the gentry present, as if it were a funeral. He padded it further with details of the dresses worn by the ladies, noted down during the performance in terror lest he forget something. 'Miss Beatrice Palmer affected a gown of white net and a white appliquéd opera cloak. Miss Diana charmed us all with . . .' You can understand, therefore, that the quiet note of disapproval that I received was heard as a thunderous put-down, intended to demolish my career.

It was the end of my theatricals at Lumb House. But I found myself the talking point of that valley and neighbouring ones for months. I was a hero; but to be honest, they were wrong. At first I had thought myself a revolutionary, but I realised that I was merely indulging my weakness for pleasing people, except that I was playing to the workers instead of to my patrons. I was so carried away with what for me was a theatrical opportunity that I hadn't stopped to consider how it would upset the Palmers.

Nor had I realised how unhesitatingly they would boot me out of my nest. I felt, not heroic, but quite sick at having to leave my comfortable berth, my clean, warm bedroom, the reliable, good food, Mrs Palmer's flow of civilised conversation and alcohol.

Not even she seemed over-troubled about my departure, showing herself to be a true Palmer, for whom those of a lower class did not have the same tender feelings as themselves. '*Do* leave me your address and perhaps I will write to you,' was all she said. *Perhaps!*

Not knowing that some years later I would return in a different guise, I left Lumb House almost as I had arrived, taking away little extra but a few dresses and some underwear filched from the wardrobes; the gift of a pie, a bottle of gin and a book of poetry from Cythia Palmer; and a sovereign guiltily accepted from Mr Palmer, who had the gall to tell me that I had 'wormed' my way into his house 'on false pretences'.

Oh, and I nearly forgot to tell you. At the foot of the column which reviewed my performance, it was mentioned briefly that a young man had been sent to prison for seven days for nothing more than hawking lavender without a licence. The magistrate was Mr Palmer.

·4·

I FLED into town and went to a pub named after what might have been Mr Palmer's dream: The Headless Woman. I had discovered it one unhappy evening when fleeing Lumb House and had been there often. It had been described as a 'reet good singing oyle'. Translated, that means, 'right good singing hole'. Yorkshire villages and towns are riddled with 'oyles'; cellars, cupboards and dingy rooms, pleasant and unpleasant; coal oyles, food oyles, pea oyles, singing oyles. The word 'hole' in Yorkshire has a special darkness, depth, and dampness to it.

The alehouse is jammed between the River Calder on one side and the Rochdale Canal on an embankment above its roof. The old, damp pub is wetter still for swilling happily nearly twenty-four hours a day in the ales brewed by Lydia Dunkerly. The strip of land running between canal and river is crammed with small worsted-woollen mills, their windows as black and greasy as the stones of the buildings. It is the workers from there, those poor moles out of gas-lit oyles, who consume most of homely Lydia's ale. Plus a leavening of the barge folk who bring tales from far away. Walking to it along a dingy, damp lane that threaded between the walls of factories, I could hear, counterpointing one another, the dull clatter of looms and the higher pitch of a fiddle; a primitive and barbaric music that did not pluck at the sentiments, so much as tear at the heart.

And it was the middle of a working afternoon.

The dirty little factories along the river are the refuge of Palmer's defecting serfs, which is one reason why in The Headless Woman there congregate such independent spirits. Being beyond Palmer's monopoly, the pub is full of noise, fun, quarrels, fights, gossip, tales and music. There they love nothing better; and if there is nothing to fight about, they invent it. The customers come in every shape and size, which they do their best to exaggerate. They burp, belch and – let us say that it is not only with their *language* that they are not polite. They drink unbelievable quantities, in order to boast about it; though no one can remember anything, later. Drinking, belching and burping are forms of speech. They are also measures of manliness and of character. So is it if your stomach is huge and pendulous, or if your hair and beard are so long and greasy that they are matted into one mane; likewise, if you are bald as a coot, so that would be emphasised with extra shaving, too. If you are a 'character', you may assume licence to do anything. What a bunch. Their talk and laughter was all exaggeration, and full of life.

Jolly Lydia Dunkerly laughed as soon as I walked in and wanted to hear all about my adventures. I played up to my audience. Everyone, including Lydia, was tipsy already, but they drank me a welcome. Then another one. And another. Putting her hands under her apron, Lydia rubbed her tummy in her customary, warm gesture. It was not only because she was selling more rounds of ale. It was so motherly and welcoming, she might have been indicating the place from which I had been born. She was another Mary Shuttleworth, though not so big and boisterous, for no one could compete with Mary in these respects. But, as Lydia had suffered a less tragic existence, she approached the world with a more genial trust than had my Mary. I believe that until the end of my life I will find myself time and again being drawn into the bosoms of such women.

Lydia, not a bit surprised by my proposal to move in, gladly gave me room, board and a job, as if she had been waiting for me all along.

An odd place for the developing Sylvia to find a home in, I hear you say. You *did* say, in fact; often. The reason was that it accepted me, too, as a 'character'. Beside Lydia Dunkerly's matronliness and the work that she offered me, I enjoyed being in a place that was a cauldron of itinerants and entertainers.

Despite my taste for the finer things in life, the natural refuge for me was among the warm working class: an obvious fact that you tended to forget with your background of Rishworth School and Cambridge. The Headless Woman was the one pub where, though in the company of the sweated, rooted and prejudiced labourer, I could take an honourable place as a maverick of the theatre; the means by which I had, by repute, struck a blow for freedom.

*

I believe that nowhere else do they have anything comparable to our 'comic bands'. I don't mean that they haven't black-faced minstrels; of course they have, in plenty. Also there are mummers from the south to the north of Britain: men dressed in women's clothes, hats piled with flowers, decked with ribbons, rattles in their hands; kissing the girls, making the children laugh. Their clothes make brilliant flowerings of colour splashed against the dark mills. But is there anywhere else where they combine the mummers' dress with the songs and instruments of nigger minstrels, adding absurd, home-made instruments that make some very strange noises? Where they conduct the proceedings with a working-man's jocularity as hearty and barbaric as the music of iron-shod clogs on cobblestones? Such a combination would appeal to the lunatics of The Headless Woman, wouldn't it?

Yes, it had its own band, which had won championships; for comic bands were so common that they held competitions all over the Pennines, to which we travelled at the times of Rush-Bearings, Whitsuntide Walks, Easter Pace-Eggings and so forth. There is a photograph existing of twelve of us posing with frozen looks (for once) in two rows around our bandmaster, Alfred Bates. He it was who said that his mouth felt so stiff, he needed a pint of ale to loosen it again. We always called him the Schoolmaster, after his profession. He is holding a great silver and brass cup which requires two hands to grasp and it is tangled up with white ribbons. The Schoolmaster wears a waistcoat, jacket and tie; he also sports a distinguished, white beard. Out of respect for the occasion he wears a working-man's flat cap, the kind that looks as though it should belong to a chap who keeps ferrets.

In school this would make him look a fool, but here it is a mere token, for the rest of us are dressed up as such clowns. There's huge Arthur Micklethwaite, his spade-shaped beard hung over the lace collar of a flowered frock, the end of a

106

long, tubular, decorated papier-mâché instrument to his lips, a minute pork-pie hat on his head. There's little Bill Priestley with his concertina resting on his crossed legs that are clothed in Turkish pyjamas. There's Willie Barker in a proper minstrel outfit, with a candy-striped suit, a blue top hat, a striped bow tie stiffened with cardboard and reaching out to his shoulders, and his face blackened. There are the rest of us, holding drums and fiddles, dressed in frocks, skirts and ladies' hats.

The odd thing is that, as with mummers, you never get a real woman nor even a child taking part in a comic band. The fun is a serious, competitive, male activity; as sturdily masculine as a rugby team.

But there's a place for me. There I am, in Lydia Dunkerly's night-dress. Among all the other female dresses I stick out like a sore toe because I'm so genuine. I seem to know how to carry it, and have all the other details right.

For instance, although it was not unusual in that pub to grow one's hair to shoulder length, I kept mine as well-washed as a girl's and tied it in a feminine way. I still hardly needed to shave, yet I removed my soft, fair down most carefully.

I had in a sense made a step backwards from what I had achieved at The Lumb. There I had stumbled upon the means of floating around the building quite naturally in drag, but here, as in The Fleece, I was supposed to express my feminine self in public only by making fun of her. The feminine in me became both ecstasy and Hell. You can imagine.

I spoke this new person's secret name, *Sylvia*, only in the privacy of my room, shaping my lips softly and carefully before my mirror. It was at this point my preoccupation with mirrors properly began and I bought my first, a not very large one, but spiky with gilt and surmounted by two enamelled butterflies, for my Headless Woman bedroom. Even with the door locked, secretly to dress in the fine clothes which I had stolen from Lumb House filled my chest with a pounding heart.

Suppose a fire should break out downstairs?

Suppose some characters should raid my room while I was out and see the clothes that I would never degrade by wearing them for the band? I suspected Bill Priestley, who teased me cruelly when he'd got some ale down him. He was small and rough, like a terrier, but he clung to his big friend, Arthur Micklethwaite, as little fellows often do hang on to and inspire mischief from some big but unimaginative chap. The pair of them were just the sort to get up a raid of that kind.

Serving ale in the tap-room, dressed in male clothes and unrecognisable as Sylvia but nonetheless feeling her to be my inner being, trying out small tricks of behaviour that I hoped might be taken for either masculine or feminine, or as neither – a flick of the wrist, a toss of the head – I was tense, watching everyone and that pair in particular for a reaction. Surely I was going to give myself away with a gesture?

It astounded me that I was barely noticed. I was learning what anyone who does anything peculiar finds that they can rely upon: people observe far, far less than you fear they do, and are far less interested in you than they are in themselves.

If somebody did give me a second glance, seeing, perhaps, a trace of the make-up which I had applied for a secret session in my room and had not been able totally to remove, or a gesture that was too much like a girl's, I hurried off, blushing, before trouble could start. If they tittered, I fled to my room, shutting the door tightly in fear of pursuit.

Often I consoled myself by putting on a silk shirt or a lace collar, sitting before my mirror, or lying on my bed – the only things that diverted my mind. Dressed up with nowhere to go, what was I to do next? One suddenly feels an idiot. I tried writing letters to Cynthia Palmer, but felt too ashamed of my spelling, my grammar and my lack of a style, to post them. I couldn't get the hang of phrasing things differently when you write them down. I was also too conscious of my clothes. I feared and hated myself, until it turned to nausea. I was too ashamed to go forth again for a long time and when I did so, I pretended to an exaggeratedly boyish air. *Never again*, I'd say to myself. Keep it for the band. For pace-egging and festivals.

But Sylvia crept back to me, a delicate, shy, virgin rose, snuggling, searching to bloom in my body. *What is wrong with me*? I cried, time and again. Keeping silk blouses and stolen dress for my room, I was tormented by living in two worlds.

Still I distantly envied girls and women who were able to move with confidence through a choreography of gestures. I wondered if I dared ask one to teach me. I never did so. Alone before my mirror, I tried to imitate them.

I wanted clothes which I had not the courage to purchase and could not afford. I found it was expensive, having two people to keep! I began to think about stealing dresses and underwear, as I had already stolen from Lumb House.

I wanted perfume.

*

Perfume! You know how these longings can hurt you. If you cannot fulfil them, they become an obsession. I had discovered scent when Mrs Haigh used to dab herself, often at peculiar times – just before she was going to bed, for instance. The ladies at Lumb House doused themselves. Lydia Dunkerly had a bottle or two which she hardly ever used and I begged her for some.

'You don't need scent to do a turn in a comic band!' she teased.

'I do for the front row. I think it'd be funny.'

'You are a *one*!'

She didn't offer me any, not because she was ungenerous but because she did not take my request seriously. I had to steal it.

Surreptitious, terrified of being gaoled for an 'unnatural offence', of being hounded, pilloried in *Tit Bits* as Boulton and Park had been for going out in drag a few years before, even of stretching the patience of capacious Lydia Dunkerly, I used to dab myself before I went forth in the morning, pretending, if anyone wrinkled his nose, that it was a trace left from my previous night's performances.

In the end, I had to purchase my own scent. Couldn't resist.

It was from going into Holt's, the chemist's, that I was given, you might say, my last chance to spurn Sylvia, even though it was she whom I'd gone to the chemist's to serve. With my guilty manner of those days, I told the girl behind the counter that the perfume was for 'my sweetheart'; which was not as untruthful as all that, even though the 'sweetheart' was myself. But it aroused suspicion, for an innocent simply does not bother to explain his purchases.

109

Females other than Suffragettes, I have noticed, mostly show the world a withdrawn look; one I have tried to cultivate. It was the boldness of this girl, piercingly and unblinkingly staring, trying to work out what I was, friend or foe or freak, that was extraordinary. Especially as she wore mourning dress. Down to her ankles she was clad in black crêpe, with a row of crêpe-covered, black buttons reaching up to a tight collar. It was expensive, so I knew she must be Mr Holt's daughter.

'What's your sweetheart's name?' she teased.

'Sylvia.'

Her face lit and she laughed outrageously, for one in mourning.

'How did you know that was my name?'

I laughed, too.

'I didn't', I answered, truthfully.

'Wouldn't you say that you are a little bit wicked?' she teased.

'I didn't know it's your name. But it's a deucedly nice thing to learn.'

'You speak very nice. How did you learn to talk like that? You don't look the sort.'

'I lived at Lumb House, actually.'

'You must be a servant.'

'No, I wasn't. I was a friend of Mr Palmer. But I left, as a matter of fact.'

'Why?'

'Oh, it's a long story. I'm an actor.'

'Are you the one who does things at The Headless Woman?'

I didn't know whether to answer. I didn't want to ask, sarcastically, 'What things?' I was tempted; but it was tempting providence – she might tell me what things.

'I thought you were,' she said with a smile. 'People talk, you know! You're the famous Jacky.'

Another customer had entered the shop.

'I was going to take Sylvia to the Oddfellows Hall in Halifax this Saturday,' I said, hastily. 'To the music hall, but she cannot go. Would you care for the ticket instead?'

To be honest, I felt that, though not exactly a tart, Sylvia (the chemist's Sylvia) was perhaps brazen and cheeky enough to settle my problem once and for all. I thought that there was a bit of experience inspiring the bright look of her eyes.

She became involved in selling cough lozenges, but I carried on talking.

'They have Mr Dyson's Gypsy Choir, and a gentleman doing farmyard impersonations.'

Even though I had never yet been there, I knew the programme. But there was one item that I would have blushed to mention; one listed as, *The Great Mr de Sere, the most famous female impersonator of the day.'*

The other customer left brusquely because she was not getting the attention that she expected.

'The music hall, eh?' Sylvia said with emphasis.

'Yes. There's no harm in it!'

'Some wouldn't agree.'

'Who?'

'Well – never mind. You're a terrible tease. And you've upset my customer. She thinks I'm flirting and she'll tell the whole town. But I'm *not* a flirt, so don't expect it. I don't think I can come. It'd be wrong. But I'm not sure. You'll have to ask me later. Won't your Sylvia be jealous?'

'She could be – if she knew.'

To prepare for taking out the chemist's daughter, I went through one of my swings-and-roundabouts. It was my most determined effort to oppose myself. Fiercely I told myself, over and over again, *I am a man, I am a man and I have a sweetheart. Forget all your nonsense; just keep your joking to the stage! Be satisfied to enjoy a laugh with a band.*

I felt relief that I had made a decision. There remained my doubt about being able to cope with a sweetheart, but it was crushed under my determination.

You know how you can fool yourself. *I* know.

Sylvia Holt, still in her black clothes, a little black cloak over her dress, joined me on the tram to the Oddfellows Hall. This was the first time in my life that I had taken a girl out. You could not count my moorland walks with Ethel, for we had simply grown into accompanying one another without any ulterior intentions, like brother and sister. It was not its naivety and thoughtlessness, but its possibilities, its conceivable future, that were making this exciting.

111

I had never before entered a place properly set up for entertainment; the kind of hall that Jim the carter had boasted about; that they had talked of in the New Delight in Diggle and that had been the inspiration for ineffectual dreams in Mrs Haigh. The Fleece had consisted simply of tables in a room that had a bit of a platform at its end. The Palmers' house-theatres had been merely requisitioned attics. Here was a place where Charles Dickens had delivered a reading once and where Liszt had given a pianoforte recital. Not music-hall turns, I know, but the Oddfellows had by now, as some would say, 'descended' to that level. In its new use it retained its old splendour. The front was a splash of Greek columns painted with gilt. Inside, as well as tables, there were tip-up seats set in rows. Drink was served in a 'promenade'. The nobs sat in the auditorium as if in the theatre, soberly watching the acts. There were galleries for the likes of Sylvia and me. It wasn't that I was too mean to take her anywhere but into the gods. If you weren't the right sort, as shown by your dress, they wouldn't let you into where the toffs sat.

I led her to the promenade to buy her a drink, but she was horrified. She told me that Mr Holt was 'Temperance'.

'I didn't dare let him know that I was even going to the music hall, let alone with a chap. He would have half kill't me. I said I was going to a lecture at Square Chapel.'

However, it was while she was making this pronouncement that I took her hand and she let me keep hold of it as we settled into our seats. We were as solemn as judges because I didn't know how to conduct this holding-hands business, while she, I believe, was waiting for me to get on with something and was teasing me. Perhaps, bearing in mind what apparently she knew about me at The Headless Woman, she was interested in me as a test of her ability to allure, or as an adventure.

Anyway, the atmosphere put me off. It was not what I had expected. I had thought that a proper music hall would be like The Fleece or The Headless Woman on a larger scale. Oddly enough, the Oddfellows Hall was very like a chapel, with its polished pine seating in the gods and its gilded arches. Perhaps it was the ghost of Temperance shot through my evening that made me think that chapel must have inspired the music hall, at least in Halifax. When the chairman took his place, he was very like a parson standing in a pulpit. And very much in the style of a fire-and-brimstone preacher was his way of banging his gavel to keep order while the turns came on.

There was turn after turn and all of them professional. For a quarter of an hour, Mr Dyson's 'Gypsy Choir' sang excerpts from Carmen. The girls were all from Bradford and sang in English. They did just one gypsy love song, in a sort of Spanish which even a Halifax audience realised was grotesque. But they came on twice. Then there were the farmyard impersonations and a couple of stand-up comics.

Thank goodness it was dark, for when Mr de Sere appeared, I had to let go of Sylvia's hand and my body went rigid as a stick, without my being able to control it. My male stance collapsed. If Sylvia Holt could not see my embarrassment, I'm sure she felt it.

What embarrassed me was that he seemed a *real* lady, larger than life with a bustle and a parasol, strolling as it were along a seaside front on a summer's day. Blackpool Pier, with the Isle of Man ferry boat setting off across the blue sea, was painted on the backcloth. Mr de Sere was a towering creation of a woman, with more of everything than any real woman. Yet he was convincing. His coiffure, in particular, was exquisite. As his dress trailed along the 'promenade', at one moment he twirled his parasol and the next he dipped it elegantly.

> You can do a lot of things at the seaside
> That you can't do in town . . .

The extravagance made people laugh. The realism made others beside myself hold their breaths. Many were shocked. Some laughed or whistled, others gasped. Mr de Sere did not turn a hair.

I did more than hold my breath. I was, as I say, rigid.

'What's the matter?' Sylvia asked, probably thinking that I was feeling sick, or that I was as shocked as she was.

When I didn't answer, 'I think that sort of thing's disgusting,' Sylvia hissed.

As she had hinted at what I did at The Headless Woman, was she trying to draw me out?

I squirmed, I can tell you, all through the remaining acts,

though trying to pretend that everything was normal with me. I couldn't have come anywhere near telling her that on my mind was my doubt, suddenly returned, as to whether I was male or female.

Here I am at the ripe old age of sixteen, I told myself, and I have never thought of anything else in my life and I still don't know the answer, nor do I have anyone to talk to about it.

Because it was nice being near Sylvia, too. Oh, irresistible.

On the way home, we actually spooned. Sylvia seemed to expect it. I was excited by her. I was curious. Oh, I wanted to settle this matter of who the deuce I was. In the end, I couldn't say whether it was I who led her, or she who propelled me into a dark alley, where spooning did not fail to prove thrilling; the taste on her lips, the smell of her hair, the feel of soft skin in the dark, her intent eyes staring so fixedly, wonderingly at me, begging me to take a lead in kissing her.

All of the surrounding night seemed to conspire with this absorbing business. Drawn into my memory are the trams clanking past the end of the alley where I pressed her against the wall; the sounds of pianos and voices from public houses. She knew how to lead a chap on, all right. She had saved me from my doubts. I was securely male again.

She did it! I made a fool of myself. An utter idiot. A moment came when a shutter fell over every sound and sight in the world, and every thought, as if I had tumbled into a well. I was indeed in danger of collapsing, for my knees were giving way.

I am ashamed to tell what happened to me next. There was a brief ecstasy, the length of a spurt of flame from a match, and a second later, disgust, weariness and a sense of pointlessness. I don't know how married men can put up with that feeling, that let-down, night after night, year after year.

Coming to my senses as suddenly as I had fallen out of them, I was compelled to pull away from her, embarrassed.

Afraid. Ashamed.

We took the tram back, as we had spooned – in embarrassed silence; she not asking questions that she knew the answer to and I not offering an explanation for what did not need one. What a shameful journey.

At last, 'Why do you always wear black?' I asked.

I was curious because, to say the least, she had not behaved as if in mourning.

'My mother died a year ago and my father can't forget her. I don't think he could ever bear the shock of me changing out of black. I couldn't do it to him.'

Back at The Headless Woman I cleaned my trousers and lay awake half the night, unsatisfied and guilty. I could not stop myself being haunted by Sylvia's pale, chemist's-shop face that was like a moon among dark clouds as it rode upon her black dress and by the feel of her padded silk dress as I tried to find her.

Yet my thoughts were interrupted with exciting memories of Mr de Sere. Can I or can't I be a real lad? The question made my palms and the back of my neck prickle with sweat in the dark. I still did not know the answer: am I normal or aren't I?

In search of a solution, I went back to the shop a week later. There were several customers and Sylvia made the most of them, hardly speaking to me. But I hung around, trying time and again to get a word across to her.

'Go away!' she hissed under her breath. 'Stop bothering me!'

By departing to the back of the shop, she gave me to understand that she had delivered her last word.

But she had to come back and I still dithered there.

'Why?' I asked.

'Doing *that!*' she said. 'You know. On our first time out! Go *away!*'

I felt sure that she was experienced in all this sort of thing; wasn't she still teasing me?

As I still dithered, 'My father's coming,' she hissed her most desperate threat.

I left without even receiving her goodbye.

That's it, I kept telling myself. *If that's what it's like to be a chap, then I'd rather be a pansy! At any rate, I've tried to be different. Well, be blowed to them all!*

That walk back to The Headless Woman was, I knew, the end of my old, timid existence and the first day of a new life. One of being like Mr de Sere, though I had no idea how to bring it about. A life as Sylvia. *My* Sylvia. Why not? Why not? I kept glancing at my reflection in shop windows, or in any reflecting surface that came my way. I scrutinised how people regarded me as I tried out being camp, holding my hands out as I walked. You know; that caricature affected by our sort, which is a way that no woman ever walked. I was only a kid.

But I saw myself in a new light. I had lived my life feeling overtired, ashamed, unable to give attention to functional things, or listen to conversations, being choked by thoughts to which I could not give utterance, and it struck me that there had been a similiarity between myself and Mr Haigh. Like him, I had been suffering a draining away of my thoughts and concentration. I, too, was like a person being blackmailed. So long as I was unable to air my secret, my secret self was blackmailing me. At last I faced up to that secret blackmailer in my head who had given me nought but guilt. Once I had refused to be ashamed of the 'crime', I was relieved of the blackmailer. Sylvia walked, now, with a light step.

Though she took time to be perfected. She needed your protection for that, Mr Dodds.

*

In one leap I had outgrown The Headless Woman, which had felt so womb-like and cosy, but I had nowhere to go that was any more satisfactory for the new life which I, so dimly, envisaged.

Apart from my wander from Saddleworth over the hills, my first travels about Yorkshire were with the band. We hired a farm-cart and a team of horses, decked them and the cart with ribbons, and off we went to an Easter pace-egging in Hebden Bridge.

Though we could hardly hear him for our noises and blarings, the Schoolmaster, pontificating good-humouredly from the shafts, told us that *pace* was a corruption of the Greek for Easter, *pasca*. The simple inhabitants of Hebden Bridge, not knowing this, guessed that a 'pace-egg' was one that had to be rolled down a hill in a race on Easter Day. The first part of the race was for everyone to carry an egg on a spoon to the top of a hill.

They did other things. They danced, laughed and gawped in the streets at the bands assembled from all over the county. There I was, able to sing and dance while wearing women's clothes publicly in the streets of Hebden Bridge!

We also went to make idiots of ourselves in Bacup, where we defeated the Bacup Coconut Dancers (who wore half-coconuts on their knees), and we went to a rush-bearing in Saddleworth. The custom sprang from the days when, once a year, they changed the rushes that formed a matting over the stone floor of the church. So said the Schoolmaster, who was a folklorist, writing articles for the *Antiquarian Journal*; which is why he came with us. The cart, laden with rushes piled in an ark-shape upon a wooden frame, decorated with garlands and chains of flowers, was dragged for miles through the lanes by a team of stout lads dressed in mummers' gear. There was always a maiden perched on top, and that year when they'd all got drunk they decided that the 'maiden' was going to be me.

Little Bill Priestley proposed this idea. Drunk in his harem pyjamas, he sat in the pub sucking his pipe after a 'practice'. As my contribution that evening, I had sung what was known as 'The Holmfirth Anthem'; a ballad from Napoleonic times about a swain who must leave his maiden 'where the pratty flowers do grow', so as to go and fight 'yon Spaniards and French'. It was too soppy a number for the occasion and they were all a bit cross with me. I made things worse by questioning some of the Schoolmaster's theories about pace-egging, about the origins of the names of villages, of rocks upon the moors and so forth.

'And what does a pansy like you know about out?' Priestley snarled. 'Go and join the girls.'

Thus I would be sneered at if I started on any subject of importance, such as trade, war, money, politics, engineering, weaving, Empire, or history. They treated me as they treated real women. They would indulge me only if I was trivial, child-like and irresponsible, as women are supposed to be. Woman as the white man's burden.

In fact, I believe we treat women as if *they* are a sort of drag-act. As if, just like me, they exist as a masquerade for the amusement of men.

But that's by the way.

'Didn't I catch a stink o' scent on yee t'other day?' Priestley remarked.

I didn't answer.

'Aye, I think I did.'

He dropped his words threateningly into the silence.

'I think I got a whiff of it. Thou smelled like a pox-doctor's clerk.'

'Let 'im be,' Willie Barker murmured.

Priestley squeezed his concertina, to make a very rude noise.

'Lydia said she had some missing from 'er drawer last week. Does thou know out abart it?'

'Let yon alone,' Willie repeated.

'And she's lost a pair o' pants out of her washing. I'll tell thee what we should do,' Priestley snarled. 'We should dress up yon funny article,' (he meant me) 'and put 'im on top o't' cart i' Saddleworth where 'e come from in t'first place.'

Arthur Micklethwaite was glowering from behind him. I couldn't refuse. They would have done much worse to me if I had. Not tell the police. Much worse, perhaps.

My comfortable days at The Headless Woman were numbered.

Yet the band had led me out to entertain all over the Pennines. I was soon, quite naturally, doing it by myself, partly to dodge being ragged at the pub, where Bill Priestley played with me like a terrier with a rat.

For a couple of years, I became more of a rover than I have been at any stage of my life, until recently; although keeping a base at The Headless Woman. I performed and studied acts, travelling for a few weeks, then returning to sanctuary. My beat stretched from the Huddersfield, Bradford, Brighouse area, along the Calder Valley to Todmorden, to Burnley or over the Lancashire border in the other direction into Rochdale. As well as singing-rooms, I worked the new clubs set up for working men; these were self-improvement societies and naturalists' societies that had drifted into becoming entertainment centres. I was hardly ever billed, other than sometimes with a handwritten notice stuck up an hour or two, at most a day or two, in advance. I slept anywhere I could find. I could rarely afford the proper theatrical digs known to the other entertainers and I stayed in places too seedy even for them.

There were too many of us. I found the district swarming with entertainers. You'd meet a dialect verse-writer going to perform in a Wesleyan hall, or a fellow walking a moorland road with a fiddle strapped to his back. Like me, he would be following a route mapped in his head that linked a wedding supposed to be taking place here, a mill-girls' outing to a moorland beauty spot there, to a Methodist 'love feast' that sprawled over a whole village or to a Sunday School centenary celebration held in the open air so that an alternative to a harmonium was needed for the hymns. You could make a living out of nothing. I'd talk to these wanderers, walk along with them and pinch details of their acts. I'd pick their brains as eagerly as they were wanting to pick mine, to find out where things were going off, where a crowd would be drawn and how I could slip in. My colleagues could be very 'close'. Like all the other turns, I got by through keeping my ears open, spending a timely penny on ale, or joining up to pilfer an orchard or a hen's shed.

The times I've walked up and down the twenty miles of canal towpath or hitched lifts on the barges. The times I've taken the tram, the train or the omnibus to the end of the line and walked the rest of the way over the hills, night falling, clouds rolling up, not having an idea where I was heading. When no one would take my act, I, like other performers, was happy to clean out bedrooms, polish boots and whitewash stables, as I had done earlier in my life.

I practised my turns as I walked along the roads, trying them out on temporary companions. Often two of us, acquaintances of no more than an hour, now become friends, would cannily 'practise' in the corner of a public house when it was empty and as a result be given a booking, as well as a free meal.

Dan Leno, I believe, practised his acts by taking long walks – 'in the rain', he said. From Todmorden market I picked up a trunk like Dan's and I started to collect more props, here and there. That suddenly and dramatically changed my style. Up to this point, Mr Dodds, you must picture me wandering

119

the roads in Mr Haigh's cast-off worsted coat, my belongings carried over my shoulder in the seaman's bag that he gave me. But I couldn't carry a trunk on my back. It had to be either left at The Headless Woman or transported ahead. It's amazing about these things; though I'd done well enough without it, once I'd acquired the trunk it became essential. But when me and the trunk were together, no less a form of transport than the train would do for us and also I was obliged to tip porters, hire pony-traps and hackney carriages. I'd come up in the world and the change measured the improvement of my act. I had become less of a tramp and more of a 'professional' entertainer. My calling-places had become regular ones. I had a reputation to fulfil.

However, despite my trunk, my train journeys, my hunting the eyes of theatrical agents up and down the valleys and the name I had for my act, it was still rough trade.

*

Oh, what a world beckoned! But I had to go back to The Headless Woman, still to be tortured with timidity about my penchant. What a mess I was in, being one thing in the morning in the pub, another on stage somewhere in the evening. Maybe taking a glass of ale with chaps at a bar and then dashing to the mirror in my room, re-arranging my hair and trying a dab of scent. Apart from anything else, all this didn't do the act any good. One thing that drag, especially, needs is bags of confidence and not bags under the eyes from sleepless nights, worrying.

At long last, I met a fellow, if that's the right word for it.

I met Mr de Sere himself, one wet night in the dressing-room we were sharing in Bradford. He was well over six feet tall and broad, too. In his vest, he looked like a Standedge Tunnel navvy, or like a firebeater from a mill. It was Sylvia whom he was addressing that night, and she was really quite afraid of him. His accent was pure Leeds. I kept wondering how he lived and whether he had a wife and family.

Almost the first thing he did – he touched me. Frightened me to death. You remember what happened to the two chaps in Saddleworth? I moved away in terror, but didn't dare leave the room in case he chased me and became violent.

Rooted there, trying to placate him, I told him about a few of my problems. He leant a pair of hairy forearms on his dressing-table among his pots and powders and said, 'Listen, my sweet, have courage. Come out into the daylight with it. Being camp is as old as the hills. Drag-acts go back to antiquity. Do you know about shamans?'

'No, Mr de Sere, I don't.'

I was back among the occult and mystical again. The ghost of Cynthia Palmer. With another barmy folklorist like the Schoolmaster. You could rely on it: the Big Questions were coming.

'The shamans up Russia? Down Siberia way? No? You 'aven't 'eard? *Sweetie!* Among the American Indians? Where've you bin? You ought to read some bewks. They are *wise* men, my sweet, who dress up in women's clothes and their people expect it of them because it unlocks the door to hidden knowledge.' He waved two palms across my eyes as if they were those very doors opening. 'They can prophesy. All the primitive tribes dress men up as women. 'Cos they're not daft.'

'Do they, Mr de Sere?'

'Listen to me, son. The ancient theatre was full of it. It goes back in time further than anyone knows. Shakespeare was as camp as a field full of tents. He put drag-acts into his plays. Mistaken identity.'

'I know about that. I've done that.'

'You must tell me about it, sometime,' he said, impatiently. 'If it's your ambition to do drag, darlin', take a tip from me. Come out in the open, yes, but in the theatre and in the right company. I earned my living in the boxing booths before I tcwk up this lark, and *I'm* scared. You have to be a bird of the twilight. Keep it to that and don't get *too* serious about it. I say that because, looking at you, I think you're the type who might.'

'No, Mr de Sere.'

He wasn't the sort anyone would want to quarrel with. No one would want to meet him in a dark alley.

'There are all kinds of us, and I don't know if you've found that out yet. Some of us do things – well, they really will send you down for them. Some of us are quite normal in every other way, having wives and families, but we like to break out every now and then to dress up. For others, dressing up is a substitute for everything else. So long as we can wear our silk – I can see myself that you like silk – or our rubber or our leather, we don't need anything more or different. I'd say you were that sort. If you keep your common sense, you'll be a recruit to an honourable and dignified profession, one associated with the acquiring of wisdom. All our priests and vicars are still dressed in drag, just as in ancient times. Ever thought of that, my sweet?'

No, I hadn't.

'Here, have a look at these magazines.'

While Mr de Sere at his dressing-table stripped himself down to his true self, fifteen brawny stone of it, I read as much as I could understand and devoured the illustrations.

'Ever heard of Edward Carpenter?'

'No, Mr de Sere.'

'Aubrey Beardsley?'

'No.'

'Christ, you haven't lived! Pardon my swearing. I'll bet you've never opened a bewk in your life – like 'alf this sordid profession. That's what's wrong with it. It lacks any flipping refinement. Oscar Wilde?'

'No, I'm afraid not.'

'Open that drawer, kid. Take out the envelope at the bottom. That's right, open it. That's Mr Oscar Wilde in drag as "Salome". Don't tell anyone I showed you that, or mark my words, I'll finish you. You'll look like a plate of your mother's strawberry jam.'

'I don't have a mother.'

*

And then – you!

Through Deetrich's Agency of Manchester, who advertised in *Era* for 'Topliners, or anything startling', I went on in drag at Liston's in Manchester. It was a small place, as halls go. On the first floor of a block of offices for textile merchants, it was almost as unsophisticated as The Fleece, with a dusty, bare wooden floor like a warehouse and the bar, divided by iron pillars, along the side. It was situated just off the main square of the city, Piccadilly, on Tib Lane; a narrow street famous for pet shops.

I went on between a hypnotist and a bioscope operator. At Liston's it was not considered unprofessional for me to sit at a table immediately below the stage while I waited for my five minutes of singing *The Holmfirth Anthem* and there I first noticed you because you were staring at me, while you leaned at the bar drinking Madeira drawn from the barrel.

I was dressed prettily for my song about a deserted country girl of generations before; an image, I realise now, perfect for appealing to your tastes, with all taint of absurdity removed because I was in a music hall, under theatrical lighting.

You bore the haunting stare that I recognised from past men; most significantly, Mr Palmer. As the evening wore on, I watched it change to the fixed stare of one who has drunk too much, following the onset of an obsession.

Because I was the performer, I could not study you so boldly. Fixing my attention on the hypnotist and his wife on stage, I felt your eyes boring into the back of my head. Then I went on to do my piece for ten minutes in front of the curtain, while behind they removed the couch and erected a screen for the bioscope.

From the lip of the stage I took a closer look at you, my eyes flickering as I sang. I guessed you were fifty years of age. I noticed your costly, though conservative, worsted suit and the tastefulness of everything that you wore; at least, it seemed tasteful in a Manchester music hall. Age had brought its deteriorations which you were at pains to hold in. I wondered if you were wearing a corset. When you did not wish to meet my eye, you played with a gold ring on the little finger of your left hand. Also you had a strand of black hair that from time to time you stroked across your dome, believing that you could hide the baldness. The years had given you a thick moustache, dyed black I suspected. It drooped in a fashion which even today I do not know whether to describe as sardonic or sad.

Following my applause, I managed, after circling the room for five minutes, to stand near you during the bioscope operation.

The gas lamps had been turned down and the operator began showing pictures of chapels and town halls, which held our attention only because the figures in front of them were actually moving, and because we knew what was coming next. By the time that the screen was showing shots of girls falling off bicycles, or caught by a sea-breeze – any excuse for showing a bit of ankle or leg – I had reached your side.

You told me that you liked my act. Your speech, like your appearance, was gentlemanly, with an accent cultivated in places far removed from there. You remarked upon my surprise at your pleasure; but it was more that I felt hopeful than surprised. 'The critics don't always enjoy my turns,' I answered, whereupon you reassured me that they were all parrots and vipers who had crawled out of Tib Lane pet shops. You asked me to have a drink, to celebrate my coming success. Dressed in a romantic frock, I could hardly ask for my usual tankard of beer and I requested Madeira because it was what you were taking. Timidly I ventured to inquire if you were an agent, which you denied – and then you told me that you were interested in opening your own theatre! You could open all doors. You knew about everything. What else did I see about you? How much did I ever see? Not much; you were always a wall, a cypher, a door I could not quite get through; someone I've never seen clearly. Pity me: I was a dazzled tyro in the halls, desperate for chances. You have seen how actors are when they meet someone of great influence. Ours is a desperate profession, one that blinds you to other people. I don't see you clearly even now. Only as a background to my self centredness. All I've ever cared about is clothing the female me. Dressing up. Forgive me.

When you said that you lived in Halifax and I told you I lived nearby, you waved your arms as if this was not news to you. You offered your card, hinted that you usually made it to the Café Royal by late afternoon. Suggested that we meet.

·5·

ON and off stage, my inclination to be feminine was
swallowing me up. Men-women such as I have hung
themselves with washing lines or thrown themselves under
trains because of such transvestite dilemmas.

Instead, I dared the Café Royal, where the nobs were.
You know the Café Royal? Not the London one, but ours.
Halifax's; in Crown Street. It was Cynthia Palmer who had
told me first of its existence, as an 'oasis' of culture supported
by the refined families of the district trying to prove that 'life
isn't all muck and brass' in Halifax.

I would never have dared think of entering the Café a year
or two before. But off I went dressed in a silk shirt with frills,
which I covered with a coat until I arrived. It was definitely
Sylvia who haunted the Café Royal, with its polished tiles,
carpets, bevelled mirrors, great brass lamps and bowls of
flowers; the sounds of china tinkling, the sifting of silver
and a murmur of polite voices. They served lovely tea, with
pieces of lemon, exquisite. A string orchestra played among
aspidistras and palms. The Café was used by rich ladies out
shopping, stopping by to rest their corns and cluck over the
state of the Empire as revealed in *The Times*. Also by the
theatrical and artistic crowd who liked to shock them. They
had only to whisper the words *Wilde* and *Bernard Shaw* to
cause a sensation.

They were nearly all men in the artistic circles. I gathered
that they were Socialists and free lovers and free thinkers;
they seemed to be free everything, brave as the day. One
had been thrown out of the Huddersfield Choral Society
for being a Socialist. Socialists and women were specifically
banned from singing, under the rules. They wore red ties and
floppy hats, cloaks and embroidered shirts. They belonged to
a higher order of heaven, visiting art galleries, concert halls
and *proper* theatres where they did real plays and not my

kind of silly performance. Always they had just come back from Paris or they were off to Venice, whereas I thought I was something because I'd been along the canal towpath to Todmorden. Even so, they *boasted* about being bored, about doing nothing, about rising late, about sponging off hard-working parents whose fault it was supposed to be that their children were bored. They pretended to have tuberculosis and were proud of that, too. They didn't know what on earth they were going to find to do for the rest of the day. *Une autre tasse du café, peut être?* Yes, sometimes they spoke in French. Perhaps they would write a poem, they said, if they weren't too exhausted.

What a world this was! These were dandies and their true art consisted in being seen. They said stupid things simply to be overheard, not to make any sense. Like me, they flourished in the twilight and hugged the shelter of the palms. The only sun they cared about was the delight they got from the people whom they could shock and they turned like marigolds to this. The world there was topsy-turvy; I believe they have such cafés in Vienna. Remembering the manners I had observed at Lumb House, how to hold a cup with one finger crooked through the handle, how to cough into a handkerchief while my eyes were lowered, how to tuck my feet neatly under the table and not sprawl, and certainly not to spit, belch, or pick my nose, I tried to disguise any evidence that I had been dragged up in a workhouse, as I sat there most afternoons for a couple of weeks, waiting for you.

You turned up, smiling, explaining that you had been delayed in Manchester.

You picked up the traces of our last conversation; do you remember? With garrulous enthusiasm you talked of changing, demolishing and opening new theatres in Halifax, full of 'the latest art'. I had never before thought of the town as about to turn into a new Florence, nor did you seem quite ruthless enough for a Renaissance prince. Poisoning your mother was the last thing I could imagine you doing. I thought that I knew Halifax as a place of work and dirt, where no one wasted money rather than earning and saving it, but, listening to you, I was ready to believe that I had misjudged the town.

Also I noticed that you did not spike your conversation with malice, envy and waspishness, as, so I had learned through sitting in the Café Royal, is customary among artistic people. Everything that you said was generous. Your kindliness stood out a mile. All the time, Garrick, you stared at me hard and the mind behind your eyes, I felt, was restless.

'Allow me to get you some more tea.'

You had – by the way – such a deep, mellow voice and it always excited me.

'Do you take India or China?'

You flicked your fingers for a waitress.

'India,' I answered, though I had no idea of the difference. 'You are very generous.'

You seemed embarrassed by your money, even by the mentioning of it. Your eyes still on me, you instructed the waitress to clear away the litter of my long afternoon, waiting for you. Indeed, you told her to change the tablecloth. The thought occurred to me that you were promising me a whole new start in life. Did you intend me to think that?

A sweet trolley was wheeled to our table.

'I watched you very carefully at Liston's. I'd seen you before, you know,' you told me. 'You were on stage at a gentlemen's private club in Rochdale, weren't you? And other places. You have a *great deal* of potential. It's my vocation to help theatrical talent. I take a pride in being able to spot it.'

You complimented me on my stage dresses. You'll understand how pleased I was to be, for once, appreciated for such things. Nonetheless, I told you that most of my clothes were picked up for nearly nothing after funeral clearances. Like Mrs Palmer when I told her a joke, you believed me and it didn't make you laugh.

It's embarrassing not to be understood over a joke. You end up trying to explain why you are not a liar. I was on the wrong track.

'You don't take yourself seriously enough,' you said. 'I mean: that perfume! Who brewed it? A witch doctor?'

You wafted the scent away from your side of the table. I'm afraid that I didn't enjoy your humour, any more than you had appreciated mine. It's amazing how humour is a matter of class.

'You know what, young man: you need training. Your act would never make the grade outside the provinces. There's no need to try to be a comic. You can pull the strings of pathos instead. You have the ability. But what you'd be really special at is a dress-act.'

'What's a dress-act?'

I had never heard the term, but it made me breathless with excitement, to think what it might mean. I couldn't imagine anything more fulfilling than wearing dresses.

I was right.

'The audience comes simply to look at you. The songs and jokes don't matter. The dresses are what they come to see. But you must wear only splendid ones and carry them with an air. That is something you need to learn.'

You put your hand inside your jacket to pull out a thick wad of postcards. There was Sarah Bernhardt and a whole gallery of other actresses.

'*You* could look like that,' you said, specifically of a picture of Bernhardt as 'the Empress Theodora'.

'*Me?* Like that. In . . . *silk?*'

'Yes.'

'*Me?*'

'Yes. You should think in a bigger way. You could pose for artists and photographers, as well as going on stage. You could simply *be* – if you had the right setting.'

You swept me off my feet – surely you knew that; outlining a breathtaking career. Imagine what a fulfilment it seemed for Sylvia. I should set my sights beyond local singing-rooms, you told me. You would find me an agent to get me on to the Stoll music-hall circuit, don't worry, don't worry, you said, sliding back your strand of hair. You would have me trained. You would introduce me to artists who would depict me on canvas. You would buy me clothes. You would open an account for me at Rimmel's the perfumer in Regent Street, London, who was, you were the first to inform me, by appointment to Her Royal Highness the Princess of Wales; the things would be delivered by royal mail or train. An account, for perfume! I wondered if you were about to offer me a ring.

You asked where I was living and I told you I had a room at The Headless Woman, where I washed pots for my keep. You pretended not to believe that I could sink so low.

'Someone as charming as you. Such slender features. Deary me, we'll have to get you out of that. It's no wonder your clothes smell of beer and tobacco smoke. Suppose you move into my house, The Hollies, and I find a lady to tutor you? We can go into a partnership to promote you. Don't answer me now. Think about it. I'm not a married man. I live alone and have a great deal of time to fill in.'

Shouldn't I have realised that you might have something more at the back of your mind? Of course I did. But I believed that you were too kind to hurt. You were the sort who tries jolly hard to cheer a chap out of his troubles rather than harp upon your own, and it struck me from the first that, whatever else it was that you wanted for yourself, you *genuinely* desired something for me, too. Despite what you had said about waiting for my answer, I felt that I was already letting you assume that I would move into The Hollies.

By now the waitresses were closing up the Café Royal, sweeping away cups and saucers the minute they were finished with, hanging up their caps and aprons in the kitchen. Even though all afternoon they had seemed not to be even breathing, with only their clothes whispering in the scent of starch, now they were clattering chairs on to tables and letting us overhear what time it was. It was five o'clock, the hour when the place might otherwise have filled with homegoing clerks.

'What the British are quite their best at,' you said, 'is saying *No . . . I'm afraid we're closed . . . We don't have any left . . .* Saying *No* is our religion, my young friend! Thou shalt not, you know. Gets into our businesses, our theatres, even our cafés! Whatever else we do, whatever crimes we commit, we *mustn't* make life too amusing, oh, dear, no, too sensational, or that philosophy would cease to be true. What we can't do, what we don't have, what we wouldn't dare, is our pride and an institution. It supports our church and state . . .'

'Mr Dodds, do calm down, sir!'

It worried me, already, that you became red and apoplectic.

'Your heart!' I cautioned.

129

All that you said was good-humoured enough to make even the waitresses laugh, although their feet were tired, their eyes were glazed over from the coming and going, their hair was dropping out of their caps and they knew they wouldn't recover until they reached home. I'm sure they said to each other that you wouldn't harm a blessed fly, and I caught sight of one of them skipping through the kitchen door imitating you, saying, *'I'm afraid we're closed . . . we don't have any left,'* producing a burst of laughter. From the start, you had a devastating way with waitresses, didn't you?

We were the last to leave. As I followed you into the lobby, it struck me that whereas the others of the Café Royal crowd rabbited on about their painful boredom, about the difficulties of 'getting started' on a poem and worried about their coughs, you had talked mostly of prospects and opportunities for me or, if not that, of the things about society in general that made you angry; which were the negative things, the *thou shalt not* aspects.

I followed outside, where it was raining. I felt that I understood a lot about you from seeing, from the back, the way you raised your collar and pulled down your hat. The rather sad way you did it.

'Well, that's that, then,' you said, briskly. 'You know, I never could have another *lady* – I mean, a wife – in the house, because of Mother.'

'I thought you said that you lived alone?'

'I'll explain later.'

You held out your hand.

As I shook it, 'Call me Garrick,' you said.

But I never have been able to; except at rare moments, you always remained 'Mr Dodds' to me, until you died. How I wish that it had been different! That we could begin again and I could call you *'Dear Garrick'* to your face!

*

A month was needed to make preparations, you told me. In that time we met several times in the Café Royal. Besides which, your letters, fragrant with eau-de-Cologne, arrived for me at The Headless Woman. Sometimes there were two or three each week. As you know, I'd never before received a letter (for Cynthia Palmer never did write to me), let alone answered one.

'Got a sweetheart, at last?' Lydia Dunkerly teased me.

It went all round the bar.

'Our Jacky's gotten a lass to write him letters.'

'He's changed 'is mind about t'wenches. Doesn't let on nowt about 'er, though! What's she like, Jacky lad? Spill the beans.'

'Must be keen. This is t'third message this week.'

''Appen it's a fellar.'

Nobody believed that, of course. Not with those envelopes, with that scent.

Your letters, though written in lovely language, the kind you can hardly tell what a person's saying, all boiled down to inquiries about my sizes in clothing. You asked for more and more precise measurements of chest, waist, hips, inner leg, neck, neck to base of spine and shoe size. I used to borrow Lydia Dunkerly's tape measure and, after various private contortions, scribble measurements on a piece of paper before I handed them to you in the Café Royal. You never seemed satisfied. Really, you wanted me to write elaborate letters but I was shy of the style. It took me many years to realise that you can write things down in just any way you wish.

Finally, you sent your servant, Joseph, with a horse and trap to collect me. Only by the skin of my teeth had I managed to get to the end of my term at the pub without trouble. Any more baiting, and they would have tarred and feathered me. As at The Fleece, I got out only in the nick of time.

Nonetheless, what a send-off the lads gave me. It was an event I've never forgotten, and I can hardly remember a thing about it; if you follow my meaning. Lydia Dunkerly tapped two barrels of free ale and I used up all my savings in paying for a further barrel. I wanted to leave free as a bird, as unencumbered with money as I had come. Besides which, I had a definite idea that riches awaited me round the corner. I felt also that I could do something for you, who so clearly wanted and needed Sylvia; the person I longed and needed to be, anyway.

'Shake 'ands on it,' said Bill Priestley, spitting on the palm he offered me and expecting me to do the same, as if we were striking a bargain. 'Let's be mates. Let bygones be bygones, and no offence intended, eh? At 'eart, you're a decent sort and 'ave give us all a lot of fun.'

I shook his hand, then I left them all, shouting drunk, dancing and playing a fiddle and an accordion in the middle of the road and certain to be celebrating for another week after they had bundled me into the trap. Joseph was expecting me to be sick in it, to judge by his po-face.

Thus I set off for Skircoat Moor.

*

Skircoat Moor is the poshest district of Halifax, a little bit of town that is similar to Harrogate or Bath. It is quite unlike a moor. You see there an elegant park and in fact the really smart area, where the nobs have their houses, is called Savile Park. It was given to the town by Lord Savile, original Lord of the Manor, on condition that the coal smoke of houses built there be consumed inside their chimneys by means of a patent device. 'It is a great hardship that so very little trouble is taken by the town authorities in urging the manufacturers to find a means of remedying the evil of bad air and destroying vegetation,' wrote Lord Savile, wanting to do his bit against the possibility of a dire future. A Smoke Abatement Society was formed and you were on the committee. You were a great committee-man.

In Lord Savile's day, the soot of Halifax had hardly got under way. You should see it now; a lady hardly dare have her washing hung out. It falls in annual tons which are scientifically measured, even if nothing is done about it. When Edward Carpenter came to lecture on astronomy, he thought it a joke because the stars seemed to be permanently invisible.

Perhaps smoke abatement was not enforced because the 'town authorities' were dominated by the Crossley family, manufacturers of carpets by means of steam looms. Carpets paid for theatres and other magnificent buildings. Where, too, would our great Queen have been without the taxes from the Crossley brothers: John, Joseph and Frank? The steam-driven carpet-loom invented by their employee, John Collier, paid for the Crossley Chapel, the Crossley Baths,

Park, Almshouses, model housing and the huge Crossley and Porter Orphanage in Savile Park itself, but smoke abatement wasn't one of their interests; for the money was made out of eight huge mills crammed in a narrow valley, Dean Clough, employing over four thousand work people and smothering twenty-seven acres with buildings.

Imagine the smoke; but Halifax ignores its muck and goes in for luxurious things. Sykes' Subscription Concerts attended in full, formal dress were the rage when I moved there. Even the Dean Clough (Workers) Institute held formal concerts. The front page of *The Halifax Guardian* was crammed with advertisements for clarets, champagne, household linens, fashionable clothes, liveries and uniforms for your servants and agencies for them, jewellery and watches, anti-bilious pills and Dinnefords' Magnesia to 'cure' over-eating.

People enjoy themselves in Halifax. I mean, the middle classes do. But dressing the town up to look like Bath or Baden-Baden only makes more bizarre the sooting of buildings, the wilting of trees. Put your fair hand out of the window of The Hollies and black flakes will fall upon it. Cuffs and shirts and collars: the black snow keeps maids out of mischief.

In the gardens, before roses open fully their cups are stained with soot, with the dregs from the tall chimneys.

*

The splendours of the Moor are reached, from Halifax, by way of a gradual climb; or, following my route with Joseph, by a steep ascent out of the grimy manufacturing villages in the valleys.

I had to be the first to speak. Joseph would have driven the whole way in silence. He was what we call 'close'. But I couldn't sit side by side in a pony trap for five miles without speaking.

We had come through Sowerby Bridge and were climbing Bolton Brow, past the chapel. I spoke in my Yorkshire accent, to make him see that I was one of his own kind. That's always a mistake.

'Been with Mr Dodds long?'

'Six years.'

He fell silent again. I was thinking of saying that it was a fair pull for the pony, or something about the new front of the chapel.

Then he opened up.

'Doing his garden and his driving abart. Mr Dodds traipses up and down a lot, at all sorts of hours. Other folk are in bed.'

The gates of inquiry were open.

'Six years is a long time,' I remarked.

'Nay, it's nowt.'

I felt quite put down.

'Isn't it?'

'No.'

We were silent once more as we went past The Shepherd's Rest public house; it took some time because of the commotion over unloading some barrels.

'I was twenty years in my last position wi' a Catholic seminary. A girls' school. They were everywhere. You wouldn't be interested.'

He laughed.

'Then you're a Catholic, Joseph?'

'Aye, I'm Catholic born and Catholic bred.'

Strong in th'arm and weak in th'ead, I wanted to continue.

A Catholic and a gardener. I saw what they had in common. Both are lonely occupations, at any rate in this part of the world. And he was 'close' by nature. If one wished to keep secrets, he was exactly the servant one would employ.

We climbed through Pye Nest. We reached Savile Park on its plateau. At one side is a nice shopping district known as King Cross. I'd been there. At the other edge, above a cliff of dark rocks, is the Albert Promenade, a boulevard with cast-iron railings where one strolls supposedly for the sake of one's health, as one does in Baden-Baden, for instance; so you told me. So far, I'd never strolled along it, myself – never had fine enough clothes. There are breathtaking, dramatic views to Norland Moor and right down the Ryburn Valley. With the wind in the right direction, a somewhat cleaner air which they describe as 'bracing' blows off the moorlands, though it only seems clean in contrast with what comes from the other, Dean Clough, side of town. My drive through Savile Park where the houses surround a beautifully kept green devoted to cricket, band stands and trotting horses, eventually to burst again on to the edge of the cliff at the Albert Promenade, took my breath away with its wealth and elegance. For although I had combed the wilder parts of West Yorkshire from end to end, I would never have dared, never have thought, to set foot on Skircoat Moor. You'd as likely find a ragged moorland sheep strayed on to it. I had believed that it held nothing for me. Life is full of surprises.

I remarked upon the fine houses. It was summer and the gardens were in full bloom.

'There's a lot of nobs live up 'ere,' Joseph answered me.

'Really?' I egged him on.

'One of them built that silly thing!'

He waved his whip towards where, standing on the edge of the rocks, was a massive, hexagonal tower, built like a mill chimney but without a factory anywhere near it and finished off at the top with decorative stonework.

'What is it?'

'Wain'ouse's Tower. A folly. Gents go in for *follies*, don't they?'

'What's it for?' I asked, although I knew all about it, of course; it's one of the famous features of the district.

''Appen 'e'd nowt better to do wi' 'is money. Wish I 'ad some of what that cost. I wouldn't be driving this 'ere contraption. I'll tell you why the old b——r put it up. One of the other nobs built a big wall at the end of 'is garden so old Wain'ouse couldn't look over at the view. "I'll settle 'is 'ash," says Wain'ouse to 'imself in 'is posh voice and 'e put up his "Tower" with a staircase inside so 'e could go up it and nobody could stop 'im looking. Toffs are mad on what they call "views", aren't they? Nowt better to do. But all you get from views is rain on your face.

'It's a funny thing,' Joseph continued. 'I was brought up on a farm. In grandfeyther's day, they built the fronts of their 'ouses looking into the bank, for the sake of the shelter. They put 'orses and pigs at the back, to look at the "view", which is where all the weather come from. Nowadays, they turn 'em all around. Views my a——e! Old Wain'ouse wanted to see what all 'is neighbours were up to, didn't 'e? Wi' a telescope. But

Mr Crossley capped 'im over that one and built the biggest telescope in the world at Moorside just down the Moor, for spying on what folk are doin'. And they wouldn't know 'e was watching 'em, it were that powerful!'

'Perhaps it was for surveying the stars.'

'There ain't no stars in 'Alifax.'

'Perhaps it *was* for looking at the scenery?'

'Scenery! Mrs Dickenson's 'ousemaid told me she caught old Wain'ouse spying on 'er from on top of 'is chimney. Not daft are they, the nobs? That's why they 'ave a lot of money. Views my a—e!'

'Please don't speak in that manner.'

'Well, it's true. They've all nowt better do wi' their money than play wi' their follies. Mr Dodds is the same. You should make a music-hall turn out of it.'

He spoke, if anything, even more disrespectfully after my reprimand.

'That over there's the Crossley and Porter Orphanage,' he said. 'Summat like an orphanage, that. Costs ten pound a year to send a nipper to Crossley's "orphanage". Looks more like the Metropole 'Otel in Blackpool, don't it? If it wasn't black wi' soot. What it's for, is for nobs to send their by-blows to, to get 'em out o' the way. That's Mr Crossley's 'ouse, there. One of the Crossleys' 'ouses. Their seats are all over town.'

'I know.'

Now that I didn't want to talk, he did.

'I believe you're coming to stay at The 'Ollies in pursuit of your career in the theatre and the music 'all?'

'Yes.'

'Mr Dodds speaks 'ighly of you.'

'Thank you, Joseph.'

''E takes a great interest in theatrical people and 'as given a lot of them a leg up. I go to The Mitre in Market Street myself, usually on a Friday. You've never been on there, 'ave you?'

'I'm afraid not.'

'Thought I 'adn't seen you. I generally have a gill or two, no more than that, and watch from the back. Bet your time will come to go on there, wi' Mr Dodds' help. Bet you do a very comical turn, dressed in drag, though it's not my cup

136

of tea and it's not what I go there for. I appreciate the conjuring tricks more and a bit of the ordinary sing-song, when you can tell who it *is* that's singing. Whether it's a man or a woman, I mean. But I've nothing against your sort. It pleases some, doesn't it? Otherwise it wouldn't be 'appening, I suppose. Mr Dodds tells me and Mona that you'll be with us for some time, in pursuit of your training for the theatre.'

'I hope so.'

'Yes. He took us both into 'is confidence in the front parlour and gave us a solemn talking-to about it so that we wouldn't be taken by surprise. I don't know what Mona thinks. She never says nowt about out. She never goes near a music 'all nor touches a drop of stout. Bin with Mr Dodds a long time. Bin with 'is mother before 'im. I never knew 'is mother for anything like as long, but I'll tell you what, she was always a lively card. Mona watched 'im grow up. "Master Garrick", she still calls 'im. You'll see. She's chapel. But she's all right when you get to know 'er.'

'I don't think I will get much opportunity,' I said, haughtily.

'What do you mean?'

I didn't answer. We had reached the Albert Promenade, where pairs of gentlemen stroll in order to take their hats off to pairs of ladies who seize any opportunity of a gleam of light to raise a parasol. The Hollies is on the side of the road away from the view, where the deep screen of black evergreens ensures that neither the wild moorland weather nor anything else intrudes. I was thinking that, as we'd soon be turning in at the gate, I'd better adjust my tone. Even yet, I didn't know how to converse with servants.

'Oh, I see what you mean,' Joseph said. 'Well, I 'ope we can all manage to fit in together.'

'I hope so.'

'I'm only giving you an 'elpful tip, tha knows. Though I suppose we 'ave to treat you as one of the nobs, now. 'Ave to get used to seeing you around the place in your outfits, I suppose, sir?'

'I've no idea quite what Mr Dodds has planned for me.'

'It's something in that line, I believe. Some folk would say it's a bit strange, but a good servant serves 'is master and no one else, I say, so you needn't fear Mona and me taking notice.'

'Thank you, Joseph.'

'Don't know what we shall 'ave to call you, though. 'E 'asn't told us that.'

'I expect we will all get quite used to it.'

'I expect so. I suppose you 'ave to do it thorough, if you want to get on, don't you?'

'Yes, Joseph. You do.'

'Otherwise you end up in life like me, driving a blasted cart. Wish *I'd* grabbed my chances.'

*

I remember, as clearly as if it was happening this minute, my impression when I turned in at the gate and I don't think I've changed it a jot since, no matter how many times I've strolled in, been driven in, or scampered so as not to meet somebody or other who might look right through me in the cruel daylight. The main gate is absolutely, mathematically central and not an inch out, I'm sure. A straight drive passes through the exact middle of two Joseph-shaved lawns which are his pride and joy; he's a dab-hand with a scythe, or with a mechanical mower when they came into fashion. The centre of each lawn sports a trimmed holly bush, each a round blob. He makes them look as though they're cut out of a solid block of wood, they're so neat. The drive then passes through a holly hedge. Even the passage for servants and tradesmen to reach the back has been screened off at the side with a hedge of holly.

I don't know if they're different in other places, but here the leaves of evergreens acquire a skin of soot, repellent to the touch; don't ask me how they survive. Startlingly against the nearly black background of hollies were white flowers, camellia, aubretia and white climbing roses. Nothing but white flowers, the black and white garden looking oddly bridal. Not fresh, as on the wedding day, but as they become when preserved under a bell-jar. The waxy look, you know, the grime.

Through the hedge, the drive reaches a circle made for a carriage to turn in before the door. While most

138

houses are content with gravel, The Hollies uses the square, mason-cut cobblestones called 'sets'; a hard-wearing surface that would take the pounding of carthorses, laid down quite unnecessarily by your father who thought it a fitting advertisement for himself as a mill-furnisher, so you told me.

Everything about the grounds and the house is symmetrical; somebody had a mania. The two windows on either side of the door, the two bedroom windows on the upper floor, that is, your own and your mother's, with the stained-glass window ending the passageway in the middle over the front door, the two little attic dormers for Joseph and Mona. The Hollies is so well built, of such expensive stone, but so strict, so without flowing lines, without elegant proportion, without adornment. The blinds were almost completely drawn and for a while I thought that a relative had died. Inside, beyond the square porch, two sets of square rooms, same length of sides, same height as length, entered from a passageway with the stairs going up at the end. Four similar bedrooms above. Yours and your mother's at either side of the passage at the front, as I said. Behind your mother's room is the nursery, also untouched since the childhood of 'Master Garrick' and your sister, Liza. The rocking horse and all the other toys still there. The junk that's been collected in that house over – what – fifty years, perhaps longer! Stairs to the attic were at the end of the passage.

Joseph didn't put himself out to help me from the trap and I was as yet too untrained, you might say, to wait for him to do so. I scrambled on to the doorstep, still tiddly, holding back my discomfort and wondering where the deuce to turn to obtain relief. Joseph stirred himself eventually and beckoned the garden-boy, who had come scurrying round to gawp. The pair of them dealt with my trunk while I followed them in to face the music.

That is, Mona, who had come from the back, almost as far as the porch. Joseph was right; she wasn't one to say much. Her hands crossed stiffly upon the lap of her apron, she was like the verger of a church wondering if there's a reason to eject a pagan. It was one of those occasions when, without reason, two people dislike one another from the start. I sensed an enemy.

'Mr Dodds?' I inquired, foolishly. You know how embarrassed you are when you don't like someone and you are afraid of it showing.

She merely stared, in her dreary brown dress looking like an old owl peeping out of a dark tree. It was one of those looks that people give to suggest they 'think a lot'. Perhaps she expected a freak; she might even have been disappointed in my boyish costume.

Still not having uttered a word of welcome, she went off presumably to inform you of my arrival and I was left, after Joseph and the boy had disappeared with my trunk up the stairs, judging my new home from what could be learned from the hallway; taking in the powerful smell of wax polish and its gleam upon the reddish-brown woodwork; listening to the ticking of the clocks from the shadows. An undisturbed, fusty, velvet darkness was my first impression of the interior of The Hollies.

I was staring at one of several lithographs of the Queen that were on the walls, when you appeared. You shook my hand. In fact, you squeezed it. You led me upstairs, playing with your ring as you climbed. At the top was another picture of the Queen.

'I do hope Joseph provided you with a suitable ride. It must have been quite an excursion.'

You spoke as if the low public house, the name of which you could not force upon your lips, was a thousand miles away; you who, so you had already told me, were the habitué of cafés in Vienna.

'Yes, thank you, Mr Dodds.'

Then what did you lead me into, but a new *bathroom*, that is, a room specially set apart to do nothing else but wash and bath yourself in and attend to your toilet, *which, moreover, was to be entirely my own!*

You emphasised that, twice, watching me take in how pretty you'd had it made for me. The porcelain bath-tub, with blue flowers on the rim, rose up like a piece of upholstery to contain one's . . . my . . . shoulders. There were brass taps with white china centres, saying *hot, cold*. Most of the room was tiled, in white tiles with a matching blue floral pattern; which is a Turkish style, I am led to believe. The woodwork was mahogany. There was a cupboard, and another door at the far end. There were frilled curtains at the window.

The room also held – what a joke – my own *flushing toilet!* Not the first one I'd ever seen in my life, because there were two of them in Lumb House which I was never allowed to use; but still, it was *my own! My own!*

All this was what I'd had to wait a month for, before I came to The Hollies.

'You will want to wash and prepare yourself. Possibly change,' you said and I was wondering whether you wanted me in drag. Did you realise how I felt? 'Please join me downstairs when you're ready. Oh, isn't it fascinating, don't you think? Interesting, at least? Just before I leave you, let me show you . . .'

And you flung open the other door of the bathroom, which led into . . .

'*Your* room! It used to be my sister's. Liza. She didn't approve of my being a bachelor. I'm afraid she never understood that it suited me. That is why she left. Actually she was jealous because she was never mother's favourite. She was father's, and she took after him, too. Oh, well, don't let us worry about that on a gorgeous day like this. Oh, my, isn't all this exciting? I'm sure you'll be happy.'

I was peering about, for the curtains were drawn in this room, too. I saw my trunk, my bags and boxes there. Though it was summer, a fire was lit.

'Is it a little stuffy for you? Do, please, draw back the curtains. Why, open the window, if you like! This is quite separate from Mother's part. It doesn't matter so much in here.'

Enigmatic comments that I understood only later.

'I'm apt to forget. But there's no need for you to take much notice of a fusty old bachelor's quaint ways, is there? Do just as you like – in here, at any rate. The room's been made a little small because we had to fit the bathroom out of it. The bedspread, as a matter of fact, is my mother's. *Do you like it?*'

In my tipsy state, I was tempted to kiss you for such a lovely home, but thought better of it. Did you notice?

'I can *see* that you like it.'

You were hopping with pleasure at my response.

You paused.

'But *do* call me Garrick.'

I could hardly get a word in edgeways, but my delight must have shown. How had you, a bachelor, been able to assemble these feminine surroundings? The frilled curtains matching those in the bathroom, the dressing-table made, I learned, from walnut, the matching wardrobe, the innumerable anti-macassars, the several little tables and pouffes, the washstand, the china ornaments (some of them rather saucy), and yet another portrait of the Queen. I couldn't imagine Mona putting all this together and I didn't know, then, that one can hire designers to construct such things.

I was wondering if I dared take the portrait down and hang my mirror in its place, even though the room already held an unusual number of mirrors. Evidently you had anticipated my need of them, but I still wanted to use my own, the one with the butterflies, as I had so few personal possessions.

'Do you know, the cover has not been removed from her bed for twenty years, but I had it washed especially for you. How about that? The laundry maid comes from Monday until Wednesday. And what a silly fuss Mona made about having it done, too.'

I was wondering how your mother now did for a bed cover.

There was also a most interesting oil-painting of a lady over the mantelpiece. You went and smiled at her as if she was a real person.

'My mother,' you explained. 'She was the well-known actress, Eugenia Fanny Watts. That is, of course, before she was married. You *must* have heard of her.'

'Oh, Mr Dodds, isn't she just lovely!'

A confident woman in her early twenties, she held her head tilted on one side under a preposterous hat that I could have done with for a turn, and she was laughing, too, as if she appreciated how silly it was. She was making a coy gesture with her hands. As well as her lips, her eyes were laughing out at whoever was painting her. A camellia flower was tucked into her bosom and I wondered if it had been plucked from the garden. Evidently someone was particularly fond of that flower.

While I was staring at it, 'Well, then I'll leave you. When you look in the wardrobe, I think you'll find a few surprises.'

'Oh, really?'

I didn't imagine they'd be such a surprise. In my trunk were the letters you had written to me.

'Yes, really. Don't look just now. I shall leave you. When you come downstairs, Mona will have prepared our usual five o'clock tea. I should tell you, Jacky, we *do* do things according to the clock here. That's the only thing and I hope you don't find it irksome, but my mother established the timetable and I don't like it to be upset.'

You went through the other door from my room, and I saw that it led into your own bedroom.

'If I were you, I should take a bath,' you said, wrinkling your nose and laughing. 'If you want anything, you can ring for Mona.'

Ring for Mona: not likely!

As soon as you'd gone, I rushed into my bathroom, made use of the flushing toilet and, with one of the sweetest pleasures of my life, pulled the chain, watched the water swirl, listened to the sweet gurgle and receding echo of the plumbing. Then I filled the bath with hot water that made the plumbing roar.

*

I walked naked from room to overheated room; a pleasure I had never enjoyed in a house before. None had been warm enough, private or sympathetic enough. I felt I was the newcomer to a harem. All for my own pleasure, I walked as Sylvia. Not until then and, as I say, without a stitch to cover me, did I look in the wardrobe for your 'surprises'.

Among other items, you had purchased a white, silk shirt which had splayed lace cuffs and a high, frilled neck. Yes, it could have been worn by man or woman. So you had thought about covering my neck; unless you're born especially fortunate, it's an important part to cover if you want to convince in drag. I also selected a pair of dark purple harem trousers, the legs so large that they flowed like a dress. At the foot of the wardrobe were a pair of light patent-leather 'house' shoes. In drawers, I found a selection of ambiguous silk underwear. Little of the clothing was *exactly* female wear. Oh, very careful of you.

Before I changed, I unpacked my luggage and lost my previous, suddenly tawdry-looking possessions inside the drawers that slid as if they were on castors and in wardrobes large enough to make a home in them; at any rate, I in the past had slept in places no bigger. Despite your comments about my perfume, I couldn't resist applying some, only I tried a different one from my store. That, I thought, was far enough for the first time; especially, I presumed, as I had to meet your old mother over tea.

I took my time preparing myself, as a lady is excused for doing. Upon my finger I placed a large ring. I chose the little finger of my left hand, to be like you. A naughty thought. My ring held a piece of coloured glass instead of a ruby, but never mind. Most of what I possessed had been acquired as stage-props and for the time being I wouldn't want to suggest anything different; wanted to hint that this was merely a private turn for you and your mother, as she had been an actress. Just a special entertainment for tonight.

Sliding my fingers delicately along the bannister, I descended the stairs as softly as I could. Nevertheless Mona rudely stared from the kitchen, muttered something that I didn't catch and shut the door. No sooner had she withdrawn her horns, than the door opened for Joseph to take a peep. He was now in his shirt-sleeves. More calm, more ready than Mona to be frank about his curiosity, he puffed his pipe in the doorway. I was glad that neither of them dared to speak.

I had reached the bottom of the stair. 'In there?' I boldly asked, pointing to the door that was on my left.

While Joseph nodded affirmatively, your voice called from within, 'Yes, in here, please! In the parlour!'

And in I went, for tea.

What a room! Certainly it was not a bachelor's place, with its sewing tables, its massings of ornaments, its aspidistra ... but I won't, I couldn't, catalogue it all. That stuff must have taken a century to collect. One could hardly move through it safely, especially as one could barely see half of it when suddenly plunged into the dim light. The light was dim because the dark green velvet curtains were almost completely drawn. I felt like a newt underwater, at the bottom of a pond.

You were standing, waiting, rubbing your hands, watching me peer.

'I didn't expect you to live like this,' I said.

Although it was certainly theatrical.

'I have to do it to protect mother's things from fading,' you told me. 'What *did* you expect?'

'I don't mean, just the curtains. The furniture . . . I suppose I thought it would be more jaunty. Please excuse me.'

'Did you enjoy your bath?' you asked, severely.

'Oh, yes!'

The table was laid only for two, with a rack of scones, various pots of jam and everything prepared for tea. This was my first sight of the Crown Derby tea-service that was to become so familiar; the cups nestled intimately within each other upon a pile made of their two saucers. The milk was secured from flies under a tasselled cover and the sugar bowl likewise was protected with a crocheted cloth.

'Please be seated,' you said.

It was obvious where I was to sit; for one of the places had in front of it a small, square parcel tied with a pink bow.

'Oh, Mr Dodds!' I exclaimed. 'Is that for me?'

You merely continued to smile, as you sat down.

I pulled the bow, unwrapped the fancy paper which had violets printed upon it, pulled out what at first I thought was yet another box, although it had a small hole at one end, a little window in it, and a lever.

'It's a camera,' you explained. 'Point it . . . No, the other way round.'

Your hand briefly touched mine.

Touched, more confidently, my elbow.

'Wonderful invention. One can preserve days, people, memories for ever. It's the latest thing. With this camera you don't need a studio, nor even a tripod, and can photograph everywhere. Picnics. Outings. Look into the viewfinder! That's it. Point it towards the chink in the curtains, there, then you'll be able to see something. No, don't press the lever now. It's loaded and it's too dark in here for a snap. When you snap something, you must breathe in, so as not to move when you expose the lens. I'll show you tomorrow on the lawn and we'll experiment by taking each other. Won't that be fun?'

'Oh, Mr Dodds, where shall I put it?'

Handling it as delicately as the Holy Grail, I rested it on the sideboard, as instructed. Oh, but such a lovely gift!

Everything was ready on the table except the tea-pot, which Mona brought in after you had pulled the bell-cord. She covered the pot with a tea-cosy, sniffed and tardily departed, her eyes darting at me. She was still in her brown, high-buttoned dress; no one had instructed her to change for tea. There was no style about her and her nails were dirty. You expected little of her and it made her arrogant. I had thought I was going to quite a stylish establishment, even if not of the Palmers' class, and I was disappointed in Mona.

'She's old,' you excused her, guessing what I was thinking. 'She's been with me for a long time.'

We sat at the table. You poured the tea.

'So Joseph told me,' I said.

'He conversed with you on the journey, did he?'

'Yes.'

'Remark to Joseph that it is a fine day and he'll reply, "No, it isn't. It was finer yesterday." Say that the weather's poor and he'll tell you that it's the best we've had for months. Say to him that our life is rather – bizarre, shall we say? – and he will answer, "Nothing peculiar about it", and will say the same to the neighbours' servants.' You tapped your skull with your finger. 'That's being clever. Mona says nothing at all. She believes that only trouble comes from talking. That's another advantage. I prepared them both for your arrival.'

'Your mother is not to join us?' I inquired, merely to be polite; for I was relieved not to have too much to deal with at once.

'Oh, deary me, no. Mother passed away.'

'Your mother has died? When?' I asked, thinking she must have died during the month since I had seen you in the Café Royal and that was the reason for the drawn curtains.

'Five years ago. Perhaps I should have told you, but she is still alive for me, you know. The camellias were in bloom.

One never gets over such things. And why should one wish to forget? It would be a betrayal. But your own mother? Where is she? Is she alive?'

'Alas, no. Her grave was met untimely. But she was an actress, too.'

'In what did she appear, may I ask?'

'I do not know. She passed on too soon. But I believe she performed in some affecting productions on the London stage. I have the idea she was unfairly treated by mankind. In fact, Mr Dodds, my mother is with me, too, always, all the time, even though I never knew her. I understand how you feel. I really do.'

I searched for inspiration among the golden dust dancing in a chink of sunlight that escaped into the room.

'Haven't you her programmes?' you asked.

''Fraid not.'

'I have the programmes for almost everything Mother appeared in. I will show you my collection, before long.'

Across the table, you touched my hand, covering the back of it with yours, which was so much larger, fatter, warm-brown and freckled. A fatherly hand, I thought, yet the touch was a mother's, and tender.

This was the first time in my life that a man had gripped my hand so. At that moment you were everything to me.

I told you more about my own mother and of how I always see her. I described her, terribly purposeful, tense with it, waiting, standing, rocking in the railway carriage, tears petrified behind a mask of determination, *I shall go through with it*, waiting still for a better day that she didn't believe in.

'My God!' you exclaimed. 'How can you live with such grief?'

I couldn't give an answer.

'How fortunate it is that we have met,' you continued. 'Life is a vale of tears. But one can pretend that it is otherwise. Can't one? *Can't one?*' you insisted.

'Yes,' I replied.

'I'm afraid I've remained always shy of marriage,' you confessed in this room where you were sheltered by twilight, 'I mean, *real* marriage. I wouldn't mind – you know –

147

pretending. But one couldn't do such a thing with a real, female lady, could one? For she'd be sure to want something more, no matter what else one gave her. Ladies are like that.'

'There's nowt so queer as folk,' I said, to cheer you up. 'As the saying has it.'

'I beg your pardon? I have never heard that saying.'

'Two old fellars were talking in a pub, see.' I eased my elbows on the table, at last. 'They'd gone through all their neighbours. What their peculiarities were, gossiping about 'em, talking the night through. In the end — three o'clock in the morning — landlord refusing to proffer them no more ale — one of them sums up, "Aye, well, there's nowt so queer as folk. They're all a bit peculiar. Except thee and me." Then he takes a close look at his friend, see . . .' I leaned close to you. 'And says, "*And thou's a bit strange at times!*"'

'A *vulgar* story,' you said, shivering.

*

That weekend for a treat you took me to Sheffield to see Marie Lloyd.

Sheffield! It must be forty miles from Halifax to Sheffield.

'One can take a train,' you said, smiling as if it was nothing. *And* we travelled first class.

In the theatre you were in your element. You were quite a card. But the audience was full of chapel folk. You could spot them a mile away. Both of us could. Maybe they *were* in their best clothes, which were mostly of black worsted or crêpe, but they could not dress their faces. Nor their gestures. Nor their mouths.

The sight of chapel people made your blood, too, run cold. It's their combination of black clothes and smiles. The smile is not the one I was used to in the workhouse, The Fleece and The Headless Woman, which was helpless and generous. Is there anything more sinister than a planned smile? Neither are the black clothes those of heartfelt grief; they are a stylish effect, a warning of seriousness.

Because of Marie's reputation, they had come along to be shocked. '*Isn't she naughty?*' one heard on the promenades, even before she had started. You mimicked, shocking them

148

by putting on a high-pitched squeak at the bar, '*Isn't she naughty? Oh, isn't she naughty!* Making a fool of several by seeming to be as disapproving as they were.

Small women usually look ridiculous in massive clothes, so why wasn't Marie, small and dumpy, ridiculous in her florid dress and huge, floral hat? It was because of her huge presence on stage. We all expected something extreme, something more than we had ever experienced before, and by jimminy, we got it.

But the heart that beat within Marie Lloyd was no exaggeration. She meant and felt every word that she sang. Her songs were stories that she acted out. Her singing was also part-chanting that broke and rose into a brook-like warble when she hit something funny, or something that raised her spirits and that would have raised ours, too, if we hadn't all been so smugly resistant. She was a character actor as well as a singer and what shocked the po-faced audience was the characters that she portrayed.

Even more shocking were her portrayals of *women* enjoying sex.

> *I always 'old with 'aving it if you fancy it,*
> *'Cos a little o' what you fancy does you good!*

It was the women who were the most shocked by that bubbling, hot voice. The disapproval in the stalls was as taut as a bow string.

'Hussy!'

'Well!'

'I say, look at that chap!' you whispered. There was this grocer or something who was afraid of laughing because his wife kept throwing him side-glances. He tried to pretend he wasn't watching the stage, but he couldn't resist it, then red in the face he stared at his shoes.

You tapped him on the shoulder.

'Jolly good performance, what?' you teased him. 'Marie Lloyd does Sheffield proud, eh?'

His wife glared over her shoulder at you.

'Disgusting!' she hissed.

'I was addressing your husband, madam. I believe he's enjoying the performance.'

You were in your element, bubbling with – dare I say it? Love.

'Disgraceful,' the man muttered. 'And who's your friend?' he tried to hit back. Though I wasn't even in drag, then; just a little bit pansy, you know.

We spluttered with laughter.

> *And if that's your blooming game,*
> *I intend to do the same,*
> *'Cos a little o' what you fancy does you good . . .*

Oh, you were a card when you got going, Garrick Dodds! Wrap anyone round your little finger. I was in fits.

We were almost the only ones to clap at the end of the first house. Marie, used in London to the adulating audiences that she deserved, was furious.

'You don't like me, well, I don't like you!' she screamed at us, in her accent which was a mixture of cockney and posh. 'And you know what you can do with your stainless knives and your scissors and your circular saws. You can shove 'em up your a—s!'

I learned afterwards that at first she refused to appear for a second house. Apparently the manager visited her dressing-room. No doubt it was already in its notorious mess of beer bottles, fish and chips.

'Don't try to schmooze me!' she shouted.

'They'll do what you want with their knives and scissors,' he persisted. 'But can they be spared the circular saws?'

Marie laughed and relented.

'All right, then. Play "God Save the Queen" and tell them she's 'ere.'

So the Queen of music hall went on for a second house.

·6·

I T *was* exciting that my hired instructress in female appearances, Mrs Emily Simpson, knew so much about
the theatre; what was worn by Sarah Bernhardt, Marie
Studholme, Gertrude Elliot, Miss Phyllis Dare and her
sisters; what Madame This and Madame That said to the
Prince, what they did in Paris, oh lah de dah! Having been
your mother's dresser, she was a proper sport, but kept it
hidden. When one prised her open, she was a real fountain.
One couldn't stop the gossip running.

She was thin and small-featured. She took cautious glances
rather than looked boldly. She smiled to herself rather than
laughed outright. One could never imagine her indulging
anything so raucous as anger or tears; when upset, she'd
make a tight-mouthed comment or two. Her husband had
died in a fire at the clothing store which he owned and I'll bet
that when it happened, she did no more than bite her lip and
(a phrase of hers) 'get on with it, dash it!'; although I know
that she loved him deeply.

I learned that she had enjoyed a sentimental affair with
you – before her marriage, of course. It was after she
discovered that the grip your mother had on you made
fulfilment impossible that she married another. Though
Eugenia Fanny Dodds' (née Watts) 'vibrant' character had
a powerful hold upon her, too, as emerged in conversation
all these years later; on, so it seems, everyone who came close
to her, except her husband.

Yet if one met my Mrs Simpson in the street, one wouldn't
be aware of a woman distinguished by experience and
tolerance; a person able to take aboard all your eccentricities.
Women with a past invariably hide it when they reach the
age of fifty and say little about it except when their intimates
draw them out. They put on more, not less, modest and
sober appearances than their neighbours who have led less

adventurous lives. All that you might have observed would be that Mrs Simpson was more refined, scrubbed and, when she did speak, more pretentious than most. But she didn't say a lot. She kept her own counsel until asked and then she uttered well-formed sentences that you would have thought were being read out from *Vanity Fair, Tit Bits* or *The Illustrated London News*. All delivered without a trace of accent. She taught me more about how to bury mine than anyone else ever has.

Partly delayed by her affair with you, she had married late. In girlhood she had worked in a dress emporium in Leeds. For ever after, her imagination was devoted to fashions, materials and modes, as if little else existed. Even in the later days when I knew her, it was difficult to speak to her on any subject – shall we say colonial expansion, or the travels of the Queen, or which actors were booked to play at The Grand Theatre at North Bridge, subjects which interested all of us in the evenings – without bringing into the conversation chemises and cloaks, burnouses and garters, jabots and shawls.

In the mid–1850s, when she was fifteen or so, she discovered her passion for the drama, where clothes were displayed in their most glamorous lights; society balls being out of Emily's reach. I believe she regularly visited the old theatres in York, in Richmond and in Leeds; those dark, wood-lined, long-gone places that were more like penitentiary chapels, with rows of boxed-in, wooden pews. Her enthusiasm had first been inflamed by performances of Shakespeare in the quaint Georgian theatre, the Theatre Royal, now demolished, in Halifax. There the stagings in mysterious candlelight were so realistic ('effective' was the useful word that Mrs Simpson taught me; 'the word "effective", you will find, will cover a multitude of sins') that for the 'Alas, poor Yorick' scene, they used the skull of a criminal who had been hanged locally upon Beacon Hill. An indifferent actor could easily *cover a multitude of sins* when the audience's eyes were fixed upon that lugubrious object in his hand.

How the young Emily Potts, as she was then, managed to travel, all alone, to those distant theatres in that long-ago, primitive age when the railways were in their infancy, I do not know, nor how she afforded it on her miserable pay, nor how she found the time; but it shows what our little Miss Potts was made of and it led to her future employment, travelling between all the metropolitan and provincial venues with the much-reviewed actress, who was not a native of Yorkshire: Miss Eugenia Fanny Watts.

One realised that Emily had been quite a wild gal before she adopted the corsets of convention which restricted her for the remainder of her life to what she believed she ought to be as a lady of Halifax; trained in a dress emporium, that is, one stage up from domestic service, breaking on to the fringe of theatre life, married to and then widowed by a store-owner. There was a streak of gay madness inside that little body.

Mrs Simpson was paid to visit me for several hours each morning as well as to be around as a semi-permanent house-guest. The aim was to make me so perfect an imitation of womanhood that the audience would gasp even before I did a thing on stage. Oh, it was a lovely thing to do. The advantage I would have over other drag-acts would be my perfection; this would make the fame and fortune of all three of us. Mrs Simpson was not merely a stickler for perfection – she attended neither church nor chapel, and perfection was her religion. Under her tutelage I turned into Camellia Snow; the name that you invented upon drawing the curtains aside and peeping out, on our first evening together, to see the camellia blossom, 'white as snow'.

I had to agree that it was a much better name than 'Sylvia'. I had grown out of her. Sylvia had been a girl but Camellia was a woman, who thanks to Mrs Simpson learned how to hitch on a bustle, how to walk up and down the carpet; who knew the secrets of the dressing-table's alchemy, had absorbed manners and studied such books as Mrs Beeton on *Household Management*, volumes on etiquette and deportment.

Dressing the show properly would use up the whole morning. But real ladies take quite as long in preparing themselves and don't even think about it; for being a lady, of whatever sex, is a profession.

I have always found it much easier to dress when in the company of women, for they make it all seem so much more natural. Especially the practical Mrs Simpson, grim-lipped, serious, often with her mouth full of pins. It is quite difficult when alone and if men were present I think I'd find it impossible. That is why you were never at these scenes.

Oh, it was fun. Nobody could say it wasn't fun, good Lord. Imagine the three of us getting round to the subjects of artificial breasts and the holding in of private parts.

It surprised me that neither of you was embarrassed by discussing how to obtain and fit bizarre clothing; deciding upon the strategy, one memorable evening around the fire with the lamps unlit out of consideration for *my* blushes, of measuring me for these items to be delivered by rail and mail-cart from distant Huddersfield, York or London. What giggles we had over the operation of fitting them; Mrs Simpson as the expert doing some of it, or advising, as propriety dictated, and flitting in and out of the room, being entirely professional. She could have been a housewife at the butcher's. But I, I must confess, didn't know where to put myself, nor where to look, sometimes.

You offered the explanation to Leak and Thorpe of York, Kay and Monningtons of Huddersfield, and Axtons, the corsetières, of Victoria, London, that your wife was rendered too shy to make a personal visit, as the result of an unfortunate accident when riding a runaway horse.

*

In the hour or two before Mrs Simpson's arrival, modesty made it imperative for me to make my basic preparations in private. My breakfast, of toast and marmalade, I took in bed. I would have preferred it after bathing and shaving, but to have eaten in mid-transformation between male and female would have been too embarrassing before Mona when she brought the food in. Next I wandered around my room, silently working myself into the right frame of mind, enjoying this time to think my way into my role. When at ease with it, I bathed and shaved my whole body, or as much of it as I could reach. Even though most of it was hidden, the complete works were needed in order to make me *feel* as a woman. Besides, suppose I accidentally lifted the edge of my dress and you saw hairs around my ankle, oh my God!

Then I turned to my underwear: the artificial breast-former, the cover of my awkward parts and so forth. My most usual corset was made of cotton reinforced with leather, stiffened with whale bone, and it had what Mrs Simpson told me was a 'spoon busk': a thick piece of padded leather at the front, shaped like a spoon and intended to hold in a lady's stomach; in my case, the piece of leather was extended to suppress a little more besides. It had been specially made by Axtons and it laced up at the front as well as at the back, so that I could fasten it for myself. It was most ingenious and expensive. Such a garment had to be manufactured in London, for a local corsetière would have informed the police.

Over it I wore combinations of a chemise top with drawers, smooth-fitting to accommodate the tighter dresses that were coming into fashion. Mrs Simpson's nimble fingers had adapted it with a square, buttoned flap for doing something it was nigh impossible for me to perform in the expected fashion; you know what I mean. A cloth belt at my waist had my bustle clipped on at the back. Of steel wire strong enough to support heavy drapery, it was light but tough as a lobster pot so that it couldn't be crushed when I sat down.

At this stage I was fit to receive my tutoress. Ladies suffering from the present-day servant problem complain about the difficulties of dressing without the assistance of a maid. While I know that it is a necessity of being lady-like to invent foolish things to complain about, this might indicate to you the miracles of engineering I had achieved, solo, by the time of Mrs Simpson's arrival. I had overcome difficulties undreamed of by any woman and I tried not to appear fagged out by the endeavour. There was still a long way to go.

Her first task was to help me complete my appearance. You would have had me dressed up like Eugenia Fanny Watts on stage – Lady Bracknell or some such part – but in general Mrs Simpson advised against it. In 1895, when I first came to you, tailored suits for ladies had become popular and I was quite comfortable in one of these. Also they looked well on me, I think. One in brown cotton drill I remember with affection. It had delightfully puffed sleeves (sleeves were at this time blown up like balloons), and the suit was pulled in at the waist before flowing out over a small bustle. It stopped about an inch off the ground. Adding a black straw hat, I could eventually stroll around thus all day on Skircoat Moor. It was Mrs Simpson's sensible advice for me to wear clothes of an intermediate sexual nature, so that, if the worst came to the worst and I got into a sticky corner, I could be mistaken for a woman dressed as a man – something which, such is the mystery of society, is regarded as not being anywhere near so bad!

As I slowly dress, my fingers respond to the delicacy of the clothes. A transformation of my inner self begins from this touching. It is all done in a sensuous way and I am self-absorbed. I touch, I stroke my silk, my skirt, or my bosom. Mrs Simpson, having worked in the theatre, is sympathetic to the self-absorbed way in which an actor transforms himself into his role. She busies herself quietly in the wings, brushing my wigs, perhaps.

She shows me how to build my own stage-face. A base cream is dabbed on to my cheeks and chin, then smoothed out with my fingertips. I dab it on my forehead and under my eyes, on to my nose, and spread the cream there, too. I moisten it with my finger wetted on my lips. I place blue on my eyelids, and purple above, moistened also with the aid of my finger. Touch up the corners of my eyes. Brush up eyelashes. Using a soft brush, apply a blusher to my cheeks, of a faint crimson colour.

My mind all the while concentrating upon my *inner* transformation.

Paint my lips.

My appearance is completed. The butterfly steps forth from the chrysalis. There I am, perfect. And the rest of my room – discarded clothes, powder spilled, a perfect mess!

Next, I am taught movement. My instructress watches my gestures, ready to pounce and correct them. The way I put my hand over my mouth to hide a cough. How I pick up something that falls to the floor. I drop something on purpose and try again. It's only what all young ladies have to do when sent to schools in Switzerland. Merely the way to sit and to walk swallowed up hours of training. I practised in front of mirrors and then without them. More mirrors were brought in, so that I could see myself from several angles. If my gesture didn't succeed in making me feel feminine, as my training progressed I knew without being told that it was wrong and I would do it again without its being requested.

Through this part of the proceedings, especially, I steadily rid myself of any remaining assertive manner. I discovered that if I met Mrs Simpson when I was in a demanding frame of mind it created an obstacle which took an hour of repetitive feminine movements to overcome. These rituals finally jolted me from a masculine to a feminine state of mind; though feminine clothes in themselves make you feel vulnerable and dependent upon the help of others.

In this category of manners comes, perhaps, what is forbidden to a lady: perspiration. I was trained almost to stop breathing when I felt a bit of a sweat coming on. Also not to let out vulgar sounds. Not to open my legs nor scratch, not to pick my teeth, not to interrupt male talk any more.

To sit there like a d——d stuffed parrot.

Though Mrs Simpson trained me in what was possible within the proprieties of lady-like conversation.

Also to speak 'properly', that is, as she did, by making me read aloud passages out of *Tit Bits*, over and over again.

'*The great French actress Rachel had as hard a childhood as ever fell to the lot of genius. Ragged, barefooted, and hungry, she played the tambourine in the streets and sang and begged for dole. Naturally she was illiterate and vulgar.*' Who would choose to be a lady? I ask myself; well, clearly, I would! Just to wear these clothes . . . the ecstasy . . . the silk . . . but I mustn't get carrried away.

After we had spent an intimate hour together and before lunch when you would be present, was the best time to ask questions about you. I found that the way to succeed with my shy tutoress was to seem to be undemanding, with a quiet voice, but to be quite direct, so that she could not wriggle out of it. Provided I had judged the right moment.

'What was Mr Dodds like as a young man?' I asked, coyly.

A melted, happy look came over her eyes.

'Oh, my handsome, young Garrick! He used to talk wonderfully at debating societies.'

Have you ever noticed how often the first thing that women admire about a man is what he says and the sound of his voice?

'He was very smart. Slender as a guardsman. He would spend half an hour adjusting his cravat. Looking for dust on his spats. Then his mother would do it all over again for him before he went out. Brushing dust that didn't even exist off his shoulders. She thought the world of him and he of her. That was his trouble. Garrick was all that she was left with, after she had abandoned the theatre for – *that man*. Dodds, who used to sulk upstairs among his library of engineering manuals if anyone crossed him. Mother and son were like conspirators, whispering behind his back. It was she who wanted him christened 'Garrick', while his father's choice was William. While he wanted him in the business, the mother wanted him on the stage and he would have been most effective for he was wonderful before an audience.

'Do you know what it was like here in the eighteen sixties?' she continued. 'We all got up carriages to go and watch the riots. The Chartists and plug-drawers met at North Bridge in Halifax and went all the way down the Calder Valley to Todmorden pulling the plugs out of the boilers in the mills, so that it took another whole day to get up the steam pressure to work the looms. People were terrified of revolution and Garrick's own father wrote a letter to the newspaper describing a time in the near future when workers would be collecting the blood from beheaded mill-owners on North Bridge. "Nonsense," said Garrick, out in public to the debating society and not caring a fig about defying his dragon of a father. "Chartists are only poor people wanting a crust of bread for their labour." What a row there was, at home and in public.'

Mrs Simpson was fiddling with my gloves, wishing to talk about you but also afraid of being drawn into saying too much. She was hovering near the door. She was trying to escape.

'I am surprised his mother didn't want him to marry,' I tempted. 'To get him out of here.'

'She did! All she wanted was for him to find a nice girl. But that was when the other side of him showed. "I wish he'd grow some hair on his chest!" she used to say to me, many a time. "I have a husband who's too much one way, and a son who's too much the other. Why couldn't the good

158

Lord portion things out properly? If I want grandchildren, I'm going to have to depend on Liza." But all that Garrick, too, seemed to want was a nice girl to marry. Only he could never find one nice enough to take home to mother, so he thought. He was afraid of her being disappointed, as she had been with his father.'

'How peculiar.'

She looked at me with a smile, as if to say, *You should talk*.

'Surely *you* wouldn't have disappointed his mother?' I ventured. She smiled again.

'I knew too much. I understood him too well. He could never have made a good husband. What sort of wife could be second-in-command museum-keeper to his mother's career? He knew this himself and what his choices were. If he'd wanted to, he could have swept any girl off her feet with his talk and she might have followed him to the end of the earth, but instead, what did he do with a sweetheart but show her his theatre collection, shoes worn by his mother, dresses she had worn and that she would have thrown away, props she had handled in this, that or the other production; her candlesticks, and what-not-else. Stage pictures of her. We talked about it. But he's decided what he wants and has remained faithful to his ideal. Hasn't he? The Hollies doesn't represent his own character at all. It's his mother, everywhere. Grown stale; poor man . . .'

*

As soon as I had dressed, an extraordinary thing happened to me and an equally surprising change came over you. Though you knew who and what I was, yet you could not help treating me as a woman. It was astonishing; it was impossible for you to think of me as anything but a woman, no matter what you *knew*. That was quite clear. You did not need to act at all. It was impossible for you not to be gallant and protective.

I, equally without being able to help myself, turned into another character, vulnerable, shy, a bit skittish, often temperamental. Heaven knows where Camellia had been lurking within me all this time, but whenever I was dressed for the part, her personality took me over.

That gave you the confidence to take me out. My first expedition was on a misty evening when you walked me under the lamps on the Albert Promenade. I was clad in a heavy cloak. Sheltered by you, I ducked my face under my hat, out of the way of the few passers-by. We went only a couple of hundred yards before my legs felt weak from the strain. I could not help my eyes darting everywhere to spot a policeman. Yet when we reached home, I felt so elated that I couldn't wait for another adventure!

I soon began to feel more unusual when hopping around The Hollies as Jack on the following day, than I did the other way round. I no longer knew who was on holiday from whom. Jack seemed, more and more, a feeble creature.

Thus, by degrees, I was led to the point when, in full daylight, treating me entirely as a gentleman should, you led me as Camellia to one of the Leeds emporia where they adapt Paris fashions in their workrooms.

A great change took place in Leeds during those years. Jews. They were escaping from pogroms in Russia, arriving in their thousands for a most curious reason. They had purchased tickets supposedly for New York, travelling by ship from the Baltic to Hull on the east coast of Yorkshire, by train across England to Liverpool in the west and thence by steamship to America, but they found that Leeds was as far as their tickets allowed them to go. Having no money, they stayed, occupying the Leylands area. They were absorbed into the ready-made clothing trade and there was a huge expansion of the business.

The emporia that swallowed up their labour were in effect magnificent clubs for ladies. You and I sat under clouds of hanging muslin, with materials and dresses swamping the counters across which we discussed, as solemnly as real men discuss war, shipping, colonial policy or banking, the Paris couture designs illustrated in their magazines.

Something else of importance happened to me. The manager introduced the word *dybbuk* into his conversation. And what was a dybbuk, I wanted to know? I learned that in Jewish folklore it was an alien being who could enter a person's soul, change his nature and play havoc with his personality.

160

Was Camellia a dybbuk in Jack's soul, making him help-lessly follow this lunatic fantasy with you?

*

When eventually I emerged upon a theatre stage, you said, it would be to astound the world, with my past wiped out, as had happened to many a successful actress. Eugenia Fanny Watts, apparently, like 'the great French actress Rachel', had undistinguished origins in the East End of London and if knowledge of them had reached the light of day, it would have ruined her career.

One day, after about six months, when reading aloud from the advertisement columns of *Entracte*, you told me that the South Shields Empire had booked a 'living statue' act, with ladies appearing in the nude.

'*Naked?*'

'I think that their bodies will actually be covered in shellac,' you replied. 'It is something you could do, surely, Camellia.'

'*Naked* but covered in shellac! Me?'

'In your case, a *clothed* representation, of course. With others. Charles Morton staged *tableaux vivants* of famous paintings at the Canterbury in London, don't you know. You do not move. You do not speak. It would solve the problem of your voice. Of your movements which are not, my dear, entirely perfected, either. It would enable us to proceed by degrees. One thing at a time. Always the best way.'

'What's *tableau vivant* mean when it's at home?'

'*Life*, my dear. *Life.*'

'Life? That doesn't move nor speak?'

You claimed that it was a most distinguished form of representation because one had been staged in honour of the Queen in front of the town hall in Harrogate. Before a banner inscribed, 'God Save the Queen', a pyramid of gentlemen dressed up as a Chinaman, an African Negro, an Indian with a huge fan, a sailor, a soldier, a policeman, an Eskimo, et cetera, made a *tableau* of the Empire, to be recorded by a camera and sold as a postcard. The gowned Britannia, moreover, with flag and trident, was also a gentleman.

Mine 'brought to life' the famous painting, *Captive Andromache*, by Frederick Michelangelo Hardcastle ARA, of which you had an engraving upon the stairs. You had it moved into my bedroom so that I could study it and I didn't dare say 'No', although your pictures all seemed full of eyes that followed me around the room, while the frozen gestures only made me think of the agony it must be to hold them. Your pictures of the Queen, of Jesus, of Great Scenes from Shakespeare by Frederick Hardcastle, were all like that.

I went on at The Star Theatre in Bradford. Before the stage curtains opened, the chairman introduced me by banging out an art lecture with his gavel. 'And now we have the extraordinary and sensational Camellia Snow, in Mr Oscar Wilde's famous phrase, turning art into life . . .'

There followed five minutes further hectoring drivel, because you had bribed him. Then came drums and a chorus from *Aïda* played by a string band. The curtain rolled back and there I was, illuminated by one of the extravagant fads that were driving the manager towards bankruptcy: electricity.

Thank G-d I'm slim. In a loose skirt trailing over my sandals, no corset and naked above the waist apart from two metal cups on my breasts, a slave bangle on my arm, a jug balanced on my shoulder, I stood in line with half a dozen other music-hall tyros. Except for myself, all of them were genuine 'maidens', dragged in off the street. Some of them were prostitutes whose clients sat in the audience. I was the leading member, about to dip my jug into the well that was painted upon the backcloth.

Except that for two minutes none of us was to move. The sight was supposed to raise gasps of surprise that humans could have the motionless characteristics of wax. Thus a breast or an ankle could almost be exposed; through a loophole of the law, you might say! For the *tableau* didn't exactly imitate Hardcastle's painting; we showed a little more than he would, for his posh salons and art galleries. But if you moved a muscle, they'd nab you and prosecute you for indecency. That made us hold our breaths, I can tell you. I believed there were detectives in the audience and certainly there were nosey parkers from the Vice Protection Society, trying to catch one of us girls blinking, so that we could be hustled off to the clink.

I felt as much at a loss without something to say and do as a smoker is without a pipe in his hands. I hadn't anticipated what effect it would have on me to swallow my stories and jokes. My face probably showed anger. I found it very hard to hold the calm smile belonging, so I was instructed, to Andromache's aloof and dignified acceptance of her fate. But I *was* the star of the show.

The curtain fell and we all thankfully trooped off for a consoling drink at the pub over the road. And I must say that I did enjoy the company of the girls who formed the rest of the *tableau*, common as they were.

'Do you know what 'appened to f———g Sacco, the Fasting Champion?' one of them said. ''E starved 'imself to f———g death by doing *vivants*, lying for fifty days in a glass case while people filed past and gawped. 'E took his f———g act all over the world, until the day come they lifted 'im out of 'is case an' 'e was f———g dead.'

*

Being a lady *is* half way to being a *tableau vivant*, when you think of it.

I soon realised that I was not merely appearing to be, from time to time, a woman. I was actually turning into one. I was becoming 'captive Andromache' – many a serious word said in jest, as they say. My periods as Jack steadily seemed less real to me than my times as Camellia.

I confessed this to you.

'Now,' you pointed out, gleaming, 'you have no money problems and you can concentrate upon being yourself.'

Which is quite funny, when you think of it: my being 'myself'.

You saw this female shaping herself under Mrs Simpson's instruction and you worshipped it. You had an extraordinary capacity for worship. Some do have it more than others. And I, instead of being the artist of a precarious drag-act conducted upon the stage, safe from doing myself any damage because it was a mere game for a short time, was flattered into becoming the victim of another's fantasy.

I saw that my role in life was to become your Unattainable Woman. And why not? I asked myself – fatally.

Because worship, I found, is not the same thing as love. It is much colder and has no consideration for the other's desires. Worship seeks only to please itself, though it appears not to do so. That is why objects of worship can be sacrificed with ecstasy; be slaughtered and burned. Can you not see, today, old men who worship and envy youth, sacrificing it with mad ecstasy to the War?

Whereas no one gives up or hurts what they love. Though they might criticise it, they will die themselves to protect it.

*

I tenderly loved you for making my life a comforting unity of my inner and outer worlds. But I was denied the resources of real women. I couldn't join the Ladies' Sewing Circle, the Smoke Abatement Society, or the St Jude's Church Committee, could I?

In their place, I could imagine other satisfactions. You could have shown me; you were the older one. You hardly touched me. Sometimes I longed for it. When I came to your room after I had drunk too much, surely you guessed that I wanted you to show me some affection? Set in your ways, you could not unbend. You were too – *Victorian*, dash it!

And then, as my role was to excite you as 'the Unattainable One', nothing could be done anyway, could it?

The desire would come; the one I'd thought I'd had for Sylvia, the chemist's daughter, and now meant for you. What was I to do with it after you said, 'No'? What *was* I to do, to uncoil myself?

Throw off my glad-rags, become Jack Shuttleworth again and walk the streets.

Friday night, the working-man's pay night which meant a hundred music nights, entertainment nights, called with an excitement that reached me even in The Hollies, where Joseph and Mona were paid with faithful precision. I could visualise it as a sparkle all over Yorkshire. In the smoky villages under the shadows of chapel and mill, with the moorland a colossal, windy barreness all around, the respectable would be off to a choir-singing, a lantern slide show, or an improving lecture organised by their betters; the middling respectable would go to a band concert; and the disreputable would bury themselves in the public houses with fiddlers and singers. The different audiences would no more speak to one another, though they passed in the narrow village passageways and cartways, than would the brethren of differing chapels.

In the towns were the theatres and the music halls. Joseph would be off to either the Oddfellows Hall or The Mitre public house. Why shouldn't I?

I changed into Jack's clothes and left a note saying, *Don't worry about me. I have some business to attend to. Will be back soon. Do not wait up. J.*

Yes — *J.* Not Camellia; but was it short for Jack or Jacky or Jacqueline? you would wonder. I could be a tease, too.

And out I went. Out, busting with unexpected (well, not too unexpected), frightening desires. Out of the gates on to the Albert Promenade, flabbergasted to find no one took a blind bit of notice of me.

It was December; an especially grimy, damp month in the North. Drizzling. The grey grease, a solvent of sulphurous filth in the rain, coated the pavements and made them slippery. I gulped the air, so grateful for it, so grateful, even though it was cold and dirty. But it was *real* air, I said to myself as I walked downhill under the grim, bare, dripping branches that were like strands of battered lead; like pipes of leaking plumbing, overhanging the gardens.

I felt as daring and frightened as when I had first gone out in drag. Afraid that I might be betrayed by the traces of make-up ingrained in my skin, by my walk, by the way I now had of carrying my clothes which I could no longer help, by my voice as it was trained to sound, and by the cast of my mind surely revealed to all who overheard me when I opened my mouth in some public house that I would enter – soon, soon. Afraid that the desires I had suppressed, ever since Mary scared the life out of me in the workhouse, might leap out of my unguarded mouth and bring the policeman running.

I intended to drop down, down, down as far as I could out of Skircoat Moor, until once again I reached the lowest part of Halifax and the common people. *My* common people. I descended through Park Road, Savile Road and St John's Lane to Wards End. To my left were Barum Top and Barum Bottom; there's names to make a dog laugh! By the splendours of the Albert Statue and the Theatre Royal, I turned into Horton Street where it grew more seedy with commercial properties. There, too, was Dodds Mill Furnishers; not a stylish emporium but more like a factory itself, noisy and smelly with loom parts, with boxes of screws and bolts wrapped in oily paper; at one end, a frugal counter and a boxed-in office where the money was collected for you.

Woodal, Nicholson and Company's carriage factory, Bracken and Sons' paper warehouse, two or three wool warehouses, a wheelwright's and a cabinet factory were squeezed into courtyards between Horton Street and the southern side of the market hall, by the fish and game stalls. It was a place rich with the smells of glue, wood, machine oil and fish. At each step sunk into this foul, human region, I felt better.

At the end of Horton Street I turned left, where a couple of Temperance hotels face the railway station. Don't be deceived; they drink hard enough in the poverty-stricken jumble of streets behind – in between the long strands of the noisy, steamy railway sidings, and the back of the Market Hall and Square Chapel; in Alfred Street, Hatton Fold and Cripple Gate, where poverty, industry, the gas works and the workshops of industrial craftsmen swamp the gentility of the parish church; under the shadow of Beacon Hill.

Clean, brave people, fighting off dirt: that is what I noticed. They were housed in courtyards that the sun could not reach. They lived in terraces without gardens, opening on to streets where the horses left their manure, dissolved in rain, to pour in a thick yellow fluid along the gutters. Being so much nearer Dean Clough and other factories, their homes were that much more thickly coated with soot. The sky was that much more clouded. But how brave and clean the women, especially, were – their shawls, their aprons, their laughs, their bits of artificial lace! How futile but brave their efforts!

They scrubbed the pavements between their house walls and the gutters. Oh, you d——d soppy fool, Jack Shuttleworth, you wanted to kiss them, you had tears in your eyes as you saw them scrubbing on their hands and knees! You sentimental idiot, dash it, you loved them!

Do you know what they used, Mr Dodds – you, who hardly looked at the poor; do you know what they used, Mr Dodds?

They scrubbed with what they call 'donkey stone' – a yellow stone acquired by trading old rags or old iron with a pedlar who leads a donkey and cart along the streets, crying 'Any old rags! Any old rags!'

By such means, women who would do anything to hold the filth at bay scrubbed the public pavements, even in the drizzle, yes, even as the black rained down and speckled the still-damp, golden areas of cleansed stone before their very eyes. Why did they not cry at the futility of their eternal battle with dirt?

Because it was Friday when the men's wages, or some of them, came to the home fireside for an evening of bartering, bullying, humiliation, male swagger and abandon. That was why they did it. In the fading winter daylight, I wandered through the women's waiting world as they anticipated their menfolk's return. Penelopes of the scrubbed doorstep and the uncertain wage packet; that's what they were. Already I sensed excitability and tension. Uncertainty, bullying, rape and violence threatened. The man with his wages in his hand held a club, a battering organ of rape, or even (could it be?) a sweetmeat-bribe. He *could* take his wife out, or buy her a present. All the women knew what their neighbours' husbands would do with their pay, even though few would talk about it.

I was likely to be missing my dinner, so I went into a cluttered shop at the corner of a terrace, where they sold beer and lace, syrup and sugar. I went in to buy chocolate or a pie.

One woman there was telling others that she had 'a good husband'. For her, Friday was hardly a high tide at all. The only difference was that she carried herself in a superior fashion, knowing the purgatory that others suffered; those who did not follow *The Way*. She was a chapel woman. 'He hands me over his wage-packet complete,' she boasted. She would divide the contents into several tins: one for food, one towards the children's education, one for the rent, one for a little indulgence when Christmas came round and one for deposits with the Halifax Building Society. The words *self-sacrifice, deposit, savings, building society* and, finally, *death* had a spice of righteousness upon her tongue.

167

Like you, I shudder whenever I come across that tone. The other women had husbands who would fall in through the door many hours after their respectable neighbour's coins had dropped, one, two, three, four, with a sound clink into the box dedicated to the building society, so I saw them bristle in anger.

For instance, a woman with not an ounce of fat on her anywhere. Stringy hair. She looked like an old, gnawed bone thrown out to the dogs. No need for her to recount her story to me. I could tell it for her. She see her husband's pay-packet whole? For that, you know, is the great divide: between the men who bring their pay-packets home unopened, and those who keep their earnings secret. All she could hope for was that her husband would be too drunk to beat and rape her. She would gladly (well, almost) sacrifice 'breadwinning' money for the safety of receiving, late on Friday night, an impotent weakling whom she could put to bed like a child, mopping up his vomit during the early hours.

Yet, as I knew, she would despise as an unmanly pansy the husband who brought home a wage-packet complete for his wife to open and inspect. There's nowt so queer as folk.

Meeting my expectant, nervous Penelopes in the corner shop, I knew that their dependent lives at their core were not so different to mine, though superficially so.

And yet, though I drifted through their world, later on I wanted to be where the money was spent; where the men went and maybe, maybe, took the women if they chose. I thirsted for my audience, though I knew what sort they were; what tales were wanted and needed by the tired working man.

I'll tell you about the art and the audience I've given my life to so gladly. Afraid and ashamed of the impotence induced by long hours of labour, they counterfeited virility by roaring at crude descriptions of sexual failure: the cuckold; the woman who longs for it but can't get it; the man who can't. It was so as to pretend that these things were not true of themselves. They laughed at jokes about sex as they knew it, an unhealthy course through incest and semi-hidden fumblings before children and grandparents in overcrowded, thin-walled cottages. Hating the articulate wit with which their betters have brow-beaten them for centuries, they turn to the raw humour that runs out of the bowels. It was your wit that estranged you from them, Garrick. When you assayed a witticism, they turned away to growl into their beer; when you turned your back, they retaliated by saying something crude. Something as distasteful to you as your wit was to them. I saw it, I saw it, many a time in the halls! Wit that comes from the head and from the intelligence is from their point of view 'stuck up'. Physical beauty, too, is 'stuck up'. The working-man's young body being soon broken by labour, male beauty is detested as a pretension; unless it is worshipped as a private vice. You can laugh at anything that's 'stuck up'. And at anything about dirt; about f——g or p——g. Compelled to labour in filth, the working man makes having a stomach for dirt into a matter of pride.

Then, there is the morality of drink.

'How many pints have yee supped tonight, old lad?'

'Only 'bout ten. So far.'

'Ten! Get some more ale down yer, lad. Are't'a pansy or summat?'

Drink is a test of character and the important place to be king is in the tap-room. On pay day, especially, it is improper and unmanly to remain sober.

Laugh at people from somewhere, anywhere, else. Wealthy people from the South, especially. Londoners, especially. Foreigners. Full of a secret, shameful feeling that it is from lack of imagination that they remain toiling in this place, they claim rootedness as a virtue. Not to know Halifax as well as one does oneself is a matter for contempt and shame.

Above all else, my working class is a pack, reducing the ambition to leave, to lead, to be different, expressive or artistic. You must be full of hatred or at least pretended contempt for those who are not part of it. Make fun of vanity, of southerners, of pretensions, of impotence and cuckoldry; praise fighting, drinking and excrement. I had the brew of such entertainment in my heart. People would come along to hear me because they were choked in misery and wanted, wanted, to live and laugh. Like me, to be done with pain.

In the early evening, I went to The Mitre public house and music hall on Market Street, where they were making preparations. The turns to come were scribbled over the bar. As I watched the acts nipping in for a quick one before they got ready, I was aching to perform.

The landlord disappeared. He reappeared, washed, flushed, dressed in a yellow waistcoat and red neckerchief for the part of chairman.

'You've some interesting billings tonight,' I began.

He merely grunted.

'I do a turn or two myself, as a matter of fact.'

'I can see the grease paint. What do you do?'

He scrutinised me over a glass that he was wiping. He was pretending that he had something better to think about than me.

'Monologues. Comic Yorkshire tales. Have you heard the one about . . .'

'Let me tell you something, kid. Tyros are always coming in here, but we do all our bookings through an agent. I'd like to give beginners a helping hand, but they're apt to drive customers away and I can't afford to patronise at the expense of my own pocket. I'd soon be out of business and in the workhouse, wouldn't I?'

'I'm experienced. Worked the halls for years. Been at Liston's. Hen and Chickens. Done the Star in Bradford.'

Aren't you with a booking agent?'

'I was with Deetrich's in Manchester. I've not been in Halifax long. I just popped in, saw what was going on and thought you might be interested.'

'Got a letter heading?'

'I'm afraid I've not got round to it, yet.'

'Where are you living, then?'

'I'm residing with a gentleman on Skircoat Moor.'

'Oh, I see. What's your name?'

'Jack Shuttleworth.'

'That your stage name?'

'Yes,' I lied.

'Never heard of you. What turns you done, did you say?'

'Listen to this one . . .'

I threw a glance to his barman and also to an old codger sitting in the corner. The landlord understood perfectly well that I caught the old boy's eye *because* he wasn't interested, in order to show that I could reap an audience and that I was a pro.

'*There was these two brothers, see. Archibald had a terrible st . . . st . . . stutter and Cyril had a limp, wi' one leg shorter than t'other. They were walking along t'road, see, when Archibald said . . .*'

You know the rest. My three listeners were laughing. From the first word, I was in heaven once again. But the barman was making me uneasy. It was the way he looked at me and smiled.

More customers were coming in for the evening entertainment. Were gathering at my part of the bar, wanting to listen to me.

'What other turns do you do? What did you do at the Star?'

'Has your missus got a couple of old hats or an old frock I could borrow?'

'Ah! I thought there might be something o' that sort about you.' But he was smiling at me. 'Sarah!' he shouted. '*Sarah!*'

'What are't'bawling abart?'

'Get us one of your old 'ats, will yer?'

'What for?'

'And an old frock. Ne'er mind what for, do as you're told. Chap 'ere 'as a use for it.'

Sarah appeared.

'Who wants it?'

'That chap there. He's going to try a turn.'

'Two hats,' I said. 'If you can lay your hands upon them, madam. I do two women talking to each other and as each speaks I change my hat.'

She didn't return my smile.

'One o' them sort, are yee? I'll 'ave 'em disinfected after.'

'Go and do as tha's bid and stop yappin',' her husband said.

'Your lady-wife doesn't think too much of the idea,' I remarked.

'My wife thinks what I tell her to think!'

I was avoiding the barman's eye. I felt fear and excitement, though I didn't like him much. He was about my age, gingery and rat-like.

171

'Have you heard the one about Victoria and Prince Albert after the first night of their honeymoon?' I said. '"*How did you get on last night?" the Baroness Lehzen asked him. "Sometimes on von side," Albert answered, "sometimes on der oder."*'

The barman laughed the loudest. Yes, he was still trying to gain my attention.

Sarah returned with a frock and two hats. It put her in an even worse mood that we broke into laughter when she did not know what it was about. There and then, I took off my jacket to put the frock over my shirt and trousers. Rammed one of the hats upon my head. It was the kind I like; black, with pheasants' tail-feathers drooping over it.

Sarah was just the type to wear a silly hat.

'*There was this old lady walking up from Barum Bottom to Barum Top, on a wet day wi' 'er skirt pulled over her head. . . .*'

I pulled the hem of the skirt up to my neck and grimaced round the bar.

'"*Eh, Missus!" a young scamp shouts. "You're showing your legs!" "Ne'er mind my legs," she answers. "They're sixty year old, but my 'at's a new one!"*'

I was booked for that night, to go on between the conjuror and the farmyard impersonations.

'If you want scenery and props we haven't got none,' the landlord said. 'We're not the bloody Oxford. Harry'll 'elp you on the pianer.'

'Don't need nothing, old sport. I can get by just with my talent. *Ra-ta-tat!*'

I danced a few light steps while he filled my glass. I still wouldn't look at the barman. I didn't even want to know his name. Drag, once again, was saving me from something worse.

The conjuror came on and was lousy. But he did me a favour. They'd appreciate anything, now.

'"*I say, I say, I say! I believe that Prince Albert is going with the Queen to Windsor!" "He'll go further than that by morning." "What do you mean, old girl?" "Why, he'll go in at* Bushy, *pass* Virginia Water, *on through* Maidenhead *and leave* Staines *behind!"*'

If you'd heard me making jokes like this, wouldn't I have sweated! I changed my accent.

'"*A chap come to our door, Mrs Bolton, with his hair plastered back and so polite. He wanted me to go and vote in the Election. I couldn't go now, I said. Someone has to mind the baby, keep an eye on the oven, fetch in the washing. But perhaps tomorrow. Tomorrow's too late, he said. Didn't I care about my children's upbringing? Aye, I did, I told him. We've already sent one to the grammar school so he wouldn't have to work as hard as his father and all it's done for him is to get him a schoolteacher as a wife that can make a speech better than she can make a suet pudding.*"

'"*What party were he from, Mrs Sykes?*"

'"*How do I know what party? It weren't no bundle of fun, I'll tell you that. I don't know whether it were an 'am tea or a funeral. It must be like prising butter out of a dog's throat, getting folk to your party, I said to him.*"

'"*Well, I'm capped at thee not knowing what he were canvassing for. Thou should have asked him a question or two.*"

"*I did, though. I asked him if he were walking out with a young lady yet, and what her name was, or if he were wed, cos if he wasn't, I knew someone that was looking. I 'ad me scent on!*"

That brought a laugh.

'"*Mrs Slater says she'll vote for anyone who's a nice fellar and will bring down the price of gas. She cannot thoile to put a penny in the meter just to bake a loaf . . .*"'

I was paid a guinea for my night's work and offered an arrangement any time I wanted one. Kept in ale for half the night long. I was thrilled just to be earning my own money instead of being dependent. The less I needed the barman, that is, the more I fought free of him, the more persistent he was. I believe I totally rebuffed him. Thinking of you. Pickled in ale, I was hardly able to find my way home. But back in the early hours to The Hollies. Snug in my housecoat for elevenses. Feeling very sorry for myself. I wonder if you realised what I missed with you? But The Hollies *was* the only place I could enjoy dressing – properly.

'Where were you last night, Camellia?'

'Out.'

'Where?'

I did not answer.

'I know where. Joseph watched you in The Mitre.'

'I know. I saw him. He told me when I first come here that he went regular.'

'First came here. Went regularly. Why did you do it? What did you want?'

'Life.'

'*Life*? Did you find it?'

'Oh yes, I found it.'

'Are you satisfied?'

With a sneer.

'Yes, I'm satisfied.'

*

There is one feature of Skircoat Moor I haven't mentioned: electricity. The Moor was very advanced in that respect, due to the experiments of its grandest resident, Mr Louis John Crossley, a son of the founder of the carpet manufactory. Mr Crossley had died at the age of forty-nine in 1891: that is, before I came to The Hollies, therefore I never met him. For my idea of him I have to depend upon yourself who, may I say, had been invited to Moorside on several occasions. Mr Crossley had been dogged by ill-health, but the light of his life, as you put it, had been his electrical inventions.

It was not possible to live on the Moor and escape what was termed 'the romance of electricity', because at Moorside a couple of huge gas-engines developed twenty thousand candle power of electricity through a couple of dynamos. Crossley even had a copper wire laid to Dean Clough, well over a mile away, along which to send his electricity for the use of his factory. He also developed the prototype for the world's first electric tram – the one built to run along the Golden Mile at Blackpool. He designed a model tramway to take children around the Moorside gardens.

And, built upon the roof of Moorside, next to what at that time was the largest telescope in the world, was an electric lighthouse. Under a Gothic spire, a huge lens was able to project a beam for many miles. It was said that it was possible to read a newspaper one and a half miles away by its light. The light was still brought into play by his descendants and often I saw it flitting over the sky as, I imagine, the aurora borealis flits over the arctic night.

I can't make sense of the stuff myself – electricity; don't know whether it's juice flowing down the wires, or what the d——l it is; and as a matter of fact it seems to me that no one else understands it very well, either. It is my impression that the only thing you can rely on is its *un*reliability. The blessed stuff is always breaking down.

But inspired by your illustrious neighbour, you grew fond of tinkering with electrical contraptions, though thank God you were never foolish enough to rely totally upon them, for I have heard of people being killed by electricity. You mixed your lights, with their mysterious tendency to extinguish themselves, with dependable oil lamps. To some extent Joseph was trained to cope with the crises produced by electricity and the gardener cum coachman might have proved very successful at dealing with them, as he possessed a talent for mechanical things, but his natural surliness created an impediment when approaching anything new; so it was usually you, a born amateur, tinkerer and marveller at the world's new wonders, who fumbled around with a box of safety matches and a candle; who put out minor fires; and who called for oil lamps as the electrical lights flickered and died.

Mr Crossley used his electricity to develop refinements for the telephone. He had a wire stretched to Northowram Hall so as to show how sound could be transmitted along it. The first Bell telephone in Britain, let me tell you, was linked to a system devised by Louis John Crossley for Dean Clough. Then he improved upon it, patenting the Crossley Transmitter to amplify the faintness of Bell's telephone invention and give it a clearer sound over the crackle and background hum. He used his wires and transmitter to enable the worshippers in the Congregational Chapel at Saltaire, Bradford, a dozen miles away, to listen in astonishment to a service conducted from the Square Chapel in Halifax. He also transmitted a church service from Square Chapel thirty miles to Manchester, using the signalling wires of the Lancashire and Yorkshire Railway Company. Beat that!

So naturally Halifax was used to the telephone system earlier than other towns. It was ahead of the world with a whole gamut of mechanical inventions and means of production. It was that kind of town.

An interest in mechanical inventions was something you inherited from your father and you soon had a telephone installed. One wound this blessed handle, which I was told was to produce the electricity, and if one listened carefully, one could hear a voice; if one wasn't out of breath from turning the handle, one could talk down it, too.

*

A born optimist, you never could be persuaded that such cranky inventions were a waste of time. In 1897, as a further step towards 'keeping up', you bought a Daimler motor car that had been manufactured under licence in England by the Motor Manufacturing Company. That was more fun than either telephones or electricity. Together we had looked at some motor cars on show in Leeds and I had hoped that you would purchase a Lanchester . . . a two-seater phaeton which I thought a more flash vehicle. However, now we could poke among the horse-drawn traffic of the streets and lanes. We could visit theatres and explore the countryside.

A new exclamation entered our language. *'Pip, pip!'*

People waved, laughed and followed us. Well, we gave them something to follow!

Ours was one of the first motors to be seen in Halifax. In the earliest days, the garden-boy walked ahead of us with a red flag. Joseph was trained, unwillingly, to drive and given a uniform in order to take us to beauty-spots. William Wordsworth, the poet, recorded that the smoke of Lancashire tainted the air of the Lake District, one hundred miles away; but for those of us who lived in the pool of muck and dirt, it seemed that we had to travel only twenty miles, as far as Ilkley, to be clear of it; such are relative values.

Nature was so lovely, by the rivers, along the woodland paths. I have never since been able to enjoy nature and beauty as I did with you. It has never seemed quite the same to look

176

at a flower, the coils of a waterfall, or a trout in the shadows under a bridge. You would point out the beauty of simple things that no one else noticed, butterflies, dandelions, small birds, and sweep me along with your enthusiasm, as a child does.

I would take my Box-Brownie along. We were snapped at Hardcastle Crags, the Cow and Calf Rocks on Ilkley Moor; Rievaulx, Fountains and Bolton abbeys. I was charmed, I can tell you, at finding a picturesque scene reproduced in miniature, a jewel in the glass of my viewfinder. I used to shine up the little window with my handkerchief, you remember, struggling to get the dust from the corners; then, as now, never quite succeeding.

Tea-rooms were beginning to open in some of these places. We went to ones in the country from spring to autumn and in Ilkley, York or Harrogate during the winter, so that we became connoisseurs. Cyclists and hikers from the towns were also taking to the hills, many of them working-class people. The men carried rucksacks and wore breeches with thick stockings and boots, while the girls were sometimes in shocking bloomers or in Rational Dress.

You had a special fondness for tea places which had secluded gardens where they served the better class of trade. By then, almost always I went out in drag. My motoring costume, a rubber or leather coat and a veil, made me feel quite secure and when I was ready, I could peel it off and show myself as more unambiguously feminine underneath.

You were so tender and protective, and this I found *most* enjoyable. You would spring into the correct manner for a gentleman's behaviour towards a lady, asking what I wanted and ordering it; brushing against me, touching my fingers, holding my hand, even. Putting my arm through yours. Inquiring after my welfare. The other customers, and the waitresses lost in their own preoccupations, noticed nothing.

But you could be a frightful tease sometimes. Couldn't you, my dear? Admit it! More than once, you made me take your photograph as you posed, with some abandon I might say, next to a pretty waitress. Your arm around her waist, perhaps. You knew that I was burning with jealousy. That was partly why you did it.

You were completely uninhibited once you got on to your own merry-go-round, your fun fair. You could go anywhere and do anything in that mood. If society is outraged, that is society's problem, you believed. You yourself would be merely amused.

Very often the girl would be full of amusement, too, because, after she had taken a second look, she had not been quite able to make out what I was; or she'd had a quiet word with Joseph when you sent her over with some cakes for him, waiting seethingly in the motor car. In front of these girls, you would tease me cruelly, oh, don't deny it, saying that I was your sister or your niece, and I was choked with jealousy. The photograph when it was printed would show you beaming and relaxed. The girls with whom you flirted thought that the sun shone out of your —. No; I mustn't say it.

Sitting among the roses and the strips of lawn while the waitress ferried tea, scones and that northern luxury, 'rum butter', I convinced myself that an explanation of your character would help you. Perhaps I was a bit woozy from the rum in the butter; they were never so stingy with it in those days.

'If you like their style so much, why do you keep Mona on?'

I wanted to get rid of her and employ a decent-looking, young house-parlourmaid. I couldn't understand why you didn't want that, too, since neat waitresses gave you such a *frisson*.

'Because she was with Mother,' you blandly answered me as you always had. 'Maybe, if you are not happy as you are, we should employ you as parlourmaid? Maybe it's not good for you to be lazy?' You laughed at me. 'Camellia, I don't have any change. Dip into your purse, dear, and give the girl a tip.'

And the girl thanked *you*, keeping her eye on *you* while *I* was compelled to fork out a sixpence from my pocket money!

Oh, you knew how to be cruel.

Our excursion was ruined.

When the girl turned her back, 'You're showing off, just to hurt me!' I said, with tears in my eyes.

'Nonsense, Camellia. Calm yourself.'

How reasonable you could be, when it was you who held the cards.

'If I was your servant, I wouldn't be safe for five minutes,' I told you. 'It's only my being a lady that keeps me out of your hands.'

You went white and then red.

'Maybe I'd have some *fun* at last, if I was your housemaid,' I continued. 'Let's try it.'

I'd come close to the bone. Fearing you'd have a heart attack, I let the matter drop. The waitress scowled at me, of course, thinking that the trouble could only be caused by me, for such a nice gentleman could not possibly be at fault.

But letting the matter fall silent would not drive it away. As we sat together behind the glum Joseph, my eyes were pricking with tears. So were yours. The beautiful countryside through which we passed was as far away from us as descriptions of somebody else's dream.

'If you don't want me to say . . .' I began and stopped, my words choking me. I didn't want to break down. 'If I can't say what I think, then all I am is a waxwork.'

We got back into The Hollies, I don't know how. A pair of cripples.

My deciding to say nothing more exasperated me into saying *everything*. Firstly I made a dive for the bottle of Madeira and one of the glasses kept by it in the cupboard. A quick nip of alcohol before I go on stage is my source of Dutch courage, but has as often been my undoing, if I take another. As I did now, very quickly. You said nothing, afraid of violence from me, I think.

'Let me be a parlourmaid, then! Go on! Something might happen! At least it would be a change! Let's try out a new game!'

I took a third glass.

'I'll take a job as a waitress if it will excite you. Anything to stop us being bored.'

I knew only that I was missing something.

I suddenly tore off my wig. I surprised myself.

'Look at me!' I shrieked. 'Look at me, Mr Dodds! *This* is what I am!'

179

You clutched the edge of the table, staring at a mad woman, a mad man, but not speaking.

I ripped my blouse apart. My stitched-on breasts were mere lumps of padding, hanging loose. I thumped my chest.

'This is what I am, Mr Dodds! *This* and *this* and *this*!' I was almost ready to pull down my drawers. 'If we forget it, we'll both end up with the lunatics!'

We stared at each other with nothing to say; do you remember? Truth had broken the shell of our fantasy.

'You had better sit down. *Do* sit down . . .' you said, not knowing whether to call me 'Camellia' or 'Jack'. We were all at sea and I did not even own a name.

Then my greatest fear of all exploded.

'*What will happen to me when you've grown tired of me?*'

'What are you talking about, Camellia?'

'When you want someone else? Am I to be thrown out then?'

'I would never do that.'

'And what happens if you . . . when you . . . *You're so much older than I am!*'

A sentence, a gesture, could smash so frail an egg as ours.

*

At least I succeeded in reducing Mona to the ranks and in introducing a parlourmaid, whom you enjoyed as much as I did. To that extent I broke your mother's hypnotic rule. Though it was mostly Mrs Simpson who won the victory. 'A necessity if we are to maintain the degree of politeness consistent with the introduction of Camellia,' Mrs Simpson informed you in our little madhouse; pronouncing 'necessity' as if it was French, *nécessité*, and the remainder in the exaggerated RP of one hiding a native accent.

How could we find someone with more style but as much discretion to replace Mona? Unless one speaks of those in the employ of such as the Palmers and the Crossleys, who are our equivalent of the real nobs, the Asquiths, the Bonham-Carters, the Devonshires, for example, servants in Yorkshire are, like every other member of the working classes here, independent-spirited and full of Chartist principles. It's the very devil to get them to live in, for example. Many of the houses flanking Skircoat Moor have courtyards with separate entrances where reside cooks, maids, coachmen and gardeners who refuse to be tied to the homes of their employers, 'at their beck and call'. Without such an arrangement, it would be near impossible to find servants at all in Halifax. I approve of that independence and admire them for it, but it presents a terrible problem when you have been handed Mrs Beeton's *Household Management* as your model and are expected to amuse someone as contradictory as you. The candidate had to fit in with our unusual household, yet not be too unusual herself; to understand us, after it had been explained to her that I was a particular kind of artist, needing to practise at home; but not be nosey. We needed someone without a family hanging round. A spinster would be ideal. She would need to be discreet.

We all three agreed upon the above requirements, which amount to everyone's ideal servant. That is, someone who is hardly human. Also, she must be young. It was I who wanted that, having it in mind that I might find a companion like Ethel.

But not flighty. That was your insistence because you didn't quite trust my conversion from a young man.

Mrs Simpson said that she should be of 'good appearance', that is, tall; clean and 'amenable to genteel practice'.

Where do you find such a one? You suggested that we turn to the Catholic Agency for Distressed Girls, but Mrs Simpson and I doubted that we'd find there someone of the requisite sophistication, experience, intelligence and discretion. In any case, most of them had illegitimate babies, as well as parents to keep.

We interviewed five females from a more ordinary Servants' Registry and settled upon Sarah Goodband, the daughter of a coal-miner from Barnsley. She had left her home to work in a Todmorden cotton mill, but hadn't liked it, and we thought she fitted all our requirements. She was certainly a good-looker.

Mrs Beeton told me all about the duties of servants and what their appearance should be. I, as the mistress, chose Sarah's uniform from a catalogue of the Army and Navy

Stores, London, and it was delivered by rail. But apart from instructing on how to interview and then how to dismiss servants, the manual told you nothing about talking to them in between.

And you wouldn't have expected it, but — wasn't Sarah a snob! After the cotton mill, she was looking for a quite different life. She wanted to be clean, so with her background she thought herself lucky to find something much better than a housemaid's position that would ruin her hands. She wanted to have good manners. She admired Mrs Simpson and aped her.

You never knew about this, Mr Dodds; at least, I don't think you did, for I never told you; but when Sarah first appeared in my room to serve me, I, looking for a friend, told her a funny story. My first gaffe.

I was seated at my dressing-table. I was wearing one of my own favourite fantasies, a gown definitely to be worn only on special evening occasions. It was made of satin net, the bodice built on to a boned silk foundation. The gored skirt was made of seven flared panels, the rear two of them longer, being gathered in at the waist and forming a train. I wore it with a breastplate of silver chains and the whole ensemble was set off with a choker of imitation pearls, a neckpiece like Princess Alexandra's. As Sarah believed, in those early days, that all this rig was for a 'rehearsal', I thought I'd better put on a performance.

'*There was this chap was fond of going out drinking and leaving his young wife at home,*' I began. '"*I've plenty of knitting to do, I can get on with the washing and the ironing and the baking and the garden in the summer when you're out. Only I get so lonely,*" *she said.* "*Never mind,*" *he answered her.* "*I don't like to think of you by yourself, lass, so I'll get thee a kitten.*"'

Sarah smiled. But as my story continued, she started fidgeting with her Army and Navy Stores dress and wanted to be off. I would have asked her to sit down, but I knew that it wouldn't have been right.

'*Chap went out and had a skinful of ale. When he got home, she told him,* "*Ee, it's right grand wi' kitten purring on the hearth, and I can get on wi' my sewing, and my*

*washing, and my ironing o' your shirts, and my digging
in the garden . . ."*

'Some months went by, and then she weren't so happy.
"What are t'crying about, lass?" he asked her, when he came
home and before he fell asleep. "Well," she told him, "it
were grand when t'kitten stopped at home, but now it's
grown into a tom cat, it's never 'ere wi' me." "We'll 'ave
to do something about that," chap said. He took the cat to
the vet's and had it neutered. It cost him fifty shillings.*

'Next night, both he and the cat stayed at home. "Eee, it's
right grand having cat purring on the hearth again, and you
sitting at the fireside, smoking your pipe, and I can get on wi'
my darning and my washing and my ironing . . ." "Aye," says
the chap. "But if I could have my fifty shillings and yon tom
cat could get its tackle back, you'd see neither of us!"'

Sarah wanted to titter but, no, it wasn't the done thing. I
could have told such a joke to Joseph; not to Sarah. Imagine
her, dressed up like that, listening to my flipping music-hall
yarn while she was playing her part as parlourmaid. It is
only in real life that people can step aside from their roles
and still be credible.

*

However, the day came when Mrs Simpson refused to play
her part anymore. She disapproved of what you were 'doing'
to me.

She had been quiet all morning, unable to resist an unlady-
like biting of her nails.

'Garrick is behaving exactly as his own father did with
his poor mother.'

I told her I couldn't see the link.

'He plucked his Eugenia Fanny Watts off the stage, too,
where she didn't seem a real person. Where she was "clothed
in the light of theatrical glamour", as one might say. Once
ensconced in The Hollies, it was a different kettle of fish. She
turned into a real person again and her theatre passion became
a nuisance to him. He wrote his own part for her. Dictated
her life for her. I can't go through all that again, watching
it happen to you, Camellia. Garrick Dodds understood *all*
this when he was a young man and swore he'd *never* be

like his father. What's happened to him since to make him forget, I don't know. But I won't be part of it, dear Jack, and I'm leaving. I've already told him so. It isn't any good for anyone and you were meant for something better. You yourself should leave.'

'I can't leave.'

'Why not?'

'I'm too fond of him, now.'

·7·

A S we all know, 1901 is the year in which occurred the most significant event of our time. The most important in civilisation, probably, when in January our Queen died. When the whole nation turned over and went into mourning.

Well, it's a funny thing, but there's not a person you meet who can't remember exactly what they were doing when they received the news.

We were playing snakes and ladders, when Sarah came in.

Within a day or two, the whole town and every village was smothered in an extra fall of black to rival the soot. Black had been quite fashionable before because of Victoria's mourning for Albert, but nothing like this. Black drapes on the buildings, black clothes everywhere, black curtains. Your pictures of the Queen were draped. Even Mona changed her brown dress for a black one – probably envious of Sarah. Joseph and the boy strung banners of black cotton across the garden, their grey breaths blooming over the frost.

For most of the day, a band with its instruments wound in ribbons of black crêpe played funeral dirges on the Moor. Each afternoon through that week between the announcement of her death and the funeral on 2 February I was dressed in black silk, for I must have been one of the first of the nation to be clad in mourning.

The death of the Queen was much more significant for you than for most of us. You suffered, not merely as a member of a distraught nation that had lost its mother; for you, it was a personal crisis. You really believed that so long as she sat on the throne you had some consolation for the loss of your own mother.

You were made for mourning. It was your vocation. Was this huge grief our ultimate fantasy, and as far as you and I could go?

Then whatever could we do next?

185

Imagine me a day or two after the announcement. I sit at my window. It is amazing how much this discreet lady, Camellia Snow, can discover about the outside world simply by peeping and listening, supplemented with gossip and news. One river flows through you and the other quite different one comes through Sarah Goodband. Most ladies pick things up from listening in at the fringes of life.

It is drawing close to four o'clock. Joseph, some time ago, went indoors by the yard steps, for I heard him scraping his boots and coughing; he smokes too much shag. He has gone to collect you from the bank. The gardener's boy has returned home to his mother and fifteen – or is it fourteen – brothers and sisters, so I wonder what tale he tells them, the little beast. Mona has gone around the house to stoke the fires. Darkness is settling in, but I could, if I wished, switch on the electric light.

There you are! My lord and master. I hear the motor car turn in between those soppy stone lions at the gate.

You reach the house-front. After a moment, Joseph drives the car round to the back. You enter the hallway. I can hear you hand over to Sarah your hat, your black worsted coat and your stick with a silver knob. Between my door and the head of the stair, where I always am at this point, I overhear you comment to Sarah on the weather, just as you always do. I hear another voice. I look down and see what I did not expect, and it startles me. A tall, dignified gentleman.

Palmer.

I recover my composure. I pause at the top step, holding the bannister, one knee slightly projected, until you glance up. You see me smile affectionately, the sort of managed smile one feels able to achieve through layers of Rimmel's Blanc Marimon and Hebe Bloom. Framed for your benefit as you look up the stair is a composition of me in my mourning dress. This is Sarah's signal to exit the stage, left. Mona peeping from the gods.

My performance is gathering momentum as, rustling, loving the silk, I descend and reach the cold, hard terracotta tiles of the hallway.

You introduce your visitor.

'Mr Palmer,' you say, 'meet Camellia.'

You remain straightfaced as you make the 'introduction'. I cannot believe it! A joke, at a time like this? You explain, as always, that I am a 'relative who has moved in for a while'. You know that, as Jack Shuttleworth, I was in Palmer's mansion. Mr Palmer shows no curiosity. Perhaps they have been talking about me already. One must always, *always*, be on one's guard against toffs making a fool of one.

No, I don't think so.

Exuding an air of grief even greater than yours, Mr Palmer kisses the back of my outstretched hand; believe it or not, apparently without realising who I am.

But of course, how could he be expected to, with me so changed?

*

Mr Palmer had never condescended to visit The Hollies before, although I understood that you were both acquainted from attendance on committees, having the same interest in smoke abatement. Even though Palmer owned mills, he was more interested in cutting the Crossleys down to size, and most of all he cared about his park.

I knew that you did not much like Mr Palmer. However, you had found my old patron at the end of his tether, with no pride left and not unwilling to visit a mere tradesman's home in order to kill a little of the time that hung so heavily on him.

I soon realised that I could breathe again. You had not brought him here to tease, but because you could not help yourself from offering Palmer comfort. On the contrary, it was you who were anxious, glancing at one and then the other of us, half expecting the flash of recognition to pass between us, but you never caught it. If anyone was in a position to play games, it was me. I quickly realised that there was no need for me to give anything away, if I did not wish to; and I am actress enough at least for that. Mr Palmer was too distracted to recognise me in an unexpected place and guise.

The three of us took afternoon tea with full ceremony in the dining-room. After Joseph had lit a fire, Sarah served.

What else could we talk about over tea but the Queen? It would be sacrilege to mention anything else. We sat around the huge, oval table, elbows politely clear of the laundered, white cloth. You regurgitated details of the town's plans to upstage the arrangements made by Bradford and Huddersfield. Public functions had been abandoned and the music halls were closed. The D'Oyle Carte Opera Company had stopped its showing of Gilbert and Sullivan's *Patience*; it was aborted at the first interval when the news was announced by the manager. And we had planned to go to *Patience*; I hated missing a treat. The meeting of the Halifax Thursday Cycling Club and the Mayor's Old People's Tea had been cancelled. Visiting day at the workhouse was cancelled, poor devils. Flags were at half mast. The town hall bell had been ordered to be rung. Oh, this funeral would be the grandest entertainment ever.

Mr Palmer hardly spoke. I had never seen such deep gloom. He moved as if he could not take in what he was doing, nor where he was going. Anyone could have led him anywhere, like a child, but it would have to be slowly for his feet were leaden. When he lifted his hands, they weighed like iron. Nonetheless he raised them often, to smoke one after another of his black cigarettes, or to hide his face. He was so self-absorbed that I don't think he would have recognised me even if I hadn't been transformed.

Sarah's white cuffs passed to and fro briefly before my sight as she handed round the cakes and I looked up into her eyes that were longing to smile. After our first hiccup, we had formed quite a relationship and we understood one another.

You sent her for *The Halifax Guardian*. There was a black grid printed over the pages and columns. You folded it to read out a report of 'a trouncing for the Poet Laureate because of some awful verses on the Queen's death'.

'Good old Halifax! That's the style!' I let out.

You did not approve of my levity. I exchanged another glance with Sarah, who was restlessly shifting her weight from one leg to the other and trying not to let it be seen, for she knew that Mr Palmer was a very grand visitor.

'A year of mourning has been announced,' you told us. 'The nation will need every day of it in order to recover. But we never shall. I have always been able to derive comfort from saying, "The Queen's on her throne, in the end everything will be all right." Now it can no longer be said.'

I understood how you felt about the Queen. There was no mother left for any of us, but especially for you. Railway builders, generals and headmasters of public schools, all left without a mother. I could weep for them, the poor devils. Women everywhere must be weeping for their bereft menfolk.

You passed around *The Guardian*. The funeral arrangements were a vast, national music-hall *tableau*. One advertisement showed a mourning dress at ten shillings and eleven pence which looked like a heavily draped bell. Needhams of Halifax announced every kind of material and dress imaginable in black – blouses, costumes, skirts and umbrellas – to enable us to ape the Court's mourning. Purple and black material for draping churches and public buildings was advertised.

You'd have thought that Mr Palmer would at least have been interested in this; that at a time of such drastic change in the textile market, he, being a wool-man, would have trade very much on his mind. From perusing the newspaper, it seemed that everyone else had. The country was already running short of black textiles and anyone who had them ready manufactured was able to take advantage. But those whose warehouses were filled with coloured stuffs were going out of business. One could see this from the knock-down sales of bankrupt stocks of coloureds, while the blacks were rising. The West Yorkshire woollen trade had been thrown into chaos by the Queen's death. Had Mr Palmer been weaving blacks or coloureds? I doubt if he knew himself.

Mr Palmer was compelled to leave the room and during his absence you explained. Palmer's grief was because his wife, the poet, had . . . had . . .

'In fact, it is believed that she killed herself, though it has been hushed up.'

My stomach leaped into my mouth. I saw her so clearly. My dear, batty friend who had taught me so much. She might have been in the room with me. I gagged on my food.

'How?'

'Mr Palmer has influence.'

'I don't mean, how was it hushed up. How did she do it?'

'I believe that she took poison. A most painful way.'

'She wouldn't want to spoil her looks,' I remarked.

I so clearly remembered her making this very point.

Deaths other than the Queen's were either insignificant at this time, or they were absorbed into the magnificence of the greater event. For Mr Palmer, the black banners, the tolling bells and the mourning dress everywhere were for his wife. When he returned to the dining-table I watched him combat his sorrow. He was shattered and unable to take anything in.

I could play no games. I looked at Sarah. When she overheard that his was not an abstract, public mourning, she looked aghast. Coming from a coal-mining district, she knew about sudden death.

You dismissed Sarah. You put your hand across the table, as you had often done to me, and touched the back of Palmer's hand.

'I know what it's like.'

You released your touch from an embarrassingly long exposure.

'It wouldn't be so bad if I could sleep,' Mr Palmer muttered.

He had spoken little in an hour, yet his voice was as hoarse as if he had delivered a public speech. He lifted his head. At last he allowed tears to moisten his eyes.

'How *could* she do this to me! How *could* she leave me! I did *everything* for her, you know. I gave her everything she had.'

'I'm sure you did,' I contributed, trying to be sarcastic. Oh, I knew him from this!

'We had a quiet funeral. It is what she would have wished for.'

He wanted to hush it up!

Nevertheless, I put out my hand to touch Mr Palmer's other hand. You cannot ignore grief like that. He gave me a startled glance. He did not like a strange lady touching him. Perhaps he thought I was common.

'Time is a great healer.'

That sounded odd, coming from you.

'Time is so heavy! I pass hours in counting the minutes.'

The electric lights were not yet switched on, so we could sit without shyness together, each of us holding a hand while through the twilight Mr Palmer uttered his fitful, heavy sentences.

'She never trusted that I loved her.' He shifted his eyes to me. 'Please excuse me, madam. I cannot think what I am saying. She was a wonderful woman, ma'am. Highly talented. A poet.'

'I wish that I had known her.'

'I wish you had, ma'am. You might have been friends.'

'In time you will find yourself able to shoulder the future,' I told him. 'Have confidence.'

He looked at me for a second attentively and brightly; with a fleeting feeling that I was offering some hope.

*

Most of the public drapes disappeared six months after the Queen's death. Among normal people – I mean, among working people – positiveness returned, even more strongly than when Victoria was alive but in mourning. I can't speak for what happened at Court, where, for the ladies, black dresses trimmed with crêpe, black shoes and gloves, black fans, feathers and ornaments, and, for the men, black court dress, black swords and buckles, were the order for a whole year. In Halifax, the tradesmen picked up the new King Edward's gay spirit very quickly and began to anticipate summer cheerfulness lying around the corner in the shape of chapel anniversaries and strawberry teas. The surviving, scurrilous amusements of a certain class of spinners, weavers, rag-pickers, labourers and the destitute continued in smoky hovels. The more sanctimonious, self-improving poor and not-so-poor had the innumerable teas, processions and preaching spectacles organised by the Methodists.

Some of this kind of fun was on the wane. However, Halifax's blossoming prosperity called more and more for genteel forms of entertainment – concert and choral societies; theatres. On a Friday or a Saturday night, Wards End was more like London's West End.

On a summer bank holiday, 1903, we went to the private ceremony for the opening of The Palace Theatre in Horton

Street, which was part of Halifax's burgeoning theatre-land; the blossoming that you dreamed of when I had met you, and which I had not been able to imagine. The new Palace elbowed aside yet more of the seedy woollen-warehouses and small-trades establishments originally there. It was a sight for sore eyes, with its painted, sliding roof and its sixty-foot-wide stage.

The McNaughten Vaudeville Company floated shares locally for the Palace. You bought many of them and that was how I came to be taken to the opening ceremony, along with a thousand other 'prominent local residents'.

I met Mr McNaughten there. He was a real swell, related to a general. He had been born in India and, after English public school, he managed an indigo plantation in Karachi, for ever afterwards bearing himself through his music-hall empire in London and the provinces with the aloof dignity of one who has held a powerful position in the Colonies. He was known for appearing about town, also in Sheffield and in his London headquarters, dressed in a silk hat and frock coat. He was tall and had a strong, firm face. His nickname was 'the Bachelor Entrepreneur', and he claimed that he was too busy with his music halls to marry. Easy to see, then, why you were chums. I have to admit that I, too, was an admirer. Wouldn't anyone be? He wasn't the sort one normally met; not when one trod the boards and not the board *rooms*.

Naturally, when the occasion involved such a man, I went to the private ceremony in full regalia. I remember getting dressed. I bet you remember it, too. Our rooms were temptingly next to each other and you came in. You were excited and you touched me – properly. You did this so rarely. I must have been still glowing when we got to the theatre, where some asked me if I was an act booked for the public opening in the following week. And I wished that I was.

While the orchestra of the Bradford Palace Theatre played a selection of medleys, we were ushered around to inspect the building. The first thing I noticed was that there wasn't that provision for rough-and-ready people, a gallery. Instead, there was an 'upper circle' with tip-up seating for a thousand.

Lots of fine things were soon being sung, said and promised from the massive and freshly gilded stage. After one of our best local tenors, Mr Fleming, sang the national anthem, followed by Tosti's *My Dream*, the Mayor of Halifax made the claim that the theatre was 'as good as anything they have in Blackpool'. Mr McNaughten then promised that the theatre would be one where 'a man may bring his wife, where the comfort and entertainment of ladies and children are especially studied'.

'The old music hall is in the transition stage from the singing-room to the new vaudeville theatre,' he prophesied. (Or perhaps he *announced* it.)

Then – blow me down with a feather – I'm blessed if Archdeacon Brooke, the Vicar of Halifax, didn't appear on stage (yes, a *real* vicar, not George Robey with a red nose) saying, 'So long as it is the intention, and I believe it is the intention, of this company to give entertainment of a character which our daughters and sisters can attend without a blush of shame, then I say from my heart that I wish it success.'

Farewell to The Mitre and The Fleece and even, maybe, The Headless Woman.

Mr McNaughten and the vicar had rung their death-knell.

I think that you were pleased.

*

I've forgotten to tell how we used to go to church together. I was amazed at your being a regular until I realised that it fitted your capacity for worship. While Mona attended her chapel and Joseph was at St Joseph's, you with me on your arm went to St Jude's, an edifice with a sub-aqueous look because of the green algae on the stones. I could wear a large hat, a veil and a long, smothering coat. At any rate, I would be in a severe disguise and we walked across the park if the weather was clement.

In fact it was in St Jude's that I first noticed your ability to adore and I am surprised that you were not a Catholic, for Anglican sermons didn't interest you at all. You could have written better ones yourself and you soon turned your eyes to the woman, the mother, Mary I mean, with golden hair and a blue gown in the window. It was in church, too, I realised that my role was to be the Unattainable Woman;

like your mother, worshipped and cosseted, but therefore I couldn't be touched.

Our quarrels tended to occur when we were returning from church. It was the combination of the illuminating effects of broad daylight, the compulsory, boring slowness of a Sunday morning walk when all the curtains of Skircoat Moor were twitching under the fingers of Sabbatarians, and the seriousness of mind hanging over from a two-hour service; its false atmosphere of honesty and forgiveness. That Sunday, the vicar had delivered a sermon about 'being true to oneself', at which we both sniggered.

I noticed that we said the same things each week at the same points on our walk. Did you notice that? The same tree, lamp post and green-painted shelter. The remembrance of what I had last said at that gatepost or bandstand inspired the repetition.

I was as trim as Savile Park itself in my dark, worsted suit. Gloves, hat and veil. We drew level with the little green shelter; do you remember? It is divided into four open, triangular compartments so that one can face whichever view one chooses, or be protected from whatever meteorological violence is coming from the world's corners – the cold easterlies that blow from the Huddersfield or Bradford directions; from the Todmorden side, the sun that leathers a lady's skin; the drenching rains from Manchester way, over the hills. No one was sheltering there at the moment. Not only may one not work; one may not even loiter on Sunday. With their nursemaid, some children were on the grass, wishing they were allowed to play. God was a great frost. But it was a sunny day. Summer.

'You can't be a woman by thinking of yourself as one all the time,' I said. 'Because that isn't what *any* woman does. I'll tell you what a woman is. If she isn't wishing she was something else, something with more chances, in other words, wishing she was a man, she's taking it for granted that she's a woman and is trying to better herself. Forgive me for saying so, but that's not what you want me to do, is it? You want me to stay a picture-postcard. The Empress Theodora. You want a magic lantern show. Best of all, I should be an animated film for the bioscope . . .'

Because of our fantasy life we can have no normal visitors, I remind you. No normal social life. In truth, you didn't ever want a theatre career for me. Your greatest love is for *preserving*. Yes, it is. Photographs, postcards; your museum of mementos. Preserving yourself – even *you* wear a corset. All right, you taught me some French and showed me the cathedrals, took me to Blackpool and Llandudno. But you educated me because you wanted to put a bell jar over a perfect flower arrangement. A *tableau vivant*.

'I'll tell you something else, Mr Dodds. You would really have liked to marry your mother. You would have liked to kill your father, like that chap in the old Greek play who blinded himself. You want me to dress in your mother's clothes so you can pretend you are married to me. Now you want me to sleep in her room!

'And that's the truth!

'*Look at me!*

'And you never listen to me!'

'Let us sit down. I'm weary,' you said.

We sat in the shelter.

You put your hand on my knee.

'I have tried to put you on the stage, even though I risked losing you that way,' you said. 'Speaking of truth – the truth is that you are by nature too frail a plant to survive in the music hall. Jack. As soon as I met you, no matter what I said, I knew, really, that you needed to be protected from the rough and tumble of the theatre. You wouldn't have been able to make a living. You are, simply, not bold, not brave enough to face it out. You try to please other people too much. But not to please yourself. And I have been protecting you from knowing that.'

'I'm *flabbergasted!*'

'*Please* do not shout. Remember that it is Sunday.'

You gripped my arm and later I found a bruise.

'Listen to me! I am telling you the truth.'

You let go of me to mop the back of your neck. You had turned florid.

'Are you all right?' I asked.

'Yes. Give me your arm and we will walk on.'

We took the remaining two hundred yards to The Hollies at a slow pace and in silence.

If only I had known. Forgive me!

We went indoors. Sarah received our outer clothes and we were left alone again. I poured us two glasses of Madeira. I poured myself another one, before you had touched yours.

You were holding on to the sideboard. You had your strained look; the one when you could not guess what was passing through my mind and felt insecure. I put it down to no more than that.

'Are you all right?' I repeated.

'A bit winded. What about you, my dear?'

I was boiling with frustrations. That, of course, was why I was quickly knocking back three, and more, glasses of Madeira.

'You are quite, quite wrong about my being too frail for a stage career, Mr Dodds.'

'Am I? Please don't stare at me like that. You look most evil.'

I swallowed yet another glass of wine. Your eyes followed the movement of the bottle to the glass, the glass to my lips. My head was spinning. Actually, I've never been terribly good with drink.

'I'm not too "frail", too "feminine", for the music hall, Mr Dodds!'

'*Please* call me Garrick.'

'You promised me a career, Garrick, *you promised, you promised*, but you made it impossible! That's the truth. Mr Dodds, are you all right?'

For your hand was on your chest.

'It's beating a little. Never mind.'

You got up unsteadily.

'I'm so disappointed,' you said.

'So am I.'

Holding on to furniture, you left the room, still talking as you went.

No, not talking: spitting at me.

'Even your so *very* vulgar act, if you don't mind my saying so, that you thought was so good, my dear, would not have worked for long, you know! Your nature is too shy. You would never summon the power to put it across . . .'

'I'm dashed good at it!' I screamed.

'. . . But I gave you a chance to do something that at least was fascinating and strange.'

I heard a door shut and realised that you had not attempted to climb the stairs. For the first time ever, you went to the ground-floor toilet used by the servants. I stood in the parlour doorway and listened anxiously. Apart from anything else, you couldn't bear spiders. That place was full of them, holed up in cracks in the whitewash.

I heard a great banging: that of a weight fallen against the inside of the closet door.

'Garrick, are you all right?'

I ran down the passageway, lifting my skirts. I had never before run in that house and so far as I knew neither had anyone else.

'Mr Dodds! Garrick! I'll move into your mother's room!'

No answer.

'Sarah! Joseph! Mona!'

I was tugging at the closet door but it would not open because you had locked it. That's why I was not there. You died alone. Forgive me.

The servants arrived all at the same time. While we three women pulled in futility at the door knob, Joseph fetched a crowbar. 'Miss Camellia, you had best sit down,' he ordered; this was his way of telling me that he wasn't my servant anymore.

Sarah sat with me in the parlour. Yes, *sat*.

All the pretences had already collapsed. She put her arm around me, and I felt like a small boy. We did not say anything. I did not need to see what had happened. Your heart, your heart . . .

*

It is when you lose a loved one that you realise, what you had taken for granted, that the whole world was focused upon him. I was like one cast out of a tribe. I wanted only to hide in my room – the place in which, when you were alive, I thought you were imprisoning me. Every detail was now so poignant – the portrait of your mother, the Box Brownie on the sideboard with an album of snapshots. After the hollowness and fear in my chest, my first reaction was exactly as Mr Palmer's had

197

been to death and which I had thought so selfish: I was angry with you for having left me. Of all emotions, that was the last one I would have expected.

I looked for something to be angry against. I used my nail scissors to cut up some of those snapshots, the more ambiguous ones, tearing the corners out of the album in my haste and, for good measure, burning the photographs. You with all those blessed waitresses! How funny that you never flirted with Sarah. I choked at what was recalled by some of those snaps, but wished that I had not lost my control at the time.

My face drowned in its first tears. I can still taste the face-powder trickling in at my lips. I can still feel the smudged mascara prickling my eyes. I'm sure that crying's bad for one; ages one.

I have heard people describe grief as like being in a dream. To me it felt even more unreal than that, and more like hearing a description of someone else's dream. I began the life that I have lived ever since; one of trying not to think of you *every* minute of the day. Sometimes I have succeeded for a short time. Even so, as I fall half-asleep at night and drop my guard, the thought of you steals upon me with cruel and tearing hooks. You were the fullest thing in my life.

My memory was shot to pieces. Familiar places, familiar duties, dropped away into the grey sea of amnesia, yet I recalled, vividly and unasked for, the most minute details of life with you since the beginning. I could hardly walk because my balance was so shaky. How I wished that I had called you 'Garrick' more often.

I stayed in my room for several days. My lack of interest in life filled me with terror and I planned diversions; Sarah to come, for instance. Then I would be filled with panic lest the diversion did not occur, or lest it failed to divert.

Your sister Liza came bustling over to supervise the household. Whatever it was that *you* felt for her, I saw only a dry, unimaginative female, with even her flesh distributed in an unimaginative, mean way, clinging tightly to her bones. There were hairs upon her lip which she was without the vanity to shave. Since that day, years before, when she unwound the trail of rumours and came to find out what her brother was 'up to', she had always looked at me as if I was something she had trodden on in the street; as if I was something brought in by the cat. We both could not forget her wedding day. Jealous, I suppose, of the *real* bride it was possible for her to be, I had tried to upstage her with my dress. She took it badly. Finally I blotted my copybook by getting drunk with the groom and swopping smutty stories about Queen V. and Albert.

Only Sarah visited my room, bringing me food; not expecting me to eat it, but to have an excuse to enter and try to draw me out into the world.

I wanted only to talk about your wonderful qualities, but I knew by the way people looked at me that they did not know how to tell me that they were not as interested in you as I was.

I was nervous of boring Sarah, my only visitor, with my obsession and I tried not to speak of what was breaking my heart, though real pain easily broke through her veneer of domestic service. Sarah tried to talk me out of my pain by speaking of things which, she must have realised, could not touch me. She told me stories about Barnsley and her family. It sounded like Saddleworth, except that in a coal-mining community, death was even closer and therefore so was love; all other passions were more likely to break through the skin. Sarah persisted with her tales. Her words floated, somewhere; somewhere else, in the room. I had only to mention you and I was in tears. I dreaded the onset of convulsions.

It was warm weather, and she looked uncomfortable with her collar and cuffs fastened with studs.

'There's no need to keep up appearances now,' I told her. 'The pretence is over.'

'It's all right, Miss. I don't have much else,' she answered.

'Neither do I,' I said.

'What are you going to do now?' I asked her.

'I don't want to leave you, Miss. It's a rum business but I'm used to it now and you're good fun, if you don't mind me saying so. You and Mrs Simpson have shown me another life. Most of the girls I knew in Barnsley are scrubbing floors as housemaids, or . . . if you knew what it's like in a cotton mill! The fluff . . .'

'I think I know.'

'I suppose you've had it rough, too. What will *you* do?'

Of course, I didn't know.

Although it was then, in that loneliness such as I had never experienced before, that I began writing down what happened to me.

*

I had symptoms of lassitude, fractional attentiveness, loss of appetite, nausea and a constant trembling in the stomach which was possibly out of panic at the thought of having nowhere to turn, no one to care.

I longed not to have face anyone, but that is precisely what funerals with complicated arrangements are for – to give those who grieve something to do. If I could, I would have provided you with a funeral like Queen Victoria's; draped carriages and a yearful of mourning just as you would have liked.

I did my best. Couldn't be so difficult, I hear you say – a bit petulant. You left enough money. I already had sufficient black outfits. Not difficult if you have a gift for it! It'd be easy for you! It was different for me, who had to deal with your Liza, Mona and Joseph on a new footing.

I couldn't face it. I kept out of the way of all of them. Coming out of my room at last, all that I heard from Liza was my marching orders, given in such a variety of expressions I would never have guessed that there could be so many; though usually I heard myself referred to, rather than spoken to directly, as 'that person', or 'that thing'.

I stayed in drag. I was obstinate about it, partly to flaunt it before Liza and others; relatives and friends who suddenly crawled out of the woodwork. I thought about changing. I thought that I might have to. But such is the perversity of human nature, now that you were not forcing femininity upon me, I did not wish to go back to being Jack.

I did try. In my bedroom, with the door locked, Sarah's pot of tea going cold on its tray on the carpet, I stripped, scraped, washed and scrubbed. With cotton wool soaked in solvents, I dissolved what had become ingrained. In the mirrors I looked at the front, back and sides of what I had once in anger tried to show you as my 'true' self, but found that it wasn't so anymore. Mark my words: drag when half scraped off is a terrible sight. The thinner male hair flattened upon my skull after having being compressed under a wig; moreover I was now going bald at the temples. The skinned, vulnerable appearance of a face with its make-up removed.

Too much water gone under the blessed bridge! I hated what I saw emerging after being buried for so long. That Jack Shuttleworth was not me, and I could not adopt him. He was so much less a person; had so little personality compared with Camellia. Jack was merely the husk from which Camellia had emerged. The thought of going out as him was now as frightening as it had once seemed to go forth as Camellia Snow. *All* my joy was in Camellia.

What was I to do?

I was not merely powerless. When I did put in an appearance I found I was getting my nose rubbed in it. I was treated as I feared I would be when you died; as the whim of an old man in his dotage. My grief was regarded as being in bad taste. Liza, Mona and Joseph looked at me as if they had lemons in their mouths. Especially if they had to speak to me, which, sometimes, they could not avoid. They told me as little as possible.

For instance, I found out later that Mr Palmer, after so many years, had telephoned several times, but I was never brought to the telephone. If Sarah got her foot on the stairs, Liza managed to be there to prevent her from fetching me. What policemen they were all turning out to be!

For the time being, I watched impotently through my window. There was a great deal of to-ing and fro-ing with lawyers and other official or professional people. The L—d only knew who they all were.

My being unable to face them was a great mistake, as it turned out. Instead, Liza took it upon herself to deal with them and her right to this went without question.

She told me again, and again, and again, that, now you were 'at rest' and 'at peace', I wasn't to be given long, so I'd better pack my bags.

'He's dead,' I said. 'He's dead.'

'You're nothing but a ghoul,' she answered. 'You're not natural.'

She shuddered – which was all put on; I hadn't been on the stage for nothing.

I retreated to my room as often as I could and I watched them in the garden, where they did what no one would have dared do when you were alive. Mona hung the washing to dry over the hedges when the lines in the yard were full. I even saw *underwear* over a *camellia* bush! Liza Buckton had a chair brought out for her to sit on the lawn, and Sarah sometimes sat in the sun after she had washed her hair.

However, being able to lip read, I knew very well what they were saying about you and me and your affairs.

*

I was even prevented from attending your funeral at St Jude's. I let them keep me away and pretended that from grief I was unable to face it.

I watched a band of people, many of whom I'd never seen before, troop down the drive. Distant relatives, employees of Dodds Mill Furnishers, and some theatre people whom I had seen before. I had not guessed that you knew so many. I wonder if I was mentioned? And the people whom we had met every Sunday in the congregation? Probably they whispered behind scented handkerchiefs, hinted and sniggered.

They tried to leave me out of the reading of the Will, too, but I hung on, because of what I knew they had said to each other in the garden. There was, at the very least, a question hanging over my future.

I had wondered about your Will. As I understood it: while leaving a redundant testament with the family lawyers, Briggs & Co., you had unknown to them made a different one through another lawyer and deposited it in the bank. It was this later Will that made provision for me. It was I, also, who told everyone of its existence. Threw the cat among the pigeons, you might say.

I boldly walked into the dining-room. Mr Briggs sat at the head of the table where you used to sit. Mona, dabbing her eyes, was on one side. Liza, at the other, was slowly, noisily, sucking a humbug. Sarah, who was not present, had provided ham and cucumber sandwiches. These were on a small table that had always been covered with a cloth and with your mother's ornaments; a change of use that you would never have permitted, so that I was given quite a start.

'This has nothing to do with you, young man,' Liza said. 'I've told you before: get out o' them silly clothes and pack your bags. You've a living to earn same as any other man now, so grow up!'

I answered calmly, 'If the servants are here, I believe that Mr Dodds' wishes might concern me, too.'

'And who are you?' remarked Joseph, which raised a sneer from Mona.

'Humbug,' Liza said, and I laughed.

'Oh, my!' I said. 'Humbug, yourself,' I said. 'Why don't you stop sucking them?'

At the threat of the law's majesty decaying into this lower-class squabbling, Mr Briggs coughed. What a cough. It carried the dignity of the law. If you could have weighed it, it would have been as heavy as the stones of The Hollies.

Mr Briggs was ten years younger than you, but in his manner he was centuries older. He was the son of your father's lawyer, and the business relationship of Dodds & Co. with Briggs' law firm went even further back. From living in a madhouse with you, I had forgotten what the real world was like, the one of patriarchs like Mr Briggs, and he gave me a shock, just with his cough. I knew that he was an adversary. I knew from lip reading at my window as he talked to Liza Buckton that he was going to do all he could 'to keep the family fortune together', as he had put it, despite the surprising new document. That could mean nothing other than keeping me out of something to which you had given me the right.

I understood human nature better than I grasped the working of the law, and Mr Briggs' character leapt out at me at first sight of his polished head smiling above his immaculate suit. When *you* smiled, it was in disingenuous welcome, as a child does, not as this lawyer did. I would have felt better if he'd snarled at me, for that I could have trusted; in any case, I knew that he would be snarling before long.

Polish is the one word that sums him up. His skin gleamed with impenetrable varnish. Nothing could get at him. You felt that if he went out into the rain, he would be waterproof. His laugh meant the opposite of laughter. It was another layer of gleaming varnish. His manner was to speak facetiously about what he knew was deadly serious to his client; to be the more circumlocutory, the more he knew that a direct answer was needed. The more desperate his client was for an answer to his case, the more Mr Briggs felt he could get away with evasive and complicated arrangements wrapped in unintelligible phrases. The more words he used, the more letters he wrote, the higher would be his bill; or his opponent's bill, because the correspondence would have to be answered. Thus Mr Briggs ground down the opposition. Either way, the firm of Briggs and Co. benefited. This game that I had never played was waiting for me around the corner.

His build, too, is that of one who could manage without the law's assistance, if necessary. He is well-fleshed, muscular, neither fat nor thin, and healthy. I felt that, even if the law made it unnecessary, he could have knocked me down with a punch.

'In point of fact, I think that it would probably help us proceed more expeditiously if this person stayed,' Mr Briggs said, with a glance that swept the room, taking in not only Liza, Mona and Joseph, but the ceiling, sideboard, sandwiches and so forth, yet leaving me out.

'Whatever for?' Liza wanted to know.

'Because it might save us all from complications and delays if we agree to put this business upon a rational footing from the beginning,' he continued to fail-to-explain, in his inimitable fashion.

He had lost us, but no doubt every unhelpful sentence would have its price tagged on to the bill.

Meanwhile I took my seat at the foot of the table, staring at Mr Briggs. Talk about water off a duck's back; he wasn't in the slightest perturbed by me. He plucked at his documents as skilfully as an experienced fishmonger gutting a cod. He selected a sheet to peruse. He did not read it to us. He 'explained' it.

'Let us get the smaller things out of the way first,' he began, and he told Mona and Joseph about their annuities.

I thought that they amounted to sizeable pensions. They were both identical, so when Joseph looked pleased while

Mona was flushed with disappointment that she could not at the moment find the words for, their reactions had more to do with character than with justice. Whereas Joseph never expected anything good to turn up, certainly not in the form of gratuities, for Mona nothing was good enough.

'After all that we done for 'im,' Mona complained, when her wits returned; I think she believed he should have left her the whole house.

'You mean to say we get all that wi'out 'aving to work for it?' Joseph questioned, dazzled.

'I'm afraid so,' Mr Briggs chuckled. 'You're now a member of the leisured classes, like it or not, while I'm sorry to say that we others have to continue toiling in Adam's orchard.'

'I'm hoping not,' Liza said.

'We get that every year?' Joseph still could not believe.

'Yes.'

'Well, I'm blowed!'

'If you have no further questions, you may go now.' Mr Briggs was pleased with himself at having dealt 'expeditiously' with this matter. Mona and Joseph stood up. Then they froze, as I interrupted with, '*I* have a question.'

'*You* have?' Mr Briggs twinkled. 'Spit it out. What is it?'

'What about Sarah?'

'Well!' Liza exclaimed.

'The beesom!' Mona said.

'Sarah is the house-parlourmaid?' Mr Briggs asked, examining me.

'Yes,' I answered.

'There is no provision for Sarah. She has apparently not been in Mr Dodds' service for long enough.'

I didn't point out that you would have wanted her to have, say, fifty pounds, even though she had not been with your mother. You were never mean, but she hadn't been with us long enough for you to change your Will. The point was that they were showing no respect for what you would want. Sandwiches on your mother's table! Washing on the camellias! But I thought that arguing would only make things more difficult for myself.

'You may go now,' Mr Briggs repeated to Mona and Joseph, and out they trooped, leaving me to tussle with

Liza, while Mr Briggs glared at me as a schoolmaster does at a naughty schoolboy.

He told us that The Hollies was left to Liza, who merely shrugged, awaiting more.

'The major part of this strange legacy is more difficult to deal with,' Mr Briggs said. 'It has been left to some person previously unknown to any of us and named "Camellia Snow", also "Jack Shuttleworth".' He smiled at me. 'That, presumably, is the person who you claim to be?'

'That's who I am,' I answered

'You will need to provide proof of that.'

'Proof?'

'Proof.'

That stunned me. I had never thought of needing such a thing.

'I was in the Diggle workhouse. It'll be in their records.'

'Then produce them. You will also need testimony that you are the same person as the one in the records. Jack Shuttleworth, alias "Camellia Snow". There is no birth certificate for her, either, of course?'

Mr Briggs allowed himself one of his smiles.

'What's "testimony" mean?'

'A magistrate. The workhouse keeper, perhaps.'

'I ran away.'

'Did you, indeed? Well, without your producing proof of identity, I cannot proceed. In your case, a sum of approximately ten thousand pounds is involved.'

'Ten thousand pounds!'

'Do I detect a certain amount of greed over this matter?'

I was shamed into silence.

'The majority of Mr Dodds' fortune is in bonds of one kind or another,' Mr Briggs said. 'It will take some months to release them. You have plenty of time to get your case together, Mr – er – Shuttleworth, if we may assume for the time being that is indeed who you are.'

'Case? What case?'

'Mr Shuttleworth,' he began, folding his fists upon the table. Have you ever watched a prize-fighter in a booth getting himself prepared for a tussle? 'Quite without prejudice, you understand, I will assume that is who you are, until or unless it is proved otherwise . . . Mr Shuttleworth, there is also the question of whether my dear friend Dodds was entirely in his right frame of mind when he made his later Will and deposited it so secretively. You can hardly say that yours was a normal relationship, can you? Mrs Buckton, in her own defence as the next of kin who would otherwise have inherited, would be well advised to question the sanity of her brother in his latter years, and I will tell you now, off the record, Mr Shuttleworth, that, as her family lawyer, that is indeed what I shall advise her to do. Let us assume, for the time being, that you intend to contest this case – though I believe you would be well advised not to. Would you be prepared to appear in court dressed as a woman in order to demonstrate that you are the aforesaid "Camellia Snow"?'

'If I must. That is who I am.'

He made a clucking noise with his tongue against his palate.

'Mrs Buckton might in fact call upon you to appear thus in order to prove the infirm state of her brother's mind. What do you say to that? I'm afraid you might find yourself having to deal with something even more difficult than a contested Will.'

'It's not illegal to dress as a woman!'

'Other things, not unconnected with it, might have something to do with corrupting Mr Dodds and with unsettling his mind. Possibly there could be criminal charges.'

'We did nothing!'

'Mr Dodds' legacy is unfortunately hedged with pitfalls and I would be failing in my duty were I not to proceed with the greatest circumspection and caution. Nothing, apparently, is what it seems. Is it?'

He was staring hard at me.

'If you wish to take action over this matter, you will need a legal adviser of your own,' he told me.

'Is there nothing that can be done in the meantime?'

'You mean to let you have something "on tick", as they say?'

'I haven't any resources at all.'

'You'll have to work honestly for your living. For a change,' Liza interrupted.

'There isn't anything that *I* can do for you, if that's what you're asking,' Mr Briggs said. 'So far as I am concerned, the assets must remain frozen, at least until you have proved your identity, and possibly longer if Mrs Buckton brings an action to prove that her brother was of unsound mind.'

'So what about her?'

'Do you mean, *vis-à-vis* Mrs Buckton's inheriting the house?'

'Yes. If – '

'As she is the next of kin, and would inherit The Hollies in any case, I see no reason why she should not possess it. Someone has to take care of it.'

'First thing you can do, young man, is to pack your bags and get out of my house, with your dirty ways,' Liza said.

'So you see what the rightful owner thinks,' Mr Briggs said.

'I've heard her before.'

'I think you would do best to obey.'

*

It wasn't, in fact, much of a problem. Mr Palmer's persistent telephone calls, it turned out, had been to offer me a home, 'until Miss Camellia overcomes her bereavement'. When he eventually got hold of me directly, he spoke of 'somewhere to rest your head for a while, until you recover'. 'Stay as long as you like,' he said. His voice, which I felt obsessively tugging at me, even through one of those crackling telephone machines, was quiet, merciless, understated, deliberate and persistent. I knew what he was like, for I remembered the form of his grief, which was unbelievably self-centred. *How could she do this to me . . . I gave her everything.*

Even while offering me comfort, he could not help bringing into his conversation hints of permanent domestic arrangements, for example the names of stores where one could buy the clothes that he liked, and matters to do with what he called my 'education' (again!).

It transpired that he knew who I was, that is, who I had been, and that I was not 'real'. But one of his major talents, if you can call it a talent, was for not speaking of matters and for preventing subjects from being raised, for years if necessary. I realised from the start that, at least in Mr P.'s ambience, my pretence to be a woman had to be total.

There was some reason why, like you, he could not satisfy himself with a real woman, so that he needed a pretend one. Clearly it was not, as in your case, that he was afraid of marriage. The childlessness of a man with an estate to leave and two wives who were suicides had another explanation.

I, for my part, used tears and sulks to force my side of the bargain: that he should help me with my legal case and that I should take my Sarah with me to The Lumb.

Lip reading as I watched Liza Buckton and Mr Briggs strolling in the garden, I first saw the phrase 'antique collector' formed upon Mr Briggs' contemptuous lips.

·8·

FIFTY pounds came to me from Mr Briggs, via Liza Buckton. 'After this we don't want to hear any more from you,' she said. I was to assume that this was my pay-off, but I intended differently. Perhaps I'd invest some of it in a lawyer, for a start. I didn't at all feel that I was leaving with my tail between my legs.

I had by then acquired enough belongings to fill several trunks and suitcases. I filled one case with nothing but postcards, loose photographs and albums. Besides my own dresses and so forth, I helped myself to some of your books and a few of your museum pieces; your mother's shoes and candlesticks. Also the pot, two cups and saucers, milk jug and two plates from the Crown Derby tea-service which I knew would remind me of so very, very much every time I looked at them. One sad trunk that I took the liberty of using had belonged to Eugenia Fanny Watts and had labels still pasted to it directing it to different theatres.

Liza Buckton took no interest in my removing her mother's possessions and the mementos of her brother; I knew she wouldn't. She wasn't sentimental, like me. Also she pretended that everything to do with me was too filthy for her to touch and she was too much on her dignity to bring herself to demand an inspection. 'Seeing the last of a bad lot' was her comment to Mona, for me to overhear as the pair of them folded their arms against me upon the doorstep. Two of a kind, they are. How she must have enjoyed shutting the door.

Joseph, who had brought me from The Headless Woman, first drove Sarah to The Lumb and a day later took me. I doubt if the service would have been rendered had it not been for Mr P.'s benefit. Away I was swept, out of my prison.

'Eee, thou'rt a case!' Joseph chuckled. ' 'Ow does tha get away with it? It'll be in the papers some day.'

'I'm not the first, nor will I be the last.'

'It takes all sorts to make a world,' he chuckled. 'It'll be something to tell my nephews and nieces now that I'm retired. I suppose, in a way, thou's still working, aren't tha? "'E who laughs last," as they say.'

He hesitated over whether to drive me to the front or back entrance of Lumb House, but I told him firmly where to go. Sweep up to the front porch where a footman was coming to meet, if not to greet me. Billowing with put-on confidence, I left the servants to deal with the luggage. I have learned how they expect and like to be treated; otherwise, it's you whom they trample into the ground.

I tipped Joseph and he performed his act perfectly. 'Thank you, ma'am,' he said, touching his cap without a trace of a give-away smile. 'I 'ope I 'ave the pleasure of seeing you upon the stage again, some day.'

Clearly, I was a bit of a chump to retreat to The Lumb. The moment I got there, I sensed that it wouldn't work. Even with my Sarah as a buffer between the servants and myself, it was expecting too much of me to be 'real' all the time, while in The Lumb. I was in for a lot of retreating to my room, making mostly evening appearances, with afternoons of 'headaches' and 'indispositions'. But what else could I do? After all these years, I had no wish to give up my life in drag. I doubted that I could cope without it and I did not know of anywhere else I could turn where I would be acceptable. Here, at least, the air of the servants and of other people I had to deal with was ambiguous, as if they were conspiring, or they were quite unsure of what sex I was, or they did, indeed, accept me as a woman. It was better to be here than to have to hop about between Jack and his crude stage acts. I did not want to go back to that!

A superior, starchy maid, following behind the footmen who carried my luggage, led me up the staircase, along the glittering corridors to my room. I was fagged out by the time I got there. She explained that Mr Palmer would take me down to dinner in an hour. Oh, I like all that, you know: to see well-dressed servants, the stylish life. The only thing was: none of them looked me in the face. I wondered what their turned-away visages hid.

She and the footmen left, but Sarah was waiting for me. The housekeeper had changed Sarah's uniform. The cap was almost

211

a bonnet, the apron larger and the strings longer; in a word, more old-fashioned. Remembering my past experience of the staff of The Lumb, I was worried about how she was getting on, but apparently she was happier here because she had more people to talk to. She was also still dazzled at finding herself in this fabulous, fairy-land museum.

A less elevated girl in more functional dress brought in a ewer and a jug of hot water. She turned down the bed-sheets to insert a warming-pan. She attended to the fire. She did not speak; she could have been a jailer, or a keeper in the zoo. Soon she, too, left me alone with Sarah, to think about who I was to become and to prepare myself, in just the same way as you had left me once, to acclimatise myself in The Hollies.

For the time being, Sarah unpacked just one trunk before she left. It was the one filled with immediate requirements. It would have seemed an incongruous collection to anyone else, like something assembled for a jumble-sale, but my mementos were what I needed to feel at home. Mounted in a silver frame, a certain snapshot of you and me on a picnic at Bolton Abbey . . .

I had arrived in my black, tailored suit, my black hat, boots and veil. I stripped to my corset. I shaved, even though I had prepared quite carefully before leaving home. I built myself up again as a new person. I did not know who, yet; not quite. Talk about a chameleon! I had got used to not knowing who I was even before I went to The Hollies, so that to change again in order to satisfy a new dependency was not such a crisis. I had never known anything to be permanent, so I didn't expect any of my roles to be so, either.

Love – if that is what all this business can be called, roughly speaking – seems to consist of making yourself dependent, so that someone will salve your loneliness. Love consists of giving, in hope that you will be given to, when you are in need. But with it comes the tight grip of the fear of abandonment and grief, eventually. I wondered, as I tried on different wigs to match a new life, how long it would last with Palmer and whether I could love him. I was full of fears, wondering what I would have to be.

This room prepared for my coming was, just like the one that had awaited me at The Hollies, lavishly furnished with mirrors. They hinted that I was not a real person but a reflection and a creation, changeable at will. *Like a true woman*, you might say, I was dependent, frivolous, marginal to the men's world and having to adapt myself to it. Whereas with you I had been expected to be a biddable and sweet toy (prescriptions which as you know kept breaking down), I anticipated that with Mr Palmer I would be required to be both a biddable and vivacious one; paradoxical switches that were going to take some managing.

For a start, I decided to change my wig. I chose a more extravagant one, with ringlets. Soon afterwards, Mr P. came for me. With very few words, as if the pair of us were in a dream, he presented me with a pearl necklace. Though I had decided not to abandon the mourning in which I had arrived, yet I lightened it considerably with only a few slight alterations – wig, necklace, and doubtless another expression on my face.

I had met Mr Palmer only a few times since Cynthia Palmer died. I saw now what I had not realised over the telephone. The old man, grey and stooped but still firm as he led me on his arm down the long, broad staircase, was quite gaga.

'So glad you have decided to join us at The Lumb. It's quite a jolly place, you know. I'm sure you'll be happy when you've found your way about and have got used to us. We have lots of fun.'

Little else had changed. There seemed no additions or alterations to the *objets d'art* and the furniture – except for myself; for what else was I but a curio on a shelf? Did anyone ever look at them, or at the pictures? I doubted it, except perhaps for the occasional new, awestruck servant like Sarah, who was all agog. Before long, would anyone be taking a second glance at me? Drifting through the mirrors lining the long passage – was I a bird, was I a fish? – I felt surprised by nothing.

Into the dining-room. Instead of only you and I in the twilight where the clocks ticked, I was to be seated at a brilliantly lit table, its white cloth itself like a mirror. Once again I was with Booboo, Didi, Nana and Uncle Clarence.

It is always a shock to meet people after a period and be stabbed with the realisation that you, yourself, must also have hideously aged. Old Clarence's skin that had suffered from the sun of India was more than ever wrinkled and yellow, like the skins of the old men who used every year to mix lime to whitewash the walls of the Saddleworth mills and workhouse. The family and about ten guests or other relatives were waiting for me in the vast room lit by crystal chandeliers. All were formally attired. I noticed at once how old-fashioned everyone's dress was. The servants, each with a different function for each course, were, like Sarah, in dated uniforms or livery; the ones I remembered from years before.

As I came in, the guests and relatives fell as silent as the attendants until, '*There* you are!' Booboo exclaimed, to ease the tension.

It sounded as though I had been absent only for a day and that after all that time, she remembered who I was. It was a kindly lie, intended to make me feel at ease; an old-fashioned politeness, but it had become frozen in the sealed world of The Lumb and none of them seemed to realise how absurd it was, in its excess. Her face, and those of the other ladies and gentlemen, held welcoming beams that unfortunately were more than was appropriate and they were held for too long, so that they turned into threatening leers. The ladies' expressions were exaggerated by make-up.

During the intervening period there had grown a desperation about the family around the table, as if they were all drowning and I might be their rescuer, or at least a diversion. I realised that no one was going to show that they knew I was a male and that probably they intended never to show it; but that someone, some day, just for a bit of a tease when he or she was tipsy, would let it out. 'I know what you are, you know!' I should always be prepared for it, so as not to blush.

They had all gone a bit loopy; it was not only Palmer. In their fine house out of touch with the incomprehensible, dirty factories increasingly surrounding them, they were like a party stranded on a luxury liner, one frozen into the arctic ice, say, when, having enough food and dance-band music aboard to survive for many years, the travellers had grown old in isolation together.

I know I made the usual novice's mistake of talking too much over dinner, but I believe that I was forgiven and they were apparently enraptured as they listened to my tales.

It didn't take much to amuse them. Uncle Clarence had his female cousins in stitches describing the 'apple pie bed' that had

214

been perpetrated upon him, yet I remembered hearing the same story when I was there before.

After the meal, the gentlemen retired to the smoking-room and I spent an hour tittering, gossiping and in what they called 'catching up' with the ladies. I needed to be careful. Clearly, no one was going to admit a single thing of importance and neither should I. To say anything at all about my peculiar position in this household would be a most serious gaffe. How glad I was of Mrs Simpson's training!

And yet, the old bats broke me.

'How nice your hair would look tinted!' Didi said. 'The latest thing, I believe, is a a henna rinse for dark hair.'

I perceived that they didn't guess that I was wearing a wig, didn't see that I wasn't a woman. Either that or they were playing a more thorough hoax than I had realised.

Then Booboo leaned over, pretending to whisper in my ear but in fact saying very loudly, 'What Sampson really needs, you know, is a woman who will love him. A wife to provide him with children *before it is too late for her to do it.*'

Either they were teasing me cruelly, or they did take me for a woman.

I believe it was the latter. I had to run out of the room, my handkerchief to my face, and burst into tears.

*

I saw less of Mr P. than I expected, after what I was used to from *our* closeness. His memory apparently shot to pieces, Palmer would forget me and everything. With a lost, drawn, hunted, even starved look, a lit cigarette in his hand and perhaps dangerously to be abandoned somewhere, he would wander about the mansion doing things for himself as if he was still a soldier adventuring beyond the fringes of Empire; a place where he had no servants and had to do for himself such things as turning lamps on or off, finding his clothes or boiling water. He would steal into the kitchen at servantless hours, in the middle of the night or on Sunday morning when they were in church, would boil water and forget to remove it from the stove. He would turn on gas jets and forget to ignite them. Also, this house, too, was illuminated by electricity and we know how freakishly inclined that is.

Not surprising, then (I hear you say), that Mr P. could not remember whether I was in truth a man or a woman.

The trouble was that, as is sometimes the case with those who appear to be deaf, blind or gaga, he gave me reason to doubt; for about many of the things that interested him, he was most acute.

Legal affairs, especially those appertaining to his money and possessions.

Fishing.

Bioscope and animated film.

Practical jokes.

An interest in getting up theatricals had died as the denizens of Lumb House grew older, but Booboo, Didi, Sampson and Clarence never tired of playing tricks, the same ones time and again, upon one another. They took almost the same trouble, spent as much time and money preparing some of these, as they had once done over their theatricals. Booboo thought it a frightful giggle to sew nettles or mustard leaves into the crotch of Clarence's trousers and watch his unmentionable discomfort throughout a polite dinner-party. Another jape was to smear asafoetida inside Clarence's shoes. As soon as his feet warmed, the stuff smelled awful and he would be looking around, sniffing, examining the soles for the source.

Clarence was most often the butt of these jokes because he was so eager to prove himself a 'sport', having been in India. The aim was to test his patience, but he always laughed. Apple pie beds were commonplace for him, yet he always behaved as if it was the first time it had happened. He was like a kind uncle determined to amuse children.

One of *his* jokes upon Booboo or Didi was to stop the maid on her way upstairs, give her half a crown to say nothing about what he was about to do, and sprinkle sodium in the bottom of the chamberpot; the sodium exploded on contact with water.

Sampson Palmer's humour was distinctly more cruel. He couldn't get under tough old Clarence's skin. Didi, too, was strong and wily. Booboo was the soft one and therefore most often the object of his officers'-mess humour.

She was fond of cakes, having the most elaborate concoctions delivered from Ilkley, Harrogate or Halifax. She would plan the designs over months until, with such silly, bright-eyed pleasure, she would have sent to her confections mounted with fairy-tale castles, or trees crowded with birds, fashioned out of icing-sugar. More than once I watched Sampson Palmer get drunk and, with that glaze of apparent forgetfulness as he stared at Booboo, take hold of birds and palaces to crush them slowly in his hands, being never too drunk to examine the tears welling in her eyes. She always half expected this to happen to her deliveries and as a result he would, hawk-like, inspect her pain.

I was there, partly as yet another joke, partly as a curiosity that did not require much of anyone's emotional involvement, and partly to complete Palmer's masquerade of being capable of entertaining a mistress. Nothing was said about anything! Principally from watching him with Booboo, I realised that Mr Palmer hated women, which was why he could not give them love, which was, at bottom, why two of them had opted out. Determined to have a family, or the appearance of one, at any price, he had bribed his wives, as well as other relatives, with status and wealth, thus gathering this zoo around himself. Then he preyed upon them and destroyed them. Offering them only his possessions, it led him to accusing his wives, who behaved so 'badly' when they realised that they were starved of love, of ingratitude.

I, as a fake woman, had a curious perspective upon this, being able to feel the dangers that they were vulnerable to, and also to feel as a man; although, I trust, never such a man as Palmer.

What Palmer did to women was to bring them down, swallow them up, leave them bereft – mere scarecrows; sticks with rings on their fingers.

Did there have to be a victim for every one of his passions, I wondered?

A female victim?

Women, to Mr Palmer's reasoning, were irrational creatures who were for ever spoiling his image of his perfect family and home. If they showed themselves to be sad, angry or frustrated, especially in front of others, they were ungratefully fouling his picture of himself as a man of nobility, kindness and honour. He wanted a partner who could be a mask for him; a partner for him to wear like a suit of clothes.

I realised that my attractiveness was that I was *not* a woman; that I could be made into what he wanted and I had the advantage that I could move and speak. Here we go again, I said to myself.

It showed while he was fishing. He took me with him, as you had taken me to tea-rooms. He wore all the correct clothes and he simply wanted me there to admire him, to prop up his vanity. He did not appear to be gaga on the river bank. For a time I became a fisherman's widow, sitting decoratively while he paced up and down his private river, flicked his artificial flies until he had decided that he had fished out that stretch, then flicked his fingers at me in exactly the same manner, as a signal that we were to move on.

Fishing seems to me a cold-hearted occupation. I watched him pull out of their element these vibrantly living, clean beings and, once they had served their purpose of exciting him, he would end their lives with a thoughtless blow. It occurred to me that thus he had angled for me and thus with one insensitive blow he would end me.

*

If one of her fancy cakes was on its way from Harrogate, only to be threatened by Mr P., frightened Booboo, with a sly giggle, would sidle up to me and offer me a fiver to 'put in a good word with the old man'. On other occasions, Didi did the same thing and so did Nana. I'm sure that none of the ladies knew about the others. I amassed quite a lot of money this way and did not let on, adding it to what was left of my fifty pounds; which was most of it, for I had little need to spend.

But it was terrifying to see the fear of Booboo and Didi.

It frightened me, too, to see my turn coming round for madness and death, after Pamela, Cynthia, Beatrice, and Diana.

A victim is exciting only while she is being manipulated. Then she starts to imitate the image that has been made of her, for she has nothing else to offer.

During afternoons when I made use of what Miss Shingles long ago had taught me to call 'indispositions', afternoons when I attacked The Lumb's massive store of alcohol before creeping secretly to bed, I dwelled upon what I'd heard of the two Fielden brothers of Todmorden. I told this story to Didi and she simply commented that the Fieldens were 'common and not our sort of person'. She didn't understand, and I missed Cynthia Palmer. I told my Sarah and it quite broke her heart.

As I had heard, the Fieldens made a fortune in the cotton spinning industry and both fell in love with the same girl who worked in their mill. She said she would marry the first one to build her a castle, whereupon Dobroyd Castle, a black, Gothic pile like The Lumb, was erected upon the hills. The girl was duly prepared at a finishing school in Switzerland and married. Thereby the poor creature was disinherited of her own background and couldn't be at ease with the nobs, either. Like me, she took to drink and was put away to go mad in a Swiss chalet built for her in the grounds, as Marie Antoinette had her Petit Trianon.

If I wasn't to be a drunken wreck and a toe-rag, I had to fight for something. I felt that I must not leave The Lumb before possessing the full resources that you had left me, Garrick, and I fought for my life by daring to remind Mr Palmer of my need of legal defence, which had made me agree to come to his ice-palace in the first place.

How fierce old Palmer's silences could be, but I wasn't going to be put off. I reminded him that I had still not resolved the delicate matter of having to prove that I am Jack Shuttleworth and also Camellia Snow, without giving Mrs Buckton the evidence to question your sanity.

'Yes, yes!' he muttered. 'Must have a word with Buckton. She's a stingy old cow. Leave it to me.'

Although it had been left with him for months.

'What will you do, sir?'

'Why, speak to Ashcroft, of course.'

Mr Ashcroft was his own solicitor, who was no less forbidding and procrastinating than Mr Briggs.

'*When* will it be brought to his attention?'

'It has been so, already. Damned dilatory fellow!'

'Is nothing happening?'

'The problem is to bring it to court and not be laughed at, damn it.'

'But surely something can be done in the meanwhile to release my funds? Briggs is simply holding them back. That can't be right. It isn't *his* money. Nor anyone else's, other than mine.'

'It's increasing for you at compound interest, damn it! You don't need any funds while you're with me. You're damned lucky! Don't I provide for you? Are you short of anything?'

'No . . .'

'If ever you are, just let me know. That's all you have to do. In the meantime, do as you are told. I keep you to *smile* and be perfect, not to pull a long face.'

His dark eyes threatened me under what had now grown to be bushy and neglected eyebrows. The only thing I feared was a real argument with Mr Palmer, which might end with my being cast out without ado. If I knew anything at all, I knew that. But, expected as it was, no such quarrel occurred.

For one thing: about the proper gentlemanly matters he was considerate, delivering flowers and presents on the correct occasions, opening bottles of champagne, making sure that I was comfortable in my room, that I was not short of money, company and entertainment – just as he had pandered to Cynthia Palmer's poetry.

For another thing, it proved impossible to put on a temperamental show with Mr P. He was always calm and firm; though I tried hard to follow that difficult razor's edge between the two chasms, disastrous argument on the one side and boring lack of vivaciousness on the other.

The reason he was so calm, that we had no arguments, was that there wasn't a person there to argue with. His inner life was as mechanically, perfectly organised as his outer one. I have never met another of this type. Usually people are quite different on the inside. They hide there all the secret, inarticulate thoughts, which burst out under strain and set fire to things. He *had* no inner life. Because of this, he was imperturbable and if I opened the subject of the subtle matters of the heart, he didn't know what I was talking about. I might as well have gone out and talked to his horse.

At bottom, your problem had been that you adored women *too* much. Mr Palmer's was that he hated them. The result in both cases was to desire a woman who did not make feminine demands. You showed your feelings through your mausoleum devoted to your mother as well as through your masquerade with me; also through your love of the capacious motherliness of the theatre and the womb atmosphere of church services, the soothing lullabies of 'hymns', the images of a celestial mother.

It's interesting that I knew everything about your mother; the sizes of her clothes, details of every theatre production she had appeared in. I had not a single detail of Mr Palmer's. He could tell me nothing. I think this illustrates how dead he was inside. He had no gift for introspection. Whenever I asked him about anything personal, he could not 'remember'. He could not talk about anything intimate.

Let me put it this way. Mr Palmer had no female component at all. He was suave on the outside, yet his inner person totally lacked confidence. When I looked underneath Mr Palmer's polished surface, no one was there.

*

Mr Palmer, also, had a large collection of theatre magazines, programmes and picture-postcards of actresses, though I doubt if some of them had appeared on any stage other than in a photographer's studio. Take it from me, all the toffs have these semi-secret archives. Mr Palmer had a locked room devoted to his. I had not known that it existed, the first time I was at The Lumb.

Among the mahogany filing cabinets and drawers was exhibited what Mr Palmer told me was called a Filoscope. From the Greek meaning 'leaf', apparently. Leaves of pictures, all slightly different to one another and forming a sequence of movements, were bound in a metal casing. You flicked them with your finger, to give the impression of motion. It was *most* startling. One showed a female dancer. Another was a girl undressing as far as her underwear. A third was of a girl coming out of a bathing-cabin to take a dip, and I was told that the young lady had been prosecuted for allowing herself to be photographed thus.

There were other types of moving-picture projection. Whetstone's Moving Picture Stereoviewer was more sophisticated and used a drum with a handle, which could be turned rapidly to show quite complicated actions, for instance a maid peeping through a keyhole at a couple preparing for bed, and a horse jumping a fence. Mr Palmer had other variations; a Tachyscope, a Zoetrope ... the possibilities quite made my head spin.

Mr Palmer had among his friends a Mr Bamforth of Holmfirth, who was a house-painter and decorator, as well as a photographer. They say of Yorkshire folk that they'll never buy a penn'orth of mussels because they cannot find a use for the shells. Mr Bamforth, determined not to waste anything, including a skill, combined his by producing lantern slides and picture-postcards of which he painted the backdrops. He was such a dab-hand with his brush that he could slap in a background in half an hour; generally a country view inspired more by the scenery at the nearby Huddersfield Palace than by nature. Sheet-music publishers got him to promote their new songs with slides and postcards. He had produced two million slides and was turning out six hundred more per year. Soft focus, floral festoons and romantic gazes conveyed every desired message. Mr Bamforth could sentimentalise anything: religion, war, mining disasters, poverty. I had been introduced firstly because Mr Palmer wanted studio pictures of me and I was photographed, caressing a rose, among Mr Bamforth's grotto and rockeries which had been built for his scenes of fairies, nymphs, or maidens yearning for a dead mother.

Mr Bamforth also made animated films for the bioscope. He produced, for instance, a series called the 'Winky' films. *Winky's Ruse. Winky's Weekend.* These were ten-minute comedies showing a local actor in embarrassing situations.

Mr Bamforth wanted to make a film called *Kisses in the Train* and he sought out Mr Palmer because of his influence with the Lancashire and Yorkshire Railway Company. Bamforth had his own actress in mind, a young lady from the chapel he attended, but Mr P. in return for providing the train, two carriages and the use of a tunnel, persuaded him to give me the part instead.

No one was in the compartment but myself, made up to look like a nervous tart, and a young man, a cad if ever you saw one, who sat next to me. You could tell by his dress that he was a bank clerk or something like that. He was, in fact, a clerk and a supporter of the Hade Edge Chapel, from which Mr Bamforth plucked most of his actors and, especially, his child-actresses. You could tell that I didn't trust this fellow, by the way I rolled my eyes, clutched my handbag and kept my knees pressed together. He was poking a finger into his celluloid collar, while with his other hand he stroked his brow. No caption was needed to show what *he* wanted that made him so nervous.

It takes a whole day to make an animated film. Early in the morning I was led to the site in Mr P.'s Rolls-Royce motor car, oh lah-de-dah, while Mr Bamforth and his assistants, including the male actor, turned up in the motorised commercial vehicle which carried the camera, tripod and mercury flood-lighting. It was quite a cavalcade and it brought out a whole village to watch us. It needed a policeman to keep them in order, and the shooting itself was photographed for the newspaper.

Spending the morning practising this little scene over and over again under Mr Bamforth's direction, Mr Palmer standing by, made me quite testy. I could see that if ever I was going to show temperament, it would be on a film set. I was not used to the constant repeating of a single scene. I had to wear a heavy, yellow make-up that I wasn't used to and that stunk of lard. I could not get the hang of the exaggerated mime that is necessary in film work, to make up for the fact that no one can hear what you are saying. In fact, I was confused by everything that was happening; and at the time, I couldn't possibly grasp how this ten-minute film was going to come out. For instead of merely setting up a camera and shooting what was before him, as it would appear on a stage, Mr Bamforth was fascinated by the possibilities of splicing together bits of film, shot on different occasions, from different points of view. The way the bits were put together told a story almost without the aid of captions, because one guessed what was implied by the various shots.

In the evening, they showed what were called 'the rushes' in the Valley Theatre in Holmfirth, which Mr Bamforth regularly used for displaying his films. When put together, spliced at the beginning was a bit of film showing a view from the train so you could tell that we were in a tunnel, and at the end was another piece showing the view from inside the tunnel, looking out to the fields.

It was a most ingenious technique. Thus one understood that the scene took place inside the tunnel. Each time the train rocked, the cad took advantage of the motion to sway closer to me. The film went dark for a few seconds, to show that we were in the tunnel, and when all was lit up again you saw me in a fluster, tidying my clothes, and him wiping smears of make-up off his face.

Something else showed when it came before a public audience in that same theatre. At first they were quite bowled over by our little performance, especially as we two actors were sitting there, watching it, too, just like real people. Then someone twigged, and the whole theatre was laughing at me, with lots of *oohs!* and *ahs!* Mr Palmer was furious at what had come out in film although it was not visible in real life. He was *most* furious.

There was only one line of caption, supposedly spoken by me:

'Hands off, you cad!'

*

You know when it is that prisoners lose their wits? It is when they remember their happier past; especially if they believe their sentence to be eternal.

All through the winter of 1913–14 I satisfied myself with optimism that the pain would go. It did not go. Memory was Hell; and I learned why Hell was conceived as an infinite burning.

Sometimes it seems that my only defence in life has been a capacity for overhearing, for reading the signs; for reading upon people's lips what they do not intend me to hear; and for spying. Putting two and two together as the winter months wore on, peeping into letters (I didn't like doing so, but I *had* to), I realised that Mr Palmer was not fighting my cause. On the contrary, he was instructing his lawyer to hold off any solution. Mr Briggs and Liza Buckton privately – 'without prejudice', as it was put – agreed that I *did* have a case; whereupon Mr Palmer came to an agreement with them that nothing would be done to prosecute it – his purpose being to hold me prisoner at The Lumb. I could not face being kept for ever dangling on the thread of an unsolved legal case. Moreover, his holding me made him the more irksome; made me love you the more.

The straw that broke the camel's back was when Sarah married a soldier. She had met a second lieutenant at the draper's I used to send her to. So it was my own fault. As she left, I still could not help thinking; well, you know, he could have been me! Sarah and I had grown very close. But I was glad she had found a young officer. The War had not yet started, though it was on the horizon. Now, I believed, she could afford to keep her own maid.

From believing that I might eventually win justice for myself, I had come to realise that I could be blackmailed with a horrible fate. Palmer was enslaving me with the threat of it. I could only run. I would turn from hunter into hunted, but better that, than slavery.

Apart from my own money, I had saved up quite a lot of Booboo's and Didi's fivers, so I could last some time by myself. On a tempting spring morning in 1914 I could not help myself strolling across the park to purchase Taffy and the caravan from the gypsies.

For another five pound note, a gardener used his under-world knowledge of the kitchens and the servants' quarters to organise the delicate, secret extraction of my belongings. Thus I began my fearful but exhilarating life as an exile in my own country, as a refugee.

I knew that, after I had left, Palmer would join forces with Liza Buckton, wanting to find me and gain his revenge for having opposed him.

·9·

IT is 24 May 1915. The weather is roasting and it doesn't suit me. I'm the shady type. The sunny brilliance might have been a fine prospect for me at one time, but as things have turned out, I belong to the shadows. Now it is the Western Front that is, I believe, bogged down in rain and thick mist, the men trapped in mud at the bottom of those trenches, the action desultory. It is the towns and villages here, in the sunshine, that are like active war zones.

War, war, war; there is nothing else, anywhere. Something you would never have imagined has happened, Garrick: men pouring war from the air. Zeppelin raids on the south east coast. While from Ypres, privates have written home about the gas attacks and bits of their letters have been printed up in the newspapers. 'It creeps into the trenches like steam from a kettle. You feel it tightening in your chest. You cannot escape it. It's the nerves that it attacks. Your nerves are shot to pieces.'

The soldiers are also printed up if they complain about all these strikes we're having in England and Wales, especially among the miners in South Wales, or the tram strike that is at present 'crippling' London. 'Here are we fellows preparing to lay down our lives for the sake of King and Country for no more than a shilling a day, while over on the home front – it doesn't seem right.'

The women are solidly supporting the war effort. They, behind their curtains, are knitting socks, raising money and urging their men, 'for shame', to leave their marriage beds and go to fight.

What a summer is beginning! The heat makes everyone madder, faster, more violent, more noisy. It's our rain and soot that gives us our normally sombre temperaments. As soon as the sun shines, we turn into those same Latin types whom we despise as 'dagos' and 'wogs', don't we? You used to notice it.

Just to show the kind of thing that's going on: in Burnley, three days ago, I was delayed by a lunatic. I had left Taffy and the van at the edge of a common. Had tidied myself up, changing out of my gypsy tatters. Although underneath I wore lady's silk underwear to make myself feel nice while I walked through the streets, on top of it I was clad in respectable trousers and jacket, a straw boater for the sun, but the scarf still knotted at my neck. I had put a few of my other bits and pieces in a bag. Swinging a cane to help work up my confidence, I went round to the Palace Theatre at the end of the morning, at Band Call time, hoping for a cancellation so that I could squeeze on to the bill.

I would have liked to have offered the manager something a bit outrageous; the kind of thing I might have done in pre-War days. Something belonging to the fun we had for just a few years, after Queen V. died, with Edward on the throne and before this War came.

However, I carried with me a sombre outfit. What the stores call 'matron's wear'. An ensemble one would don for shopping in Harrogate. A navy-coloured suit and a dark hat, plus a veil that I could pull over my eyes and dramatically convert my clothes into widow's weeds. I proposed to do *There's a Long, Long Trail A-Winding*. Something sentimental to suit the times and also fitting for my age.

I thought it would appeal in Burnley, after Ypres and the gas attacks. No such thing. The concert was booked out, all the artistes had reported and were secure in their lodgings around town. The manager wouldn't even audition me for a later engagement.

He was as solemn as a judge. Burnley didn't require defeatism, it needed songs to inspire more recruitment. Hadn't I read Lord Kitchener's appeal in the papers?

In which case I'd sing a different number, I said.

Scowling over his spectacles, he told me that it was none of his business, it was a matter between me and my own conscience, but looking at it merely from a business point of view, what the people of Burnley would be wanting to know is, why was I fooling on stage in this fashion when I was young enough to join up? If he was younger himself, nothing would keep him back, he said. Questions were already being asked in Parliament about how many men of military age were being wasted on the stage. They'd be throwing things at me. Et cetera, et cetera. Blimey; didn't he make me feel small.

In the waiting room there was a chap offering bird impersonations. When I'd listened to him chirruping for ten minutes, I remarked that now all the birds of Yorkshire and Lancashire had been choked with smoke, the only place to hear linnets and warblers was in the music hall.

'Christ, where you bin brought up? Swallowed a f——g dictionary?' he said.

Thereupon a gentleman, a proper gentleman named Mr Nutton, recognising one of his own kind because of my voice, interrupted in order to agree with me. I knew his name because it was in gold letters on his Gas Fighting Appliance. He was about sixty, dressed in the knickerbockers and tweeds belonging to the country, and he had the ferocious face of a retired officer.

> Although I'm not a chicken,
> I'm pretty good at clickin'
> When I see a nice old man like you

– You know the song. He understood the temper of the Burnley Palace better than I did, but he was quite mad. In the mean little anteroom to the manager's office, when the chirruper was in and while we were both waiting, both of us hopeful at that stage, he wore for my benefit the ponderous headgear and mask made of leather and rubber which he had invented. He wanted to demonstrate its use on stage, within a cabinet filled with what he called 'German gases'.

We others agreed that his act was especially timely after Ypres. But he could not demonstrate it without fetching a cylinder of gas and his cabinet, as well as the pump with his name on it that he had brought with him already; and when he went into the office to propose hiring a coal-cart, there and then, the manager would not agree to it.

While the bird impersonator was taken on, Mr Nutton and I both ended up crestfallen and in a mood to console one another.

Mr Nutton, who was obsessed, wanted me to go with

him to his home to open a few bottles of ale and to see his invention. I was wondering what his home would be like. This could have been the beginning of an adventure. As we walked through the streets, I swung my cane jauntily. I tipped my straw boater to a lady with whom I accidentally collided; and I wondered what Mr Nutton would make of it if he knew what I was wearing underneath my other clothes.

The trouble was, I was realising that his biggest problem was not the unwieldiness of his act but his insane jingoism, so rabid that it even put off theatre managers who as a matter of life and death had to pull in patriotic crowds. I had been rejected for one extreme, and he for the other. For the time being, this somehow made us friends: neither of us was making accurate marketing calculations. We were a pair of idealists. But there was no mileage in it for us.

His performing on stage was not to make a career of it, but to recruit what he called 'gas fighting battalions', and he had apparently been so incautious as to tell the manager that he was an amateur.

On our walk through the streets, he railed about 'the bloodthirsty Kaiser and the work of his hellish hordes'. 'We all now know it means murder and mutilation, ruthless tyranny, sensual lust, rape and rapine, piracy and poison, debauchery, gluttony, lust and loot . . . ' he said – shall I go on? 'The desolation of the once happy homes of the innocent Belgians, the wreckage of cathedrals, works of art, our *dear* maidens murdered in cold blood, little children hacked and violated, and our brave and honourable combatants *tortured by the fumes of hell . . .* '

He was obviously rehearsing his act. Salivating over it.

'Why do our music halls and theatres not do more for the patriotic endeavour?' he asked, glaring at me.

'I do not know,' I replied.

'Instead of which, they poison the wine of life with the lees of lasciviousness! They sepulchre their chivalry to women in a slough of suggestiveness! They are ribald renegades, sir! *Smut*!'

I decided that, once he had got me into his house and discovered what I truly was, he would probably take me to be an ally of the Hun.

Fortunately for me, he lived among such a tangle of cotton-spinners' terraces that it was easy for me to give him the slip by darting down an alley and across some waste ground, while he was still walking a few paces ahead, declaiming to me.

*

Especially from feeling my silk underwear, I had been lusting to slip into those clothes which in Burnley I merely carried in a bag, and be seen, be seen! All I could think of was to find a private place and dress up. Perhaps, in the twilight, I would venture among people, walking through the streets.

This idea took entire hold of my mind. I tried not to think of what I would *most* like to wear; nor of the spacious, mirrored rooms in Lumb House and The Hollies where I could have worn them. Instead, I concentrated upon what was possible. A modest disguise, but it could be very satisfying.

I have got clear of the factory regions. I am now west of the waste-tips, the chimneys and the filthy rivers:

> *The Irwell*
> *Will smell well*
> *If you stir well*

– as the children like to chant. Today, I reached the edge of the park at Salmesbury, a few miles short of the town of Preston. There are avenues of magnificent trees planted in the last century, copses, pools and grassy parkland like a music-hall backcloth or a Bamforth postcard. Taffy enjoyed a rest, the rough grazing at the edge of a wood and a drink from a pond, while I hid the caravan under the trees, down a track where the grass had clearly not been pressed down for a week or two.

I wound up the gramophone and played the new Regal record that I had bought in Accrington: Marie Lloyd singing *A Little Bit of What You Fancy Does You Good*. I dared to leave open the caravan door and window, to let what breeze there might be blow through while I changed. I shaved my face for the second time that day. I stripped myself of trousers and shirt, and got right down to the foundations, building myself up again from the front-fitting corset which you purchased for me. The same silk underwear as before; that was the really delicious part of the exercise. I put in nothing like the effort I used to for your benefit, nor for Mr Palmer's, but my act is smoother these days from years of practice. I wore the navy cloth suit and dark stockings, then a black, short-haired, page-boy wig. The hat with the veil awaited my going out later. If I got into a tricky spot I could pull down the veil and masquerade as a widow; of whom there are so many these days. I cleansed my face with glycerine cream. I made up. The stage-whitener, enlivened with rouge. Something on my eyelashes.

The skin and lines that can't be hidden under powder remain ... I know, I know ...! The age of the face is exaggerated by the very devices one has to fall back upon to try to hide it.

My enlarged eyes, which were supposed to suggest innocence, projected the alarm of an old tiger in the night. What a mess our minds, choosing, make of us. I tell you this: a history of womankind is dramatised in the face of a made-up drag artist.

I have to rely, these days, upon being able to draw the veil.

I wound up the gramophone again and played Eugene Stratton singing *I may be crazy/But I love you*. I sat on the caravan steps, folding my dress across my lap, stroking my arms, feeling the silk move under my clothes next to my skin, quite at peace and harming nobody, thinking my thoughts, working myself up to add a little more to my writing. Happy to fill in the time until evening when through a warm twilight I would take a stroll through some nearby village.

I believed that no one would find me under these beech trees now breaking into leaf. I loved it there. The little points of beech buds, you know how late they come, poking like bits of reflecting, emerald glass out of the brown casings and the beech twigs shining like silver.

I believe I could live in a caravan for ever.

But I was no sooner settled, than I was disturbed.

It was because I fell into the clutches of some *real* women, Garrick, that I firstly found it difficult to get beyond Salmesbury, and then had to fly as if the devil himself was after me.

231

It's my own fault: I should have known better than to pull up on the edge of a country estate. It's on estates like this that they soon come nosing after you. I've had a year of it and I know.

You'd think that, in a thousand acres, they'd be glad of a few living people to remind themselves that they still belong to the human race. You'd think they'd want to share a bit of their own good fortune. No such thing.

Settle up near the packed streets of cotton-workers and no one will bother you. The operatives have few possessions in the whole world and half of these are scattered around their doors and yards. They leave out their washing, their perambulators and babies, dolly-tubs and brushes, tin baths and bicycles; anyway, their houses often aren't locked. They leave their back doors open for the neighbours because someone might be ill and in need, or wanting to borrow a spoonful of sugar, so you could easily nip in and pinch the family Bible and the clock given to grandad for three quarters of a century's labour in a cotton mill, if you were so disposed. Yet no one among these streets will chase you away. But pitch camp at the corner of an estate where there's nothing but a few rabbits that the owner regards as vermin, a few fallen logs belonging to a man who has hundreds of acres of timber, and in ten minutes some bully will be there suspecting you of mischief. It'll be a gamekeeper with a shot gun. Or a woman, probably a schoolmistress or the vicar's wife, who comes prying.

If a gamekeeper comes, I pack up without more ado. The less they see, the better.

With a woman, it can be touch and go. With her you do have a head start; for if she herself has walked across to visit a solitary 'gypsy' caravan, rather than sent a policeman, it's because she's been unable to restrain her romantic nature. She's arrived more than half prepared to see me as a scholar gypsy, free as the wind. There's no greater slavery than being 'free as the wind', but her kind doesn't know that. I never attempt to disillusion her. On the contrary, I feed her illusions; it's one of my techniques of survival. Real gypsies and tinkers are hounded away without more ado and they know that the less they tell about themselves, the better; but I lay it on, as

232

quickly as possible showing her how genteel I can be, so as to get her on my side.

When she's ceased to be stiff with authority, which is the more rigid because underneath she is quivering with fright, I generally invite her to squeeze into my caravan, to view my Crown Derby tea-set and my objects from the stage. It is then that I announce what I divine has been observed already; that I'm not 'really' a gypsy, 'I worked in the theatre.' After this, there's a fifty-fifty chance of being left in peace, or even of being invited into a kitchen, or into a parlour to enjoy tea and scones. My visitor at the least departs appearing to be charmed and pacified, saying that I've quite made her day and it's an honour to have met such a remarkable person.

The trouble is that she's likely to change her mind later. She reflects that we have not been introduced, that I am not 'known' and that I do not belong to a family. She tells the police that she's frightened for her silver. This I invariably do not discover until about three o'clock the next morning, when a couple of bobbies arrive on bicycles and hover some distance away, whistling *Roses of Picardy*.

This is to see if I'll come out and confront them. Perhaps I'll perform a foolhardy act, thus giving them an excuse to arrest me. I never fall into the trap, so next thing, one goes to the front of the van, the other to the rear. They simultaneously shine their torches and shout 'police' – the idiots! This is when, for their benefit this time, I light up my books and china, before I confront them.

Sometimes it works. They apologise for the 'nervous old lady' who complained about me, and they leave me in peace to pursue my 'studies'. Or they move me on. Again, I never argue. But either way, I have suffered a disturbed night, and that is why they come at such a time, rather than immediately after I have been reported to them.

*

At Salmesbury, it was the vicar's wife who strolled across during the early afternoon. My third choice of record was winding to its end: Marie Lloyd again, singing *Every Little Movement Has a Meaning of Its Own*.

Through meadows packed with flowers, lady's smocks and marsh marigolds in the damp places, buttercups where it was drier, I spied, through the loops of branches on the edge of the wood, this lady coming. She swayed uncorseted; I could pick that walk out from quite a distance. She was wearing a light silk dress of pale blue stripes, a yellow sash around it, and a straw hat which she held on to although there was not a breath of wind. They are going to be making hay early this year; the grass already came up beyond her knees. Don't laugh; but I was thinking of Aphrodite rising out of the sea.

It's not easy to lock the door and pretend you're not at home in a caravan; not like in a house. I hadn't time to change my clothes. Though I am used to bizarre situations, they have always occurred either among cognoscenti or at night-time among dim lighting and shadows. But a woman sitting in elegant mourning, wearing stage make-up, on the steps of a gypsy caravan: imagine!

As I waited for her to approach, I thought of the explanations that might spring to her mind. What should I do? Put on the hat and pull down the veil? That, in the circumstances, would be more preposterous. I would have to brazen it out.

I did not take a direct look at her until she had reached me and had paused. I caught her staring at me as one does at inferiors, without feeling the need to disguise one's stare, nor to say anything. In an instant, I knew her type.

But I felt safe, for she was as mad as a hatter, as I could tell at a glance from the twinkle in her eye; though she was not as far gone as Mr Nutton; she was just gay with it. As she was possibly even superior to the middle classes, I felt the more secure; she was likely to be tolerant. She could be the daughter of an Honourable. She could have been one of the owners of the hall, but I didn't think so; she wasn't as disdainfully proprietorial as all that. I therefore guessed that she was from the vicarage. Vicars often marry such types, don't they, and women in country vicarages are often jolly strange – think of the Brontë sisters. Their cloistered way of life encourages fantasies. There's nothing like it to create lurid imaginings, as hectic fungi grow in damp, dark cellars; I know all about that. But she also had the kind of arms, soft and thick and healthy, that I know I can trust, and an oceanic swelling of the breast to match. And I liked, I envied, her silk dress.

'What are you doing here?' she asked, with aristocratic deliberation. 'And who are you?'

But there was a distinct sense of fun in her voice.

'I am an actress, in the music hall.'

She was the type to whom you could come out with it.

Of course I was wondering when, or if, she would guess what was *truly* peculiar about me. Her eyes were darting everywhere. I was wondering what she thought of my caravan that she was inspecting so carefully. It's really quite smart and I'm very proud of it.

'This is *my* secret place,' she said with a smile and like a little girl. 'I come here often, to read. I thought that no one else knew about it. What were you playing on your gramophone? I could hear it right across the fields.'

'Marie Lloyd.'

'You know that this is private land. Why are you dwelling in a caravan?'

'I have a romantic disposition.'

'You are taking an unusual holiday?'

'It suits me. "There's nowt so queer as folk."'

My changing my accent to quote a dialect saying put me on the same side of the class divide as herself: we were both laughing at the same thing.

'Are you a famous actress?' she asked, staring me in the face after having searched all around me. 'Might I have heard of you?'

'I don't know. I'm Iris Vane. I was due to appear at the Burnley Palace.'

'The name isn't familiar, I'm afraid. Isn't the Palace rather low?'

The upper classes can say the most rude things in the most charming fashion.

'One has to take whatever one can get, these days. Anyway, it fell through.'

'You must be glad, really. Inside.'

'Yes.'

'Gosh, it's hot, isn't it? Seventy-four degrees, my husband said. And only a week ago there was a frost that ruined the crops.'

235

She removed her hat and shook her hair free. I've never been able to do that properly, yet I've practised shaking my hair for *simply ages*. You should try it; a most difficult gesture, yet girls do it without thinking, from about the age of five.

'Do you mind if I look in your caravan?'

She was already looking. Again, I recognised class. Nowhere was private to her, not unless she reminded herself to be polite – when they want your vote in an election, for example – and my home might have been a doll's house in an exhibition. All she had to do in order to get her own way, so she believed, was to smile.

'Please do.'

'Thank you.'

From the top of the steps, her knees close to my face, she stepped right inside.

'Oh, how very charming! And you really manage in so little space?'

'I do. One gets used to it. After a short period, a house, even a single room, seems too big for a single person.'

'How amazing! But how charming! But how super!'

Fearing what she might pry into next, I got up and joined her. Her eyes were already upon my writing things.

'I am composing my memoirs,' I confessed.

'What a most extraordinary thing to do! For publication?'

'I hope so. Eventually.'

'Then I trust that I will get to read them. I will be able to boast that I know you, won't I, when the War is over.'

I opened all the cupboard doors before she did it for herself. I let her see my rows of jams, mustards and pickles, packed to stop them shaking on the road; my wardrobe, and how my bed slides; the little stove; my method of packing china; the elaborate equipment of my dressing-table; my photographs of you and me on picnics.

'Who's that?'

'The only man who was ever kind to me.'

'Was?' Her eyes picked up the hat and veil. 'Oh, you're in mourning. I beg your pardon. I thought there was something. I didn't know. I do beg your pardon for intruding.'

Women are always eager to talk about intimate things to one another; so different to men, even old friends when they meet, and it surprised me all over again. It was one of the things I have had to get accustomed to whenever I deck myself in drag.

'It's all right. It was some time ago. He was a friend. I dress this way out of habit.'

'A friend?'

I couldn't tell what she was thinking. I wasn't afraid. I felt that perhaps I could be honest with someone like this. However, she skirted her thoughts.

'And that's your horse outside, too!'

'Yes.'

'What's it's name?'

'Taffy.'

'It must be lovely to be a gypsy.'

'Sometimes.'

She was laughing at me.

Had she *twigged*?

'My throat is a little sore,' I said. 'I do apologise.'

'Warm weather can be very treacherous. It can affect the voice.'

'Yes.'

'Do you tell fortunes and make pegs and things?'

'No, I'm afraid not.'

'I'm glad you don't. Most of them are fakes. I'm glad you are not a fake, Miss Vane.'

Yes, she had twigged.

'And I'm sure you don't steal clothes off washing lines,' she said.

'Wouldn't dream of it.'

She walked out of the caravan, having inspected. She spread herself on the grass, plucking at the flowers, while I took to the shafts again and wondered whether she was going to leave. She had told me that this was *her* place, and she was obviously one of those ladies who have hours upon hours to fill in. You could see how used to such a way of life she was, by her utter unconcern about time or whether what she was doing was worthwhile. Another person would be looking at a watch and hinting at what was to be done next. She had no more concern for time than a cat enjoying the sun would.

She anticipated me.

'I know why you like taking to the greensward and things. I often lie here for hours. I'm not interfering with your privacy or anything, am I?'

The thought had at last crossed her mind and it made her sit up with alarm.

'No.'

It was a bit late for her to say so, even if she had been. Put-on guilelessness is characteristic of her class, too. It was a good job that I liked her. For no reason that I could understand, she made me smile.

I know what it was. She was like summer itself. Warm and casual; the light dappling her fair skin and dress, just as it speckled the meadows and woods. She was such a contrast to the War seething in the streets and along the valleys.

Also I was relieved because she was kindly. By this stage I knew that she was no more going to have me chased away, than to fly.

'What do you do on stage, then?' she asked, lying back again, an ox-eye daisy between her teeth.

'I sing popular songs and folk songs. I do funny turns, telling dialect stories, too.'

'In an accent?'

She seemed surprised that I could actually speak in the way I was brought up to talk in Saddleworth!

'Aye,' I answered, very broad.

'How long are you thinking of staying here?'

'I don't quite know.'

'I mean, are you heading for anywhere in particular, or are you just filling in time?'

'I'm going to Blackpool. But I'm not in any hurry.'

'You can stay as long as you like, for all I care. But I don't own the land. Would you like to stay?'

'Yes.'

'Look! We are getting up a concert this evening in the hall of the Technical Institute.' ('Getting up', again!) 'I don't know if I dare ask, but – well, it's for such a good cause, you know. To raise money to send cigarettes to the tommies. Would you contribute your talents? If you were to agree, it would probably put you in good standing with the local families. That would surely be a good thing from your point of view.'

'I'd be glad to do a turn.'

She sprang to her feet.

'How lovely! How absolutely splendid of you! My name's Mabel Bradley. Please call me Mabel. I'm married to the Reverend Archibald Bradley, parish encumbent. To a wanderer like yourself that must sound awfully boring, but it isn't, not always. One meets people. You, for instance.'

'No, it doesn't sound boring.'

'Do let us shake hands!'

She brushed at her dress and we shook hands like gentlemen.

'Is "Iris Vane" a name you adopted for the stage?'

'Yes,' I admitted. 'My given name is Jack Shuttleworth.'

She smiled.

'That sounds just as unusual – a man's name.'

'I am a female impersonator,' I announced. 'Obviously quite a good one. I was practising when you arrived. I'm sorry if I've led you on, but I couldn't help myself.'

'Good Lord! You're a *chap*! I thought all the make-up was just because you were in the theatre.'

She stepped back a few paces. She stared at me openmouthed, then put up the back of her hand as if to hide a gasp of horror. I at first thought that I'd thrown away my chances and that she was going to call the police. But I had not mistaken her underlying, lively character.

After a suspended moment, she sat down and doubled up to grasp her knees with the abandon of a fellow stage-artist. She burst out laughing.

'I shouldn't have sworn like that. Archibald would be most displeased. But it just slipped out. I've never met anyone like you! But I did think there was something different about you.'

She gave me a severe look.

'You're not a deserter, are you? Because if you are . . . '

'No, I'm not a deserter,' I hurried to tell her. 'I haven't signed on. Yet. Until Lord Kitchener's appeal I've been too old for the endeavour. I told you, I'm a music-hall artist. It's simply what I do to earn a living. My profession.'

'You *are* going to join up now that you may – aren't you?'

'Yes,' I lied.

'Because, I must tell you, I've no time at all for grousers and shirkers. Neither has anyone else of the respectable womanhood of this country. We believe that we're worth fighting for. Swinging the lead disgusts me.'

She had stopped smiling.

'Yes,' I agreed.

'How does one get into that sort of thing? Impersonating. I can't imagine it.'

'That's a long story.'

'Well, at least you'll be able to feel that you're doing your bit on the Home Front. *Won't* you liven our stuffy concert, and don't they just need it! We have awfully small horizons here, you know. Terribly parish-pump and all that. I mean, some are. *I'm* not.'

'I didn't think you were. Otherwise, I wouldn't have told you about myself.'

'Sing one of your songs for me.'

I got off the caravan shafts and proceeded to strut up and down the grassy track through the wood.

> *Up to the West End,*
> *Right in the best end,*
> *Straight from the country*
> *Came Miss Maudie Brown . . .*

'Marie Lloyd!' Mabel screamed out, and clapped her hands in delight. 'Her to a tee!'

I nodded and continued.

> *And if you should want a kiss*
> *She'd droop her eyes like this,*
> *But now she droops them just one at a time!*

I gave Mabel one of Marie's stupendous winks. I don't know how good I was at imitating her, really; an awful travesty, I expect, but Mabel was pleased.

> *And every little movement has a meaning of its own,*
> *Every little movement tells a tale . . .*

I performed for some minutes, then I stopped and took a curtsey.

'Actually, we – some of the girls – used to dress up in drag in the school dorm and my brother, Jonathan, made a spiffing girl for some of his school productions. Plaits and everything. Little rosebud lips. I saw him. We have a photo at home. He's a High Court judge now, but he was absolutely super when he was fourteen. Almost as good as you are. Lots of the chaps did it, you know.'

'Yes, I've been told.'

'Is that where you yourself learned?'

'Yes.'

'Are you going to come to our concert dressed as a man, or as a woman?'

'Whichever you would like. It won't be taking place until after dark, will it?'

'Eight o'clock.'

'I'll come along dressed up to the eyes, if you like.'

'It'll shock our local society, but they won't mind when they know you're doing your bit on the Home Front, and it'll be *such* fun! I'll do something in drag, too. Black coat and tails, you know. Vesta Tilley sort of thing. Wouldn't *that* be spiffing!'

'What do you suggest we sing?'

'I don't know. I don't really care. You're the artist. Except it mustn't be *too* saucy for Salmesbury. And the concert *is* for the war effort. We need songs that will support the chaps and give them courage, don't we? There aren't nearly enough of them.'

She sat next to me on the shafts. From a pocket in her dress that I hadn't realised was there, she pulled out a notebook and pencil. The notebook had a marbled cover and the thin pencil was threaded into the spine.

'I have a secret pocket,' she remarked, making me wonder why she had confided in me. Also, she winked, repeating my gesture from the song. Not many ladies wink. She opened her notebook and I saw pressed flowers.

She wanted us to compile a programme for our part in the concert. My suggestions were such numbers as *Are We to Part Like This?*, *I Was A Good Little Girl Till I Met You* and one of my favourites, *Little Yellow Bird*. Hers were so jingoistic that the words of them stick in my throat. But I have to survive. In minutes, we had made our list.

After she had left, I packed up, harnessed Taffy and went down the road to the Technical Institute. I turned into a short and un-made road at the side, and parked the caravan, tethering Taffy on waste ground.

I went back into the caravan and made myself up in full glory, to emerge when I could hear a hubbub of voices from pathways and hall. I wore a dress that Mr Palmer had given me. It consisted of South American beetles' carapaces stitched over glittering silver mesh.

Yet I managed to walk unnoticed through the shadows at the side of the building. Made of shiny Accrington bricks, it was as gauntly functional as a cotton-mill, but I could not resist being excited by the yellow lights through door-glasses and windows, and by the nervously jolly people also making towards it, wondering what the coming performance would be. My name, 'Mr Jack Shuttleworth, alias Iris Vane,' had been plastered over the top part of the poster, right next to Lord Kitchener, with his fierce eye and moustache and his menacing forefinger; a recruitment notice phrased in that brutal manliness that does nothing to woo. Its 'appeals' are mandates. '3rd/4th Duke's. Men of good physique over 5ft 1ins are accepted for the above Battalion. Enrol at once.'

In the second year of the War they were accepting dwarfs! Taking anyone. There was a hectic, vicious need, and you could feel it in the atmosphere of the Institute, which doubled up as a recruitment centre. There were copies of the same Kitchener poster and several others – TAKE UP THE SWORD OF JUSTICE and YOUR COUNTRY'S CALL, ISN'T IT WORTH FIGHTING FOR? and IT'S OUR FLAG.

I threaded my way through to where the concert was to be held in the dining-room. It was already quite full. Many of the village men, little fellows, or older ones who had not until today raised their right hands and accepted the King's shilling, and who had not yet been carted off to barracks, were there with their nervous wives.

The room smelled dusty and was very bare except for a platform at one end and a small table at the other for collecting entrance-money and other contributions, in boxes with Union Jacks pasted on them. Also there were some boards on trestles, covered with tablecloths and refreshments. None of your Institute staff; for this important event, two maids from the vicarage were acting as waitresses, giving the evening performance a little tone. There was to be a dance, with the music provided by a small band, mostly brass. There was a rope stretched down the middle, the full length of the hall; it was important that, even though they were fighting a war side by side supposedly for the same thing, the 'better classes' of the district be separated from the lower.

The lower classes, those members of it not occupied preparing teas or working the mechanical functions of the concert, were expectantly and uncomfortably seated on wooden chairs side by side around the walls; an arrangement that doesn't encourage conversation. Staring into the blank space between themselves and the dividing rope, they had the mute, nervous expressions of cattle dimly apprehensive of slaughter.

The better classes appeared to have no such fears, although they and their loved ones could be slaughtered, also. It was clearly *their* War. They stood confidently talking in groups and occupying the whole space on their own side, making the other side of the rope seem like a great hole. The ladies were eager and gleaming at the thought of feeding their chaps to the butcher. Don't some women just love sending their menfolk off to war!

You couldn't say that my entrance caused a hush, because the one half was quiet and nervous before I got there, and dominating the other part of the room were such figures as the vicar, the schoolmaster and the recruiting sergeant, who was a big, bullying character carrying a swagger cane. It appeared that there was a rumour that one of the 'People from the Big House' might put his nose in, and most were looking out for that. But I also think they were astounded at how convincing a lady I am. I don't suppose they expected me to be so expert and professional, and certainly they didn't know how much practice I've had!

Naturally, I myself was most curious about the vicar. I'll bet that if it had been put to Mabel Bradley that she had given me any idea of what her husband was like, 'Nonsense' she would have replied; and for certain I would not have recognised him but for his collar and suit. The reason, though, was that he was the opposite to the strong impression that she had created in my mind. As women instinctively do about a man who has a grip on them, out in the meadows she had created a portrait of someone larger than life and a bit terrifying. In fact, he was weasel-like, timid and small.

Mabel was with him when I entered. 'Coo – eee!' she called and immediately came over to me. Thereupon it was decided to which side of the rope I belonged; not that I would have hesitated to make the same choice for myself, because since early days I've not forgotten on which side all the benefits lie.

She whispered that she'd *explained the position*, then she introduced me to some of those on her own side of the rope. She was quite proud of knowing me. Mr Palmer's fabulous dress made it impossible for such snobs not to accept me for a person (if not exactly a lady) of breeding. One after another embarrassed, half-embarrassed or overbearing figure said to me, 'Glad to see you doing your bit for the Home Front!' or something of that sort; even addressing me as 'old chap'. I think that mostly they were trying to reassure themselves that the world was as they 'knew' it to be.

'We've got to see the Hun off, by fair means or foul, eh, what?'

'You're one of the Shuttleworths, I hear? One of the Saddleworth Shuttleworths? Didn't know there *were* any people out there. Thought there were only weavers. Hill-billies. That sort of thing.'

'That's rather a smart frock you're wearing, Miss . . . er, Mister . . . I don't know quite what to call you, eh, what? You didn't know my cousin at Winchester? Renwick. Clive Renwick. He used to dress up in all sorts of rig at end of term.'

'A lot of the chaps are doing your sort of thing out there, you know. Makes the other chaps laugh. You're not on leave, I believe? Are you going to sign up, now that the times are calling?'

'Are you going around the whole country doing this sort of thing for the troops? How *brave* you are! I mean, I wouldn't

244

dare dress up like that, not for a king's ransom.'

They made me welcome, in their own way. They could cope with me when I reminded them of their school days. But it's maddening when people get you on their own side by assuming that you already are, in the way that they talk to you. You have to answer them back jolly smartly, or you find yourself committed to their way of thinking.

I tackled the problem mostly by not answering at all. I kept my head down, smiling and concentrating on my coming performance. I do get nervous, you know; I haven't told you about that, and you never quite realised what it was like, did you, Garrick?

And I could already feel the unanswerable jingoism building up in the room. *Their* patriotism, not mine; though perhaps that will shock you, dear. Nor that of the poor cattle on the other side of the rope, with whom I rightly belonged.

But to be frank, I couldn't *stand* the way that they stared dumbly, asking to be hit. I preferred the facetious nobs; even though I didn't like them, either.

Though one or two of them, over there on the other side, allowed themselves to titter.

After I'd swanned around for a while, it was announced by the Reverend Bradley that the concert was about to start. The band played *Onward Christian Soldiers*. It was clear that there was going to be some serious stuff before anyone could relax by dancing. The vicar was fiddling with a sheet of paper. The band having finished its rousing number, he coughed once or twice until silence fell, like a stone over a tomb.

'This poem was written by Harold Begbie in August 1914,' he announced. 'I think one can say that its moral is even more true today, now that we are almost one year into the conflict. It is entitled *Fall In*.'

The Reverend Bradley read the poem, very dramatically.

> *What will you lack, sonny, what will you lack*
> *When the girls line up in the street,*
> *Shouting their love to the lads come back*
> *From the foe they rushed to beat?*
> *Will you send a strangled cheer to the sky*
> *And grin till your cheeks are red?*

But what will you lack when your mate goes by
With a girl who cuts you dead?

The Reverend knew to lift his eyes from time to time off the paper. His eyes sometimes swept the ceiling, making his spectacles glitter. At other times they dwelled upon his peers. Mostly, when he was not reading, he stared at the lower-class horde. He was singling out individuals for the longest and most unnerving glances. I expect they hadn't signed up yet. At any rate, there were certain men afflicted with the fidgets. But he wasn't having it his own way, either.

'All high and mighty, safe home in blighty!' someone whispered.

The poem grew steadily worse. It ground on into its moral like a tank pushing through mud.

Where will you look, sonny, where will you look
When your children yet to be
Clamour to learn of the part you took
In the War that kept men free?

'Here, here!' broke in the recruiting sergeant, to lead on the others. His glance, too, swept the ones on the other side of the rope, who more and more looked like captives.

' 'Ere, 'ere,' some sycophant shouted.

'Here, here,' supported my friend Mabel.

By now, her husband looked a foot taller than he had seemed before. You couldn't say that he wasn't good at performing.

Will you say it was naught to you if France
Stood up to her foe or bunked?
But where will you look when they give the glance
That tells you they knew you funked?

'Quite so,' said the old Jingo who had asked me if I had known his cousin.

'Sschh!' Mabel hissed, not wanting him to upstage her husband.

How will you fare, sonny, how will you fare
In the far-off winter night,
When you sit by the fire in an old man's chair
And your neighbours talk of the fight?

Will you slink away, as it were from a blow,
Your old head shamed and bent?
Or say –

The vicar rose on his toes and his voice reached a crescendo.

– I was not the first to go,
But I went, thank God, I went!

The nobs began to clap, quietly. The Reverend smiled at them. Some of the others clapped, too. But the vicar had another verse to go and he got on with it quickly lest he be cut short. He held up his forefinger. Left it sticking there until the end of the verse.

Why do they call, sonny, why do they call
For men who are brave and strong?
Is it naught to you if your country fall,
And Right is smashed by Wrong?
Is it football still and the picture show,
The pub and the betting odds,
When your brothers stand to the tyrant's blow
And Britain's call is God's?

There was no mistaking which section of the audience had a weakness for football, the picture show and the pub. The vicar didn't take his eye off them. He roared out those words, *Right, Wrong, Britain, God's*; one could never have imagined he had such a powerful voice.

The audience was most appreciative. The vicar shrank to his usual size and smiled, while the schoolmaster, who now appeared on the platform, led the cheers.

The schoolmaster believed himself to be good at being MC but he was terrible, parodying some music-hall chairman he must have seen, once, somewhere. He was nothing but another bore and a bully, like the sergeant.

While he was talking, the sergeant and others were going around the room and along the rope, collecting money. I could see bank-notes sticking out of a couple of boxes.

A chap who looked like a banker came on to do conjuring tricks with cards. Then Mabel was introduced and she was as good as her husband. During the previous turn she had slipped away and had changed into a Vesta Tilley outfit.

An officer's coat and cap, with immaculate uniform-trousers over shiny patent shoes. Swinging a cane in martial fashion, she rendered one of the numbers that have caused Vesta Tilley to be called, with Lord Kitchener, 'England's Greatest Recruiting Sergeant'.

> *I'll show the Germans how to fight,*
> *I joined the army yesterday,*
> *So the army of today's all right.*

A young woman went on stage to sing *Jolly Good Luck to the Girl Who Loves a Soldier*. Next, we had *The Girl I Left Behind Me* and *Sister Susie's Sewing Shirts for Soldiers*. An old buffer appeared to quaver through a Boer War song, *The Boys of the Old Brigade*. His struggle to do his bit had a few mopping at their eyes. The money was rolling in. I overheard it being said that they'd already collected £13 for the purchasing of Woodbines.

Then a sandy-haired little fellow made his way out of the plebeian section of the audience. I hadn't noticed him before. Though undistinguished, he was respected. To guess at his profession, I'd say he was a craftsman; a local carpenter or a roofer. He was thirtyish, dressed in civvies but with a soldier's haircut, and he had that unmistakable, sallow look of the prisoners of barrack room and trench. The haunted, the hunted look, too, that I have seen in those who have been at the Front for a while; and he must have lied about his age to have got there.

He was introduced as Corporal Knowles, but everyone seemed to know him. So far, the performances had been by the better sections of society, directed towards their inferiors, and it was quite brave of this little chap to have a go. He was evidently appreciated for it, and was encouraged with smiles and clapping. Though his betters patronised him, he looked weary and as if life was a struggle. But could he shock them!

> *If you want to find the Sergeant,*
> *I know where he is, I know where he is.*
> *He's lying on the canteen floor.*
> *I've seen him, I've seen him*
> *Lying on the canteen floor.*

His accented voice and his crude, plebeian style of singing

as well as the comedy of the song brought him the first laughs of the evening.

It gave him courage. Though his own crowd were enjoying this and had started to sing with him, on my side of the rope they were growing uneasy.

> *If you want the Sergeant Major,*
> *I know where he is, I know where he is.*
> *He's tossing off the privates' rum.*

I could see that the recruiting sergeant was wondering whether to stop this performance. He was trying to catch the eye of the MC or the vicar but they were not looking in his direction. He glared across the rope. Under his fierce look, most listeners seemed to recollect where they were and what was supposed to be their proper attitude. It didn't put Corporal Knowles off, though. He'd got the bit between his teeth.

> *If you want to find the CO*
> *I know where he is, I know where he is.*
> *He's down in a deep dug-out.*
> *I've seen him, I've seen him*
> *Down in a deep dug-out.*

'Get off, Harold!'

'Get back to the Front and stop swinging the lead, old chap!'

Some of the ladies were laughing.

'Give him the white feather!'

'You should be ashamed!'

'My goodness!' Mabel was turning to the nearest men at hand. 'Aren't you going to stop this?'

Not before Harold Knowles got through his last verse; even though he was clearly about to break down.

You know what it is like when you feel that someone is near to breaking with nerves on stage. The excruciating, unsettled feeling it sends through an audience. He was near to tears as they tried to shout him down, but his words were mercilessly realistic.

> *If you want the Old Battalion,*
> *I know where they are, I know where they are.*
> *If you want the Old Battalion, I know where they are.*

I've seen them, I've seen them
Hanging on the old barbed wire.

Mostly they were shouting him down, but there were one or two other men there who knew the words; just one or two, but that was enough to give him courage. Apart from these, his own sort were almost worse than their betters, who seemed rather glad to leave them to the business of driving off stage someone who was being yelled at as a 'coward', a 'traitor'. The brass band struck up in order to interrupt the singer. The recruiting sergeant, assuming the duty of removing Corporal Knowles, was red-faced and bursting with anger.

Harold lost his nerve and ran out of the back door. This was laughed at as yet another act of cowardice. Yet in all the reckless war-fever that I had witnessed, I had not met anyone braver.

They were all talking about it, while the MC and the recruiting sergeant tried to get through this sticky patch as quickly as possible, and move on to the next turn. You couldn't say there was pandemonium, but the hall was distinctly livelier.

'What a disgusting performance,' Mabel said. 'But you're not listening to me! You've a faraway look in your eye.'

'Have I? It's those things he's singing about.'

'He brought that song from the trenches. Most unpatriotic, *I* think. He should have left it there.'

'Why?'

'Because it lowers morale, of course. And any officer will tell you that a drop in morale means more casualties.'

'I suppose that's so.'

'Well, then. The MC's looking at us. I think it's your turn to go on. They hope you can set the evening back on course again. Go and do your stuff!'

The MC was all smiles for me. He was longing to change the mood of the audience. He borrowed a cap, so that he could doff it to me as I came on stage.

On the spur of the moment I decided not to risk songs but to play for laughs. I came on stage slowly, turning to blow a kiss and smile. Chaps were whistling at me, women were cackling and the upper crust of society was exchanging smiles, glad to find all the unpleasantness apparently evaporating. But they were wrong.

In my spectacular dress, I put on a grotesque Yorkshire accent.

'*There was this old lady walking the streets on a wet day with her skirt pulled up over her bonnet, see. 'Eh, Missus!' some young scamp shouts –*'

Not a laugh. Nothing more than a titter. Try again!

'*Chap come to our door collecting, says " 'ave you got anything for the Children's Home?" "You cheeky thing," I says, "We've only been married six months!"*'

Again, only a titter.

'Lend me your hat, Missus,' I said to a woman near the front.

'What, me?'

She blushed and pointed a finger at her breast.

'I'm not going to pawn it.'

I got some laughs with that.

She passed up her hat. I sniffed at it.

'There aren't any mice in it, are there?'

I dived into my two-person act. I put on the hat.

'*I'm sorry I arrived a little late for the reception committee in Salmesbury, but I was arrested by the police.*'

I took off my hat, looked in another direction and changed my expression.

'*Arrested by the police? Whatever for, may I ask?*'

'*For drinking eau-de-Cologne.*'

'*For drinking eau-de-Cologne! What was the charge?*'

'*Fragrancy!*'

The better people almost liked this one. The vicar smirked and so did the sergeant.

I had it in mind to do my 'parrot' story. Perhaps Mary and her sampler. But nothing was going to work, really. Corporal Knowles had left hanging in the air the odour of foot-rot in the trenches, the smell of blood pouring from a bayonet thrust, of bodies hanging like rags on barbed wire in the rain and of limbs blasted over the mud. The things that many who were present knew of but didn't speak about. I'm sure that they had heard rumours of what happened to 'shirkers'. How they were shackled to carts during bombardments, suspended on

251

crucifixes, imprisoned under fire in barbed wire compounds without beds or bedding in the rain, compelled to stand for days up to their waists in water or sewage and threatened with the firing squad on the following morning.

Thousands are shot for desertion, even for minor offences, as everyone knows though it isn't in the papers nor mentioned in Parliament, because soldiers out there are under orders not to communicate with Members. Who's at war against whom? Is it merely English against Germans? Then why torment, shoot and sacrifice our own men? Rumours get out. I have heard a great many in public houses. But the words for this real pain are resisted, by the nobs because they are 'unpatriotic', and by those on their way to become gun fodder in the ranks because truth makes sacrifice and heroism difficult.

A woman who had been staring at a recruitment poster suddenly pointed a finger at me and shouted me down. 'That's a fellar! What's he doing here? Why isn't he with the boys? He's swinging the lead! *He's a deserter!*'

I, like Corporal Knowles, had to flee. If you can talk about 'fleeing' in a horse-drawn caravan. Under cover of darkness, I moved five miles down the road. I have my experiences of how those who have noticed where you are camped come creeping up on you in the dark.

·10·

AND so, after a partly delicious, partly hideous little episode as Iris Vane, I changed back into a raggle-taggle gypsy fellow.

The next Lancashire village I reached, no one cared what I was. I met the old postman who had delivered telegrams, having to go from home to home with his black-bordered messages. He was weeping in the public house. All the young men of the village, belonging to one battalion, had been slaughtered with one burst of machine-gun fire. All gone, within an hour, somewhere. By being careless about German spies, by taking no care to cover up signs of preparing for an attack, the General, it was said around the bar, had let Jerry know that his lads were coming and the lines of machine-guns were waiting for the boys equipped with nothing better than rifles and bayonets. 'They should 'ang the generals,' they said.

It was in this pub that I met a chap sitting alone before two glasses of beer. He drank one, then the other, then he filled them both. He stared at the glass he was not drinking from and spoke to no one, until I broke into his reverie. I found that the second glass was for his friend who had been shot from his side in Flanders.

I reached Preston. There the Socialists were out. It was very daring of them to put their noses forth in Preston: a town devoted to armaments and also holding the huge Fullwood Barracks. On the western edge of England, it is safe from Zeppelin attacks. Also, being isolated among square, flat miles of potatoes and celery, any spies and fifth columnists, conscientious objectors and Socialists, are easily spotted as they approach. If they can't be disposed of by using the Emergency Regulations, it would be easy enough to dump them in the River Ribble which flows deep, sluggish and tidal over deposits of mud. If there's anything unusual about them, why, over a wall they can see the wide, black river to remind them of what could happen.

But, God bless my soul! There were the Socialists, braver than ever I was in drag, with banners and a rickety platform. (Socialists are like that.) Defended only by a cordon of Suffragette ladies with ribbons across their breasts, their orator was declaiming to a small audience of munition workers, mostly women; also to a few officers, one or two circumspect gentlemen in good, black suits and Homburg hats, and three policemen.

'This war is not about justice. It is about the struggle of the Great Powers to dominate one another,' he declared. 'The ravaging of little Belgium is not the work of the pillaging Hun but because of financiers, capitalists and manufacturers on both sides competing with each other to take raw materials on favoured terms from the colonies that they rule.'

'Your sort should shut your f——g mouths! We're the f——g civilised ones!' a woman shouted. Her clothes were stained yellow, her skin too was ineradicably yellow from TNT poisoning. Such fated munitions workers were nicknamed 'canaries'.

The orator did not even change his tone; not even when the crowd laughed because he quoted Mr Keir Hardie, '"Had the workers been consulted, war would not have happened; why were they not consulted?"'

I am sure you would have admired his style. But as a matter of fact, I was sceptical of this philosophy, because of what I had listened to every day along all the valleys from Halifax. 'What would you do if you saw Jerry pointing a gun at a baby?' 'What if 'e were 'aving a go at your sister?'

Doubtless the happy dead are still saying this up on the clouds where you are. I wonder if you are listening? You being such a patriot. At any rate, this crowd parroted the same things. One might have no hope of convincing a worker in armaments that the only likely reason for Jerry pointing a gun at a baby is that someone is poking a gun into *his* back; that this could only be prevented by soldiers having the conscience and bravery to refuse to fight.

However, number one: not many of these women *were* committed munitions workers. The industry had been minimal before the war. Just as the Government had made use of unemployment to raise a 'volunteer' army among the men, so most of these women had been forced by starvation, inflation and delays in receiving their separation allowances, into the work of filling shells with gunpowder – as other females had been hustled into the sweated labour of sewing uniforms and kit-bags under corrupt army contracts that were making a fortune for profiteers. Women unable to afford a halfpenny for a loaf of bread had been expected to find seven shillings to purchase a copy of a marriage or birth certificate that had been lost by bureaucrats and that they needed before they would be given allowances for the children or for their husbands at the Front. It happened so often, it was difficult not to believe that the losses of bits of paper were deliberate; many times I have asked myself, who was at war with whom, in this war to end wars?

However, number two: I had heard the same words from textile workers and miners in Blackburn, Accrington, Burnley and Halifax, where some people were still suffering near starvation. Women, whose husbands and sons had been among the first reservists to go, who were unable to buy food or pay their rents because they had not received their separation allowances through the inefficiency and heartlessness of the Government, whinged pitifully, 'It was them as started it, we canna let them get away wi'it.'

Women whose funds had dried up for weeks because their amateur-soldier husbands had committed some trivial offence; elderly fathers who had seen their sons return home on leave with that same haunted silence, those same dark-rimmed eyes, which I had observed in Corporal Knowles, were the very ones to shout down anti-war 'agitators'.

I felt sorry for them; I really did. Think how many times through the centuries the boys have gone off, upright and singing, down these same Preston streets and have come back broken, if at all, with nothing but another war waiting over the horizon. As the Socialist CO orator declared, the War would not have happened had the workers been able to learn from experience and had not been as bad as its promoters.

Or so it seems. But, if I may point it out, there's another factor. Look at what I see, Garrick: the fathers, the mothers, the boys eager to acquire a haunted look in Flanders, shout these things with a flushed recklessness. They are not uttered with the deliberation of true thoughts. The newspapers, the clergymen, the schoolmasters and the town-mayors have told them to think thus. Mabel had confided to me, in the meadow, that the clergymen of the country had received government directives as to what they should preach in their sermons.

As any other ideas in these times are too difficult to hold, and one must think *something*, those handed out by Parliament and by Kitchener will do. Only: you damage yourself by not knowing truth from lies. Even more so, by choosing lies because they are the simplest. I should know.

*

Blackpool! As far westward as I can go, to get away from it all. I have to make a decision about my life. This is *my* Western Front.

I break on to the coast at the South Shore, but eagerly travel northward. The lower classes occupy the south of Blackpool, the genteel classes are in the north, where you used to take me.

I remember our first outing. As it was for Camellia, I had to be protected from the rabble and we went first class, though you would have sat in a first-class compartment, anyway. Three coaches left Halifax. After the most alarming shuntings, clangings and blowing of whistles at every major junction, third-class carriages joined us from Bolton, Rochdale, Manchester, Blackburn, Oldham – from all the 'cotton' towns – so that the train seemed a mile long when we steamed into Central Station, four hours later. We had our compartment almost to ourselves, but outside some stations there were half-mile queues. Children waving flags, toy buckets and spades were squeezing out of the windows.

But the real excitement began after Preston, when everyone competed to spot Blackpool Tower, and the shouts travelled the length of the train when someone saw it: a pepper pot on the horizon. I thought it had been a clear, sunny day in Halifax, but as soon as I put my head out of the carriage window, I saw the difference. Halifax was so permanently dirty that one had ceased to notice. I felt as though I had clambered out of a coal cellar. Here the sky really was blue. I was intoxicated by it; by the thought of Lilly Langtry at the Opera House in the Winter Gardens; and then by the sea, which I had never visited before. We came out under the glass-covered station canopy, Broughton's Dining Room on our right. Instead of hiring a cab to the Imperial Hotel (in Claremont Park, which the lower classes are discouraged from invading, because of a twopence toll) you insisted on sending the luggage ahead and walking the short distance to the Promenade and taking the tram. I was so glad that you did! The tide was almost in. Oh, the sound of it! The silver restlessness, brighter than the sky! The screams of the white, white gulls!

Once Taffy and I have passed the barrier of the sand dunes, reaching the first boarding houses and the Pleasure Park, I pause to stare at the sea. But now, the tide is out. In Blackpool that means *out*. It is far away beyond ribbons of brighter water threading the sands. One could not reach it without wading. Also, because of the haze, the horizon is invisible, except by peering. The sea is something receding and eternal; seeming ever held back. Like truth. There's nothing like staring at the level, damp sands, and then the sea, for thinking out the truth about oneself. It is like staring into a mirror; one misted over so that there exists no clear image, except the one that the mind puts there, dimly; but it grows clearer through peering.

The town of Blackpool, on the other hand, is all distraction. What a contrast on the right-hand side of me! It is the biggest, most devoted entertainment centre in Britain. From the rough dunes of the South Shore where the gypsies and tinkers used to camp until they were driven off as 'insanitary' (but really to make way for the Pleasure Park), five miles up beyond the mid-town where the million per year of textile workers and coal miners gather in their best Sunday clothes around the Central Pier, to the North Pier and Talbot Square, the town is nothing *but* entertainment – apart from a few churches and chapels embedded in it, like stony raisins in a fruit cake.

Dare I, a 'tinker' who has bridged the class divide, take my caravan and horse three miles to the north? Daren't I just!

Though not to park among those sisters of the caravan,

the horse-drawn bathing cabins along the shore, but half a mile inland on a place left waste behind Central Station by the Lancashire and Yorkshire Railway Company. Where there is chaos and the movement of strangers bent upon entertainment, I am safe.

Nevertheless, I am still boldly parked among streets of prudish boarding houses, each named after the town where the proprietor likes to advertise – usually the one from which he hailed. 'Wakefield House', 'Elland House'. . . . Their scrubbed and donkey-stoned steps, their plush, theatrical curtains pulled aside with golden cords to reveal tables laid with white damask cloths ready for tea, and their familiar names bait the cotton workers and the miners who pour out of the 'excursion trains'. If you come from Wigan, go to Wigan House so that you don't have to spoil your holiday by mixing with strangers. I believe that abroad there are hotels named 'Hotel Great Britain' and 'Hotel Swiss', upon the same principle. While for those who are pretentious without being parochial, who want grapefruit before their fish and chip supper, there is 'Windsor House', 'Balmoral House' and 'The Regent'.

The brick-strewn ground, growing mostly thistles, offers little grazing for Taffy; moreover, someone could steal her while I'm working. But I have a friend, a music-hall fan who works as an ostler at the stables belonging to the Princess Hotel where they keep horses and landaus to take guests to and from evening performances at the theatres and the Opera House. I offer him a shilling per week, but don't tell him how long it will be for. 'We'll see how we get on,' he says, with a wink which promises nothing and everything. With a smile and a joke about my glad-rags, he says he'll also keep an eye on the caravan, because he lives nearby.

I walk seawards, into Talbot Square, which, genteel as it was once, has been invaded more and more by the lower classes. You did not like that. On all our visits you remarked how things had changed, meaning, of course, as people always do mean, for the worse. No matter what class, visitors to Blackpool are well dressed; the working men in caps, the women in straw hats and elegant gowns, despite the War. They are here to show off, to pick up a girl or a fellar, to have a good time. That's all they're interested in. Only I, it seems, stare at everything. Here is a stiff young man with a limp and a pallid complexion despite the fine weather we have enjoyed. He has a puzzled look and a brutal haircut. He is in civvies but I know he is a wounded soldier convalescing at one of the requisitioned hotels. Here is a young woman coming along staring at the ground; though it is none of her business, she tidily picks up an apple that has rolled off a cart and despite her fine dress, I know that she is a holidaying maidservant. I, in my gypsy tatters, am taken for someone touting for a living along the beach. You can get away with anything in Blackpool. I could walk through town in drag and only be taken for yet another person earning a living in a show.

I rest myself against the railings between the public drinking fountain and the horse trough. On the North Pier behind me, Professor Speelman is valiantly persisting with his concerts of classical music. An elderly(ish) gentleman is making his way towards the pier. He looks kind. I smile at him, but he does not smile back. It is too late for me, for that sort of thing. Or is it? He changes his mind, gives me what might be the glad-eye, and makes for the Metropole Hotel.

So many memories! Looking up the Square, there is Yates's Wine Lodge into which you were fond of nipping for a schooner of sherry straight from the barrel. A flag, I'm sure it's the same Union Jack which used to cheer us of old, is flying from the cupola. Around the corner to the right are the Winter Gardens. One hundred yards southwards along the Front is the Palace Theatre. Florrie Forde and G. H. Eliot, the 'Chocolate Coloured Coon' who comes from Rochdale, are starting tomorrow, 26 May, while at the Grand Theatre Mr Max Allen's Company is performing in *Hindle Wakes*.

Oh, I just cannot help a sudden wash of tears embarrassing me before the crowds. Such a womanish thing to do.

When I've dabbed myself with my hankie, I realise that what I must think about is work. On the Central and South Piers and all over the beach are groups of clowns and pierrots, performers with fiddles and melodions, collecting money in hats. As a last resort I could get myself up and try to grab a pitch near the Central Pier entrance, where the crowds make for the Isle of Man ferry.

Or I can do better for myself, at least be under cover if it rains, in one of the song-plugging booths along the Promenade; along the Golden Mile. Right among the phrenologists, palmists, ventriloquists, midgets, bearded ladies, the 'fattest woman on earth', the thinnest, strongest, hairiest, et cetera, are the song-plugging booths belonging to Mr Lawrence Wright and those of Mr Bert Feldman.

Mr Feldman's my man, for me to get a hearing.

*

Mr Feldman, the Blackpool music publisher, has this week placed a full-page advertisement in *Era* to tell us that his 'biggest ballad in years' is *A Little Bit of Heaven (Sure They Call It Ireland)*.

That, I could never sing; not without making it farcical. But there are other numbers I might have a go at. Since Mr Feldman bought the copyright of *It's a Long Way to Tipperary* he has become one of the biggest publishers in the business; much bigger than his Blackpool rival, Lawrence Wright. Not even Stoll and Moss take out full-page advertisements but Mr Feldman grabs your attention with a page holding little more than the title of the song, as bold and unavoidable as a recruiting poster. That's the kind of man he is.

I am lucky that he is not at present in the Isle of Man. Yes, *Mr Feldman. No, Mr Feldman. Wouldn't I be an added attraction because I am in drag? A freak for them to stare at?*

I am signed on, my payment being part of a halfpenny commission on each song-sheet sold. I share the halfpenny with three others: a pianist, a salesman and a hustler who works the street. With luck and hard work, so I am told, I could make one pound per day.

Such as I can at least pour our pain into our art. At eight o'clock on the following morning, while Florrie Forde and G. H. Eliot are oblivious in their beds in The Metropole, I put on a summer dress of pink and white gingham check. It has a fitted bodice and a lace frill around the hem, which reaches almost to my white boots. It has a high 'cossack' collar and long sleeves, with lace cuffs reaching over my white gloves. On my blond wig, a simple straw hat with a pink and white ribbon. I carry a parasol which matches my dress, for I made it myself out of the same gingham, by covering an old umbrella. I also a carry a draw-string bag, made of gingham.

By half past nine I am ensconced on the platform of Feldman's Music Stores, a dark little place that it would be grandiose to describe as a theatre. There is a large placard outside declaring, 'Song Successes! Come Inside! Admission Free!', while the remainder of the space on the building's front is smothered with notices of what I will be singing, all day, in almost continuous performance until six in the evening, if I want to make any money. The room holds, at a pinch, fifty people on hard wooden seats, although at this time it is almost empty. It is a sunny day and the first people abroad are making for the sands. Later, children will be brought in after they have eaten too much candy-floss, Blackpool rock, or fish and chips, while drunks will shelter there in the afternoon when they have spent their beer-money, and by the end of the day the singing booth will probably stink of vomit. Thank God for the fine weather, which keeps out those who are only sheltering. On the other hand, it is in bad weather that one can make money at this game, for who wants to be crouched in a dark cave when he has come to Blackpool for the beach and the sea air?

The words of the songs are projected on to a screen behind my head. This is operated by the salesman. I must get the audience singing along with me, so that they'll become involved enough to want to buy the sheet music afterwards. It's a real test as to whether I can still create what you once called 'a subcutaneous shiver'. (I had to look it up in a dictionary.) But songs with rousing or catchy choruses are naturally the best sellers in Mr Feldman's booths.

Nonetheless, flogging a song is hard work. I have to believe in it and must convince each person that I am singing to him or her alone. Though the audience is coming and going, I somehow have to raise the temperature of attention, hunting through the indifference; throwing out a joke, shaking an ankle, strutting with my parasol, making a smutty suggestion at the expense of my own ludicrous self, in order to bring back the attention of someone about to walk out. I soon know when I have touched a nerve, for people behave differently, without realising that they are doing so. Someone whom I could never imagine dancing, gets up and prances about. An arm waves with an unexpected animation and her partner turns to her with surprise and delight. An old girl who has probably not done such a thing for thirty years plays coquettishly with her necklace, moved by a melody. Knowing that I am winning, my pace eases. My pianist believes in me and grows as relaxed as a rower going downstream. Though the customers bawl the choruses as if they are hunting songs, no matter; the point is that they're excited and will buy. The floorboards bounce and the pianist's ale quivers in its glass upon the piano. All the emotions of all the people in the room are gathered into one feeling, like the different fingers of a hand gathered into one glove; and I am wearing the glove, I can wave whichever finger I like. I am Napoleon taking an army to Moscow. I could drown them all in snow. But I bring them back. And they are sorry when the song is over; they want to take it away with them.

Here I was, in the twilight of a life that had been so much despaired of, singing for my salvation in a stinking hovel, but thrilled to be in gingham. On my fourth day, at twenty past eleven in the morning, when some instinct made me look at the clock, I became aware of a woman staring at me from the half-filled theatre. At the end of the number, when the pianist and I enjoyed a break for five minutes, drinking glasses of beer while the salesman went round with the sheet music, I observed the woman speak to him, before she dipped into her bag for a threepence-piece and bought a song.

When he came within reach, I asked what she had said. She had wanted to know my name. He had told her, of course, only that I was Rose Gay, which is what she would have read on the notice outside the booth.

She watched me through another number, hardly taking her eyes off me. She was only a couple of rows away. I studied her as well as one can from the stage, knowing how everyone is looking into one's eyes. She was slender, modest, well-dressed, about my own age, and probably married to a successful tradesman. Making no concessions to the summer weather, she wore a dark suit, that of a woman who attends chapel regularly; but also, a large, black hat. Though plain, apart from a little black lace and two artificial cherries, it was saucer-shaped and reached down to the tips of her shoulders. It was an extravagance, but a tentative one.

I hoped that her attention was because I had met her somewhere on life's journey, though I couldn't think where. But I began to sweat with fear that she had something to do with Liza Buckton. She was staring with half a smile that hardly changed upon her small lips and it made me especially uneasy because, I felt, it was to cover her distaste. I was already thinking of how quickly I could get out of Blackpool. My commission wasn't paid until the end of the week, but I must leave that afternoon.

I finished my last song of the morning. The pianist, the hustler, the salesman and I had planned to go to the pub for an hour.

The woman came up to me, nervously rolling her sheet of music into a baton.

'Rose Gay? Is it Jack Shuttleworth, by any chance?'

She could tell by the way I clung to the edge of the stage and, probably, went white, or red, or both, that she had hit her target.

Her smile vanished and she looked completely serious. Was it with distaste, or even, could it be horror? She put me out of my misery.

'Ethel Ferret,' she announced. 'So *this* is what you are doing!'

I was still unable to respond.

'I told you I'd come to hear you in the music hall, one day. I knew that I would. I knew you'd be famous.'

But she did not speak with delight.

'Ethel Ferret! Good heavens!'

I could stare at her more calmly now, looking for something to recognise. I began to find it then; to wonder, in fact, how I could not have known her, even though she was a little plumper; even though she was so upright and well-dressed.

'This place is just to sell Mr Feldman's songs. There are better places than this,' I said, recovering.

'You've been on at the grand halls?'

'Yes,' I exaggerated. Well, to be honest, I lied.

'You been on at The Palace?'

'I'm hoping to be.'

'Oh, my! Fancy me having known someone who is appearing at The Palace. I never thought that those people on the stage were quite real. At the Winter Gardens, too?'

She spoke drily. Did she mean what she said, or was she having me on?

'I might be appearing there. Nobody knows, do they?'

Her voice, though not without a trace of accent, was quite refined and I tried to match it. I felt pleased that life had been kind to her and, to be honest, a bit envious. I was unsure what she thought about me. Well, not too unsure. She didn't much like what she saw.

For the first time in years, I was embarrassed by my drag. I found myself plucking at my dress, trying to cover myself more completely and not be seen. I would have liked to hide my face, suspecting that she found it hideous.

'I must go and make up,' I excused myself and forced a smile. 'I must look a sight. This is just my act, you know. Ethel Ferret, my word! Will you wait a moment?'

'Yes,' she answered, heavily, as if decisively making a promise she wasn't sure that she wanted to keep. I sensed the chapel woman whom her clothes declared.

Whether she waited for me or not, I had to escape, at least for a moment. I left her and went into the little dressing-room and toilet behind the stage.

I looked at my face in the mirror. I was tempted to escape by the back door. I had been so hopeful but now my own repulsiveness flooded over me. As strong as my instinct was to bolt like a rabbit, I wanted not to be cowardly and to go and talk to Ethel. As I doctored my face with balls of cotton wool and with the emergency cosmetics that I had brought in my bag, I realised that I felt strongly about her. I had missed her. I had always known that Ethel could be quite beautiful, at least to me, if only she had a more forthright disposition, was less bedraggled, held her head high, was better dressed and fed. All that indeed had happened to her.

I felt something that I thought I would never, ever feel in my life.

I realised that I had not looked at her hand to see if she was wearing a ring.

As I had nothing to change into out of drag, I did the best I could with my created self and returned, reminding myself that I was a craftsman of the stage, and smiling.

She did not smile back. I saw the old Ethel Ferret. I used to feel sorry for her, but now her expression unnerved me because I thought she was solemn, not from being crushed, but because she did not much like me. Yet she had spoken to me.

I took a furtive glance at her hand, although there was no need for me to be furtive. I saw that she was, indeed, married.

Unless she was widowed.

'How on earth did you recognise me, in my stage dress?'

'By the way you stand. By your face. By the way you express yourself, even though you speak quite well now. By the way you move.'

'After all these years?'

'You haven't changed so very much, Jack.'

'Even in drag? You must remember me very well.'

'Oh, yes, I remember you very well. I used to think that you were wonderful. We were nobbut children at the time, weren't we?'

'I'm not always like this, you know.'

'Aren't you?'

She looked full into my face. I thought it was to detect whether or not I was lying.

'No. This is my stage dress. My proper clothes are – I live in a caravan.'

'You do?'

The pianist, the salesman and the hustler had departed, detecting something urgent or tender between the pair of us. The hall was empty apart from Ethel and me.

'Yes. Can I take you to lunch?' I asked.

'My dinner, do you mean?'

She looked puzzled. Working people call their midday meal 'dinner' and only genteel people refer to 'lunch', so I knew that she had not risen very high in the world, despite the money that had been spent on her clothes. But she thought that I had climbed to the middle classes.

Just as in the old days, she let me lead her, towards the exit from the booth. But at the door, she froze.

'Are you going out *like that*?'

'Yes. Why not?'

I suddenly felt foolish.

'I thought it was your stage dress. Are you out of your mind? Have you gone out looking like that before?'

'Sometimes. This *is* Blackpool. If anybody notices, they'll know I'm working.'

'Some work!'

'Nobody ever notices anything, anyway. You'd be surprised.'

'You must have done it quite a lot of times, to have found that out.'

But she walked on with me. I took her northwards along the Promenade. Despite my dress, and all the years, it was a most peculiar sensation of what I believe is called, in the French, *déjà vu*. Yes, it was just like the old days, on the moors above Saddleworth. From not having recognised her, it was now as if no time at all had passed since our last meeting.

Almost. The obvious questions which I was dying to ask, I didn't dare to raise. No doubt she felt the same, so we were stiff and almost silent.

'Do you know Robert's Oyster House?' I asked.

'No. I'm only ever here at Wakes Week, like everyone else.'

'Do you like sea food?'

'What's that?'

'Mussels. Cockles. Oysters. Clams.'

She started to laugh.

Ethel Ferret, *laughing outright*!

I don't know what could have given me more pleasure than that.

'I thought you was talking about sea-weed or something!' she said, still laughing. 'I've never had any o' them things!' Her voice had lapsed into the accent that I remembered. I wonder if you believe me, Garrick – it wasn't that strange floating feeling that we experienced during happy times, as if there was no skin between us, but I so much wanted to touch her. Yet the very intensity of my feeling prevented me from even brushing against her; although by being casual

I could have got away with it, for people might assume we were sisters. I longed to nip back to the caravan and change into male clothes, but felt that I couldn't trust her to keep a rendezvous.

We ducked into Robert's Oyster House, on the Front between the Palace and the North Pier. The whole, dark little place was moist and cool with sea-food. The dishes of cockles, prawns, clams, mussels and Anglesey oysters were displayed in trays on marble slabs.

I took Ethel into an inner room where we sat at a marble-topped table. Few other people were in this back room. I pressed an electric bell-push and, as Ethel had no idea of what she would like, I ordered a selection. Ethel's only request was for bread and butter, and, if it was at all possible, might she have a pot of tea with her dinner? She had become even more polite among strange company, in a café. She was shy and over-polite to the waitress. I had to show her how to eat oysters, as you had shown me, my dear Garrick, in this same room, in fact at this same table. Just as when we went there, they were served already split, in a shallow dish. I slid one on to my tongue, my head tilted back. My mouth, throat and nose were filled with the taste and smell of sea water as if I had dived into a rock pool.

Ethel tried an oyster, timid about letting go of it, then she pulled a face.

'Spit it out if you don't like it.'

But she swallowed the oyster as if it was medicine.

'I'd rather not have any more, thank you.'

'Try the cockles.'

'No, thank you.'

'The mussels, then.'

'No, thank you. I'll content myself with bread and butter, thank you, if you don't mind. Perhaps we could have a little more of that, if it is no inconvenience?'

She was as timid as ever about strange things, but stiff politeness was her substitute for bravery. I rang the bell.

'Just one round, perhaps?' Ethel requested. 'I like to keep my weight down.'

Ethel Ferret keeping her weight down!

'You don't seem much fatter than when I last saw you.'

'My husband doesn't think so . . .' she began, and stopped.

I couldn't bear the silence that might show her how I felt, so I hurried on to say, 'Have you any children?'

'Five.'

I think I was blushing. I wanted to hide my disappointment but I don't think I managed. My heart was in my little white boots.

'I told you that you would have lots of children.'

'And I told you that you wouldn't know me if we met again! That you wouldn't even remember my name. Would you have remembered, if I hadn't told you?'

'Of course I would.'

I would have done, too, but I felt that she didn't believe me.

'You *didn't* recognise me, though.'

'No. You didn't give me time.'

'I knew you, all right. Straight away. Even in – disguise. You couldn't have been surprised at me being in Blackpool. I mean, it is Wakes Week. Quite three-quarters of the town is in Blackpool on excursions at the moment. My family and I are staying the full week at the Balmoral. A most superior guest house.'

'I didn't know in which town you were living.'

'Oh, no, of course not.'

She didn't tell me, either. Was it because she wanted to ensure that I wouldn't follow her?

'So what has been happening to you?' I asked.

'Oh, a lot. A *very* lot. Only three of them are mine,' she added, realising that I was thinking about her children. Women are very quick about these things. 'Jack is a widower and had two children already.'

'Your husband's name is Jack?'

'Yes.' She smiled. 'Just like yours.'

For some reason, I was pleased.

'Isn't that strange?' she said.

'Yes. Where did you meet him?'

'At chapel.'

'When did you start going to chapel?'

'After you left, the Welsh miners who built the new tunnel took me because I was lonely.'

'What does your husband do?'

'He's a butcher.'

'Is he doing well?'

'He has his own shop, with fifty acres for keeping sheep and bullocks. Perhaps you could visit when you are . . .'

'Not in drag?' I interrupted, nervously.

'I was going to say, "appropriately dressed",' she said, humourlessly. 'But what have *you* been doing all these years?'

'I could never begin to tell you.'

'Are you married, too?'

'No.'

She smiled, knowingly.

'I didn't expect it. Are you doing well in your stage career?'

'Yes! Yes indeed! Prospects are opening.'

'Yes?'

'Yes. I am working for Mr Feldman.'

'Does that mean that you might be famous?'

From believing (perhaps) that I was famous, she had moved to the assessment that maybe I could become so. At The Fleece, I think she had been awestruck by what she regarded as my romantic nature. Now, I saw, a great deal during the intervening years had disillusioned her, but also it had made her strong, 'her own woman', you might say, and armour-plated. For all my experience, I felt quite naked and vulnerable still, compared with her.

'Mr Feldman made a fortune from *It's a Long Way to Tipperary.*'

'Yes?'

'Yes.'

'I don't know about it. I know our soldiers sing it on their way to meet the enemy.'

'Would you like to hear? I don't want to bore you.'

'Yes, please.'

Having finished her bread and butter, she wiped her fingers on her napkin and folded her hands on her lap, sitting upright and beaming, not exactly expectantly, but patient. I guessed that she was used to being told stories. Her husband probably recounted his day's doings at length, when they were together in the evenings. Perhaps having to listen to them was the price she paid for security and married bliss.

269

'Jack Judge – you know Jack Judge?'

'No.'

'Well, he wrote the song in Stalybridge in Lancashire in 1912 for a five shillings bet. He'd been doing the local theatre and at the bar afterwards he bet his friends he could compose and sing a new song at the Grand Theatre on the following evening. He'd no idea what it was going to be until he was on his way to his digs when he overheard someone say it was a long way to somewhere or other, so he stepped aside into the Newmarket Inn and wrote the most famous song in the world, just like that. Feldman bought it for twenty pounds and Florrie Forde sang it in the Isle of Man. It didn't do very well. But workers on holiday took it back home to Lancashire with them, and when the regiments were disembarking at Boulogne last year the *Daily Mail* reported that all the soldiers were singing *It's a Long Way to Tipperary* so Mr Feldman printed thousands of copies and made a fortune. That's the way your luck can change, if you take a chance.'

I got excited.

'Just look at Charlie Chaplin. When I first met him he was part of a troupe calling themselves "Eight Lancashire Lads" and I performed a sketch called "Casey's Court Circus" with him at the Halifax Palace. 1906. He was at the Keighley Hippodrome as "Jimmy the Fearless". Jimmy did daring feats, rescuing a maiden bullied by a cruel stepfather, saving an old lady's cat stuck in a tree. But he wakes up and finds he's been dreaming. Eugene Stratton was on the same bill. The last I heard of Chaplin, he was on at the Oldham Empire in 1910. Then he sailed to America and did all his acts on moving film. *Laughing Gas*. Haven't you seen it showing all over the country, now? That's what you can do with animated films. It's what I'd like to do, and leave the theatre. If you must know.'

'You always were a dreamer.'

'I thought *you* were the dreamer, sitting in that kitchen, by the well. Do you remember? I always believed you'd have no future.'

'No, you were the dreamer. Never making up your mind.'

'*Me* not make my mind up?'

It was, after all, I who had shown the determination to leave and take a chance at The Lumb.

'Yes. *I* knew what I wanted. I knew I'd know what it was when it came along. You never even knew what you *were*. You were always trying to please everyone.'

'I was?'

'I suppose that's why you're an entertainer. You're very good at it, I'm sure. You always were. But you'd be even better if you didn't try to please too many people. You have to satisfy yourself, sometimes, in order to please anyone else. What time is it? Goodness gracious, I believe I must be going. The children's nursemaid will want to go out for a breath of sea air herself, by now.'

I paid the bill. We went on to the Promenade. I still wanted to touch her. Didn't dare, of course. A married woman.

'Do you mind if I walk along with you?' I asked.

'No. But please don't see me right to my boarding house. I mean – I'm sorry to be blunt.'

'That's all right.'

'I've hurt your feelings.'

'No, you haven't.'

We walked in silence, southwards.

'I mean, I couldn't let myself be seen from the windows of a respectable boarding house with you, could I? Not when you're like that.'

'No.'

'I'm sorry . . . I mean . . . I didn't mean . . .'

'I know.'

'It's not my fault.'

'It's nobody's fault.'

Another silence that lasted for the space between two lamp posts. Would have been three, but I started to sing, quietly.

> *I may be crazy, but I love you.*
> *So why don't you come right down,*
> *And say goodbye,*
> *Because you may not see me anymore.*

'*What*? What's that?'

'Eugene Stratton's song that he did in Keighley with Charles

Chaplin.'

'After you left Standedge I could hear you still talking to me in my head. That went on for weeks. You can't imagine – I can still remember it. What a shame, that it should have turned out this way. What a mess. It's such a pity. It's nobody's fault, but it's such a shame.'

I felt most miserable and Ethel was as saddened as I was.

'What do you think of this War?' I asked her.

'Think? Excuse me, I don't understand. Is there anything to think? It's in a just cause.'

She spoke briskly, glad of something else to talk about, obviously.

'Is it?'

'Of course it is!' She almost stopped in her tracks. She almost shouted. 'Who doubts it? My eldest son went off gladly.'

'*Your* eldest? He was old enough?'

'Jack's son, I mean. He was killed. But I'd feel the same about the War even if it were my own son! His younger boy has answered the call, too. Unfortunately for myself, I have no one to give. I merely have three daughters, out of my own body.'

Ethel Ferret talking about 'out of my body'! But she said it drily, as a parson might say it, quoting the Bible.

It was all going wrong. We didn't even agree in our opinions. The more of her husband's sons were killed, the greater the inheritance for her own children, was my uncharitable thought. But she had become the kind of woman who would plan in that way. From my being sentimental about her, I began to see that I'd had a lucky escape. I was the one who had lived; if not in the sense of having a family and children, at least in my imagination and in my head.

Yet some of the things she had said touched me to the quick. Perhaps it was sensing this that made her say something that was really cruel; she knew that she had a victim. Though I believe she would have considered herself merely to be giving way to proper, patriotic sentiments.

'Of course, they wouldn't want you, either. Not with your nature. Any more than they'd want a girl. You have a good excuse.'

'Oh!'

She could not have hurt me more. She knew it, too, though I looked away.

'And I suppose the butcher's business is doing well because of the War?' I answered her, sarcastically.

'Why do you say that?'

'Isn't it so?'

'I don't know why you make such a remark.'

She had stopped at a street turning.

'Profit,' I said.

She stiffened.

'I must go on alone from here,' she said. 'But I *don't* think it is a pity that we've met.'

I stayed rooted while she stepped away from me. Without turning around, she waved her sheet-music roll and said, 'Thank you for the music, I think that Mary will enjoy playing it.'

'*Mary?!*'

Hearing that she had named her daughter Mary made my heart leap even more than when she had informed me that she had chosen to marry a man named Jack.

I watched her go to the end of the street, where she turned up some steps to a boarding-house door, still without glancing in my direction although she was now at right angles to me and could hardly avoid sight of me.

She disappeared and I turned back towards the sea front, to return to Mr Feldman's booth.

I had taken a longer lunch hour than I should have done. My colleagues would be cross with me, yet I could not keep myself from staring towards the sea for a few moments.

*

I got out of drag. Dash it, I did everything to scrub off the traces.

I went to The Palace which was full of men, many of them officers and soldiers in uniform either on leave or convalescing in the hotels-turned-hospitals. They were attending the concert given by Florrie Forde. She is a huge woman, the Brunnhilda of the music hall strutting in tights, sequins, necklaces, feathers and her short warrior's tunic

273

dress, while waving her diamond-encrusted baton to lead us in singing the choruses to *Pack up your troubles in your old kit bag, And smile, smile, smile!* Next, she sang *Tipperary*, which brought tears to the eyes of a one-legged invalid sitting next to me. The men were all but bowing to her. I'm sure they would have done so if she'd told them to and if the hall hadn't been crammed with seats.

I am amazed at men's wilful desire to abdicate before a powerful woman who knows what she wants; but maybe this kink is what keeps the world turning. I'm sure it has something to do with why the men are in this War; one that's less a fight, I hear, than a grovel in the mud inspired by Vesta Tilley, singing *Jolly Good Luck to the Girl Who Loves a Soldier* and *I'll Show the Germans How to Fight*, and by Marie Lloyd, urging men to Flanders by singing of how she loves her man, *Now You've Got Your Khaki On*.

My eyes, like all others, were glued upon Miss Florrie Forde. I, too, hung upon every note and word of *Goodby——ee, don't cry——ee* and *Hold your hand out, naughty boy!*

Seeing this huge, laughing, larger than life woman was like seeing Mary, Mary my mother, reincarnated upon the stage. It was quite uncanny. Telling me not to cry. Swept me away. Though I knew all the tricks, still I could not believe that she wasn't singing only to me.

*

I knew, too, that after a quarter of a century's experience of the halls I could never move an audience as she did, no matter what it was that I sang about. Nor as Marie Lloyd, nor as Vesta Tilley did. Nor Eugene Stratton, George Formby, Dan Leno. I, being a freak, neither man nor woman, could not inspire the sympathetic human passions that men felt for women stars, that women felt for men. I had neither what was required to appeal to those of the opposite sex, nor what was needed to reach my own.

It was because I was not *real*. I am a freak trapped by a flaw in his own nature. An actor trapped in his role; or in the role chosen by another. A freak of doubt and questioning. Genius is, above all else, I believe, a capacity for being *oneself*. That is what Marie Lloyd possessed. The real stars are those with the courage to multiply and scatter that essence which is themselves.

I had meant to make more of my visit to The Palace. Perhaps hang around the stage door afterwards. But I left quickly. I detested my hermaphrodite existence that had lost me to all normal relationships. I hated my wrecked plumage that had horrified Ethel.

I remembered your quoting to me, 'The road of excess leads to the palace of wisdom.' My dear, has our excess of fantasy and pain led *me* there? I would have thought that wisdom would glow more brightly than this – than trailing through the streets, regretting.

*

I went to the caravan: that was last night, when I slept so fitfully. I have never curled up with another person in my whole life, except, I think, I can just remember the feel of Mary's body, though I could be imagining it. Simply to dress as I wish has been enough for me. Better than having to put up with someone digging their knees or elbows into you and snoring! To create fantasies has always seemed more exciting than anything could be in reality. Tonight I really missed the experience of another body though. I have felt and wondered about this lack many times but never so strongly as now. You and I could have done so much. Do you remember when, after we had been drinking, I tip-toed to your room and, when you had stared at my drunken, perhaps agonised face, you would not let me in?

Do you remember how we once lay together on a sunny river bank while you spoke to me your beautiful thoughts?

You murmured that Anglo-Saxon poem about life being like the flight of a swallow which enters out of darkness through a window in the hall, passes through the light a moment and then vanishes into darkness again through another window.

Do you remember how, one sober morning, I brought you your breakfast in bed because you had a chill? I sat upon the covers for a while and before I left, we kissed, on the mouth. 'I really think you ought to go now, Camellia,' you told me. The Unattainable One, of course!

In place of you, I now imagined Ethel Ferret, the feel of her small bones and thin flesh. I held a pillow against my side, imagining it to be her. I spoke her name to it. Ah, well, that was mere foolishness. I do not even like Ethel anymore.

Though I have experienced so little of love directly, I have witnessed much, in Mary Shuttleworth whenever she talked about Joe Gaukroger. Also in Mr Haigh, unfathomably enduring his distress over his faithless wife. His mind distracted, it is hardly surprising that, as Ethel told me, he put his pipe down somewhere and set fire to his own home.

Dear Garrick, we, too, suffered from the disarray of our senses; especially from the mind-wrecking of the fantasist, inventing, inventing, for love's sake. We knew what it was like to push one another to the edge of a precipice, judging the distance more and more finely, just to gain a reaction, didn't we? Schemes for cheating one another such as in ordinary life one would hesitate to use against an enemy are sometimes employed by lovers. I have seen it! The predator moving in for the kill, falling mercilessly upon his victim's weak points. A different being took over and this irrational dybbuk of love was terrifying. One found that one didn't know a person.

No wonder that, in so many of the pictures around your house, artists depicted love as a mad-eyed huntress; Cupid as a baby with a quiver full of arrows. No wonder that poets describe lovers as lost, sick and out of their minds.

I was stranded upon the isle of your creation, Garrick. There we wrecked our hearts on fantasies. Pieces of jagged glass rubbing against each other. Yet out of love we kept it up! Coals smouldering within the ring of dark hollies.

I developed my special relationship to the light and the dark, seeking always the shadows in which to hide. Experiencing so much of daylight's beauty through my veil or by looking through the window; for me its play upon trees, flowers, grass and roof tiles became like bright jewels in the window of a shop where, comfortably off though I was, I could not afford to buy.

When we quarrelled, the clocks in The Hollies seemed to tick more loudly. Oddly, it was the clocks that made you feel it was such a timeless, unchanging house; the clocks living in their places, tick, tock, might as well have been death-watch beetles in the woodwork, tick, tock. The silence apart from them made our turning the pages of *The Halifax Guardian* sound like the fall of a ton of coal. Were we going mad? I noticed that you developed a nervous twitch, your cheeks inflating and deflating like a rabbit's, while I used to talk to myself – did you hear me? Trying to get used to being Camellia, for you.

As a hermaphrodite, I had one half of me split off into a person who could hate the other half. Perhaps the reason I have come to be what I am is so as to be able to step outside, criticise and reject part of myself.

For two years, I went through terrible swings. Often at first I could not sleep for thinking, *Camellia Snow, Camellia Snow, what a turn!* until my name became a meaningless sound like the words such as *grass* and *moor* that I used to say over for the fun of it when I was a boy in my workhouse bed. I'd think myself into being this transvestite female and spurn the male, but just as I felt triumphant my act would slip. I'd miss The Headless Woman and The Fleece. Creep out of the house. Do you remember when I found out that, while pretending to disapprove, you had secretly advanced me up the bill at The Mitre, purely for my sake? Oh, I kissed you then. Collapsed into your demands. Found being female exciting and fresh again. Yet once more, became revolted by its dangers.

If I rebelled in the form of Jack, it was never long before I was back in my queen's robes. Weak and vulnerable though I felt, I knew that my hope of remaining with you depended on holding to my goddess role. Once again, brave the dangers of living in another's fantasy world.

The claustrophobia.

The nervous tension.

The tiredness that comes from constant self-consciousness.

The physical debility that comes.

The gunfire of our briefly flaring hatreds.

'I'm going! Pack my trunk!'

Then the reconciliations.

*

Dawn came over Blackpool and I had made up my mind. I gave the caravan and Taffy to my friendly ostler, in return for his looking after my mementos for me to retrieve them 'when the struggle is over'. I asked him to sell my clothes for the war widows. Mr Palmer's dresses should fetch a packet. When I come back, I told him, I am going to start another life.

How happy I felt to be uttering clichés, like everyone else. I walked down the Promenade, a man. My problem in life had been to choose what to be and I had chosen once again. With, in my breast pocket, the letters you wrote to me during our first month while I was still at The Headless Woman, I chose to go down to take the King's shilling at the recruiting booth in order, at last, to be *real*.

The recruiting station was another dusty hall of unvarnished, wooden boards; this time, a market hall. It was busy and I ended up trapped at a table with an NCO who was taking down details; except that I kept interrupting with questions. He was impatient, hinting that it was unmanly to hesitate.

He showed his intolerance by abandoning me to attend to a slender gentleman not unlike yourself, who was a concert pianist, so I learned from overhearing him. He kept stroking his fingers, right up to the point when he took the King's shilling in them and swore the oath. Then he carried on stroking them again, until he was directed to another part of the market where a huddle of recruits were being thrown into their first experiences of military discipline: being bawled into line even before they received their uniforms.

I kept thinking about his hands, which were now at his sides and which he was therefore not allowed to stroke. He had decided to destroy them, through handling mud, rifles, trench-props and barbed wire.

I returned to the NCO, who smiled at me, smugly.

I asked him again about pay. He admitted testily that it wasn't much, but as he pointed out for the n'th time I'd heard it, I was joining up for King and Country; not for selfish reasons.

I took the shilling in my hand.

The oath was there for me to swear.

'What if I find it doesn't suit me and I change my mind?' I asked.

'You can't,' he snapped.

'I haven't sworn yet.'

'I mean, after you've swore – o' course.'

He was restraining himself because I was not yet a soldier, but he was dying to bawl me out. I knew that he was waiting only for a few sworn words from me, and then he was going to make my life Hell.

I put the shilling back on the table.

'I'll come back tomorrow,' I said. 'I must think about it. I have to see a man about some clothes.'

CHRISTOPHER BURNS

THE CONDITION OF ICE

In 1936 Ernest Tinnion leaves England for Switzerland to climb, with his childhood friend Hansi Kirchner, the awesome north face of the Versücherin. As they prepare the ascent, unforeseen pressures mount: from Tinnion's lover, who has left her husband to join him; from a too curious, menacing German photographer; and from a rival Italian team. In a breathtaking climax, Tinnion is forced to weigh survival against loyalty, neutrality against love and friendship, and to recognise ominous parallels with the looming global conflict.

'Christopher Burns' harsh, beautiful novel employs a number of unforgettable mountaineering images to dig deep into the condition of the European soul on the eve of the war'
Kazuo Ishiguro in The Sunday Times 'Books of the Year'

'Put Burns' imagination on a perpendicular cliff of stratified black rock with the cracks filling with snow and he'll have you feeling for a toe-hold in the carpet'
Nicholas Shrimpton in the Independent on Sunday

'Burns writes with a marvellous lightness of touch . . . a novel whose living perfection is triumphantly removed from the icy rigidity that is its subject'
Savkar Altinel in The Times Literary Supplement

'Excellent, exquisitely crafted . . . One of Britain's finest writers has written a gripping, many-layered story'
Val Hennessy in the Daily Mail

'That rare thing: a novel of action and emotion which is also a novel about the way people think . . . it is a tremendous achievement'
D. J. Taylor in The Independent

sceptre